Praise for
Forks, Knives, and Spoons

"*Forks, Knives, and Spoons* is the perfect marriage of wit, romance, and, above all, heart. DeCesare's writing is simply delectable and sure to woo any woman who has ever wondered if there is such a thing as Mr. Right."

—Nicole Waggoner, author of *Center Ring* and *The Act*

"Full of 1980's nostalgia, DeCesare's ambitious young women protagonists meet campus 'Forks, Knives, and Spoons' as they navigate how to ultimately place themselves firmly at the head of their own tables."

—Ann Imig, Founder of Listen to Your Mother

"A book (and dating concept!) I had to stop reading multiple times to text my sisters, often snapping pics of laugh-out-loud passages. The 80's nostalgia is spot on. High bangs? Yep. George Michael, Alex P. Keaton? Both. And when my laughter settled, my heart took over. Fans of Sarah Jio, Allison Winn Scotch, Phoebe Fox, and Hannah McKinnon will find a new favorite in Leah DeCesare."

—MM Finck, Women Writers, Women's Books

"The sounds, cultural references, and scents of the 80's will envelop you as you read DeCesares's debut. I felt like I was right back in my dorm room where the biggest decision was whether to play Squeeze or Blondie as I got ready for a dorm party. This page-turning romp through the college years and beyond follows Amy as she navigates a cutlery of cuties in search of the perfect steak knife. I made me want to plan a reunion!"

—Robin Kall, host of *Reading With Robin* podcast
and Point Street Reading Series

FORKS, KNIVES and SPOONS

a novel

Leah DeCesare

SparkPress, a BookSparks imprint
A Division of SparkPoint Studio, LLC

Also by Leah DeCesare

Naked Parenting: 7 Keys to Raising Kids With Confidence

Naked Parenting: Guiding Kids in a Digital World

For my dad

Published by SparkPress, a BookSparks imprint,
A division of SparkPoint Studio, LLC
Tempe, Arizona, USA, 85281
www.gosparkpress.com

Published 2017

Printed in the United States of America

ISBN: 978-1-943006-10-6 (pbk)
ISBN: 978-1-943006-11-3 (e-bk)
Library of Congress Control Number: 2016954658

Cover design © Julie Metz, Ltd./metzdesign.com
Author photo © Erica Shea
Formatting by Katherine Lloyd/theDESKonline.com

Part ♡ne

1988–1989
FRESHMAN YEAR

Chapter 1

THERE ARE THREE TYPES of GUYS: forks, knives, and spoons. Amy unpacked her dad's words along with her yellow Sony Walkman, turquoise Benetton sweater, and peach comforter set. His lesson was tucked carefully in her memory, the details recorded in her reporter's notebook, available for labeling the college guys she was about to meet. She would adhere to her father's advice—she always did—though she wasn't about to let any guy distract her from her dream of being a journalist, not even a perfect steak knife.

Thomas York had been animated in his utensil descriptions, and Amy sensed an aging single father's wishes for his daughter lingering behind his words. His enthusiasm that night at Bella's restaurant swept over her in a feeling of homesickness before she had even left. Now, Amy pushed down a nervous longing for home. She plugged in her new Brother word processor (her father had splurged for the large-screen version with fifteen lines visible at once) and worried about him alone in their house. The two were knotted together with trust, love, and household chores, and while he encouraged her writing, she always heard his old-fashioned hope for her to find a husband wiggle into his advice. As the machine powered on, she mulled the idea of a feature story on men as they fit into the Utensil Classification System. Her undeniable romanticism mingled with her journalistic inclinations, and she envisioned her byline: Amy M. York.

Car horns and hollers splatted against the glass. Amy startled and, with a yank, slid open the window overlooking the vast patio sprawled between two dorm towers. Puddles of freshmen in stiff new Syracuse T-shirts turned together like flocks of birds facing the wind. As the honks of the cars slowed, shouts from the courtyard circulated. Amy scanned the scene. To the edge of her sight line, she saw a flutter of guys encircling a blond pouf. As they shifted and helped, it was clear the girl had fallen, purple suitcases splayed around her, and Amy noticed a bright purple skateboard, wheels up, just beyond. *The story is in the details,* she thought, turning away from the fading commotion outside and refocusing on her new home.

She kicked her Tretorns under the desk and walked around the wall that divided the room, which had shelves and a long counter built into each side. From the doorway, Amy examined her roommate's half with a journalist's eye. All she had was a hint from the assignment letter: Veronica Warren, Newport, Rhode Island. Veronica's side of the room was tasteful and meticulously neat. Practical and serious, her bed had only one deep-blue pillow that matched her Laura Ashley floral bedding. Amy glanced at the heap of pastel-toned throws on her own peachy, pinky, paisley comforter, knowing this might be the only time her bed would be made. A small lamp with an inky shade was beside Veronica's bed, spotlighting a framed photo of a bulky guy with a round, boyish face.

Without stepping fully onto Veronica's side, Amy hungrily sought clues of the person she would be sharing this small space with for more than nine months. In another picture she saw the same puerile face pressed against a fair-skinned girl with a starburst of red hair and a thin nose that came to a pretty, slightly turned-up point at the end. Red curls spilled around her face and around half of his, too. The photo gallery displayed scenes of the couple in aligned rows of dark cherry frames. Curls flung about her on a sailboat, cascaded at a prom, escaped from a woolen hat on a snowy peak, and were the only thing out of place on her entire side of their dorm room.

A crescendo of noise in the hallway was punctuated by slamming doors. A cheer of "Woo-hoo! Class of '92 rocks!" drew Amy from her room. Coming toward her was a girl with blond bangs curled under onto her forehead; the hair just behind was curled up and teased into a feathered dome. She wore white shorts, frayed at the edges, and a boyfriend-sized football jersey. One knee was raw with scrapes. Heads bobbed out of doorways to see what they were missing.

The girl glided down the gray carpet that barely softened the concrete floor beneath it and shouted, "Go Brewster Floor Eight!" She streaked toward Amy on a skateboard, tugging two purple suitcases behind her.

"What's your name? Where are you from? I'm from California. It's going to be such an awesome year! Go class of '92! Don't you think it'll be awesome? I'm so psyched! I'm Jenny. Jenny Callista," she said as if she loved saying her own name.

Amy tried to slip in an answer, not sure Jenny was still interested. "Hi, I'm Amy York."

Jenny leaned past Amy and pulled the dry erase marker from its Velcro. In swirly letters, she formed a *D,* changed her mind, erased it, and then wrote *Jenny Was Here* on the message board affixed to Amy's door.

"I'm in the single room at the end of the hall. See ya later!" She pushed off and Amy watched as she skated four doors down.

"Your first college friend."

Amy whirled toward the voice, coming face-to-face with a blast of red curls.

"Veronica!"

The roommates left the continuing bustle of the hallway, where families lugged armfuls of geometric-patterned area rugs, red-and-black comforters, and wooden-framed futons, trying to give personality to the stark, white-walled rooms. Plastic bathroom buckets spilled with toothbrushes, pink Daisy razors, and containers of blue Sea Breeze toner. Bottles of Jhirmack and Vidal Sassoon shampoos, tubs of Noxzema, shiny cans of Aqua Net, and atomizers of Love's Baby Soft tumbled from stacking baskets on wheels.

In room 808, the girls felt at ease together, talking and laughing like old friends even as they asked the basic get-to-know-you questions. Amy sat at Veronica's desk, watching her tidy something in her already organized closet. Navy-blue towels were stacked like a department store display on Veronica's shelf; beside them were baskets of folded underwear and bundled socks. In an effortless rush of words, the two chattered over and between each other, at once hearing, asking, listening, and answering.

"Who's the guy?" Amy asked, pointing to the pictures.

Veronica sat on her bed and tucked her fleshy pale legs beneath her. "Eric, my boyfriend," she said. "Our families have been friends forever, but junior-year prom was our first date."

"Is he your steak knife?"

"What?" Veronica pulled her knees to her full chest.

Amy laughed and twisted her straight brown hair around her finger; she was forever trying to make it curl. She had been thinking about the Utensil Classification System since her father's college send-off talk and categorizing guys as utensils already seemed normal, like something that should make sense to other people.

"Oh, right, the Steak Knife Theory. This was my dad's idea of a last-ditch birds-and-bees sort of talk."

For the first time of many to come, Amy retold her father's lesson, elaborating as she went.

THE HOSTESS'S PERFUME STILL swirled and menus balanced in the air as Tom York anxiously dove into his lesson. "There are three kinds of guys: forks, knives, and spoons," Amy's dad said, laying out the silverware in front of Amy on the white restaurant tablecloth that August night.

"There are the forks, they are the smoothies." Her dad took a deep breath, pacing himself. "The forks are the guys who are cocky, they'll poke you. These are the guys to be especially careful of, the forks," he repeated for emphasis.

They sat in the front window of Bella's restaurant, their favorite spot overlooking Main Street in Newtown. Amy had lived in the same house with her dad her whole life, and the small Connecticut town was a part of who she was. It seemed the precollege dinner was supposed to be the "Big Talk" before Amy headed out on her own. It was her dad's Cliffs Notes version of *A Dad's Guide to Guys* in the way only Tom York could deliver.

"The forks," he explained, "are the guys who won't care about you. They will make you think they care, but they won't have any problem playing the field."

"So, the forks are the 'fuck-and-chuckers'?" Amy concluded after his description, laying the napkin in her lap. Not one for cursing, she shocked herself by blurting out the biggest possible swear in front of her dad. He laughed and nodded, and his exhale seemed to say, *Maybe she gets it a little bit.*

Amy thumbed the menu and noticed the sweat on her dad's forehead in the air-conditioned restaurant. A tenderness swelled in her chest.

"The Yorks! Ciao!" boomed Giovanni's unmistakable voice across the dining room. "What's the occasion tonight?" he asked, tucking a silk handkerchief into his jacket pocket before slapping Tom on the back and kissing Amy.

"Amy's heading off to Syracuse next week," her father said with pride and sadness. "I'm going to miss her."

"Ah, and so will I! I remember when you were only a little one! Here in your white christening gown! And now! Off to college!" Giovanni enthused every phrase.

Her dad tapped the knife as Giovanni exited to the kitchen, bringing Amy back to the lesson. With his index finger leaving prints on the shining blade, he continued his instruction. "This is the biggest group of guys. The knives are the middle of the road, they're not cocky like the forks. They may be a little less confident, but not necessarily lacking in confidence." As he did with the forks, and would again when he got to the spoons, her dad warned, "You still have to be careful, but the knives are the guys with potential. The nice guys will be in the knife category."

The knives are the good guys? Amy thought. *Where is he getting this? Knives cut, slice, dice, and carve. This is the perfect guy? Maybe he hasn't thought this through.* She was puzzled by his logic and wondered if this was all off-the-cuff. It seemed to be spontaneous, but had he sat up nights deciding how to give his only child this crash course in men?

She challenged him about his choice of utensils: "Seriously, Dad? Knives cut—they can't be the 'good guy' category."

"The ideal guy is a knife, Amy," he said with certainty, and stuck with his label. "The knives are right in the middle, they have an edge and can be sharp when they need to be. Not too sharp and not too dull. They're smart. They have drive, fortitude, strength of character, and they may not be as sure of themselves around girls as the forks are, but they will find their confidence."

Hmm, maybe he has given this some thought.

The waitress swished by with sparkling water and warm bread. Amy chuckled and added traits and descriptions to the forks and knives, but before she could elaborate much, her dad interrupted, determined to get through the coaching session. He adjusted the silverware laid out before his daughter, tidying the row: the fork to the left, the knife dotted with smudges in the center, and the spoon to the right.

As if he couldn't stop, her father eagerly went on with the demonstration. "Then you have the spoons. Simply put, these are the nerds, the geeks. They don't poke, they don't have edge, they're maybe even bland. Spoons may be wimpy and dull, boring and nervous. Spoons are what you kids call the dorks."

Names came to her head to fit the categories; she knew examples of each. Amy nodded at this simple Utensil Classification System and she felt impressed with her dad in a new way. He was an entrepreneur and a sharp negotiator. *Maybe sharp isn't such a bad trait in a guy after all,* she acknowledged. He was also a numbers whiz, and with his going-away chat, Amy got a glimpse into a less visible side of her dad. Unless he was talking math, she had never known him to speak in symbols.

He leaned forward, appearing drained. He looked his daughter in the eye. "Amy, I'm not a young man and I want to know you're cared for, that you have a companion to love. I've treasured raising you, but it's not easy doing this alone." He lifted his glass to her. "Go out there and bring home a good knife."

Amy smiled and her blue eyes shone with admiration. Her dad carefully rewrapped his silverware into the cloth napkin and bestowed the final moral: "And remember, Amy, every guy is thinking about getting a girl into the napkin."

Chapter 2

VERONICA NODDED AND LAUGHED politely at Amy's descriptions of cutlery guys. Her new roommate wasn't anything like her friends back in Newport, but she liked her.

"Speaking of dads, my father should be back home now. He asked me to call him tonight," Veronica said, and excused herself to the floor pay phone.

Susan Warren answered on the fourth ring.

"Hi, Mom. Your voice is hoarse, are you okay? You sound like you've been crying."

"Oh, hello, darling, yes, I'm fine. Your father just got home a short time ago. I hear you're settled in."

"Yes, I'm all organized and I like my roommate. I wish you could've come, too."

"I'll just get your father, I know he was waiting for your call. Have fun at school, sweetheart. Gerald . . ."

Veronica perched on the stool and fidgeted with the silver phone cord. The elevators pinged past and she coughed from the scent of ammonia and newly painted cinder block walls. The small lobby was furnished with a fake-wood-grain Formica table and wood-framed couches, which were covered in pilled maroon fabric with evidence of past freshman classes stained into them.

She heard her father clear his throat. "Hi, honey."

"Hey, Dad, thanks for helping me move in. I really wish Mom came with us."

"I'm sorry your mother couldn't be there, too. You know how hard these milestones are. She's always thinking about your brother," he apologized, and she pictured him tugging the sleeve of his custom-tailored dress shirt.

"I know, Dad, but I wish she'd be happy with my milestones," Veronica whispered.

"We both know you'll be great."

"Thanks, Dad." As she gently replaced the receiver, she felt a familiar disappointment and a subtle envy toward her brother that made her feel guilty.

SORORITY RUSH BEGAN SOON after classes started, and on the final day of parties, Veronica woke early to pounding on the door. She and Amy had stayed up late with Kate Anula, who lived down the hall, watching the Steve Martin movie *Roxanne* until two in the morning. The romantic comedy left Amy in tears and had her new friends teasing her as they handed her tissues.

"Who's knocking at eight on a Saturday morning?" Veronica muttered, getting up when the rapping persisted. She shuffled to the door to find Jenny smiling, already showered, made up, and hair sprayed high.

"Let's go! Up and at 'em! It's the big day!"

"But we don't need to be there until nine thirty," Veronica grumbled, moving to close the door on her, but Jenny slipped in with her hyper, radio-static wake-up call.

Jenny plunked herself at the foot of Amy's bed and started prattling. Veronica shook her head as Jenny chirped a morning narration.

"So what are your first parties today? I think we're together for the first round. I really met some great girls in Kappa, I so want to get into that house. Who did you meet there? Didn't you love the songs they sang? I like Tri-Delt, too."

Amy had no choice, so she rolled into the day and hopped out of bed, grabbing what she always grabbed first: her toothbrush. Veronica still marveled at how her roommate could be perky and full of sunshine, even when she was tired or the Syracuse weather was dismal and dreary.

All the girls who were rushing bustled about the bathroom in varying states of undress and wakefulness. Aqua Net filled the air and curling irons sizzled split ends. For the longest day of rush parties, Jenny wore a dress with a ditzy floral print, Amy had on her favorite Esprit skirt with her gold Add-a-Bead necklace, and Veronica settled on a navy V-neck dress, trying to downplay her plentiful breasts.

They fell into step with the parade of young coeds and found themselves on display. Neighboring fraternities dragged out living room couches, lined up lawn chairs, and hung along porch railings to view the prospective pledges marching before them. Whistles and cheers erupted and waned above the music that blasted from window-sized speakers and echoed off buildings.

The hours were filled with nibbling, smiling, and chattering. At the end of the day, as the rushees walked along Comstock Avenue, they were given a glimpse, or a full exhibition, of college-boy behavior. On the sidewalk, a naked masked man jogged by, swinging around to whoops of male encouragement. One pass wasn't enough, so the disguised streaker dashed across the girls' path again, earning smirks and discreet but curious stares.

Amy leaned toward Veronica and said, "I wonder what kind of guy is under that gorilla mask. Do you think he's a poor spoon being suckered into this? I bet a nice knife wouldn't bare all and run around campus, right?"

Veronica hesitated, unsure if Amy was seriously evaluating this guy with a code of cutlery she'd assumed was just a lark.

"I bet an arrogant fork would drop his pants and swagger around like that, but maybe a fork wouldn't use the mask," Amy continued.

Veronica wrinkled her forehead and was saved from responding by Jenny's howl.

"Woo-hoo!" Jenny shouted, and pumped her fist, moving closer to the naked gorilla. "Take off your mask! Let's see all of you, hunky!"

The guy turned back around, standing just outside of Jenny's arm's reach. The flock of girls shrunk away from her. Jenny looked directly at his crotch and then took a deliberate step closer. Whispers flitted and eyebrows raised.

"What is she doing?" Amy asked Veronica.

"I have no idea."

With her hand cupped, Jenny reached for him. His peripheral vision was impaired by the mask, and he startled as she clenched his parts. He grabbed her wrist and pulled her away, but Jenny's other hand yanked at the mask. She tugged it up, exposing his chin then his mouth before he released her, grabbed at the gorilla head, and ran off toward Phi Delt.

"What are you afraid of, hunky monkey?" Jenny called after him as the crowd of girls dispersed, perhaps a little worried about what house she would be joining.

When Bid Day came a few days later, both Veronica and Amy pledged their first choice, Kappa Kappa Gamma, and excitedly pulled on sky-blue T-shirts printed with a deep blue fleur-de-lis. Jenny had listed Kappa first on her pref list, too, but instead of becoming their sister, Jenny put on a stiff smile and, with a protective word of criticism toward the house that had declined her, accepted her bid from Alpha Phi and skipped off with her pledge class.

AS WAS ALREADY PART of their routine, whenever they returned to Brewster, they crossed the lobby to their mailboxes. Amy insisted on the daily mail checks like Veronica insisted on weekly laundry room trips.

Veronica had never seen anyone her own age write so many letters. Her mother sent handwritten notes by the dozen for her philanthropic duties, but Amy wrote long narratives nearly every day on brightly colored stationery. She was a writer through and through, Veronica supposed, reporting her college days to her dad and friends afar. As Amy reached into the metal cubby and fanned through the stack of envelopes, searching for the hallmarks of a letter—the licked stamp, the paper sturdier than bills, her address written in script—it seemed to Veronica that Amy worked to delay opening them to savor the wondering of what lay inside.

Veronica smiled at how quickly they'd become aware of each other's quirks and habits. Besides being a letter writer, her roommate wrote articles and quietly submitted them to the school paper; she was a sucker for romantic comedies, brushed her teeth constantly, and had an optimism that Veronica found slightly annoying if she was being honest, which Veronica always was.

"It's a letter from the *Daily Orange*." Amy carefully slid the letter from the envelope. "They accepted it, V, my article profiling the National Panhellenic Conference."

"Congratulations! That's awesome." Veronica searched her stack of mail and tore open the envelope from Rhode Island. "Eric's coming to visit next weekend," she announced. "I didn't think he'd be able to visit before Thanksgiving. Is it okay if he stays with us?"

"Of course. I'll stay down the hall with Kate and I'll clean up my side of the room, promise," Amy said. "Then when he leaves on Sunday, we'll have to analyze if he's your steak knife."

"Amy, you're not really serious about this Utensil Classification thing, are you? I thought it was just for fun."

Amy looked up from her pile of mail with a confused expression. "Well, it is fun, but it also works. This is how I'm going to find the right guy. When my dad told me about the different categories, I could totally fit my high school friends into each group. It works, V. Think of that cute guy, Andrew, I told you about from class. He's sweet, smart, and confident, too. See? Knife!"

Chapter 3

AMY MET ANDREW GABEL in marketing class, by chance sitting next to him on the first day. His sandy-brown hair was swept to the side and cut short around his ears, and he wore a navy J.Crew rollneck sweater. Human nature drew them to find the same seats on the second day of class, and by day three, everyone had created assigned seats for themselves. Because they had randomly sat beside each other on day one, they ended up in the same group for their first assignment.

"Please pick five people for your group project," the professor announced, and was answered with muffled groans.

Everyone looked around awkwardly, tentatively trying to assess one another before a history had been established, before anyone knew who were the slackers or the overachieving, perfectionist control freaks. In the end, people formed groups with those at the desks closest to theirs, with the students in between jockeying for an affiliation.

"Want to get started together, tomorrow after class?" Andrew had asked Amy after their group dispersed. His greenish eyes were happy, if a little narrow. His smile, which shone as if only for her, reached outward across his face, creasing his cheeks, instead of turning upward. She agreed to meet him, thinking, *My dad would like him,* and recognizing that she did, too. After that first invitation, she and Andrew completed their share of the group work together. She found she was disappointed that even though she felt like the center of attention when she was with him, she got conflicting signs about whether he had a romantic interest in her.

Weeks into the school year, Amy was surprised when she then met Chase. Could she like more than one knife at a time? She met him in anthropology class and the irony of that was not lost on her. Boys were one big anthropological study, and she had been taking notes as if researching an important news story.

As she sat in the theater-style lecture hall, rummaging for a pen in her canvas Gap bag, she felt his presence before she saw him. With her head tipped forward, her straight shoulder-length hair shielded her view. His aura sidled up to her, and then he eased into the seat to her right.

"Hey there," his strong voice said with both familiarity and seductiveness. He offered his name and his hand. "Chase."

"Uh, hi, I'm Amy," she replied, clumsily yanking her hand from her catchall bag.

His hand held on to hers just a moment longer than was socially appropriate. She looked up at his face, his defined, square jaw line, a wisp of chocolate hair falling into his smoldering eyes. *How did I not notice him before?* Amy thought. No name could describe the way the blue of his eyes drew Amy to him. *They are to-die-for blue,* she thought. *Crayola should make a crayon that color. To-Die-For Blue.*

Her mind jumped ahead romantically. *This is the way it happens in the movies: hot guy falls madly in love with ordinary girl.* Amy struggled to focus on the professor. She got as far as jotting the date into her notebook, but she felt Chase beside her and the smell of his Drakkar Noir distracted her from any logical thought.

By the time class ended, he had entranced her into scribbling her name and the floor pay phone number into his notebook. He told her he would call to take her on a date, and Amy silently congratulated herself. He leaned away, allowing Amy to exit the row of seats first, and his arm brushed against hers. As they parted ways in the hallway, Chase winked and blessed her with his smile. She walked away, still gazing over her shoulder at his magazine-model face, and slammed directly into a body. The impact sent her stumbling back; she could see only the Led Zeppelin logo she'd met with her cheek.

"Sorry," the guy said to Amy before she could apologize for crashing into him.

"Oh, it's me, I'm sorry," she corrected, but she was talking to the side of his exiting head.

Timid spoon, she thought, immediately labeling him as she watched his tall, lanky frame and his red backpack trundle away. She noticed small details, like she envisioned any good journalist would.

"Amy, over here." Veronica waved.

In one long, nonstop sentence, Amy told Veronica about Chase. She analyzed his handshake, his leaning into her, and their date.

"I wonder where he'll take me. I hope we go somewhere to eat."

"You're always thinking of your stomach. I don't know how you stay so skinny."

Amy laughed. "Come on, let's go get lunch."

The two roommates chose a table by the windows. As Amy opened her mouth wide to bite her sandwich, Veronica slapped the table. "Oh, I forgot to tell you, I got an invitation to our first big fraternity party. I'm not counting that beer-funnel thing we ended up at, or the one on that porch where we only stayed for a little while."

"So is he cute?" Amy smirked behind her sandwich.

"Cute? I've got a boyfriend, remember?" She pulled out a neon-orange square of paper splashed with Greek letters.

"Fun! A frat party, we should—"

"It's uncool to say 'frat,'" Veronica interrupted. "Some of the sisters told me that. We don't want to stand out as clueless freshmen. It's 'fraternity,'" she corrected, taking a spoonful of soup. Veronica was orderly in her space and her words. Somehow getting the language right aligned with her innate honesty.

Over Veronica's shoulder, Amy noticed Andrew standing to leave. She leaned into the space between the banquet-style tables and waved. Andrew spotted her and changed his course. He put down his tray then encircled Amy in what she already thought of as his signature tight squeeze, pulling her snuggly to him and resting that way for an extra beat. Amy liked to think that he reserved those deep hugs for her.

He released her and greeted Veronica, who waved her fingers, her mouth full. He dug into the back pocket of his jeans, which fit him just right, Amy noticed, and extracted a bunch of orange papers, molded together. He peeled off one square and handed it to her.

"You're both invited, Friday night, ask some of your Kappa sisters, too. It's my first big party as a pledge," he said, focused on Amy.

"That's the same party." Veronica tapped the other orange invite on the table. "Eric will be here, he can come with us. We'll be there."

Andrew looked into Amy's eyes. He seemed sincerely glad that they, or that she, would be there.

"Want to meet at the library tomorrow after lunch?" he asked.

Just as Amy pulled out her Filofax organizer, a high-pitched voice yanked their attention to the side like three marionettes.

"Hey, Andrew," a light-haired girl cooed, walking past and twitching an eye at him.

Amy's lips parted slightly as she registered that the girl had winked at him. A twinge of jealousy fluttered across her heart. Andrew's body drew taller, his affection redirected toward the girl. Things moved slowly in Amy's consciousness while they moved too quickly in her sight. He was hugging the girl, giving her the same whole body wrap he'd pressed her into only moments before.

Amy blinked her eyes without removing them from Andrew's back. She tried to glance away, tried to dismiss the feeling nudging at her, when she saw him lift the orange wad from his butt pocket again. Winky's hair looked model perfect, poufed high and crimped down to her shoulders. Her blushed cheeks and dark eyeliner were flawless.

Andrew turned back. "See ya later, Aim." He scooped up his tray and followed Winky.

"Did you see that?" Amy asked Veronica, and sulked, thinking of Andrew retracting his attention from her.

Veronica pursed her lips, nodding. She dabbed her mouth with a paper napkin. "Maybe he's not a knife after all. I'm still not convinced your Steak Knife Theory works," she teased, winking a dramatic wink.

"It works, you'll see."

"Besides, you're having a date with Chase, remember?"

Chase, Amy thought. *How did seeing Andrew make me forget gorgeous Chase?*

"Now that's a good day, one orange invitation and two shiny knives," Amy said as Veronica rolled her eyes.

Chapter 4

ERIC SHERIDAN AND VERONICA had been going out since junior year of high school, though they had played together since the time they were toddlers. Their parents golfed and arranged charity events together for their Newport society friends, and Eric and Veronica were volunteered by their mothers time and again. One night, as they worked side by side at a gala registration table, it all changed. That night, Eric flirted. And Veronica flirted back, noticing the boy who had dappled her childhood in a whole new way.

Veronica was looking forward to his visit, eager to introduce him to her new friends and her life away from home. Amy flopped on Veronica's Laura Ashley comforter and glanced across the now-familiar pictures on her shelves.

"I've heard so much about him that I can't believe I don't even know him yet."

"In a few days you will and it can't come fast enough," Veronica said, finishing her nightly tidying before they turned off their lights for bed.

A BLARING BUZZ SHOT Veronica from sleep. "Ugh, I guess it's true," she groaned.

Their dorm, filled mostly with freshmen, was known for frequent fire alarms; that this was the third one, so early in the year,
supported the rumor.

Amy shifted in bed, and Veronica jiggled her to keep her from
going back to sleep. Pulling on sweatpants and oversized Syracuse
sweatshirts, they slid on shoes and walked into the screeching,
brightly lit hallway.

"Um, Amy, you still have those curlers in your hair," Veronica
said. "Hurry up, we have to evacuate."

Amy muttered a single, sleepy "Hmm," as she yanked at the
spongy pink rollers she sometimes slept in with hopes of waking
up with curls. Inevitably, the waves that thrilled her in the morning were nearly gone by the time she brushed her teeth.

Other drowsy, confused girls shuffled out of their rooms and
herded toward the stairs. Ahead, Veronica saw Jenny walk out
of her room, holding her door open with her hot-pink toes. Her
blond hair was tousled around her shoulders and her bare legs
peeked out between flip-flops and a long T-shirt. Jenny glanced
back into the room as if she were waiting for a roommate, though
she had the only single room on the floor. Amy walked leaning
sleepily against Veronica. Suddenly, Veronica felt her stiffen. She
was fully awake and grabbed at Veronica's sleeve as an incredibly
hot guy sauntered out of Jenny's room buttoning his fly.

Unable to divert their gaze, they stopped and watched Jenny
look up at him, giggling. He casually swept the fringe of hair from
his forehead. Even all rumpled he was gorgeous. His hand neatly
cupped Jenny's butt. She was chatting away like his hand was just
a regular part of her body.

"No way," Amy said. "I guess I can't really blame her for being
drawn into his shiny silver force field, too."

"What?"

Amy elbowed Veronica as if she didn't already have her

attention and she pointed to the guy. In a whisper-shout she said, "That's Chase. *My* anthropology Chase." Amy's eyes widened impossibly. "With Jenny, that's Chase," she clarified, though Veronica already understood.

"Oh, man, I'm sorry, Amy."

Veronica held the hair back from her eyes and squinted toward them. "He's hotter than you described."

They laughed.

"Yeah, but he's such a fork. Damn, my father was right."

Veronica linked her arm around Amy's elbow as they followed the radiant couple toward the stairs, and Veronica played along.

"Okay, so Chase is a fork, Andrew is a knife. When's the spoon going to show up?"

"Oh, I bumped into one today," Amy said without hesitation as they descended the dreary brick stairwell toward the chilly night air.

"IT'S SO GROSS DOWN here," Veronica said as the elevator deposited them in the basement, her pockets jingling with quarters. Amy trailed behind hauling her drawstring mesh bag full of dirty, smoke-smelly clothes.

"We really could've waited at least a few more days, you know," Amy protested one final time.

"I told you last time, we're doing this once a week."

"Well, I *will* be happy to not smell cigarettes on everything we wear out."

"I knew the optimist in you would win," Veronica needled.

The unfinished cement walls of the laundry room were pocked with small bubble holes and striped with lines where the cement had oozed. They filled the machines as the fluorescent lights buzzed overhead, their cold light making the girls feel vaguely dizzy. Sitting cross-legged and face-to-face on the wooden bench, Veronica recognized Amy's reporter face.

"Is Eric your steak knife?"

Veronica thought about the boyfriend she had left behind and Amy's Steak Knife Theory, and she couldn't bring herself to connect the two. "I'm sorry, Amy, but I really can't compare Eric to a utensil."

She felt a pang like the faint smell of mildew around them for rejecting Amy's labels, but Amy was undeterred.

"That's okay, I'll take notes and help you figure it out." Before Veronica could explain that's not what she meant, Amy continued, "I was telling Kate and Jenny and a bunch of girls on the floor about it the other night. Listen to all the details we've added to the UCS."

"The UCS?"

"The Utensil Classification System," she said, like it was a known and generally accepted acronym.

The machines whirred behind them like a drum roll as Amy took a deep breath and began with the first definition. She started with the perfect guy: "A steak knife is right in the middle of the knives, in the center of the center group. The ideal. The fulcrum of balance. The steak knife is sharp and edgy in just the right amounts—bright and shiny, strong and confident, capable, dependable, and trustworthy." She ticked off the qualities as if listing what she wanted in a man.

"Given this some thought, have you?" Veronica teased, but Amy barely stopped to hear her. Veronica imagined she was just as excited as her father had been explaining the UCS and relented as her friend shared her faith in the system.

"He's durable, reliable, and has a solid handle; he can cut through games and crap. A steak knife also works as a team player, he knows how to get along with others, and, really, he is anything a girl defines as her perfect guy. He fulfills 'the list.'"

It seemed most girls had a list, even if they didn't talk about it. Countless hours in high school were spent enumerating the traits wanted in a boyfriend or future husband. Whether on paper tucked somewhere safe, crafted neatly in the back of a diary, or stored privately in her head, girls had a list and Amy's mention of it released a burst of laughter from Veronica.

"Oh my God, yes! I have a list."

"I knew it. That's your steak knife. Now, a butter knife is plainer, he's kind of missing a little something that the perfect steak knife would have. He's softer around the edges, a little weaker. A butter knife is closer to a spoon, so he may be a bit insecure or just less edgy."

As Amy illustrated different types of guys, Veronica found that, as ridiculous as it was, she could picture high school friends and college boys falling into some of Amy's categories.

"Then there's the butcher knife who's almost a fork. Bold, single-minded, severe. A butcher knife hacks instead of using finesse, he comes in for the kill without any fanfare. He has a hard time seeing around his big blade to pay any attention to how other people feel or think."

Veronica laughed wildly and chimed in, knowing she was encouraging this silly system: "So the less cocky forks are like salad forks, and the real bohunk assholes, they're like . . . like pitchforks!" They had veered out of silverware altogether and onto a farm. That *is* where the biggest forks belonged, after all.

Amy picked up the thread: "And there are the huge geeks who are like serving spoons, and the really timid or dorky guys are like teaspoons. They're kind of small and they do what other people want without standing up for themselves. You know, like a teaspoon just serves by scooping or stirring."

Shaking her head at herself for playing along, Veronica challenged Amy with a utensil she hadn't yet defined: "And what about a slotted spoon?"

With barely a moment's hesitation, Amy invented a new

description: "He's is a loser who makes excuses all the time because he's lazy. He's really picky about jobs so he never has one. He blames it all on other people and lets good opportunities slip through his slats because he's unmotivated or, oh, I know, because he's a burnout, stoned or wasted, and doesn't care about responsibilities." At her own definition, Amy collapsed into hysterics. "I know that guy. I definitely dated a slotted spoon two summers ago. He was a very cute slotted spoon who I had high hopes for in that I-can-save-him kind of way. That didn't last long."

Despite herself, Veronica laughed with visions of fork, knife, and spoon guys dancing in her head. How was it that sloppy Amy had created an art form of organizing guys into the silverware-dividing tray, while neat Veronica tried to keep them in an uncategorized jumble?

Amy swiped her fingers across the lint screen, then fed another quarter into the dryer to remove the lingering dampness in her clothes. Pensive, Veronica hugged her knees to her chest and asked, "What if there's someone else out there for me?" She paused and lifted her thick red curls off her neck, the steamy laundry room heat making the strands stick to her back. "Do you think I'm missing out on the whole 'college experience' because I'm still with Eric?"

Veronica was truthful and a realist. She was a rule-follower and she had a knack for pulling things back to center and grounding worries in logic. "I mean, I love him and we have fun together." She rested her chin on her knees and with a softer voice continued: "I don't know. He's from the 'right' family, his parents and my parents golf and do charity stuff together, we have fun, but sometimes, I feel like he's . . . distant."

"Can you see yourself with him, happily ever after?"

Veronica let her lips creep into an almost-smile. "You and your romantic comedies and happy endings." Then breathing in the soapy air, she nodded thoughtfully. "Yeah, sometimes I can picture us in the future, Mr. and Mrs. Eric Sheridan Jr., but I still have a lot to figure out and, of course, we're still young. I want to live in New York City, have a career, and live in my own apartment, away from my parents and away from Newport."

Veronica popped up, opened the dryer door, and folded her staticky sheets and clothes, tucking them into her basket as she went. She winced as Amy gathered her warm clothes from the machine and crumpled them into her laundry bag.

Leading the way to the elevators, Amy pointed out a white spork kicked into a corner. "V, a spork." She closed her eyes for a moment, then stated, as if reading the definition directly from *Webster's,* "A spork is a cocky spoon; a nerd who acts like a fork."

Veronica just shook her head.

As Veronica and Amy crossed the eighth-floor lobby to their room, they passed Jenny. Her tanned legs hung sideways over the edge of a couch and a cluster of eager boys jockeyed to be nearest to her. She bit her pinkened lip and threw her blond head around, giggling with interest at every word the boys uttered. Veronica and Amy rolled their eyes at each other. When they were safely out of earshot, Amy said, "She's collecting a whole place setting," and Veronica had a hard time disagreeing.

Chapter 5

VERONICA STOPPED IN FRONT of the mirror, a routine pause in her pacing, and adjusted the clip holding the curls away from her face. *It's only Eric, why do I feel so nervous?* She touched her stomach and talked aloud to herself, "Butterflies, shoo."

Amy had already left to spend the two nights with Kate, and the small room felt vast without the security of her friend. Another lap and back in front of the mirror, she tucked a stray curl into her pulled-up hair.

At last the digital clock radio on her nightstand turned 7:30. Considering Eric's call from the rest stop, he would arrive soon, so Veronica moved her waiting downstairs. She began a new course of pacing in the lobby, looping past the mailboxes and around the couches. Past the mailboxes. Around the couches. Finally, she spotted Eric in the glass doorway. She rushed over then greeted him with a reserved kiss. His preppy madras pants were paired with a button-down shirt, wrinkled from the drive; a cotton sweater hung loosely over his shoulders. His slightly formal style both contrasted and fit his round, youthful face, and his cheeks had their usual rosy blush.

"I'm happy you could come." Veronica squeezed his hand, the butterflies still flapping around. "I missed you."

"Missed you, too," Eric said, looking around the lobby. "It's different from Brown."

Eric stayed closer to their Newport home and attended both of their fathers' alma mater. Eric Sheridan Sr. and Gerald Warren had been Phi Kappa Psi fraternity brothers at Brown and remained comrades and colleagues decades later.

"Want to go out? I can show you around, we can find some friends, get some food." Veronica proffered her suggestions politely, still sensing the unfamiliarity as she signed him in and led him up to her room.

Eric patted his neatly parted hair and scanned Veronica's new home. "Man, I can't believe you brought that awful prom picture, I look terrible." He picked up the frame and examined it closely before putting it down behind the other photos.

"So, should we go out?" Veronica repeated tentatively.

"Nah. Let's just hang out here. Can we order in some pizza?"

An hour later, they were dressed comfortably in dorm wear, sitting feet to feet on Veronica's bed, laughing easily together, the butterflies having flown away.

"Okay, pizza should be here soon, let's head down." Veronica hopped off the bed and slipped into sneakers.

"The guy can wait. You don't always have to be so prompt and organized, you know, Roni." The comment stung, but his use of the familiar nickname was a salve; he was the only one who called her Roni. He smiled as he stood to follow her and wrapped an arm around her waist as they stepped into the elevator.

"Hold the elevator."

Eric put his hand out, stopping the door, and they watched as Jenny bounded toward them. Veronica made introductions and noticed Eric's gaze venture to the rounds of Jenny's breasts, pressed against her white T-shirt.

"Very nice to meet you, Jenny," he said, stepping closer to

Veronica with noticeable deliberation. "Where are you from?"

"Oh, me? Southern California. It's so different here already and I'm a little worried about the winter. I'm not used to wearing so many clothes." Then, in pure Jenny fashion, she touched Veronica's arm and in a mock whisper said, "You never told me your boyfriend is such a hottie."

Veronica stiffened, both threatened and proud, and was grateful that the doors opened to the lobby. She noticed a subtle smile on Eric's lips, and when Jenny had bobbed away, he draped his arm over Veronica's shoulder. "You've got a hottie, you know that?" he bragged. "Don't roll your eyes, you're stuck with me, you know. It would ruin our parents carefully constructed plans if they didn't become in-laws."

She relaxed into his lightness, feeling their comfortable connection return. As he paid the pizza guy and collected their food, Veronica asked, "How is it living in Providence? Do you go home a lot?"

"Nah, I've only gone home once to have Linda do some laundry for me."

They returned to the elevator and he stabbed at the eight button.

"Your mom hates when you call her Linda, and seriously, when are you going to learn to do your own clothes?"

"Why? I'll never need to do it myself. I'll just pay someone to do it."

Veronica winced at his arrogant remark. She hated those entitled expectations of so many of her friends back home. They arrived back at her floor and she opened the dorm room door for him.

Once settled, Eric picked up a triangle of pizza and asked, "Hey, I almost forgot, have you met a kid named Scott Mason? He rows for Syracuse, he's a Phi Psi, too."

Veronica shook her head and dabbed grease from her slice. Eric not only dutifully went to their fathers' alma mater but was also pledging their fraternity.

"A rowing buddy of mine knows him from home. Cool guy. He was at Brown for a regatta so we hung out a few nights."

"I'll look out for him," Veronica said.

After they finished eating, she tidied the mess from their dinner, sweeping crumbs from her comforter into the empty box.

"You can throw this away down by the bathrooms," Veronica directed, handing Eric the empty box, used paper plates, and napkins.

ERIC SAUNTERED DOWN THE hallway to his left. He bent the corner of the box to fit it into the garbage can, and as he turned to head back to room 808, he heard the click of a door and saw Jenny leaving the room at the end of the hall. She was walking his way for the second time that night. This time, she bounced, unsupported, in a baby-doll nightie that barely covered her hips. Her nipples poked at the pale lavender silk and hinted at the dark circles around them. She smiled at Eric outside the bathroom and stood blocking his path.

Eyes wide, he froze, stunned and unable to retrieve words. He forced himself to look at her face, at the blond hair that hung loose around her bare shoulders, and away from the rest of her.

"Oops," she purred as she let the hand towel drop from her basket. In deliberate slow motion, she bent to retrieve the purple towel without bending her knees. The silky fabric fell to the side, revealing the curve of her bottom. Eric stood paralyzed, hoping his baggy sweatpants would conceal his rise.

"Night, Eric, sweet dreams."

As the bathroom door eased shut, he hurried back to Veronica.

Chapter 6

ON SATURDAY NIGHT, Amy and Veronica grabbed their bathroom buckets and headed to claim a shower. It was almost nine o'clock and the bathroom air was filled with the scent of shampoo, steam, and the drone of girls' voices. Amy tugged the white plastic shower curtain to close the sliver of space on the left only to create a peek hole on the right side. Hot shower air met the cooler bathroom air, luffing the curtain like a sail. However she adjusted it and tried to stick it to the moistened tile walls, it refused to conceal all of her and she settled for even space on both sides of the curtain.

"SHIT!"

"OUCH!"

"Who forgot to yell 'Flushing!'?"

Amy heard the screeches just as her skin burned, forcing her out of the water flow.

"Oops, sorry," came Kate's sweet voice around the corner. "It was me. I'm really sorry, you guys."

Amy peeked her sudsy head out from the curtain to acknowledge her apology. Kate had a familiar, gentle face; her thin hair hung flat and straight to her chin, and her bangs cut a line across her forehead. Rinsed off, lotioned up, and back in their room, Amy got ready hiding behind the wall, out of Eric's view.

"Can I borrow your houndstooth blazer?" Veronica asked Amy.

"Sure, over there." Amy pointed with her hairbrush, shouting slightly above the hair dryer. She flipped her head upside down, trying to blow height into her roots and bend into her hair's straightness. Then she set it in hot rollers, smudged on a little eyeliner, and glossed some pink on her lips. Veronica cuffed the sleeves of the oversized men's blazer and used a final spritz of hairspray to tame the volume of her hair. After reining in the curls, she turned to Eric.

"You're really not coming with us? Just for a little while?" she pleaded. She and Amy had been looking forward to this party, and Veronica couldn't believe that Eric just wanted to sit around in a dorm room instead of going out—it wasn't like him.

"No, I'm fine. Go. I won't know anyone. You girls have fun and I'll be waiting when you get back," Eric assured her. "I brought a problem set and a paper that are due Monday, I've got to get them done. Don't worry about me, I'll keep busy here."

After uncoiling the rollers and admiring the temporary curls, Amy pulled on her pointy-toed cowboy boots under her slim jeans, belted high at her thin waist, and tucked in her favorite mismatched plaid shirt. "Ready to go?"

Veronica answered by kissing Eric, then sticking a twenty into her pocket. Out they went, coatless and bagless, up the hill into the chilly Syracuse evening to the Sigma Chi fraternity party. It was still only late September, but the night temperatures had dropped.

Amy and Veronica spilled into the fraternity house, oozing into the spaces between people. Amy spotted Andrew at the foot of the grand staircase. She grabbed Veronica's wrist, pulling her forward, and admired him as she touched his shoulder, solid beneath her hand. His face brightened at the sight of her and he pulled her into his full-body, hold-on-tight hug. Even knowing she wasn't an exclusive recipient, she melted into his hold.

"How's the first party as a pledge going?" Amy wondered into his ear.

"It's awesome! We're taking shifts serving beer and I'll be cleaning up after."

Whitesnake's "Is This Love" wailed through the house as Andrew, doing his pledge duty, delivered red plastic cups full of beer into their hands and then turned to introduce them to a cute guy standing beside him.

"This is Paul, a brother, he's a junior," Andrew shouted. "Paul, this is Amy and Veronica."

As the vibrating crowd mushed around them, both Andrew and Veronica fused into the party and Amy found herself alone with Paul, pancaked against the wall, separated only by the width of two cups. He wasn't talking, so Amy started with a basic opening question.

"What school are you in?"

Paul was studying engineering, and that one question seemed to turn on his talking. He launched into a description of the latent heat of condensation, drily moved on to recarbonization and abrasion resistance, and then on to the yawn-inducing thermal electromotive force, all while Amy discreetly but frantically searched for someone to save her.

Gracelessly, Paul lurched into Amy. His hand brushed against her chest and Amy backed farther into the wall. She couldn't tell if it was intentional; he seemed too gawky, too amateur. The motion made his beer slosh over the outside of his hand, and he wiped the wet spot on his geometric-patterned sweater. He cleared his throat, audible above the blaring Guns N' Roses.

As Paul moved closer and yelled into Amy's ear about

Bernoulli's theorem, she felt a tug on her sleeve. Amy turned grate-fully to see Veronica, who urgently pulled her away. She leaned toward Paul's ear, keeping a distance, and shouted at him, "Sorry, excuse me. Nice to meet you." With a weak wave and her back half turned, Amy slipped away.

"Nice guy? He was kinda cute," Veronica said.

Despite being completely dull, Amy supposed he was nice enough. Nice. There it was. She wondered why girls say they want a "nice" guy but then are magnetized to the forks. Specimen A: Chase. *Maybe Paul could outline the phenomenon of human attraction and polarization,* she thought.

"You saved me from a total spoon. A gigantic, dorky serving spoon." Amy spoke directly into Veronica's ear as she dragged her toward the living room and the source of the loud music.

Veronica yelled back, "Did you know that Andrew is the pres-ident of his pledge class?"

Amy raised her eyebrows, impressed. One song melded into another, not a second passed music-free as Van Halen overlapped the end of "Sweet Child O' Mine." The girls joined the dancing crowd, and beer splashed down Amy's back when a group of guys jumped with David Lee Roth.

From behind, Andrew grabbed Amy's waist, she turned to him, and they leaped in unison. She was conscious of his hands lingering on her hips, and she fixed her eyes on his. Jumping to the chorus, someone bumped into Andrew, who fell into Amy, who knocked into Veronica. Together they stumbled, laughing and grabbing one another for balance. Somehow, Paul was beside Amy as she steadied herself. He was grinning broadly as she watched Andrew join a group of permed and ponytailed coeds.

Paul moved beside Amy. She watched his oafish version of dancing: his feet stuck to the floor, his shoulders hunched, his knees bobbed offbeat as his hands flailed. Any remaining cute spilled right out of him. Their single conversation had bored her—her accounting class was a suspense novel by comparison—so before he could speak again, she danced away, letting the volume of the music and the thickness of the bodies distance her.

The jumping hadn't finished when the fraternity DJ morphed the music into "Paradise by the Dashboard Lights" and the boys started to belt out the words. In the dim lights, the shouty singing began and Amy thought about the lyrics as the girls stopped the boys, asking for commitment the boys refused to give, dodging the question of love.

As she danced with the girls, Amy thought, *Meat Loaf doesn't look like a classic hot fork, but this song could be the fork anthem. Maybe Meat Loaf would be a butcher knife since he really doesn't have the sexy stuff of forks.* Utensil Classification wasn't an exact science, Amy realized. She imagined that would bug spoony Paul.

Coarsely acting out the lyrics, the room divided into a glob of girls facing a glob of boys. Pitiful to watch as an observer, the enthusiastic participants dramatically lifted their hands, questioning. *Will you love me forever?* girls pleaded, and grasped their hearts. Boys bought time, begging, *Let me sleep on it.* The whole group of lying forks leaned in and sang out.

At the end of the song, Amy motioned to Veronica from across the room that she wanted to find a bathroom and Veronica followed. Struggling to keep her friend in view, Amy navigated the unknown fraternity house. A trio of blondes, linked arm in arm, paraded into Amy. No red curls in sight. After asking a brother for directions, she shuffled toward the staircase as Aerosmith rolled into the dense party air. She searched for Veronica from the higher vantage to no avail, and her bladder led her on alone.

From jumping to pleading to walking, Amy and Steven Tyler sang "Walk this Way" until she reached the landing at the top of the main staircase and turned left into the bathroom. The stench of urine made her cover her nose with her sleeve, and the heels of her boots felt tacky on the tile floor. Two girls leaned toward the smudgy mirror, adding more eyeliner to their dark-rimmed eyes.

"This bathroom is grody," said one of the girls, sounding loud in Amy's throbbing ears.

Amy chose the stall farthest from the one that was occupied with male feet. She was still getting used to sharing bathrooms with boys. Barely touching anything, she shifted from side to side, pulling down her jeans. The lock on the door didn't lock, and she reached out with an elbow, then a knee, to tuck it closed while wiggling out of her pants. A burst of noise filled the room when the bathroom door opened to the hallway, the girls' voices receding into the party. With one hand on the door, Amy wrestled with the roll of toilet paper that teetered on a broken chrome holder and stuck to itself, bunching up enough paper to wipe.

She heard the sounds of the last person in the room: a faint clicking sound, the fiddling of a belt buckle, running water. She pulled up her jeans, leaving them undone, and lifted her foot to flush. The tightness of the denim at her hips fought to restrict her as the stall door fell open again, bumping her side. Amy leaned her shoulder back to shut it but felt a hand close around her arm.

She jerked away. Spiraling toward the door, she came face-to-face with Paul. She exhaled with a faint sense of relief that it was someone she knew. Then she tensed, uncertain as she saw his eyes.

"Oh, excuse me, just need to wash my hands," Amy sputtered as she tried to take a step past him. *Just act normal,* she told herself, feeling her pulse race.

She glanced down, avoiding eye contact, and saw that his pants were unzipped and opened. His belt hung loose and black hairs splayed from his lowered underwear. Amy lunged herself forward to get by, but he widened his stance and planted himself in her path. Paul's right hand moved up and down her arm roughly in a demanding caress, and his other hand leaned against the metal frame, further blocking her.

Amy's attempt to pass him had only brought her closer, and she tried to back away. He stepped forward. With his body filling the opening, he dropped his left hand, slipped it up the back of her untucked shirt, and yanked her to him. Fear pulsed through Amy. She felt the bulge of him press against her. He held her with the same passion he'd shown for engineering. Beer had erased his hesitation but not his awkwardness. He kept his hold on her while he reached for his crotch.

Amy struggled to pull away but Paul held her in place, rubbing against her. His breath smelled like beer and grape candy as he exhaled into her hair. "Come on, Amy, let's just have some fun. We danced together, I could tell you liked it."

She heard voices outside the bathroom and called out, "Help! In here! Please help!"

Her screams echoed wildly in the ceramic bathroom but were lost to the noise beyond.

"It's okay, Amy, come on. We were having so much fun downstairs, let's just have a little more fun," Paul slurred as his hands slid inside the back of her opened jeans. He muscled her body toward his. His sweaty hand moved haltingly, working its way down while Amy squirmed to free herself.

"Stop! No!" Amy pushed against him, digging for strength. He held firm and his grape breath blew hot on her cheek. She turned her face farther away and wedged her hands into his chest, working to escape his hold.

Seizing her firmly, he smashed his lips against her neck, her face, her lips. Amy threw her head to the side, feeling the hot wetness against her skin. "Stop!"

Her cries made him chuckle. "Playing hard to get? I know your type." He lifted her shirt and fumbled with the clasp of her bra. It snapped against Amy's back, and he clawed his hands underneath when he couldn't unfasten it. Clumsily, he clutched and clenched her breasts, he moaned and pressed her deeper into the stall. Straining against her struggle, he forced her into the cold metal and the wall shuddered. The spoke of the paper holder pressed into her thigh. In another ungainly grope, Paul lifted her bra above her chest, tangling it in her shirt, then pushed his pants down. He clasped himself in his hand then reached for Amy's jeans. She felt his fingertips on her stomach like points of fire against her skin. His touch repelled her, and in a burst of strength, she shoved him back and he stumbled.

"Help!" Amy screamed.

Paul regained his balance and grabbed her waist, worming a hand into her pants. He stabbed himself against her body, his eyes half closed and glassy. A guttural noise gurgled in his throat.

The bathroom door jiggled, startling Paul. He turned to the door and Amy used the moment to thrust forward. Paul's fingers caught in the waistband of her jeans, but she wrenched away and ran the short span to the door, trembling as she focused on unlocking it. Andrew stepped into the room. Behind Amy, Paul rushed to cover himself, snatching at his pants. Andrew stormed over to his fraternity brother, and in a single motion, he gripped Paul and landed a strong, punishing punch into his gut.

Paul collapsed onto the sticky tile, his forehead pressed into the moldy grout, and he coughed in shock and pain. With the predator down, Andrew rushed to Amy. Her hands were shaking as she worked to untangle and button her clothes. He slipped off his T-shirt and put it around her. He moved swiftly to get her out of there, leaving Paul doubled over and moaning. He guided her toward an Exit sign. Exchanging the sweaty heat of the house for the nighttime, northern New York cold, Amy felt her shoulders stiffen and a sting in her nose. She was crying. With safety, her tears released.

The fire escape landing was narrow and chips of black paint pulled away like bark uncurling from a tree. The metal bars vibrated with sound as her boot heels clicked against them. She wrapped her arms around herself feeling her thin top beneath Andrew's shirt, a favorite she would never wear again. Andrew folded his bare arms around her, pulling her into his warmth. His gentleness turned Amy's silent tears into sobs and her breath caught on itself.

"I'm so sorry that happened to you. I'm so sorry I didn't find you sooner," Andrew said, speaking the words to Amy but meaning them for himself, too. Andrew let his hand cradle the back of Amy's head, stroking her hair to soothe her.

"We've got to find Veronica, she'll be worried," Andrew spoke quietly, still holding Amy against him. "She couldn't find you in the downstairs bathroom, so I checked out the others. I'm so sorry I didn't find you sooner."

Amy whispered into his chest: "I'm glad you didn't find me later."

Chapter 7

THEY CAREFULLY TURNED THE knob and tiptoed into their room so they wouldn't disturb Eric.

"I'm fine, really, I'm okay sleeping at Kate's again. Sarah's away, I've got her bed," Amy assured Veronica in a whisper as she quietly gathered some fresh clothes.

"That's not what I meant, you know."

"I know." She took a slow breath. "I'm shaky. And I feel stupid. I guess I kind of thought this stuff only happens in the movies. I mean, I *know* it happens, but it doesn't feel real."

Veronica and Amy had reunited at the fraternity house, and Andrew walked them home from the party, his arm protectively around Amy the whole way. He left her with a hug and a kiss on her temple. "I'm sorry," he had whispered before heading back to the house for cleanup duty.

"I still can't believe that dweeb of a spoon did that to me." They sat on Amy's bed with their backs against the wall. "It's like he morphed into a pitchfork right before my eyes."

"Pitchfork?" Eric called from Veronica's side of the room.

The girls smiled at each other. "Nothing," they answered. Veronica hugged Amy again and went to him.

Eric flipped on the bedside lamp, and rubbed the hair around his ears. The soft light illuminated a collection of empty beer cans on her desk. Veronica raised her eyebrows but said nothing, wondering where he'd gotten them and how much schoolwork he'd accomplished.

"I'll be down the hall. See you in the morning." Amy waved to Eric who was lying drowsily on the bed.

Veronica gave her another hug before she left and then slipped out of her clothes and into her bed with Eric. "I'm exhausted, let's get some sleep."

"I'm going to the bathroom, be right back," he said. She noticed him catch his balance as he got to his feet. He scratched his parts through his boxers and walked into the hall.

Veronica shook her head and squished up against the wall to leave him room in the twin bed. She yawned upon seeing the hour, 2:06 a.m., and then she closed her eyes as the weight of sleep pressed down on her.

THE BLAST OF THE fire alarm stabbed Veronica into consciousness. She wasn't sure if she had just dozed off or if she had even slept at all. The bed next to her was still empty. Eric hadn't returned from the bathroom yet, so she must have just fallen asleep. The shrieking continued as Veronica tried to piece things together through sleep's haze. Pulling on her fire-alarm uniform, she noticed the red numbers on her clock radio read 4:18 a.m. Confusion clouded her mind. She rubbed her eyes with her palms and looked around the room. Amy's bed was empty; the stack of beer cans glinted silver in the lights from the window. Where was Eric?

Feeling the need to leave the building, Veronica pulled on her second shoe, hopping into the hallway and looking left and right for Eric. She paused a moment and worked her way toward the bathroom, against the crowd, to look for him. The bathroom was deserted and encased a strange pocket of calm amid the jarring noises outside its doors. Where was Eric?

Maybe he already evacuated, Veronica thought, and joined the herd to the stairs. Outside the building, she rushed toward the floor meeting space, searching as she went; Eric wouldn't know where to meet her. Amy and Kate were already by the wall with their sweatshirts, sleeves yanked beyond their fingertips in makeshift mittens.

"Have you seen Eric?" Veronica rushed to ask, concern for him leeching from her voice.

"What do you mean? He's not with you?" Amy asked.

"No, I don't know where he is. When you left, I got into bed and he went to the bathroom. I must've fallen asleep, so I don't know if he came back in or what happened . . ." She trailed off, still muddled.

Stationed at their home base, the three girls looked around.

"Let's ask the other girls to help us find him," Kate suggested.

"But no one besides you two have met him, they wouldn't know what he looks like . . ." Veronica said, her eyes still scanning the crowd of sleepy students. "Wait! Except Jenny. Jenny met him. Last night. In the elevator, we were getting pizza, and she met him. Where's Jenny? Maybe she can help?"

Kate peered around. "I don't see her, she's not out yet."

A firefighter in full gear came toward the milling freshmen. Through a megaphone he announced, "Due to the problem we've been experiencing with too many students remaining in the building during fire alarms, we will be conducting a room-by-room search tonight. Sorry, folks, settle in for a while."

Moans rose up from the crowd, the obedient punished.

"Do you think he stayed inside?" Amy wondered to Veronica.

"But where? I checked the bathroom, where else could he be? He's probably out here and can't find me."

Veronica, Amy, and Kate split up to search different sections of the evacuees then meet back by the wall. In the darkness, finding anyone in particular was a challenge; that was part of what sparked Veronica to set a meeting spot for their floor in the first place. People covered their heads with hoods and lay against one another seeking warmth and sleeping positions. Piles of people huddled together in standing circles or sitting heaps, a few roamed about solo. Those were the people Amy tried to focus on, the ones walking without aim, companionless. She followed behind someone with Eric's stature; he was moving away from her and she picked up her step to keep from losing him. As she neared him, he turned abruptly, sensing her, and she found herself facing a stranger.

"Oh, sorry, thought you were someone else," Amy said then kept looking as she navigated back to the wall.

Kate circled her area and called out "Eric?" every few paces. She was drawing unhappy single-eyed glares from the sleepers. After weaving in and among the crowd, maneuvering as through the audience of an outdoor concert, she looped back around to the stone wall.

Determined and increasingly desperate to find Eric, Veronica charged through the lazing students with organized precision. She marched efficiently up and down an invisible grid. *He must be out here,* she thought, *why can't I find him?* She strained to remember what he was wearing to help her identify him in the night. Boxers and nothing else, she realized. He was only wearing boxers when he left her room.

The doors of the building were starting to open as firemen escorted people out and then headed back inside to continue the search, looking in every closet and under every bed to discourage future delinquencies.

Up ahead, Veronica caught a glimpse of him; lit by an overhead streetlight, she saw his unclothed legs sticking out from under a coat. *Thank goodness someone gave him a jacket,* she thought. With a rush of relief, Veronica jogged over and hugged him from behind. He startled and craned his neck over his shoulder to see who was holding him. As though it were choreographed, he rolled to face her, and they both leaned apart on the same beat. It wasn't Eric.

"Oh my gosh! I'm so sorry!" The surprise in Veronica's voice matched the shock on her face.

The guy, though, wasn't upset. "Hey, where are you going? Stay with me, we can keep each other warm."

His buddies joined the chorus: "Come back! We all want a hug like that!"

Veronica went directly to the meeting spot, hoping Amy or Kate had had better luck. Her worry and perplexity escalated into fear and distress. Noticing her approach, Amy wordlessly shook her head as she curled her hair around her finger. The three sat on top of the wall where they could view the lawn and the street full of people. By then, most of the students had given in to a seated position, and the girls looked over their heads in silence.

"Holy shit!" Kate blurted out, then pressed her hand over her mouth.

Veronica and Amy followed her eyes to where a fireman was leading Eric out of the building. He was bare legged and wrapped in a purple blanket. Jenny was on his other side, snuggled up against him under the blanket, wearing fluffy slippers and matching naked legs.

THE HALL PHONE WAS ringing again. Veronica could hear it in their room halfway down the corridor. Clearly, no one was out there to answer. She put down Amy's school newspaper article on protecting yourself from assault and went to stop the ringing.

"Hello?"

"Veronica? Veronica, is that you?"

"Why are you calling me again, Eric? I told you to stop calling. It's over."

"Wait—don't hang up—please—just wait," he pleaded, and when she didn't speak or hang up, he continued. "I'm sorry, Veronica, I'm so sorry, you know that. I want to make it up to you. I swear it was just a stupid mistake. I was drunk and I was an idiot. It meant nothing. I'm sorry."

"Eric?"

"Yes?"

"Don't call me again," and Veronica slammed the receiver onto the pay phone with a satisfying clank. A dozen white notes fluttered on the message board, drawing her attention. *Veronica. Veronica. Veronica.* They were all addressed to her and they all said the same thing: *Eric called.*

She angrily untacked each one and stabbed the pushpins back into the cork. The handwriting varied. How many people had he talked to in the past week? Crumpling them into tight balls, she threw the messages into the overflowing wastebasket on top of the soda cans and Varsity Pizza boxes. Feelings of anger, disappointment, and embarrassment collided and she brushed a tear from her cheek as she returned to the privacy of her room.

Chapter 8

AMY DIDN'T NOTICE HIM at first, but he saved her when he found her. She was huddled in her usual spot in the computer lab, tucked into the corner with her back to the wall, an intentional position to hide her ineptness from the computer-proficient. It was where she sat for hours each week trying to tap out a program in a language she barely understood. It was in that seat that she first noticed his kind face and gentle voice offering to help, handing her a lifeline.

Most of the early-morning classes were reserved for underclassmen. The first week of classes, filled with eagerness, Amy was up, showered, and ready to go like she had done in high school. As the weeks passed, on early-class mornings, Amy brushed her teeth and managed to comb her hair, but it was a minimal get-ready routine, leaving pajamas strewn on the floor and her bed unmade.

On the day that she met Matt Saxon, it was raining. Mindlessly, she threw on the college-girl uniform of fitted leggings topped with a baggy sweatshirt. She lugged her bag onto her shoulder and groggily headed out. Computer programming was the worst class for Amy's nontechnical brain to face first thing in the morning three days a week. It was the worst class for her to face any time of day, on any day of the week. Every Monday the professor assigned a programming assignment that was due each Friday. Panicked about the work, the first week of class Amy launched a habit of heading straight to the computer lab after lunch on Mondays to get started. She needed to work a little every day to finish on time.

Amy knew no one in her class, not a single familiar face. She focused on taking notes, writing down every word the professor said with the hope it would help her solve the programming riddle that week and see her through the required course. She had used computers at her dad's office to type up high school papers, and she played *Pac-Man* and *Space Invaders* on the TV Atari, but doing anything more with computers, let alone writing code, was completely foreign.

She swiped her student ID, leaving the dreary fall day, and entered the dim and humming computer lab. Wide, boxy beige machines filled rows of tables, leaving just enough space for a keyboard in front and a notebook to the side. Dot matrix printers lined the far wall with hole-trimmed paper dangling expectantly from them.

The lab was nearly empty except for the room monitor, who sat behind a desk and enforced the sign-in policy, and two guys to the left of the room with their backpacks lying open on the floor beside them. Amy drifted to her usual computer terminal in the corner, trying to muster the motivation to make another attempt at the week's project.

Unaccustomed to feeling incapable of doing assigned school-work, Amy felt panic pulsing in her throat as she logged on to the mainframe computer, typing in "AMYork," and settled her open textbook on her lap. She pulled out her five-and-a-quarter-inch floppy disk and tucked the photocopy of the lesson under the keyboard. She stared at the black screen dotted with the few lines of cryptic orange characters she'd typed on her first attempt. The blinking cursor taunted her, waiting for the next commands. She flipped through the text, then through the stapled assignment, and looked back to the computer screen. One stinking comma missing and the whole program wouldn't run. Amy twisted her hair around her finger. She was stuck.

Perhaps he sensed her frustration, or perhaps her head in her hands and the audible sighing broadcast it. Near tears, Amy felt someone beside her and lifted her face from her palms to see a tall guy with thick, ruffled black hair standing over her. He had broad shoulders, and beneath his glasses she could see his eyes were lined with thick lashes and framed by even thicker eyebrows. Without a word, he smiled, revealing a dimple on his left cheek. He pulled out a plastic chair, dropped his red backpack, and sat next to her.

"It looks like you could use some help" was all he said. Tears fell down Amy's cheeks. Embarrassed, she nodded and apologized while wiping at her face with her fingertips.

"I'm sorry, I just . . . it's that . . . I just can't get this," she stumbled, grateful for this very sweet and not-so-unattractive spoon. Computer geeks were the only people she ever saw in the lab, which she had privately dubbed Spoon City. They debated the merits of Tandy vs. Commodore vs. Wang, and conversations revolved around something called electronic mail, DOS, and WYSIWYG, which no one outside of there would understand.

"I'm Matt Saxon," he said, scooting his chair closer to the table. "You're Amy, right?"

She flinched, visible in her surprise. Then she smiled and tried to recover from the rudeness she felt in her reaction. "Um, yeah, I'm sorry. Have we met? How do you—"

"I'm in your programming class," he answered, "bright and early, or cloudy and early, Monday, Wednesday, and Friday."

Amy tried to place him.

He continued, easing her discomfort. "I sit a couple of rows behind you, the professor called out attendance the first weeks to learn names . . . Anyway, I'm Matt."

"I'm Amy, well, you know. Amy York." She was acting as unsure in the interaction as she felt in the computer lab. She took in his faded jeans bunched behind his knees and hanging over the tops of his maroon Converse high-tops. The edge of a red-and-black-checkered Velcro wallet peeped out of his rear pocket.

"Thanks," she said, her voice almost a whisper, "thanks for helping me."

He was already leaning over to determine the depth of her problems. Amy noticed his masculine hands easily tapping along the keyboard. She took in his dark wavy hair, casual in its untidiness, and his wide shoulders tugging at the seams of his Rolling Stones T-shirt.

Matt patiently began his instruction. As they worked in the slow and deliberate way that Amy needed, she felt her stress trickle away. He was making sense to her in a way she wasn't grasping in class. They finished her project and it was only Tuesday, leaving her with the next two days after lunch free, opening time she could spend with Andrew. She checked her watch; he would be leaving accounting class in a few minutes—maybe she could catch him there.

With her confidence regained, she thanked Matt, gushing a stream of gratitude.

"Thanks, Matt. Thank you so much. I can't thank you enough. Can we . . . can I meet you here next week?" Amy packed up her bag, still uttering thanks. "Would you mind helping me again?"

He smiled his answer, and thus began their weekly tradition. She noticed that when he smiled with his lips still together, they formed a small heart in the middle. She picked up her umbrella, then looked up at Matt. She had to tip her head back slightly to look at his face, and peering into it, she felt embarrassed that she hadn't noticed him in class. Was she seeing him now because of his kindness? she wondered. Was his personality outshining his shaggy appearance? Maybe, she decided, but he was good-looking. Not in the Chase-hot way, but he had a handsomeness that suited him in his dark coloring, nearly black eyes, and long, straight nose. She even found his slightly crooked teeth endearing. Matt stepped aside so she could leave her corner, his eyes available each time she glanced up.

"See you tomorrow." He smiled fully, the heart of his lips open, beaming warmth into the dim computer lab. "I'm here any time you need me."

"Thank you," Amy said again, her voice full of relief.

Hurrying from the computer lab, Amy headed toward the School of Management building in hopes of finding Andrew. She stood scanning faces as a rush of students filed out the main doors. Spotting him, she started toward him then stopped abruptly, causing a few people to bump into her.

"Sorry," she uttered distractedly. Andrew was laughing, his hand comfortably on the arm of a beautiful brunette, and Amy turned to leave before he saw her.

"Hey, Amy!"

Too late, she thought as he approached with the girl, who looked like she could be an actress in one of Amy's favorite romantic comedies.

Andrew reached for Amy and pulled her into his tight hug. Amy softened, enjoying the smell of his Benetton Colors cologne and forgetting that the beauty was waiting beside them. When Andrew released her, his smile wide across his face, he introduced them.

"Amy York, this is Bree O'Connell. Bree and I are friends from back home."

"New Jersey," Bree added.

Amy greeted her politely, a rush of disappointment mixed with longing for Andrew sweeping through her core. Bree had gorgeous dark hair that muted Amy's by comparison. Her lush look merged Irish green eyes and fair, model-smooth skin with deep accents of thick eyelashes and naturally arched eyebrows.

"Come with us to Schine for a cookie," Andrew invited, and started in the direction of the student center, expecting them to follow.

Bree seemed to sense Amy's hesitation and leaned close to whisper in her ear: "Don't worry, Amy, we used to go out in high school, but we're not together anymore. We're just friends. Come on."

ANDREW HAD GROWN UP in Sparta, a middle-class New Jersey town with some affluence. His family was involved in the community. He was the only boy, the eldest with two younger sisters. From the time he was little, his father pushed him athletically and academically. Andrew was a natural; eager to please his dad and impress his sisters and everyone else. He was earnest, responsible, and excelled in anything he tried. Things came easily to him. Though his successes overshadowed his sisters, they adored him, as did the entire Sparta High School population, students, teachers, and administrators alike. Andrew Gabel was the local hero, the superstar featured weekly in the small-town paper, the *Sparta Independent*.

He auditioned and got the lead in the school play, his presence instantly making drama a coveted activity and drawing others in his wake. He was a starting quarterback his freshman year, unassumingly usurping upperclassmen but endearing himself to them nonetheless with his charm and his game-winning arm. Andrew earned straight A's and played the saxophone. He was president of his class throughout high school, led the student council, and, in his senior year, swept awards night to no one's surprise.

As his girlfriend, Bree O'Connell fit his profile. She was pretty and well liked, and though she was never quite an honors student, she was on the dance team and perkily cheered him on from the sidelines. Their breakup at the end of junior year caused a stir in the student body. He had caught her kissing Dave Nye, another football player, outside during the homecoming dance and called it quits. Bree caused a scene in the middle of the lunchroom, begging for him to understand her mistake, but his pride was hurt and he would not take her back, especially under all those watchful eyes. They hung out in the same circles—Andrew was in everyone's circle—and eventually the incident scabbed over enough for them to be friends. From the outside, it seemed he did everything right, even handling his breakup smoothly, coming out the good guy and coolly being friends with his ex.

At Syracuse, he was a blank, except to Bree. Without his stellar history as his tailwind, he set out to re-earn accolades and special status. In the absence of the adoring Sparta audience, he was just Andrew Gabel, one among thousands of other clean-slated freshmen trying to stand out. To Amy, though, he already stood out. Without knowing his achievements, her attraction to him set him apart from the tangle in the silverware drawer of freshman guys. In her eyes, he was already gleaming as a shining knife.

Chapter 9

"AMY, PHONE CALL." KATE knocked and peeked in through the propped door. "It's a boy," she sang.

Amy chuckled. She went to the lobby pay phone and lifted the receiver dangling from its metal cord. "Hello?"

"Amy? Uh, hi, it's Matt."

After a month of tutorials in the computer lab, their talk had expanded beyond school, and their time together spilled out into social settings: a meal at the student center, a night out at Chuck's or Maggie's. Matt made Amy laugh, and he listened attentively. He told her about his band at home and playing guitar with some guys in his dorm. She shared her articles before submitting them to the school paper and talked to him of her dream to be a journalist. In an easy way, their friendship grew close. They'd jotted their phone numbers in each other's notebooks, but this was the first time he'd called her. Amy hoisted herself onto the wooden stool beside the phone and smiled hearing Matt's voice.

"Hey there! What's up?"

"So, um, I was wondering. Wondering if you would, well, this weekend is our fraternity golf tournament. It's a fundraiser, and I was thinking, I was wondering, as friends, would you, um, come with me? Like, be my date? As friends, I mean, I know you and Andrew, but—"

"Yes, of course I will," Amy interrupted, rescuing him. "And, for the record, I don't think Andrew will ever ask me out."

"With the way you described what happened at that party, and how much he's around, I thought—"

"Nope. Nothing. Anyway, I don't golf but we'll have fun."

Matt's exhale was audible across the line. She pictured him rubbing his thumb along the edge of his jaw, across the stubble that seemed to appear as soon as he shaved. She felt an easy comfort with him and smiled, happy that he asked her.

"Thanks, Amy, I'll see you tomorrow. We can talk more about Saturday then," Matt said with more confidence.

"Thanks for asking me."

Amy replaced the receiver onto its cradle, thinking that their relationship proved that guys and girls can be just friends. As she gathered her books for the library, she wondered for a moment, a little smugly, what her father would say about that.

AMY SLIPPED THROUGH THE WHOOSH of the double glass doors and into the hush of the library. She looked past the information desk, beyond the librarian bent over book cards, robotically stamping each one with a due date. The modern angles of the library battled with aging bindings. Fabric-covered books, their edges powdered with a dust that had become one with the paper, juxtaposed rows of sleek new volumes. High-tech microfiche machines stood beside wooden card catalogs and gray metal carts. Beyond the librarian were the guarded and undesirable first-floor study carrels. The rules there were strictly enforced, any breath above a whisper reprimanded. They were a last resort when all of the hidden stalls were occupied with studying spoons or flirting forks.

With a brisk step, Amy slinked past the library watchdog toward the elevators. Reaching for the button, her bracelets clinked noisily down her arm and elicited an admonishing glare. On the third floor, she spotted Andrew from behind and sighed at his profile as he referred to an open textbook. She approached, enjoying the muscles of his forearm as he made notes. Amy plunked her bag on the floor and slid into the chair Andrew had set up for her.

He turned and they sat knee to knee, looking at each other wordlessly. Amy felt something thick in the space between them, something vibrating in the silence. She tickled inside with anticipation, wondering when, if, how.

Andrew smiled at her, first with his lips together, and then he let them part slightly. He leaned toward Amy; she felt a breath-catching quiver in her chest as his face hovered near. She leaned in, just a small shift. Andrew moved to meet her but held his lips in front of hers, close without touching, taunting. Amy felt his heat mix with hers, felt a tingle in her stomach that moved lower with the faint brush of his lips. He slid his hand beneath her hair, onto her neck, and pulled her to him. She felt the moisture of his breath and savored the sweetness of his touch. Her bracelets jingled down to her elbow as she reached for Andrew's cheek, and they smiled without releasing their kiss. He cradled her head in his palms and ran a thumb along her hairline. Everything in her was responding; she was aware of every sensation in her body. Time slowed and the world narrowed to just the two of them.

Reluctantly, the kiss slowed and returned to softly parted lips before they separated. "Hi," Andrew said, kissing her again tenderly. "Wow!"

Amy beamed at him, the fluttering in her chest blocking any words.

"Wow, Aim," Andrew repeated, and leaned back in his chair

catching his breath. He exhaled deeply and Amy watched his cheeks crease in contentment at their first kiss.

"So, I'm not sure what this all means—" Amy started.

"It means I like you. I really like you." He grinned and leaned forward again. "Let's be a thing."

"A thing?"

He laughed. "We don't have to call it anything, but yeah, let's be a thing."

Amy reeled. She'd been fantasizing about Andrew asking her out since they first met, but did this mean he was asking her out? Since he'd saved her from Paul at the party, she felt a certain bond with him, an undeniable link. He placed a single, lingering kiss on her mouth.

"Okay," she agreed. "Oh, wait."

"Wait?"

She shook her head with a small laugh. "No, not that. It's that Matt called me earlier; he invited me to the Phi Psi golf tournament this weekend, as friends, of course. I told him I'd go with him, just thought I should let you know."

"Sure. He's harmless." He kissed her ear affectionately. "Besides, we're a thing now."

Amy nodded, wishing for a little more definition.

KATE WAS WAITING ON the maroon couches for Amy, books spread on her lap.

"Can we talk?" Kate scooped up her papers and they walked to room 808, greeted Veronica, and plopped onto Amy's bed.

"What's the matter?"

"I don't know, I'm just feeling sort of bummed. I feel like everyone has a boyfriend, or dates, or is at least mashing with someone, and I don't have anyone."

"I don't either," Veronica chimed in, using her dramatic

breakup to cheer Kate. She joined them on Amy's side of their room.

"Most of the time I'm fine, but today it's really bothering me."

"What about that guy who you're always hanging out with? The guy who sat with you in the dining hall last night?" Amy asked.

"Richie? No, he's just a friend." The phrase rang familiar to Amy.

"Are you sure he thinks so?" Veronica asked, and Amy heard her father's words in the question.

"Well, I kind of like him . . ."

"Is he a knife?" Amy nudged. The Utensil Classification System had continued to spread and grow among their floor mates and friends.

"Oh, brother, here we go," Veronica muttered.

"Well, he is really sweet and good to me, but I feel like he hides behind humor. I see the way other people act around him, calling him Dick even though he doesn't like it, but he doesn't stick up for himself. It's like because he's heavy, he plays the funny guy, and I worry that he's not happy even though he makes everyone around him laugh. So what's that in the UCS?" Kate asked.

Veronica rolled her eyes to the ceiling. Amy covered her face with her hands, tapping her fingers against her forehead.

"I've got it! He's chopsticks!"

"He's not Asian, Amy," Kate protested.

"No, no, he doesn't have to be. He's tricky like chopsticks can be tricky to use. He doesn't fit neatly into a category and he can make other people laugh like when things drop from chopsticks right before getting into someone's mouth." Amy began to piece together her reasoning. "Chopsticks can be awkward, clumsy, and a little messy if you don't know how to use them right. Richie still needs to figure out how to put his true self out there. It sounds like he's fun but still a bit unsure of himself."

"Well, that seems like Richie," Kate agreed.

"Hey! I have an idea." Amy stood abruptly and grabbed her toothbrush. "Let's go out tonight. Come on, maybe we'll even see Richie. It's Pub Mug Night at 44's, people will be out."

"No. It's Tuesday. I have tons of work. I can't go out on a Tuesday," Veronica protested.

Kate and Amy both laughed.

"There are no rules that you can't go out on a Tuesday, V," Amy joked. "Come on, just for a little while."

"But I—"

Kate perked up and joined in on the convincing. "For me? Please?" They watched Veronica's brain calculating and deciding as Kate continued: "You know that my parents are teachers, they would die if they knew I went out on a weeknight. 'School is your job' was all I heard growing up."

Agreeing with Kate's parents, Veronica enumerated the reasons she couldn't possibly go out then she started to talk herself into it. "Well, I don't have too much, actually, I did a lot already today. All right. Okay, let's go out!"

"Cool beans," Kate said, clapping her hands, then focusing on Amy. "Are you seriously brushing your teeth again?" She laughed and left to get ready.

Primped and perfumed, the girls gathered at the elevators with a few others joining in, and the group headed out to M Street. At 44's, with coy smiles, flashes of fake IDs, and a flip of the hair, the bouncer let them past his guard. They paid a cover and were handed plastic pub mugs, their ticket to free beer until 10:30. Waiting to get them filled, and swaying in beat with Def Leppard, Kate nudged Amy's arm. She was grinning and holding out a tattered shoelace. Amy looked down: Kate's Keds were bare, the tongues bobbing between the empty holes. She laughed, tying one end of the string around her wrist, the other around her mug handle. All around them, thin ropes and colored lengths of yarn tethered the precious mugs to arms, forcing bartenders to use pitchers to refill outstretched cups.

Arcade games blazed with colored lights at the end of the long, sticky bar. Bodies pressed against bodies as more people were granted their mugs. The odor of sweat mixed with the smell of yeasty beer. The group of girls hovered and swayed with the crowd like sea grass with the tides. The bar swallowed their voices, so they occupied their mouths with their mugs. They emptied them and emptied them and emptied them. Before disappearing, Kate yelled into Amy's ear, "Richie's here! Oh my gosh, I'm so freaked out!"

Amy felt a hand grasp her waistband. She whirled around, knocked the hand off her, and clenched her fists, ready to fight off the offender. She couldn't see among the mash of backs and chests, and then she saw Andrew.

"It's you. Sorry I hit you, I guess I'm a little jumpy."

"Oh, man, sorry, Aim. I wasn't thinking. I saw you and was just trying to surprise you."

"You did." She rested her forehead on his chest, trying to slow the beating of her heart. His hands were around her waist again, pulling her hips to his. The beer made her light-headed, and she felt a surge being up against him.

"I never asked, did you get in trouble for knocking Paul to the ground?"

"Nah, I brought him to fraternity council. He got a slap on the wrist if you ask me, but there was no way I would take any heat because of that asshole. Sorry I scared you."

Over Andrew's shoulder, Amy saw Richie embrace Kate, patting her back in a friendly but awkward way. Kate, open to his hug, clumsy or not, was laughing as she threw her arms around his neck. Richie had a wide waist and wore too-large shirts. His face was perpetually cheerful and his eyes smiled even when his mouth didn't. With only a moment's pause, he clasped Kate's face between his hands and careened over the friend line. Andrew turned to see what Amy was watching.

"Come on, let's do that, too," he teased, and Amy felt his lips tender against hers, even as his intensity was fierce. Their mouths moved in sync, and he maneuvered them as one toward the wall. The crowded bar veiled them in privacy, and she felt the beat of the music equally in her ears and heart. Deep into their making out, Amy thought only of him until they slowed to a sweet kiss. Their faces rested an inch apart and their eyes held them together.

Kate found Amy. "Oh, sorry," she interrupted.

"When you're done, let's book." Andrew nodded toward the rear alley door, opened to let in air, then left Amy alone with Kate. Amy leaned against the wall, feeling its coolness seep into her back.

"Richie kissed me! He kissed me, Amy, I'm so glad we came out. Go without me, he'll take me home," she gushed, and hugged her friend before giddily returning to Richie.

Amy scanned the back of the bar for Andrew. Her visibility was only one sweaty shirt deep, but she craned to see above shoulders and through armpits. At last, she caught sight of him resting against the doorframe and Amy shuffled slowly closer. Then she saw it.

Jenny lingered by his side; she held her hair seductively off her neck and tilted her face up to his. She leaned into him, and her chest touched his shoulder as she whispered into his ear. Amy's face dropped as Andrew raised his hand and cupped Jenny's shoulder. She pushed against bodies to move toward them faster. She lost her view and jockeyed around people who were rooted in place. Close to the door, she burst between two athletes, tall and solid, in time to see Andrew peeling Jenny off him, holding one of her hands away from his crotch and the other from his waist.

"Knock it off, Jenny. Come on, time to go," she heard him reprimand. Relief mixed with guilt as Amy wondered why she had doubted him, and her feelings shifted to anger at Jenny. Amy reached Andrew's side and Jenny stepped back with a startle. Without a word, Jenny turned and fused into the crowd, her empty mug dangling from her wrist.

Chapter 10

IT WAS TWO IN the afternoon and Amy felt like she had the floor to herself. She had finished writing her weekly column for the *Daily Orange* and had moved on to typing an essay on her word processor for Owen Chen, a fraternity brother of Matt's and a friend of Andrew's. Some of the guys had started paying her to type up their papers. It was mindless, easy work for Amy, though she couldn't help but clean up some of their grammar as she went.

Her fingers clicked across the keyboard but stopped abruptly when she heard a shrill "No!" from down the hall. A sickness bubbled in her stomach thinking of Paul, and she knocked over her chair pushing it back and darted toward the cry.

The hall was deserted and still except for a rhythmic sobbing coming from the floor lobby. Amy ran, her bare feet padding silently on the carpet until she saw Jenny, curled into herself on the stool, her back to Amy. She clenched the phone receiver with both hands. Her hair hung loose, covering her face like a curtain, and her shoulders visibly hiccuped in sync with her sobs.

"I can't believe you did that without even talking to me, Mom," Jenny spat. "How could you just throw it away? Don't you know what it means to me?"

Unseen, Amy's first instinct was to go back to her room; her

71

fury with Jenny was raw and palpable. She felt disgust thinking of Jenny hitting on Andrew only a few nights before, and she needed no reminder of what she'd pulled with Eric their first month at school. Amy started to backtrack to her room, to leave Jenny suffering in the lobby, when a wrenching, guttural sob gripped her. She stopped midstep, dropped her shoulders, and, looking up at the ceiling, turned back toward the pay phone. Her decency led her forward and she laid a hand on Jenny's back. Jenny spun, startled; her eyes were framed pink and her pale lashes clumped with tears. Amy stepped back to leave once more, but Jenny clasped her wrist, mooring herself to Amy.

"Don't say that! It's all I had of—" Amy could hear the voice talking in Jenny's ear but not the words. Over her shoulder, Amy noticed messages for Veronica pinned to the board. Each was scribbled with the words *Eric called,* and she looked back at the distraught girl who had hurt her friend.

"Yeah, I know, I know he's not. But you still could've saved it, I could have fixed it, I could have kept the pieces. Why did you even have to be in my room?" Jenny sounded like a whiny teenager. Still secured to Amy, her mauve fingernails sculpted half-moons into Amy's skin. The voice garbled from Jenny's ear.

"I get that it was in a million pieces, but still . . . it's all I had." Jenny spoke with a resigned finality. "I'm gonna go now, Mom. Bye." She held the phone in her hand for a moment longer, still hiding behind her blond screen of hair, before she placed it onto the hook.

She released her grip on Amy and looked numbly past her, not meeting her eyes. "Thanks," she said, and walked without perkiness to her room, leaving Amy alone again with the silence.

AFTER DINNER AND NO SIGN of Jenny, Amy went to brush her teeth before checking on her. In place of her toothbrush in her bathroom basket, she found a rolled-up piece of paper. The note was made of letters clipped one by one from magazines and glued into sentences.

We have your precious toothbrush. If you ever want to see it again alive, deliver one unopened chocolate to the third sink in the bathroom. Come alone. Do not call the police. Or else. Pay up or the toothbrush gets it.

Amy played along and grabbed a handful from her stash of chocolate minis. Then she pulled out a spare toothbrush and scrubbed her teeth while delivering the candy to the bathroom sink. On the way back to her room, she tied a small bag of chocolates to the dangling pen on Kate's door then knocked without waiting for her to answer.

Amy shored herself and walked to the end of the hall. She struggled, reluctance weighing against sympathy. In her heart, she knew Jenny was hurting, and that truth allowed her, in the moment, to put her own betrayals aside and knock firmly on Jenny's door. She waited; the door wasn't propped open like it so often was. It didn't take long to cross a dorm room, so Amy tapped again after a pause, with less conviction. She was uncapping the purple dry erase marker beside Jenny's message board when the door cracked. Jenny peeped out and darkness poured from behind her. She sniffled and dabbed at the redness of her nose with a bunched-up tissue.

"I wanted to check on you," Amy said. "How are you doing?"

Jenny opened the door a fraction wider, accepting Amy's kindness. She stepped in, and Jenny tugged the chain on her bedside lamp, casting a golden luster. The dimness made Amy woozy, and she eased herself into the beanbag chair with its fuzzy purple cover. Jenny's room matched her personality and had a phosphorescence about it, but there was not a single photograph of family or friends, Amy noticed. Tones of violet filled the space. Round paper lanterns hung at different heights from the ceiling above her desk, which was full of pencils topped with feathers and pens coated in glitter. A huge painting hung by a wide ribbon and was surrounded by smaller paintings, all in shades of purple and all signed in the corner *Jenny-Doe*, Jenny's childhood nickname, she had once explained. Amy admired the images again, thinking she had a true artistic talent.

Jenny plopped onto her bed, stomach down, and hugged a lavender velour pillow under her chin. "Sorry about before. I mean, thanks for being there, but sorry you had to hear it."

"I don't know what's going on, Jenny, but I'm here to listen if you want."

"My mom, well, it's just my mom and me, you know," she began.

Amy nodded. "I just have my dad."

"And she threw something away that really mattered to me . . ."

Amy thought of how her relationship with Jenny had been arm's length, polite, skeptical, and had only skimmed the surface like a dragonfly lilting over a pond. She had the distinct sense that they were hovering at a shifting point.

Amy recalled one of their first nights on campus and how much Jenny had revealed to complete strangers. She had scoped out a few couplets of roommates and gathered them in her room. Then, sitting cross-legged on the corner of her bed, she had opened court.

"So, how are we going to meet some guys?" she began.

Leaning in conspiratorially, she told the group about how she snagged a gorgeous guy on the beach that summer. As he walked by, no doubt looking her way, she pretended her bathing suit top had broken. Jenny coyly asked him to get her tank top draped over her bag, and then she rolled to her side, giving him a good peek.

Amy was surprised at the stories from a girl they had met only days before. Oblivious to her audience, Jenny continued with tales of her California flirtations. Her litany of exploits and experience gushed forth tinged with a wisp of fiction. "The Jenny Callista Legends," Veronica had said to Amy when they were back in their room.

Situated again in Jenny's single months later, Amy realized that even the coarse details she had shared that night might not compare with what she was holding back now. She watched as Jenny teetered between divulging and concealing.

Jenny tiptoed in to the subject: "My mom was dusting my bookshelves. I don't even know why, it's not like she was always cleaning my room when I was home or anything. But she knocked over a stack of books and a tea set that really mattered to me went crashing and every piece broke . . ."

Amy sat still, intent on Jenny's face and words, allowing her space and time.

"I loved that set. All the pieces fit on a china tray. It was purple with white flowers and I loved to pour water from the teapot into the tiny cups. I would take sips and serve my stuffed animals and my dad." Jenny hesitated and took a breath. "It was from my dad. He gave it to me when I was little. It's all I had when he—" Jenny crumbled, crying again.

Amy leaned out of the beanbag chair and kneeled beside Jenny. "It's okay, go ahead and cry," Amy whispered as she stroked Jenny's back. The lamplight cast long shadows up the walls like ghosts overlooking the scene.

"I should have hidden it. I always kept it in my room," Jenny choked out between sobs, "but I should have protected it and put it in my closet or wrapped it into a box before coming here. I can't believe she threw it away. She threw it all away."

"Could she get it out of the garbage?" Amy suggested, knowing it was a stupidly obvious idea, but she wanted to be helpful and didn't know what else to say.

"Gone. The garbage is already gone."

Of course she had already asked that of her mother.

"She just dumped everything." Jenny's voice faded: "It's really gone. I'll never find it."

Chapter 11

THE GOLF TOURNAMENT WAS Veronica's first date with someone other than Eric in years, and she woke easily with anxious excitement, dozing in bed and daydreaming long before she had to be up. She'd met Scott Mason when he and Matt sat with them for lunch one day. They quickly discovered that Scott was the Phi Psi who rowed crew for Syracuse, the great guy that Eric had mentioned meeting at Brown. "Sorry he turned out to be a jackass," Scott said, and the coincidental connection prompted him, in that moment, to ask Veronica to be his golf tournament date and she accepted, feeling a rare impulsiveness.

Veronica's dad was a Phi Psi and would approve of her going to the fraternity's philanthropic event, she told herself, even if her parents remained dubious of her breakup with Eric. When she told them the news, she'd intended to withhold the fact that he had cheated on her to protect him from the Newport chattering, but when she was met with their disbelief and hints of fault, the truth burst from her. It wasn't that her parents blamed her, really, but she felt their disappointment seep into their attempt at support.

As Amy's alarm clock radio went off in the middle of Joan Jett singing, *I hate myself for loving you,* Veronica thought of Eric and shook her head, trying to dislodge him. She got up and draped a towel over her shoulder, then laughed, seeing Amy's toothbrush hanging by its neck, spinning above her desk despite the chocolate ransom. She flip-flopped to the bathroom, still rubbing sleep from her head. She claimed the middle shower with her towel then waited for a toilet stall to open. She shifted from foot to foot and stood on tiptoes. Finally, Kate emerged from a stall in her high-necked, lace-edged Laura Ashley nightgown, her bangs still neat across her forehead defying a night's sleep.

"Morning, Veronica," Kate said, her genuine smile softening Veronica to the day.

Veronica rushed past her. "Morning. Sorry, I'm dying, I've got to go so badly."

She squatted over the toilet and peed grandly. Even though this was her home now, it was still a public toilet and she could never sit on the seat.

"FLUSHING!" Veronica hollered before stepping on the handle and sending scalding water to her showering friends.

"WHO'S YOUR DATE, JENNY?" Sarah asked as a group from their dorm walked to the quad together. Veronica hung back, still keeping her distance from Jenny since that fateful fire alarm.

Owen Chen, whose papers Amy had been typing, responded: "Biggest douche bag in the house! And he's been talking about the hot girl he's bringing nonstop."

Jenny turned toward Owen with her hands on her hips, appearing angry at his assessment of her date and flattered by the compliment.

He cautioned, "Watch yourself, Jenny, I'm telling you, Greg's a dick."

Jenny instantly started to defend him. "Seriously, Owen, how could you say that about him? He's been through so much. You don't even know," she argued, as if she knew Greg intimately. "He's survived hypothermia from hiking one of the biggest mountains, his dad died three years ago, and he had to work through high school to help support his family. Isn't that so sweet? He didn't even get to do anything for himself in high school because he was so busy working since his mom couldn't because she was so depressed from his dad dying. He couldn't even go to his own prom." Jenny said this last part like that was the worst part of the whole list. She continued spilling the secrets he'd offered her, sounding more fantastical as she went. Owen let a disbelieving puff of air rush through his lips and quickened his pace.

"Really," Jenny insisted, falling back a step to walk with the girls, "he's a knife, he's a really nice guy. I met him at 44's and we talked and talked. He walked me home and we just held hands, the ones that weren't attached to our mugs, and we talked the whole way. We didn't even, like, really hook up that night, we just made out. Isn't that, like, so adorable?"

"44's? You only met him on Tuesday?" Sarah blurted out. They knew what night 44's doled out cups that became affixed to their owners.

"No, it was *last* Tuesday," she retorted, the extra week an important detail. "We didn't stay long, but we talked a lot, and then he asked me out for this golfy thingy."

The girls exchanged a collective eye roll and continued without further commentary; what they said wouldn't matter. As Jenny rejoined the boys ahead, Sarah said to Veronica and Amy, "Let's try to keep watch on her, just in case." Wordlessly, Veronica looked at Amy, who nodded at Sarah in agreement.

"Seriously, Amy, I'm not sure how you can still be nice to her," Veronica said, not maliciously but matter-of-factly.

"She's got something going on. I don't know what it is but there's something up," Amy explained quietly. "I'm not excusing her actions, but I think she needs some empathy. I'm starting to think that maybe she doesn't even get how awful she's been."

"You are a hopeless optimist." Veronica shook her head at her friend, but she said it with a smile. She appreciated Amy's kind heart and idealistic nature even if she didn't feel the same way about Jenny. "For the record," Veronica added, "she's probably going to get wasted and make a spectacle on the quad, and one of us will have to pick up her pieces."

"You're a hopeless realist," Amy retorted, leaving them both laughing as they arrived at the temporary country-club setup.

Matt spotted them and half jogged over. He timidly kissed Amy's cheek, and his shaggy hair tickled her nose. His torn jeans and endless concert T-shirts were replaced by crumpled khakis and a navy polo shirt.

"You look good, Matt," Amy said as he handed her a golf club and tucked their scorecard into his pocket.

Chapter 12

THE QUAD LOOKED LIKE minigolf minus the ramps and windmills; Matt gently put his hand between Amy's shoulder blades and guided her to the first stop: beer. Though never one to skip a meal, Amy had only had time for a granola bar for breakfast and she was already hungry. Somewhere inside her, beer for breakfast seemed like a bad idea, but her hand grasped the royal-blue plastic cup and she took her first gulp.

The morning air felt soft around her, a plushness that eased away as the crowd of golfers aggregated. Teams of four gathered by the leaderboard to find their starting holes. Veronica tapped Amy's shoulder and waved a scorecard.

"We're together."

"We who? You and Scott?" Either the early hour or the first sips of beer made her thoughts slow.

As if answering, Scott appeared and kissed Veronica's temple. *That's sweet,* Amy thought, feeling that kissing sensation flutter through her.

As the sun grew higher, Amy stripped off her cardigan and tied it around her waist. She felt a subtle floating in her head as the last gulp of that first beer hit her empty stomach. It was that dangerous, playful feeling—the kind that seems as though it will last in that exact, breezy, contented state forever. In a nonthinking thought process, it was clear to Amy that just another sip would make the happy feeling last longer, and she tipped the empty cup again, letting the last drip trickle into her mouth.

"Not so fast, Amy, we have a long day ahead," Matt cautioned.

She looked at his hand touching her forearm and noted, not for the first time, how masculine it was with faint veins pushing through the skin. She took his hand in hers and smiled up at him. He returned her smile but reclaimed his hand, finding a stubby pencil in his pocket and scribbling something on their scorecard.

Hole by hole, sip by sip, they golfed and laughed their way through the course. Matt could always make Amy chuckle with his witty comments and his well-timed one-liners. The damp morning warmed to a rare sunny Syracuse day. The campus yawned into wakefulness and groups of students passed, their necks craned at the golf course that had sprung up on the quad overnight. Shouts of celebration wove between mournful "awws" and occasional curses. Teams meandered, drank, stroked, scored, and jotted down numbers.

As they looped the holes, Scott brought another round of beer-filled cups. The delayed realization that the previous cups had worked their way into her head didn't stop Amy from accepting one. It was her turn to putt again. She balanced her beer on a nearby bench and took her stance at the tee. She wasn't doing badly and was actually having fun pushing that little ball around.

Amy lined herself up and took aim. She swung and hit the dimpled ball, sending it sailing past the hole, past the bench, past the next hole and straight into the hole beyond. Hole in one! She swung her club in victory out to her side, nearly smacking Matt in the head, and the whole foursome cheered wildly. The stunned group, whose hole Amy had used, turned toward the celebration and joined in as understanding dawned. Amy skipped over to the hole to retrieve her ball and discovered it was Jenny's team.

"Way ta go, Amy, you got it in the hole," Jenny slurred. She looked like she was about to reach out to hug Amy, but instead she abruptly changed direction and wrapped her arm around a nearby tree. She leaned forward and Amy saw her shoulders heave in even bursts, as used beer splattered along the trunk. She handed her club to Matt and went to Jenny, pulling her hair up and rubbing her back. *Veronica was right.* The reflex of Jenny's heaving back beneath her hand transferred a feeling of nausea to Amy. Her stomach lurched and churned. She turned her head away from the vomit smell and claimed a few deep breaths of air.

She wondered which guy was Jenny's date. No one on her team seemed to be concerned or to even notice that Jenny was getting sick. As Amy glanced around, Jenny pulled herself to standing and meandered away. Amy followed and clutched her shoulder.

"Where are you going, Jenny?"

"I've got her, don't worry," answered a brusque voice. Greg, Amy presumed. He put his body in Jenny's path and wrapped his free arm around her possessively.

Jenny gazed up and smiled. "See, don't worry, all set, I'm fine I'm fine I'm fine, s'okay, Amy, s'all okay."

Matt was beside them. "We should take her home," he said to Amy, then turned to his fraternity brother. "Greg, we'll take her home, you can stay."

"Butt out, Saxon."

Undeterred, yet without aggression, Matt reached out to Greg, who pitched forward unsteadily. "We've got her, Greg," Matt said firmly.

Veronica and Scott approached, and, with Jenny's other teammates, gathered into a messy half-circle. Greg postured and drew his fists to his chest as he swayed to the side. Losing interest, he turned away from Matt, dropping his arms limply. He staggered to Jenny and pulled her to him.

For a moment, everything seemed to stand still. Amy glanced around the circle; she knew that Veronica was savoring her time with Scott and the earnest attention he was giving her. The day passed speckled with small kisses that got longer and handholding that crept into waist-holding. Of all the golfing couples, only Matt and Amy seemed to still have a cushion of space between their bodies. Amy watched as Veronica's deep sense of right emerged. Despite wanting to stay, despite her acrimony toward Jenny, she took a turn at trying to take Jenny home.

"Come on, Jenny, let's go," she said, and tried to pry her away from Greg. "Time to go."

Jenny pulled away, showing a forcefulness they'd never witnessed. "I dote wanna go, I'm staying."

A golf cart hummed up the hill toward the growing crowd and stopped at the edge of the crescent of people. The men who got out were muscled and clearly in-charge kind of guys. Matt whispered to Amy that they were alumni there for the tournament. They converged on the group, and Greg took several stumbling steps back. He threw his golf club on the ground and stormed away, forgetting Jenny and retreating even before either alum could speak.

Veronica joined Amy. "We'll see you later."

"What do you mean? You don't have to go." Amy insisted that she go back with Jenny instead, but Veronica dismissed her with a wink.

"We'll get Jenny into her bed all safe, then Scott and I will get some time alone," Veronica explained. "Don't worry, she's not ruining anything for me."

The alums guided Jenny to the golf cart, Veronica and Scott hopped on back, and they rode off. As people dispersed and the sound of tapping golf balls resumed, Amy and Matt heard, "Well, since we've both lost our teammates, let's play together!"

Amy didn't feel like playing anymore. The beer was sitting in her uncomfortably, but she looked at Matt, who still seemed fresh and eager to continue.

Matt read her mood. "Are you okay? We don't have to play anymore."

How does he do that?

"No, it's okay. We can keep going," Amy reassured him, not wanting to disappoint. "Besides, I just got a hole in one, that's got to count for something." Amy rallied with a smile as the new teammates teed up.

All around, cheers, voices, moans, and screeches mixed to create a solid drone. Blue cups were strewn everywhere and another was placed into Amy's palm. Just having it there made it go into her body. Mindlessly, she putted, sipped, talked, and moved to the next hole. Putted. Sipped. Talked. Moved. A fogginess was replacing her earlier lightness.

Matt handed Amy a hot dog with a neat yellow ribbon of mustard across it. That yellow line was vivid to her even as the edges of her consciousness blurred. She gratefully finished the hot dog and cleared her mouth with a swish of beer. With each gulp, the beer tasted worse and became harder to swallow. That just-right, not-drunk space declined into a dizzy-drunken feeling. Amy clung closer to Matt and tried to appear steady. She worked to enunciate her words, hearing herself from outside herself. Her tongue was sticking and couldn't catch up to her thoughts. She felt the assurance of Matt's hand loosely at her back.

Then she was home. Dim light peeked into the room from the parted curtains. From her bed, moving only her eyes, she observed her shoes, usually kicked off in a corner, lined up by the door and her clothes folded by her bed. *Folded?* She was wearing her favorite light blue boxy Kappa T-shirt, wide at the neck exposing her collarbones. Disoriented, she squeezed her eyes together and ran her tongue over her filmy teeth; when she brushed the hair out of her eyes, her forehead drummed from the faint touch. Focusing, she threw back the covers and hopped out of bed, only to lose her balance and sit back down.

"Take it slowly," came a soothing voice. She hadn't noticed Matt sitting in her desk chair, her favorite photo of her dad on the shelf behind him. Matt had her anthropology text opened on his crossed knee in the dusky light, and he was still in his polo shirt and khakis from yesterday. *Was it yesterday?*

"Matt, what happened?"

He closed the book, exposing the crooked yellow USED sticker along its binding, and returned it to her shelf, then he sat beside Amy on her bed.

"Don't worry. You had a little too much to drink, but I brought you back here and helped you get ready."

Her mind retrieved the golfing, Veronica and Scott slipping away in the golf cart, Matt offering her a hot dog. And the blue cups. Yellow mustard and blue cups. White golf balls and blue cups. Green grass and blue cups.

Matt saw the confusion in her eyes as she puzzled over the missing hours. His hand rested gently on her shoulder. It calmed her and she gingerly turned her body to face his. She folded her leg beneath her, yanked the edge of her T-shirt over her thighs, and hugged a pillow modestly onto her lap.

"But how . . ." she began, "how did I . . . ?"

"I helped you get ready, but don't worry, you got dressed by yourself. I went in the hallway." He knew her unspoken questions and her tension softened with his answers. "I stayed to be sure you were okay and didn't need anything. You've been asleep for a couple of hours. How do you feel?" He removed his hand from her shoulder and ran his thumb along his jaw.

"I'm so sorry," she said, feeling tears rise. "I'm so sorry I messed up your day!"

Matt smiled. "Amy, you could never . . ." he started, the smile melting into something else. "I had fun with you, Amy. I always do."

Before she could respond, he said, "I left you a cup of water on the windowsill."

She gagged when she saw the blue cup by the window, and a pain shot through her skull as a knock fired and her door pushed open.

"Hey, Aim. Oh, hi, Matt, didn't know you'd be here." Matt stood and Andrew reached his hand out for a firm shake. "Thanks for taking care of her, man." His tone was even and it was hard to tell if he was being sincere or sarcastic.

Turning to Amy, Andrew leaned down and kissed her. "I just saw Owen, he said you didn't look so hot at the end of the day, so I came right over."

His smell, the smell she loved, caused a moment of nausea. She gulped for a breath. When she looked over Andrew's shoulder to thank Matt, he was gone.

Chapter 13

AMY HAD BLURTED THE INVITATION without thought and so she found herself with Jenny on the bus bound for Connecticut. She had noticed Jenny lingering in the lobby as the floor emptied for Thanksgiving break, busying herself painting her toenails and worrying an issue of *Cosmopolitan* as she waved good-bye to everyone.

"You're bringing her *home?*" Veronica was incredulous when Amy confessed her impulsive act. "Don't let her take advantage of you, Amy."

"I won't, but I felt bad. She had nowhere to go and she would've been the only one left here. Plus, it's only four days," Amy said, defending her decision to herself as much as to Veronica.

The Thanksgiving travelers were piled with luggage, bumping bags against armrests and into heads as they filed on board, searching for vacant seats.

"Thanks for inviting me to come home with you," Jenny said for the fifth time since they sat. "Sometimes it's hard to be far from home. This will be the first Thanksgiving I haven't spent with my mom."

"You can call her when you get to my house and tomorrow, too, to wish her a happy Thanksgiving," Amy suggested and tucked the snack bag on the seat between them. As the bus lumbered along, the two chattered, dozed, munched, and gazed at the other passengers.

"Do you have a list?" Jenny asked abruptly.

"A list?"

"Yeah, you know, a list of the things you want in a guy."

"Yeah, I have a list." Her eyebrows pinched together as she smiled, somehow both amazed and unsurprised that they had this in common.

"What's on it?" Jenny asked.

"Well, there's the list of things I really want, like he has to be responsible and kind, not afraid to show his emotions, and he has to support me in my journalism career and have a job of his own, of course. I want a guy who will be a true partner, who completely gets me." Amy thought of Andrew and smiled. "Maybe it's unrealistic to think a guy could completely understand me, but I want to feel like he does, or at least tries."

Amy rattled off some of the traits memorized from years of writing and editing her list. She pictured the pale green sheet of copy paper, folded and folded upon itself into a small square that she kept tucked in her Treasure Box. For her sixth birthday, her dad had built the box and painted it yellow with her name on top; she had instantly dubbed it her Treasure Box.

"Then there's the list of things I don't want, things that are sort of deal-breakers."

"Like what?"

Without hesitation, Amy answered using the language that all the Brewster 8 girls conversed in: "A slotted spoon or a fork. Someone who doesn't care about his grades or his job, or someone who's mean to people. If he can't be nice to the waiter or his own mother, someday he's not going to be nice to me. And most important is trust. If I can't trust him, forget it!"

89

Jenny whiplashed in a new direction. "Why is it just you and your dad?"

Amy paused. Her friends in Newtown knew and she had rarely had to explain, but since starting college, she'd had to share the story more often. She gave Jenny the quick version.

"I never knew my mom. They were older parents, waiting while my mom fought cancer. She finally was given the all clear and got pregnant. In her sixth month, they learned the cancer was back. They did what they could, but she died when I was only seven weeks old. It's been my dad all along; we're really close. I guess you can understand that since it's just you and your mom."

Jenny shrugged. "Not really. My mom and I fight more than we get along. We love each other, of course, but honestly, I'm not that close to her. She works a lot and goes out with different guys who aren't really interested in having me around."

There was so much about Jenny she didn't know, Amy thought, despite how—with the intensity of time together and the immersion in life's details—it seemed that at college, floor-mates got to know each other more quickly and more personally than in high school relationships. Quirks were in full view—there was no hiding them while living together—and it wasn't just between roommates that secrets were revealed and personal preferences displayed. Living together meant sharing idiosyncrasies with the whole floor.

They lived with women who could recognize one another by the feet glimpsed beneath toilet stalls, easily matching flip-flops to their owners. They brushed teeth side by side, witnessing a variety of approaches, from the closed-mouth brusher to the talking-while-brushing style. There were girls who turned off the water as they brushed and girls who left it running until the sink filled; brushers whose spitty toothpaste bubbles dribbled down their wrists and brushers who meticulously spit into the drain and rinsed the sink. Just the simple, everyday act of brushing one's teeth divulged a world of differences, but it didn't let you see into another's heart and home life.

THOMAS YORK WAS WAITING at the station to pick up the girls. His once-brown hair was heavily peppered with white and swept neatly into place. He was dressed casually in jeans and a gray sweater with a blue collar poking out. He kissed Amy's cheek as he took the biggest bag from each of the girls. Once they were loaded into the car he said, "Come here, kiddo," and pulled Amy into a full embrace. "I've missed you!"

Amy wrapped her arms around him and relaxed into being with her dad. "I missed you, too, Dad." The words vibrated into his chest as she smelled the familiar scent of him, leather and wood. The scent of home.

To her side, Amy noticed Jenny stuck in place, watching the scene as though watching a movie. Her face was frozen but her eyes followed along.

AFTER CLEANING UP from a light supper, the girls helped Amy's Aunt Joanie in the kitchen with the final Thanksgiving meal preparations. Aunt Joanie and Uncle Arthur always came down from Vermont and helped Joanie's brother hold up the Thanksgiving tradition of hosting their family. Amy felt soothed by mixing the pumpkin filling ingredients and pouring them into the hand-sculpted piecrusts. While Amy baked, Aunt Joanie put Jenny in charge of laying out the silver and crystal at the table set for eleven, wedding gifts that Amy's mother had loved and that her father insisted on each year. It took all the leaves of the dining room table to accommodate everyone.

"Wow, you guys really go all out!" Jenny admired as she fingered the cloth napkins and placed the salad fork outside of the dinner fork. Giggling, she popped her head into the kitchen. "Hey,

Amy, is there a silver fork in your silverware system yet? Maybe he's a really cocky guy who is also a total rich snob. Maybe a silver fork is born with a silver spoon in his mouth."

"Someone who treats a woman like his possession."

"Oh! And maybe a silver steak knife is the perfect guy who is also filthy rich, someone like John F. Kennedy Jr., Rob Lowe, or Jon Bon Jovi," Jenny added.

"What are you girls talking about?" Aunt Joanie asked as the phone rang.

Chuckles still bubbled from her lungs as Amy grabbed the white kitchen phone from its wall cradle. "Hello?"

"Hi, Aim, it's me." Andrew's voice caressed her across the distance. "I miss you."

She stretched the long curly phone cord from the wall, across the kitchen, around the corner, and into the bathroom. She sat on the edge of the toilet cover, threading her finger through the loops of the cord. *He called,* she thought, *on our first day apart.*

"Miss you, too. I'm happy you called." Amy dropped her voice to a hush, feeling a special intimacy in the privacy of their call. She leaned back against the toilet tank and twirled the phone cord like a jump rope, letting it slap the tile floor with every turn.

"How's it going with Jenny? You hanging in there?"

"Actually, it's going great, she's nice," Amy replied as a lilting voice cooed in the background on Andrew's side of the line before a man's voice cut in.

"Hello? Hello? Who's there?"

"I'm on the phone, Dad," Amy answered into the phone.

"Already? Okay, but be snappy, I've got to make a call."

"Dad, please! Hang up!" She blushed alone in the dim bathroom as her father replaced the receiver elsewhere in the house.

"Happens here, too," Andrew assured her. "My mom and sisters are constantly picking up the phone when I'm on it."

"Come on, Andrew, it's our turn, everyone's waiting. Who are you talking to?" Amy heard a girl flirt clearly, as if she were speaking directly into the phone, which meant that her mouth was very near his. When she could no longer make out the muffled words, Amy knew Andrew had pressed his hand over the receiver. The tip of Amy's finger purpled while she waited. She unwound the coil, releasing her finger then tangled another one into the white rubbery ringlets. She resisted acting the jealous girlfriend though her stomach felt the undeniable wobble.

"Sorry. I'm back," he said.

"Guess you've got to go." The words spilled out involuntarily and she hoped they didn't sound demanding.

"Yeah, I guess I should. Some high school buddies are over. Bree and the girls organized a game of Trivial Pursuit," Andrew explained. "Next they're planning Truth or Dare."

Amy pushed out an insincere laugh, not knowing if he was serious. Who played Truth or Dare at their age? She wondered exactly how Andrew felt about her, wondered exactly where she stood. Then she dismissed the thought, he had called because he missed her, hadn't he? And he was honest with her about Bree being there, he wasn't hiding it, she reasoned. So why did she still feel apprehensive knowing he was with his ex-girlfriend?

"THANK YOU FOR A delicious meal, Aunt Joanie," Jenny said, scraping the last plate and stacking it into the sink. "And what a great family you have."

Before Amy's aunt could answer, her dad walked into the kitchen. "Come on, girls, let's go for a drive," he said. It was a statement more than a suggestion. Joanie smiled to herself, accustomed to her younger brother's timing, and plunged her yellow-gloved hands into the soapy water.

Jenny looked at Amy as she tugged her arm into her coat. "Where are we going?"

Amy shrugged. "Nowhere, really."

From the time Amy was a young girl, Tom York would take her out for drives around their hometown. When he wanted to talk to her, he'd announce, "Let's go for a drive," and head to the garage. At some point, she understood it was easier to approach certain topics without having to make eye contact. These drives stirred in her a mixture of excitement and dread, as it was cherished time with her dad tangled with the wondering of whether something was wrong. As he weaved the car through the wooded roads, he'd open his discussion, Amy in the front seat beside him.

"So, Dave's been hanging out at the house a lot lately," he'd begin, shifting in his seat. "You two are getting quite close."

"Not in that way, Dad, he's just a friend. He's like hanging out with a brother."

"Does Dave feel that way?"

"Really, Dad, you're not even close on this one. We're friends, of course Dave knows we're just friends."

In a cryptic, halting speech, her dad would try to clue her in to how guys think, to how they act when they like a girl. He tried to enlighten her on what Dave was really feeling.

"We're just friends, Dad," she'd insist, dismissing his analysis of the situation. She denied his words aloud and ignored the nudge in her gut, thinking of the moments when friendships had blurred into something more.

Driving a little longer before winding back home, the conversation would shift to easier subjects like school and sports. That was the general formula for one of Thomas York's drives with his daughter and, now, with Jenny.

"Sit in the front, Jenny," her dad directed, and Amy slid to the middle of the backseat where she could lean forward between them.

Sticking his favorite album into the cassette player, they drove through the back roads with only the sound of Billy Joel singing before Tom York spoke. His eyes focused on the road, and his left arm rested along the window. "So, Jenny, was this your first New England Thanksgiving?"

Amy breathed relief: he was starting slowly. Sometimes he just dove right in to whatever he was thinking. Then in the next instant, there it was.

"You live alone with your mom?"

Oh, no, Amy thought, *where is he going with this?* She worried that Jenny would feel uncomfortable and she opened her mouth to buffer the situation for her, but Jenny was already answering, her voice sounding at ease.

"Yes, it's just the two of us. Sometimes we spend holidays with my mom's sister, who lives a couple of hours away, or sometimes with a guy she's seeing, but it's quiet around our house. My mom's a nurse and has long shifts, so sometimes it's just me at home."

Jenny was sharing more with Amy's dad than she had with Amy in months at school. Amy slid back into the darkness and watched the streetlights flash squares of gold on the seat beside her.

"Where's your father?"

Amy's head flew up at the question. Jenny had never mentioned her father except for the story about the tea set he had given her as a child. Amy assumed her parents had divorced, but then seeing how upset she was over the tea set, she thought maybe he had passed away. Amy held her breath and tilted her head, aiming her ear toward the front seat.

Jenny inhaled audibly. "He left."

Amy's father kept his eyes forward. He gave a single nod and Jenny continued.

"He left when I was six. I was playing outside on the front steps, with a purple tea set—" Her voice caught but she went on. "He kissed the top of my head and, like he always did, said,

'Good-bye, Jenny-Doe'—that was his nickname for me—and he drove away. I never saw him again."

Amy's heart clenched, her hand floated unconsciously to her chest. *How incredibly awful,* she thought, *how painful and sad.* Instantly, she saw Jenny differently. Her promiscuity and flirtations, her forced perkiness and painted-on confidence, were changed with this new perspective on her past.

Amy's dad cleared his throat. "I'm sorry, Jenny, that must be very hard for you. There's something I want you to remember." He paused, choosing his words. "Remember to value who you are no matter what. Believe you are worth being loved and don't ever settle."

Jenny's head dropped forward and she swiped a finger across her eyelid. Her whole life, Amy had heard the words her dad told Jenny. She had internalized the message, having received it time after time. Her father helped shape how Amy saw herself. He had worked to build her self-confidence in moments accumulated and cemented through years of repetition, and it shocked her to realize that Jenny may never have been told by her own father that she was important, that she mattered. *Is it possible that she doesn't know that she deserves love and respect?*

Amy felt a surge of compassion toward Jenny and increased admiration for her own father. How had he known that Jenny needed one of his drives? How did he know what to say to her, how to get her to share?

Then her dad spoke again. "You know, life will bring you ups and downs, good times and bad ones, and you need to love yourself to be able to handle them." He looked to Jenny. "Never forget that. You have to love and value yourself." As they turned to head back home, he turned up the volume on "Piano Man" and asked, "So, what are your plans for tomorrow, girls?"

Chapter 14

VERONICA'S PARENTS WERE HOSTING their annual Thanksgiving eve Warren Foundation fundraiser her first night home. She had just enough time to change and pin up her hair before she was expected to wade through the crowd of her parents' friends, smiling and repeating the answers to "How is school?" "What's your major?" "Happy to be home?" "How's Eric?"

She watched in the distance as Susan Warren floated among her guests, grinning effusively, and as her father laughed grandly, slapping shoulders in a circle of men. All she wanted was to curl up in her pajamas, sit around the kitchen table, and tell her parents about school, but she smiled and moved on to the next group.

"I'm glad I got to see you, Mrs. Everett. Say hi to Bitsy for me."

"Oh, she goes by Elizabeth now, dear."

Veronica nodded and turned toward the crowded living room, thinking she could say a few final hellos and then slip away upstairs.

"Veronica."

She recognized the voice and found herself facing Mr. Eric Sheridan Sr., his familiar face turned serious. His eyes drilled into her and she felt like she was looking into Eric's.

"So you went and broke our boy's heart," he began.

At first, Veronica thought he was joking, but his gaze said

he wasn't. She opened her mouth to speak but shock stole her words.

"Mrs. Sheridan and I were very disappointed to hear that you won't take any of his calls, just cut him off," he continued, filling the space where Veronica should have spoken.

"I—he—but—it's that—" Veronica stammered, screaming at herself inside to form a sentence, to respond. "We both decided it wasn't working out." Her Newport upbringing propelled her to weave the little lie to protect Eric, to protect his parents from the truth, even as he clearly laid the blame on her. That fib battled inside her. The truth rose in her throat swimming for air. She swallowed it down.

"You know, Veronica, men have a lot of responsibility. Eric is at Brown, after all. In the end, it's the woman's job to make it work out," he accused.

Her manners tempered her words, and spinning some sugar from the bitterness, she said, "Nice to see you, Mr. Sheridan. Happy Thanksgiving." Then she headed toward the kitchen and the back staircase to her escape.

Comfy in pj's, she called to tell Amy.

"What an antique fork," Amy said, concocting a UCS label for Mr. Sheridan. "That gives us a lot to consider. Does that mean forks don't grow out of it? Once a fork, always a fork? I wonder, can an antique fork change his tines?"

Veronica caught herself smiling, grateful for Amy's perpetual cheer.

VERONICA PADDED INTO THE kitchen to the smell of turkey roasting and serving dishes laid out on the counters, labeled neatly with what would soon fill each one.

"Morning, sweetie."

Her mother was already showered, made up, and dressed with

an apron over her slim wool skirt and fitted sweater in a matching shade of Wedgwood blue. She had ordered most of the meal from her favorite caterer and would have help preparing and serving the banquet, but she insisted on the tradition of making homemade stuffed mushrooms, her grandmother's recipe.

"How are you already up and ready, Mom? What time did the party end last night?" Veronica covered a yawn with the back of her hand as she poured coffee with the other.

"Oh, I don't sleep much anymore, you know, not since, well, since, you know," her mother said, lowering her voice as if avoiding a forbidden word, and then she shook her head, shooing the thought that was always there, and continued with energy. "So, I've arranged a lovely date for you for tomorrow night."

"What? No!" Veronica moaned. "Mom. Why?"

"Now don't argue, he's the son of Daddy's accountant. I've heard he's quite a catch." Her mother rubbed the dirt off a mushroom cap. "His name is Ian Curtis and he'll be here at seven tomorrow night."

"Mom, you've 'heard'? Heard what? From who? Ugh! I can handle finding my own dates. In fact, I've been seeing a great guy named Scott, he's even a Phi Psi like Dad," Veronica protested, though she knew it was no use.

"Since you and Eric broke up, such a shame," she tsked, and plodded on, "I just thought I could help you along."

"He cheated on me, Mom. Cheated! Why is it so awful that we broke up when he cheated on me? With someone right down the hall on top of it!" Veronica's voice was reaching a shriek—the truth would not stay down. She had explained this to her parents, but they searched for reasons to excuse his actions, diluting their sympathy.

"Oh, sweetie," her mother said, "maybe he was just confused after not seeing you for so long. You know he's a good young man from such a nice family. Maybe you could give him another chance."

Veronica stirred her coffee with force, spinning it into a tornado. She stared at the storm in her mug and blew out a sigh while Susan Warren rhythmically chopped up the mushrooms and began to hum a tune.

VERONICA HEARD THE DOORBELL ring and took a deep breath before running the color over her lips and heading downstairs. The sounds of her mother greeting him wafted up the two-story foyer.

"Oh, Ian, it is so lovely to meet you," she gushed.

Veronica rolled her eyes and turned the corner of the steps where her date came into view. Ian Curtis wore a neatly ironed button-down, a navy blazer, and a burgundy patterned bow tie at his throat. His khakis hung on his thin frame, and brand-new boat shoes peeked out from the professionally cuffed and stitched hems. He looked like the debate team champion or the stock sitcom character of a young boy acting too mature for his age. He was Alex P. Keaton from *Family Ties,* only not Hollywood cute like Michael J. Fox. He was ordinary, his face long and skinny like his body. As she approached him, hand extended to introduce herself, she noticed shaving nicks and a few pimples dappled his narrow face. Veronica felt no sense of attraction for Ian, but she felt an immediate fondness for him.

Ian opened the car door for her, and when they arrived at The Mooring entrance, after handing the keys to the valet attendant, he helped her out of his father's Mercedes. He placed a hand on her back as they followed the hostess to their table by the window overlooking the water. Ian made Veronica feel more adult than student, and she straightened her posture.

They talked easily and naturally, uncommon with the typical

freshman guy. Ian carried himself with a confidence that didn't fit his scrawny body. Veronica couldn't identify it, but he seemed secure and had a maturity that comforted her. His demeanor commanded her attention, and even in those first moments she knew they would be friends. They talked eagerly, and he entertained her with his quips and observations about the people around them and the events in the news. She laughed at his pithy remarks about Margaret Thatcher and Ronald Reagan, about *Phantom* winning at the Tony Awards and Cher winning at the Oscars, and about the Hollywood marriage of Jeff Goldblum and Geena Davis. Veronica silently thanked her mom for arranging the meeting.

When she excused herself to use the ladies' room, he stood with her like her father still always did for her mother, but no date had ever risen for Veronica, not the other well-bred sons of her parents' friends, not Eric. She smiled gratefully. Alone in the restroom, her mind wandered to Amy's Utensil Classification System. She tried to ignore it but hearing it endlessly, she found herself entertained with the exercise. He wasn't quite a spoon; he was interesting and poised, not dull or unsure at all. He definitely wasn't in the fork category.

If Ian wasn't a spoon and wasn't a fork, then he fit in the knives, but he was softer around the edges. A butter knife. *That's it*, Veronica thought, pleased with her placement so she could share it with Amy later. *Then again, maybe I won't tell Amy—it will only encourage her.*

Veronica flushed the toilet and smoothed her dress down. With her bag on her wrist, she reached for the slide lock.

"Oh well, I've tried to talk with him about it, but you wouldn't believe how stubborn he can be. Just keeps saying she left him . . ." Veronica instantly recognized the voice. She froze in the stall and jerked her hand away from the lock to prevent her body from accidentally releasing it and exposing herself.

" . . . his father even tried to talk to her about it at the Warrens' annual fundraiser Wednesday night, but we got no answers on her end, either," Mrs. Sheridan continued.

"Maybe they just need some time," a voice she didn't know responded as Veronica heard two clicks. She glanced underneath the stalls, saw four heeled feet safely corralled and she made her escape. After a quick swish of soap and water—unable to skip hand washing even in a situation from which she wanted to flee— Veronica grabbed a paper towel and rushed out of the restroom to the sound of flushing.

Keeping her head down, Veronica hurriedly returned to her seat. Ian was promptly behind her, pulling out her chair. "Thank you," she said as she collected her napkin and placed it on her lap.

She felt him sit back down across from her and she looked up. Eric sat in Ian's place. Ian was still standing to her right, confused but waiting politely. Before Veronica could arrange words or formulate a thought, Eric leaned across the table toward her.

"What the hell are you doing out with this geek? And how dare you go out with Scott Mason and never return my calls?" he hissed at her. "You are my girlfriend, I don't accept this breakup. You're making me look bad, Roni."

Ian pressed his hand to Veronica's shoulder protectively and stepped toward the small table ready to speak, but Veronica stood up and looked down at Eric. Anger rose within her, his nickname for her stripped of all meaning.

"It doesn't matter what you accept. You are a cheater and this is over." She pointed her finger in his face and her voice didn't betray the nervousness she felt. "Stop calling me, stop lying, and stay away from me." Veronica's strong words and stance attracted nearby eyes, but unaware, she continued: "I am not your girlfriend, that ended when you cheated on me." Her gaze left Eric and fell on Linda Sheridan, standing three feet away.

"Cheated?" Mrs. Sheridan exhaled, barely forming the word. She diverted her eyes from Veronica then clutched her son's sagging shoulder. She marched Eric away, leaving her friend, mouth agape, to follow behind.

♡
Chapter 15

THE WEEKS BETWEEN THANKSGIVING and winter break whirled by as Veronica and Amy studied texts and drafted final papers. At last, exams were over and the campus was emptying for the break. Veronica and Amy ran errands before meeting up for an early dinner. It was Wednesday, December 21. They sat in the dining hall of the student center, among the dwindling students who mingled and ate.

"Oh my God!" A cry screamed into the quiet of the dining hall as a young woman ran in wailing, not making sense. Veronica and Amy joined the exodus, as everyone streamed out of the dining hall to the nearest television. Tom Brokaw looked out seriously at the gathered students listening in absolute silence.

"Carnage tonight in the Scotland village of Lockerbie, where a Pan Am 747 headed for New York crashed and exploded. No known survivors on the plane, they are still trying to determine the number of survivors on the ground."

Gasps broke the quiet, but no one looked away from the TV mounted in the corner as the NBC news anchor continued: "Pan Am Flight 103 from London's Heathrow to New York's Kennedy airport was at 31,000 feet and just 52 minutes into its flight when air traffic controllers suddenly lost contact. A short time later, the

747 crashed into a Scottish village and exploded in a ball of flames . . . It is believed that all 258 people on the plane were killed."

Amid the stunned students, someone reached up and changed the channel to ABC, acting on everyone's urge to know more, to grasp at answers and understanding that would never fully come. A somber Peter Jennings reported, "The simple facts are these: Pan Am's Flight 103 had been in the air for an hour. The 747 was en route from London to New York and then Detroit. It was after dark. For reasons we do not yet understand, the plane with fifty thousand gallons of fuel on board plunged into a small Scottish market town. Pan American is not aware that any of the passengers or crew have survived."

Images of flames and Scottish firefighters, close-ups of airplane debris and more flames, filled the screen before Peter Jennings returned delivering new details.

"We have been told from a variety of sources that among the people on board were a number of Syracuse University students who were returning from London, where Syracuse University has an overseas program."

Strangers hugged each other; sobs stabbed the stillness. People collapsed onto one another; a girl fainted and three peers prevented her from hitting the floor. Pained howls, horrified shrieks, and unguarded weeping replaced the air in the room as the tragedy came closer.

"Amy Shapiro would be on the flight," Veronica realized. She was a sorority sister who had been studying abroad during their semester as pledges. A sister they had never met; would never meet.

"Oh my God, yes." Amy pictured the girl with the same name, her face smiling from a box on the composite. So many lives gone. The shock was numbing.

"Andrew. I've got to find Andrew before he leaves," Amy said as tears crept down her cheeks. Veronica understood the compulsion to be with loved ones. "I wonder if anyone's still at the Kappa house or the administration building. I have to start a story for the *D. O.*" Veronica watched her leave, already thinking like the journalist she aspired to be.

Veronica slowly returned to Brewster, taking the long route through the quad and past Hendricks Chapel. The crisis drew her to that building and what it stood for; she longed for something she couldn't identify. She sat on the chapel steps, letting her head fall into her lap. The chilled limestone made her shiver, or perhaps it was the news as it settled deeper. She heard a sniffle behind her and ignored it as an offer of privacy. The sniffs became sobs, and a male voice whispered words of comfort, their sounds approaching Veronica from behind. In her peripheral vision, she saw bobbed hair beneath a worn woolen cap; the girl's eyes a fantastic blue, brightened from tears. Veronica noticed that her coat looked shabby, her boots out of date and scuffed, and then she winced as she caught herself making a judgment like her mother might have. Beside the girl, Andrew supported her in a hug, rubbing his hand up and down her arm.

"Andrew?" Veronica spat, harsher than she'd intended, but more gently than she felt.

He spun to face her, nearly slipping on the stone steps, dragging the girl in his arm as he pivoted.

"Veronica. This is Donna, we're in the same dorm," he introduced soberly, as if her being from his dorm explained their togetherness. "Horrible news. You've heard, right?"

She nodded and stood to leave. Stepping away, she said, "Amy's looking for you," then she turned toward Brewster and away from Andrew and Donna, another sick feeling stirring in her.

VERONICA WAS PACKED UP and lying on her bed with a book she couldn't focus on when Amy burst through the door, a dampened notebook tucked beneath her arm.

"Found him. I had to see him before I left. What are you doing?"

Veronica had been formulating and editing and deciding what and how to tell Amy, but before she could begin, Amy continued.

"I talked with someone in Chancellor Eggers's office—they couldn't tell me much more than we heard on TV—then I was waiting outside of Flint, not for very long, when he came back up."

Veronica hedged. "Was he alone?"

"No, he was with some girl named Donna. She was really shaken up, like we all are, and so Andrew walked her back to their dorm."

Veronica squeezed her eyes closed for one breath, then said, "I saw them, Amy. Donna and Andrew."

"He told me he saw you."

"No, I *saw* them. At Hendricks Chapel, they were there together." She swallowed. "Amy, he had his arm around her."

"You sound so serious about it, Veronica, it's no big deal, we're all upset. Andrew explained it to me: she was crying hysterically, he was just trying to help a friend. You know he's a good guy," Amy insisted as Veronica stared at her, her lips pursed. "Stop worrying, I know you're thinking about Eric, but Andrew's just being nice. He's not cheating. He wouldn't."

Veronica wasn't sure if she heard conviction or question in Amy's voice.

VERONICA ARRIVED HOME LATE for the Christmas break and slept in the next day. She drank her coffee, dismayed and unable to read the front-page story of the *New York Times* resting beside her. The headline sickened her: "Jetliner Carrying 258 to U.S. Crashes in Scottish Town: All Believed Dead; Syracuse University Had 36 People Aboard—Causes Unknown." She pushed it aside, her breath catching in her heart, her thoughts and feelings tangled together.

"Good morning, dear." Susan Warren floated into the room. "It is just awful, isn't it?" She touched one hand to the pearls peeking out at the neck of her peachy blouse and the other on the newspaper. "All of those mothers without their babies, I just can't bear to think about it."

Veronica nodded as her mother grabbed her handbag.

"That polite boy, Ian Curtis, called for you. I have a meeting for the foundation, I'm off." She handed Veronica a slip of paper with Ian's phone number written in her neat penmanship and kissed her daughter's forehead before she whisked out the door.

Grabbing the cordless phone, Veronica extended the metal antenna and dialed the number.

"Tonight. Movies. I'm getting you out. We're seeing *Rain Man*. I'll pick you up at seven," Ian announced. Veronica welcomed the smile that sprang to her mouth; she would feel better being with Ian.

AFTER THE MOVIE, VERONICA and Ian sat at a corner table sharing a plate of fries. The small pub was dim and smelled of old wood and salt.

"My favorite line was when Tom Cruise says, 'I like having you for my big brother,' to Dustin Hoffman. I don't know how you didn't cry at that part," Veronica said.

Before Ian could respond, a gust of cold air and a crescendo of voices drew their attention to the entrance of the restaurant. A pack of young guys clad in business suits sauntered and stumbled their way to the bar, leaning against the nicked and carved wood, sticky with age and ale. She recognized a few as friends of her older brother's from high school—decent guys, she remembered.

"Looks like they're having fun. That group of girls they're surrounding doesn't have a chance," Ian said.

As they observed the drunken interactions with sober eyes,

Ian narrated the scene, making Veronica chuckle: "Gray Suit is vying for Big Earrings, see that? He's in; she rested her hand on his arm, checking out what's under that suit. Oh, and Red-Tie Guy is going in for Ruffles, but she's not having it, shooing him away with those long, pointy painted nails. *Outta here, fella,* she sure gave him the shoulder."

Veronica's smile stilled. She watched as Red-Tie Guy didn't give up; he moved in closer to the girl with the ruffled top and leaned toward her face. Ian noticed, too. "He's not getting it. What a jerk! Leave her alone, asshole," he half hollered across the noisy pub.

Even from across the room, they could see that the guys were drunk and laying it on heavy, as if working to impress and lure in some girls for the night. Veronica distrusted the gushing attention oozing thick from the group.

"Let's get out of here," Ian suggested.

Veronica agreed and watched as Ian marched right into the center of the group and said something to Ruffles. Ian returned with the bill and two of the girls who'd taken him up on his offer of a ride home.

IN THEIR DAILY CALLS, Amy filled Veronica in on the long-distance calls to Andrew and how he wanted to pay for them so he had her call his house, let it ring twice, then hang up. Veronica laughed at Amy's excitement over their secret code. "What if he doesn't call you back after the signal?"

"He does. It's like we're in a movie, sending messages only we understand."

"No more discussion about Donna?" Veronica asked, still unsettled by what she'd witnessed and by her friend's bland reaction.

"There's nothing to discuss."

After coming home from seeing *Rain Man*, Veronica called Amy.

"Ian? He's the butter knife, right?" Amy asked, making Veronica regret sharing that thought with her.

"You would love the movie," Veronica continued, "but I'm telling you, these guys at the bar after were so drunk and total jerks."

"Pseudo-forks," Amy explained. "They're good guys turned jackass. Knives who act like forks when they get drunk."

"Amy, this is getting out of hand. You cannot simply label every guy as a kind of utensil," though as always, the discussion prompted involuntarily thoughts. Tonight Veronica remembered times when some of her guy friends became idiots under the influence, but she couldn't imagine Ian becoming one of Amy's pseudo-forks. Then she thought of Eric. Since the fire alarm, Amy had pegged him as a fork, but she challenged his label through the lens of Amy's new UCS addition.

"So if that's true, maybe Eric is only a pseudo-fork since he was drunk when he hooked up with Jenny. Maybe your system doesn't work after all, and maybe he's just forky at times but not a complete jerk. He did try to make it up to me for months."

Questions darted in her mind with an unexpected spark of hopefulness. She admitted to Amy that she was a tiny bit sad about not seeing Eric at all over the break, which sent Amy into a dissection of whether he was an authentic fork or a pseudo-fork.

"Even if he were a pseudo-fork, it doesn't explain away his cheating on you."

Whatever Amy called him, Veronica knew Amy was right. In her heart, his infidelity battled against their history, leaving her both angry and longing.

As winter break progressed, Veronica told Amy about the books she read, the dinners out with her parents, and her movie nights with Ian to see *Beaches* and *Working Girl*. Amy told Veronica about seeing her aunt and uncle in Vermont, analyzed her conversations with Andrew, and even relayed the details of her dentist appointment: "No cavities, of course!"

The night before returning to campus, Amy told Veronica about her day in Westchester County visiting Matt and his family in Tuckahoe.

"Matt's mom has a beautiful collection of Santa figurines. She told me all about the history of Saint Nicholas, his secret gift giving, and how he represents the spirit of good cheer at Christmas."

"So should Andrew be worried about Matt?" Veronica chided.

"Seriously, V? You know he's just a friend, cut it out. Anyway, Mrs. Saxon is the sweetest lady. She makes you feel welcome and loved just being near her, sort of like Santa Claus..."

When she hung up the phone a while later, her father entered the room smiling. "How can you two have anything else to talk about? Didn't you and Amy talk last night for an hour? And the day before that?"

"An hour a day is still at least twelve hours less than we're together every day at school." She kissed her dad on the cheek and headed upstairs to pack.

In the hallway, she reached high on a shelf for the antique Santa Claus that she used to play with at Christmas as a child. She and her brother would hide it for each other to find until their mother scolded them, taking it away because it was fragile. *There's so much in life that is fragile,* she thought, *but it only means you should love it more, hold it closer, instead of keeping it at a distance worried that it will break your heart.*

Chapter 16

THE SIGMA CHI WINTER formal was an antidote to the January drabness. "Amy! Amy!" Jenny waved from the back of the idling school bus waiting to take them to the Finger Lakes Country Club. Her blond hair contrasted with her ink-black dress, which dipped so low in front that her chest risked full exposure. Andrew walked down the aisle behind Amy, holding her hand, her taffeta strapless dress shimmering between black and violet in the dusk lighting. He leaned forward and whispered, "Go ahead, looks like there's a seat in front of them." He squeezed her fingers in a private communication.

"Amy, this is Keith. Andrew, of course you two know each other."

Leaning over the back of the green plastic seat, Amy quietly spoke to Jenny as the guys pounded fists and fell into conversation. Back on campus between Thanksgiving and Christmas breaks, the girls had fallen back into their separate schedules. The thread that bound them over one long weekend was stretching despite an unspoken connection. The temporary closeness had faded with the leaves.

"So, Keith, huh? What about the fireman? Thought things were hot and fiery with him," Amy joked. Jenny had started dating one of the firemen who had escorted her out of the latest fire alarm, alone, draping a reflective slicker over her bare shoulders.

"Smoldering! He stokes my embers. He's got a great hose." Jenny cracked up delivering the string of punch lines. "Stevie's smoking hot, but no biggie, he totally gets that Keith and I are just going as friends." She ducked behind the high back of the seat and took a gulp from a silver flask, then slipped it back into the pocket of Keith's sports jacket. "Besides, it's not like we're exclusive or anything."

At the country club, Andrew helped Amy check her wrap and left her to join the mass of bodies clumped in front of the bar. She glided closer to a girl in red, also standing alone. Her hair was crimped high, her bangs curled under across her pale forehead. Her ruby dress reflected red on her face, giving her a splotchy appearance.

"Hi, I'm Amy."

"I'm Stacy," the girl's red lips said. "Who's your date?"

"My boyfriend, Andrew Gabel." Amy glanced toward the bar, searching to point him out to Stacy. She saw his profile, his face creased with the smile she loved. A fraternity brother stepped toward the bar, and in the snip of time before someone filled the space, Amy saw Bree O'Connell. Andrew's high school girlfriend twinkled back at him in a jewel-toned dress that highlighted her everything. She looked beautiful, as always. In the months since meeting her, Bree was friendly and Amy liked her, but she often felt a small stab of envy. Their history made Amy feel like she was on the outside of something when Bree was around.

"Which one is he?" Stacy spoke, reminding Amy that she was in a conversation.

"Oh, right. Over there, the cute guy in the green tie." Amy hadn't thought to tell Andrew the color of her dress so they could coordinate like most of the other couples at the formal. His tie would've looked better with Bree's emerald gown than it did with her midnight-purple dress.

"You mean the guy talking to that knockout in green?" Stacy didn't mince her words, and they poked right into Amy's weakness.

"Um, yeah, that's his, um, friend from home."

"You'd better hope they stay just friends, he's pretty hot himself."

"Who are you here with?" Amy asked through a forced grin, George Michael's "Faith" bopping in the background.

Stacy's lips pursed, ready to speak, then instead she pointed behind Amy. "Oh, here he comes now."

Amy turned and was face-to-face with Paul.

Fear pumped through her chest. There were no thoughts, only feelings coursing through her. She ran. She ran out of the banquet room, down a corridor to the country club's lobby, and she burst outside into the frigid night. Panting, she paced right, left. She looked behind her.

Uncertain of herself, her body moved without direction and without mental instructions until she settled on a stone bench nestled among leafless brown plants. Her blood was thumping loudly in her ears; she was sure she could see her heart beating through her bones and skin. Trembling from the inside, she was barely aware of the icy granite beneath her.

She gripped the stone, a hand on either side, buttressing herself against invading images. She was sure she smelled grape candy and sweat in the frosty night air. She exhaled deliberately, slowing her breath; a puff of vapor obscured her vision and vanished. Why hadn't she expected to see him at his own formal? Thoughts of that night penetrated her sleep and pierced her security, yet, in preparing for the evening, he hadn't even crept into her mind. She leaned her head onto her palms and pressed hard into the bones above her eyes. Her elbows dug into her thighs but she pushed harder.

Without knowing how much time had passed, she emptied

her lungs as if snuffing out a small flame. Her skin was pink and textured from the cold, her nipples stiff inside her bra. She smelled distant smoke in the late January air.

Standing, she swept her hands down the back of her dress then went to find Andrew. As she walked past the tastefully upholstered couches of the entryway, she felt on edge, like a spy, hunting for one man while hiding from another. Every sense was heightened, her breath felt thick, and she tasted bitterness at the back of her tongue. She swallowed and walked toward the ballroom.

"Amy! There you are! Thank God!" Andrew jogged toward her and brought her body into his embrace. "You're freezing. What's going on, Aim?" He hung his body-warmed jacket over her small shoulders.

Bree rounded the corner, joining them in the hall. "Oh, you found her," she said with genuine relief. "Are you okay, Amy?"

Amy nodded then shook her head, still unable to speak.

"Need anything?" Bree asked Andrew, lightly resting her hand on his arm. He shook his head without releasing Amy, and Bree reentered the darkened party room where music thrummed with vigor.

Andrew led Amy away from the ballroom into an unoccupied event room. The only light seeped in through the edges of the door. He pulled two chairs from a stack in the corner and sat her down across from him, knee to knee, holding her icy hands in his.

"What's up, Aim? Tell me." His voice was like baby powder on a hot summer day.

"Paul." It was the first word she'd spoken since meeting Stacy.

"Oh, shit!" He hammered the air with a fist. "Shit, Aim, I'm so sorry I left you alone. I didn't see him getting on the buses, I didn't think . . ."

She shook her head and pressed her palm onto his chest. "It's not your fault . . ."

Whispered giggles then a shush came from the darkness. Even with their eyes adjusted to the dimness, they couldn't see anyone but knew they had interrupted. Andrew took her hand to lead her out. The clank of the door lever echoed and a channel of light spotlighted Jenny and Keith, who toppled into the room, already locked at the mouth.

The chords of Dire Straits pulsed as Amy and Andrew returned to the ballroom to dance away her angst. Amy held on to his arm. "Stay with me, please."

"I won't leave you. I promise."

Chapter 17

RED HEARTS DOTTED THE windows of the school store, peppered the walls in the dining halls, and dangled from the ceiling in the dorm lobby. Amy left the outdoor darkness for the artificial brightness and went directly to her mailbox. She turned the key and nearly shouted aloud when she saw the red and pink envelopes. A single slip of paper fell loose from the pile and fluttered to the floor. The photocopied poem with her name handwritten on a blank line read:

> *A.M.Y. Amy York—Brewster 808*
> *Roses are red,*
> *Violets are blue,*
> *Happy Valentine's Day!*
> *From, Can you guess who?*
> *Please see the mailroom for a flower from your secret admirer.*

AMY ROUNDED THE CORNER and handed the note to the student working in the glassed-in booth.

"Oh! You're so lucky! I've wanted one of these for two years now," she said, looking at the Secret Admirer Ticket and disappearing into a side office. She returned with a single red rose wrapped in cellophane and tied neatly with a red bow.

"Can I interview you about balancing work and school for the *D.O.*?"

"Sure, any time, stop by. Here you go. Happy Valentine's Day!" Then Amy heard the girl say quietly to herself, "She's so lucky."

Amy grinned; she felt lucky. Andrew was so thoughtful. How happy she was that he was hers. She was proud at how involved he was on campus; besides being an honors student and president of his pledge class, he served on the student government, led an Interfraternity Council committee, and managed an intramural football league. She couldn't wait to see what he had planned for their first Valentine's Day, and she staccato-pressed 8 on the elevator button, willing it to move faster. She clutched her mail with that familiar anticipation: there were cards she couldn't wait to open.

There was a detail she wanted to return to, and she reread the note attached to the rose. Her initials were there before her name: *A.M.Y.* As a kid, she had loved that her mother's name, Melissa, was her middle name and that her initials spelled her name. She had created a special logo-like way to sign it, with the loop of the *Y* encircling the *A* and the *M*. She had an AMY necklace and an incorrectly monogrammed sweater, because if you monogrammed the right way, the *Y* ended up in the middle. Amy proudly told anyone who would listen, and any new acquaintance, that her initials spelled her name. She signed her class papers in all capitals, pleased that she could be known in her small Newtown school by a single name. Then she turned thirteen and it felt childish, and she quietly became Amy with only the *A* capitalized.

No one at college knew, so how was this on the note? Analyzing the facts like a reporter, she supposed someone could figure it out from a class schedule or her student ID, which listed her middle initial. But no one really sees those and no one had pointed it out to her like everyone did once they figured it out.

As the elevator doors parted, Amy saw Andrew sitting with his feet on the Formica coffee table. Beside his heels was a patch of glittery neon purple where Jenny had spilled nail polish and smeared it trying to clean up. Andrew turned toward the sound of the elevator and she bounded to him, surprised he was there. He sat up, put his feet on the floor. His smile didn't reach his eyes and he patted the couch to his right. Silently, Amy sunk into the maroon cushion, allowing her knee to fall into his.

Amy eased words into the quiet. "Thanks for the flower."

His shoulders and eyebrows rose in unison. "But it's not—"

"It's not from you?"

"Geez, Aim, shoot, no. I didn't think, I mean, I couldn't . . ." He rubbed his forehead. "I forgot."

Amy didn't understand. He forgot to order a flower? The student government fundraiser tables had been set up in the dining halls and student union buildings for weeks, and he was on the student government. How could he possibly forget?

"I'm sorry, Aim, I forgot about Valentine's Day being today. I have this huge project due and I'm really behind on it. That's why I came over here, to tell you in person."

Amy couldn't help her chin dipping to the hollow in her chest. She blinked quickly as she adjusted her mind to the news. Andrew tucked his thumb beneath her jaw, tilting her face toward his. Now that he'd told her, he went on with urgency to explain. "I don't know how I messed it up. I wanted to take you out for a special dinner—I *am* going to take you out to a special dinner. We'll go out this weekend, okay? I promise."

She nodded. "It's fine, Drew, I've got a few pieces to work on for the paper and I'm pitching a story to the *Syracuse Post-Standard*—I'll work on that." Then she laughed a little too loudly and forced a lighthearted tone. "It's a bit ironic, really, that I finally have a boyfriend on Valentine's Day and I'll be home alone."

"It's just a day, we'll go out Saturday," he said with a hint of dismissiveness. "I need to finish this project for my consumer behaviors class. It's taking longer than Bree and I expected. We're going to have to pull an all-nighter to get it done."

Amy stared at him; her ears prickled and that ugly gnaw of jealousy punched her gut. He was spending Valentine's Day with Bree, not with her? Disappointment pressed down on her and twisted inside until she felt dizzy. She would have been fine, until she learned about Bree. He looked sincere and Amy was sure he felt sorry, but she fought to make her heart understand. His words poured into the space between them, each one bouncing off Amy's heart, barely being absorbed.

Don't cry, she told herself as a tear fell onto the cards in her lap, darkening a spot of red.

"Oh, Aim, I'm so sorry. I promise I'll make it up to you." Andrew pulled her to him, the clear wrapping of the rose crinkling between them.

"It's fine. It's just a day," she lied.

"I love you," he told her, speaking the syllables right into her ear, giving them a direct route to her heart. The words filled her veins, her organs, her bones. She nodded into the crook of Andrew's neck and held those words tightly. It was the first time he'd said them.

AMY RETURNED TO HER room to find Veronica dressed in classically tailored black velvet pants, a red satin top, and a black cashmere wrap draped around her shoulders. She dumped her stuff onto her side of the room and plopped onto Veronica's bed, telling her about the unexpected change of plans. With supportive nodding and definitive words of agreement, Veronica affirmed Amy's emotions like only a girlfriend could. Soothed, Amy diverted the conversation as she changed into pajamas.

"Did you see Cupid run across campus today?"

"No, I missed him, but I heard a Delta Tau Delta brother does it every year. Oh! I heard it from you. I read your interview with him in today's paper. Great story."

"Thanks. It was hilarious seeing this guy dressed in boxers with hearts, a DTD baseball shirt, and sneakers with red socks running after all the girls. I think he kissed almost every girl on the quad."

"He got you, too? I wonder what Cupid's kiss means."

"Not much, since I'm home alone on the day that's meant for sweethearts."

Veronica sprayed her perfume, ready for her date. Since her breakup with Eric, Veronica was enjoying the freedom of not being in a relationship, and when she was invited to the Valentine's semiformal by a classmate, she accepted. Amy was happy for her friend having a Valentine's Day date, but surprised that suddenly she didn't.

Veronica hugged her friend and headed out, her floral scent clinging to Amy's pajamas. She wore the set Aunt Joanie had sent her last Valentine's Day. The fitted camisole dappled with hearts and cozy flannel bottoms were unintentionally perfect for the overheated dorms. For as long as she could remember, on Valentine's Day, her dad would set the dining room table with a tablecloth, linen napkins, and red and white candles, and he would do his best to prepare a special dinner for the two of them, from appetizers to desserts. Her place always had a single package tied up in ribbon.

"Love is in the details," Thomas York would say.

Amy sat on her bed, twirling her poker-straight hair. *Love is in the details.* She remembered her cards and found the fan of mail on the floor, along with her bag and coat. Leaning to gather them, she noticed the stem of the rose beneath the pile. The rose she'd been so giddy over, forgotten in her disappointment. Amy held it to her nose, carefully untied the bow, and wondered whom it was from; she had been so certain it was from Andrew. Searching for something that would work as a vase, her gaze landed on the tall glass etched with SIGMA CHI WINTER FORMAL 1989. That didn't feel right to use, since the rose wasn't from Andrew, so instead, she tucked it into her SU mug sitting on her desk with an inch of stale water at the bottom.

Spreading out the envelopes on her bed, she felt like a third grader examining the valentines from her classmates. Which should she open first? She picked the one with her dad's handwriting and smiled: of course he had sent something. A check floated to the floor as she pulled the card out. "Thanks, Dad," she said aloud, grateful for some extra money.

There were cards, right on time, from her aunt and her best friend from home. Last, she opened the one without a return address. The envelope was a perky pink and the writing familiar. She saw his neat handwriting, artistic almost, perfectly angled but not severe. Amy had admired it when he jotted notes for her, listing some series of computer strokes she needed to remember. Her notebook had his steady print sprinkled throughout. She smiled and carefully tucked her thumb under the corner of the sealed flap. She unstuck the triangle and wiggled out the Hallmark card. She felt a tug at her heart. Was she allowed to feel so attached to a friend if that friend was a male? Was she feeling warmer toward him because Andrew had left her alone on Valentine's Day?

The factory-printed words read: *I'm happy we're friends.* He let the card speak for him and signed only, *Love, Matt.* She looked at her name written across the top in his handwriting and it struck her. Matt knew her initials spelled her name. Her computer login was *AMYork*.

"WHAT DID YOU DO for the most romantic night of the year?" Amy asked Matt as they finished lunch. "You won't believe what I did." Without waiting for an answer, Amy went on. "I sat in my room alone, wrote a profile on a new professor, and read my public communications book. Thank you for your card and the rose; that was my highlight. But yup, I was all alone, in my pj's, on Valentine's Day!"

"Is something wrong? Where was Andrew?"

"Yeah, well, he had a big project." Amy's voice lowered; she didn't want to complain about Andrew to Matt, and she instantly shifted to defending him without Matt breathing a sound. "It's not that important anyway, it's just a night, right? I mean, it was a weeknight and it's better that he's a good student. We're going out this weekend instead."

"That sounds good." Matt looked away and zipped up his backpack. "All set?"

"Sure, hold on," Amy said, glad for the way Matt never judged her, or Andrew, or anyone else, either, she realized. He was kind and diplomatic, empathetic and forgiving, and he didn't dwell on other people's behaviors. Amy balanced her bag on one arm and her lunch tray full of empty bowls and dishes on the other. Matt grabbed it for her, tucking both trays onto the conveyor belt.

"So, you didn't tell me, what did you do on Valentine's Day?"

"It was no big deal," Matt answered.

"Where you home in your pajamas, too?"

Matt hesitated, then held the door for her to step outside onto the snowy sidewalk. "I was out."

"Out? Out with who?" Amy found herself speaking in a high voice and louder than she intended.

"I don't think you know her, someone from my dorm. She's a theater major." Matt took deliberate steps around the fresh snow that concealed the slush beneath it.

"What's her name?"

"Laura."

Amy nodded. "Oh" was all she could verbalize, though questions ricocheted in her mind. *Who is she? Are they serious? Why hasn't he mentioned anything about her? Matt has a girlfriend?*

Chapter 18

ON A DREARY MARCH afternoon, Amy entered the bathroom clutching her toothbrush and Crest Fluoristat toothpaste, ready to brush away a snack. She heard giggling from the shower stall as she passed, barefoot and silent. She recognized the bath towel hanging beside the industrial curtain and thought she heard whispering through the sound of running water. There was a thud followed by an "Ouch!" The wet, lower voice was definitely male, and Jenny was loudly shushing him.

As the shower turned off, Amy brushed quicker, hoping to escape before them, but she saw a corner of purple pass in the mirror. She could see a wedge of Jenny in the reflection, the towel wrapped around her naked and dripping Barbie-doll body. Peeking from behind the tiled wall toward the hallway door, she motioned with her hand, waving the boy on. He stepped forward, into Amy's mirror view, a matching violet towel hugging his hips and high-lighting a rippled physique. Ken-doll ab muscles sculpted into him, his build was incongruent with his boyish face. Amy backed deeper into the bathroom to remain unseen, holding a mouthful of minty spit. From her vantage point, she could not avoid seeing Eric Sheridan tiptoe out behind Jenny. Wet hair clung behind his ears, and his bare feet slapped the floor puddles as he snuck out with the arrogance of the unobserved.

VERONICA WAS WALKING THROUGH the Brewster lobby when Eric snuck up and covered her eyes from behind like a schoolboy, coaxing, "Guess who?" His voice pierced her lungs, letting a sigh escape. She had once loved him and, caught off guard, those feelings surfaced.

Their history tugged at Veronica's emotions, even as she noted that his scent was not his own. His hands above her nose smelled fresh and slightly of jasmine. She turned, and forgetting herself, she fell into his hug and pressed herself against his chest. For a moment she wondered if she had been too harsh; perhaps he had paid his penance and she should give him another chance. She floundered and wavered, thinking he must feel remorseful and committed since he was persisting and had come all this way.

Since their breakup, despite the dates, fraternity events, and formals, she missed the steadier connection and comfort of a boyfriend, of him. Someone who knew both her silliness and her seriousness, someone who knew her family and her home, someone who knew her in jeans, dresses, or panties. Despite the hurt and betrayal, Veronica missed Eric and the idea of Eric. Time and distance softened her heart and let him slide back into it.

AMY PACED THE ROOM. Her gray sweatshirt shouted SYRACUSE, and its bulkiness hid any sign of her small breasts. Her thin legs peeked out beneath it, snug in black stirrup leggings. She wondered where Veronica was and how she was going to tell her about Eric. Passing the door on her loop of the room, it swung open, nearly missing her. *Thank God, she's home,* Amy thought, then froze as she saw Eric enter behind Veronica.

"Look who I found waiting for me in the lobby," Veronica

said, her tone clear that it was a good discovery. Her eyes had a sparkle and Eric was in their room, grinning. Amy squinted her eyes at him, unable to speak, but he was effervescent and charming in his greeting.

"Amy! So great to see you." He embraced her, pinning her arms as Amy resisted the hug.

Amy turned to her best friend, trying to understand what was happening. She had to get her alone, even knowing it might break her apart all over again.

"Hey, where are all the pictures of me?" Eric asked, scanning Veronica's bookshelves, desk, and nightstand.

Inside, Amy was starting to seethe. *What a complete fork. Does he really not get that he's been an asshole? That he is still being an underhanded, lying player?*

"My parents have really missed you. They send their love," Eric said, letting his question fade like old film while Amy stood frozen. "I've really missed you, Roni, you know I need you."

"Veronica, can you come here a minute, please?" Amy spit the words out, unable to calculate a better strategy.

"Now? But Eric just got here."

For a second, Amy questioned whether to tell Veronica at all; she even momentarily doubted what her own eyes had witnessed, as if her wishing that it wasn't Eric stepping out of that shower would make it so. Then she pictured him wrapped in Jenny's towel, bold enough to be fooling around publicly within yards of Veronica's room.

"Yes. Now. Please."

Veronica unraveled herself from Eric's arms. He held her fingertips and fastened her to him for a moment. Veronica followed Amy out of their room and down the hall toward the stairwell.

"Where are we going? What's going on?" Veronica quickened her pace to keep up.

Amy's heart was pounding; she knew she was about to deliver a blow. Steeling herself, she moved swiftly to the gray door at the end of the hall, aware that it was across from Jenny's room, but she needed to talk to Veronica where they wouldn't be interrupted, and the stairs were the only immediate option.

"Amy, you're freaking me out! What's going on?"

Amy hit the chrome bar and pressed the door into the stairwell that they had descended too many times in the early-morning hours. She walked up one flight. Veronica climbed behind her, silent now, and sat beside Amy on the ninth-floor landing. When their footsteps stopped, the only sound was the hum of the lights. Amy squeezed her eyes shut, then quietly told Veronica the truth of her ex-boyfriend's surprise visit.

Veronica let out a long, voluminous scream that bounced above and below them, and then she stood and bolted down the steps two at a time and flung her body around the bend. She reached the entry to the eighth floor then called up to Amy, her voice echoing, "Come on! I need you!"

THE DOOR OPENED TO ROOM 808 with such force that it slammed against the side of Amy's closet and rebounded back toward Veronica. She straight-armed it open and rushed over to Eric, who sat upright on her bed, startled and confused. Amy watched Veronica pound the side of a single fist into Eric's chest. She was crying and yelling at him while he sat looking perplexed.

"What the hell did you say to her?" He ignored Veronica's barrage of anger and glared accusingly at Amy.

"The truth, Eric," Veronica shouted clearly. "She told me the truth."

Veronica slid her desk chair in front of her closet. Standing on it, she reached to the top shelf and pulled out frames from under a stack of sweaters. One by one she threw the pictures of Eric and her smashing to the floor at his feet.

"You want to know where your pictures are? Here!" Another one shattered, frame parts and shards of glass skidding across the floor. "I am embarrassed that I ever loved you! You made me doubt myself and what I knew to be true." Her words caught and she threw another picture at Eric. The cherry frame Frisbeed from her hand and the corner caught Eric's forehead. He folded forward holding his head but remained silent.

Amy stepped over the Erics smiling up at her from the prom and the slopes and took Veronica's hand. Veronica's shoulders crumpled and she stepped down from the chair and into Amy's hug, sobbing. The door slowly opened and Jenny peered into the room.

"What's going on in here?" She gasped as she saw the blood dripping down Eric's face. He fixed his eyes to the floor.

Veronica pulled free from Amy's arms. Seeing Jenny in her room ignited a new fury. As if she didn't know where to direct its energy, she turned between Eric and Jenny. Her red curls freed themselves and whipped around, accentuating her rage.

"You! Are you coming to check on him? Because you can have him!" In the hallway behind Jenny, others had gathered, drawn by the commotion. "You two deserve each other," Veronica spat. "Get out!" she commanded, looking at Eric but speaking to them both. He didn't move, just sat on the edge of Veronica's bed, stunned and still. His face, hand, and shirt were covered in red as the small cut kept bleeding. Veronica felt like she was bleeding, too, her pulse beating wildly in her throat and at her wrists.

"Get. Out. Now." She spoke in rhythm with her blood.

Eric stood, hanging his head and pressing his hand to his wound. He bent down and peeled a photograph from the floor. He wiped the glass from the faces: Veronica and him squinting and salty at the beach, carefree and happy. A drop of blood rolled down his wrist and fell onto his tanned summer face. He wiped his sleeve across the image, smearing the blood and making the face in the picture match how he looked now. He tucked it into his shirt pocket and walked toward Jenny. She backed away as he approached, her face stricken. Jenny looked from Eric into the room at the red splotches and shattered glass, and at Veronica's eyes. Jenny brought her hand to her mouth, turned, and ran down the hall to her room. Alone.

Chapter 19

AMY SAT ON ANDREW'S bed as he zipped his duffel bag, ready to leave for his spring break trip. She handed him a package that looked like a giant Tootsie Roll wrapped in tissue paper. Andrew tore into the crinkly paper and shook out the thick beach towel striped in red, yellow, and blue. He lassoed the towel around Amy and drew her to him, covering her face in kisses.

He tucked a new bottle of Coppertone suntan lotion into his bag with the towel. She didn't want to cry. She had told him to go, encouraged him even, as evidence of her being the understanding, easygoing girlfriend, the way she thought she should be. But now that he was leaving, she felt deserted and lonely.

"Don't look so sad, Aim, it's only a week." He tried to comfort her with a voice that was cheery and full of anticipation. "Come on, walk me out to wait for the guys."

Andrew slung the bag over his shoulder and held Amy close to his other side. The spring break trip had been planned months ago with eight pledge brothers. They were driving a rented Winnebago to Daytona Beach and Amy was spending the week in Newport with Veronica. She was looking forward to a restful week with her best friend, mixing lazy hanging out and touristy fun. Still, a pang struck her gut sending Andrew off to the hub of spring break madness without her.

"OH, GIRLS! I'M SO excited that you'll be staying with us for the week," Mrs. Warren said, greeting Veronica and Amy with kisses on their cheeks. She couldn't wait to share her surprise: "I even arranged for the Bennett boys to take you out. A double date. One's a sophomore and one's a junior, older men, and they both attend Yale. They already had their spring break but they're home next weekend. I can't understand why Barbara isn't expecting them home this Sunday for Easter, but either way, they'll be here next weekend before you girls head back. Isn't that wonderful?"

Veronica rolled her eyes as Amy mouthed, "Andrew." She answered with a silent, "Sorry," then turned to her mother. "Mom, Amy has a boyfriend."

"Oh, don't worry about that, girls, it's just a friendly evening. One of the boys, I forget which one—Zach maybe, or Doug, no, it's Zach—has a girlfriend. Just go and have a nice time." And that was that.

Throughout the week, Veronica and Amy enjoyed quahogs, lobsters, and steamers and walks along Bailey's Beach and Gooseberry Beach. They slurped Del's Lemonade and Rhode Island clam chowder, and Amy had her first taste of coffee milk. They dyed Easter eggs and celebrated Easter Sunday with the Warrens at church, followed by brunch at Rosecliff mansion. They crossed the bridges to spend days in Providence shopping on Thayer Street, as well as touring the Rhode Island School of Design Museum and the domed state house topped with *The Independent Man* statue.

The Bennett brothers picked them up on Friday evening and drove along the waterfront cobblestoned streets to an old park overlooking the Atlantic and the Beavertail Lighthouse. Polite chitchat filled the car as the foursome honored their parents' setup, making the best of the required date. The boys pulled out a picnic basket and blankets and led Veronica and Amy to an edge of the park above the smashing water. A father and two young boys were flying kites in a field of barely green, almost-April grass.

Veronica wrapped her sweater tightly around her and kicked off her shoes. She sat at the corner of the large quilt and tucked her fleshy legs under her long denim skirt, grateful that she'd shaved her winter legs. The boys were naturals at entertaining and without effort put the girls at ease, as they laid out a board of cheeses, pâtés, and fruits and poured merlot into four elegant picnic wineglasses. Veronica caught Amy's eye and knew she was enjoying the storybook romance. She raised her eyebrows a fraction; the Bennett brothers really knew how to impress, even the daughter of Newport socialites.

"So, you're home for the weekend. Why?" Veronica grinned flirtatiously and took a sip of wine. "Couldn't find a girl on your own at Yale?"

"No, we need our mommy to make all of our social arrangements," Doug quipped in response.

An evening of laughter and shared stories of college sagas and drunken friends, of fire alarms and dorm pranks followed. They skipped pebbles and searched for halo rocks: gray stones ringed with a white band. Walking along the huge boulders of the jetty, they balanced and held hands, teetering four in a row as the sun set early in an orange blur.

Though Brenton Point State Park closed at dusk, not a single patrol was seen as the sun eased below the water and darkness nestled in. The new friends sipped, lounged, and joked as if they had known one another for years. They lay in a circle on their backs, covered in the extra quilts the brothers had packed. Their heads touched in the center and they fixed their eyes on the sky. March 31 was too early for meteor showers, and the distant lights from land dimmed the stars, but beneath the glowing darkness, the conversation grew intimate and more serious. Eventually, Doug reached for Veronica's hand, and she felt a rush of excitement as their palms met and his fingers enclosed hers.

"We're going for a walk," he announced, hopping up and leading Veronica toward the tree line. "Have you ever been to the old carriage house? See it there? Through the trees?"

"Behind that fence? We can't go in there, it's closed."

He smiled.

"I went there once in Girl Scouts; they told us there was a fire there in the sixties."

"I think you're going to like this field trip better." Doug tugged her toward a broken rule and all that remained of the historical manor home.

ZACH ROLLED ON HIS side, propping his head in his palm. His good looks shone in the dim haze, forcing Amy to glance away, removing her eyes from his. If she let him look into her eyes, surely Zach would know her heart. She worried that she was being disloyal to Andrew just by feeling an allure to this handsome, witty, and confident guy. A solid knife without a doubt. The two had enjoyed flirtations, feeling safe in the knowledge that the other was taken, off-limits, committed to another. Somehow, alone in the dark, lying side by side, she felt vulnerable and exposed, as if the security of "having a boyfriend" wasn't enough to protect her from her own attraction. Amy felt silly worrying, believing that Zach was simply being friendly to her and loyal to his girlfriend back at Yale. He had done nothing to cross a line with her. Amy dropped her head onto her folded arm and let herself look back up into Zach's face.

"I worry that you'll think it's a corny come-on, but you are really beautiful," he spoke, barely above a whisper.

Amy's heart raced with the compliment. Then her mind joined her heart in racing and wondered where he was going.

His hand crossed the narrow space between them, softly touching her cheek and sending a warm chill through her body. Amy closed her eyes and inhaled, savoring the moment of tender seduction; there was no longer a question about his intentions. As he slid his palm behind her head, Amy fell into his kiss. She was still, though her entire body pulsed with sensations. She felt only his kiss, heard only his breath, until a crash of waves startled her. Opening her eyes, she saw the faint moon, the same moon that shone above Andrew's head. Amy stiffened and stopped him with her hand on his collarbone.

"No, we can't. You have a girlfriend and I have a boyfriend . . ." she began.

"A girlfriend? Wait, you have a boyfriend? I don't have a girlfriend. Why did you think that? We broke up months ago."

Amy felt her perceptions of the evening shift, their interactions colored by this news.

"But Mrs. Warren said—"

"Well, the moms don't always have the latest updates." He smiled and rolled on his back. "I didn't know you had a boyfriend. I'm sorry."

Wow, this guy is incredible and so respectful, Amy thought, and she liked him even more, but Andrew had rescued her and she couldn't be unfaithful. Realizing she already had been, guilt coursed through her heart beside the beat of desire.

THE GIRLS LEFT NEWPORT later than planned so that Doug and Veronica could delay good-byes. The four had spent Saturday morning together with breakfast at the Hotel Viking.

To give his brother time alone, Zach took Amy to the Cliff Walk and they meandered along the Newport streets, talking like old friends. Both of them consciously tried to ignore the attraction between them, but as Amy pulled her jacket tighter around her, Zach looped his arm around her and she leaned into him. He slowed and looked into her face, an invitation. Remorse tugged against want as she allowed herself to be swept into another sweet kiss.

"I'm sorry," Amy said aloud to Zach and silently to Andrew.

Zach nodded and added space between them.

THE WHOLE WAY FROM Rhode Island to Syracuse, Veronica talked nonstop about Doug while Amy suppressed her parallel emotions for his brother. Of course, the previous night, Amy had told her best friend about the kiss. They had interpreted its meaning in the context of Andrew for hours, but as they traveled back to school, Amy was relieved to downplay Zach and focus on Veronica's connection with Doug. Still, thoughts of Zach intermingled with the anticipation of seeing Andrew, but she wouldn't let herself verbalize any more about him. She guarded against elevating the ethereal night to something more important than she could allow it to be. She protected that glimmer of enchantment and kept it only for herself.

AMY AND VERONICA ARRIVED back on campus late Saturday night, then lost an hour for daylight saving time, as if some April Fool's Day trick. After sleeping in, Amy spent Sunday in the Brewster 8 lobby waiting for Andrew's call. Midmorning, Amy jumped up, thrilled by the sound of the ringing, but the message was for Kate and the phone didn't ring again for hours. She painted her nails, studied for her news-writing exam, munched snacks, and wrote letters.

Amy's mind drifted between Andrew and Zach, between the boy she loved and who loved her and the novelty of the guy she'd just met. She blew out a breath filled with wisps of worry and wonder. Fighting to deny her feelings, she kept vigil by the pay phone. While all was quiet, she scooted to the bathroom, moving quickly. As she was washing her hands, she heard the sound she'd been wishing for all day. Two rings, she wiped her hands dry on her jeans; three rings, she flung the door open; four rings, she ran toward the lobby; five rings—*Hold on, keep ringing*—she raced to pick up the receiver. On the seventh ring, Amy answered breathlessly: "Hello? Hello?"

"Amy?" Andrew's voice sounded strange to her, but she exhaled with relief at hearing him. "You got back safely," he commented.

"Yes. Wait. Who is this?"

She heard his laugh and smiled in recognition, sliding onto the stool to catch up with Matt after a week apart. He'd visited his cousin in Washington, D.C., and they swapped tidbits on the monuments and mansions and the things that reminded one of the other.

"You would've liked the band we saw," Amy told him.

"I thought of you from the top of the Washington Monument—there was an incredible sunset and I know how you love a good movie-scene sunset. Oh, and we ate nonstop, you would've loved all the food," Matt teased. They shared the stories of their spring breaks and Amy avoided any mention of Zach, though he tiptoed at the edges of every thought.

Veronica padded down the hall and mouthed to Amy, "Andrew?" Amy gasped. She'd forgotten that she was waiting on his call and had tied up the line for how long? The sun had blinked out from behind the clouds and she'd watched the square of light move along the wall while she talked with Matt.

Shoot! Now she wouldn't know if Andrew was returning

as expected between six and seven that evening. Amy hurriedly disconnected with Matt, showered, and sprayed on Anaïs Anaïs, Andrew's favorite. She crossed campus and sat on the front steps of his dorm building a half hour before the anticipated time of his return and waited again. Amy zipped her jacket higher and wished she'd brought something to sit on as the cool cement made her shiver. She forced herself to read one sentence in her textbook before glancing up to check for him. Finally, the Winnebago ambled up the road and a jumble of raucous boys spilled out to stretch. Seeing Amy, Andrew broke away from the pack and lifted her into his arms, squeezing her so tightly that she stopped breathing while he held her.

"I tried to call you like we'd planned, but I got a busy signal." He was golden brown and his eyes twinkled like someone who had just made memories. He was relaxed, rested, and he was licking her ear, whispering, "I missed you."

In his room, Andrew dumped out his bag beside Amy on his bed and went across the hall to shower while Amy waited some more. A stack of photos beside his dirty laundry fanned out toward her. Amy knew he didn't own a camera and was surprised that the guys would be organized enough to have already developed their film. Leaving her textbook untouched, she thumbed through the pile mindlessly, scanning through pictures of every combination of the guys. She chuckled to herself upon seeing the familiar faces playing beach volleyball, sitting by a pool, eating hot dogs, riding mopeds, and drinking beer. Every picture was dotted with beer cans or beer bottles or cups of beer. They were all variations on the same picture, but as she went to lay them down, her thumb hit a bikini-clad blonde.

Amy put the pictures at the beginning of the deck upside down on her lap and slowly flipped through the rest of the pile. Images of spring break that were shown on TV sat in her hands:

perky girls with perky boobs between googly-eyed boys. One after the other peered out at her. She was disappointed to see one of Mark Goldberg, who had the sweetest girlfriend, with his tongue in a girl's mouth and his hands cupping each of her breasts. Another revealed the guys at what had to be a strip club, posing in the darkness in front of busty women in G-strings and flirtatious positions. Amy felt an odd nervousness in her stomach; the whole scene unsettled her. She whisked through the pictures quicker, not wanting to focus on them but propelled by curiosity, and then she saw it.

It wasn't in the nightclub or even at a bar. It was a beach shot, palm trees and surf in the background. She would've passed it except she saw Andrew in the background of the picture. She noticed those solid arms that she loved to be in, loved to touch. His colorful bathing suit drew her eye and she lifted the photo closer. He was standing with his side to the camera, but it was unmistakable. It was a picture of Andrew holding out the new towel she'd given him to a shiny, wet Bree O'Connell.

Amy's eyes burned and her heart felt jittery as if filled with caffeine. She didn't hear the room door click open over the faint vibration in her ears. She felt sick. She hadn't been completely faithful; had he? Emotions swam through her, splashing in her heart and out her eyes. Amy was crying and clutching the picture, the stack spilled in her lap.

"Aim, what's wrong?"

In only his towel, Andrew sat beside her and tried to glimpse the picture in her hand.

"Mark bought a few disposable cameras and we all passed them around during the week," he started to explain. "You saw them. Some of the guys didn't want their girlfriends to see, but since there's nothing of me, they picked me to keep them."

Amy thought she could see his mind scanning the images. Was

he preparing to defend himself as she was? She couldn't stop her tears and she couldn't speak; only a hiccup escaped between sobs.

"I know there are strippers in there, but I just went because all the guys wanted to go, it was just for fun, Aim."

She sniffled.

"Why are you crying? What's wrong?" he asked again with a tenderness in his tone that pulled Amy's eyes to meet his even as her heart ached with guilt.

"Bree was there?" Her voice was a whisper but the pain seeped through—pain as she wondered about Andrew's fidelity and pain as she felt her own disloyalty.

Andrew fell back onto the piles of stuff on his bed. He stroked the wet hair above his forehead. "Bree? You're upset about Bree?"

He put his hand on Amy's back and rubbed her, then sat up again. She'd deliberately worked to keep her doubts and insecurities about Bree to herself, but now everything was bubbling out of her and she couldn't stop crying.

"There's nothing between us. It was high school, it was a long time ago, and it's completely over. I've told you, she's just a friend. She was in Daytona with some other Tri-Delts and we hung out one day at the beach." He spoke the words calmly and without defensiveness. "You have nothing to worry about."

"You didn't hook up with her?"

"I told you, you have nothing to worry about, Aim," he said with finality, then kissed her and turned to get dressed.

Amy felt the rush of tears and her shoulders shuddered. She had been prepared to be left behind for him to go away with his friends, but with Bree? Had he known she would be there? Within her confusion and hurt, Amy worried. *I'm the one who kissed someone else. But did he, too?* Why did Andrew's relationship with Bree keep unsettling her? Before she could decide, she spoke.

"I kissed someone."

Andrew stopped putting on his socks and turned to her with an unbearable slowness.

"What did you say?"

Amy bit her lip and she lowered her head, heavy with tears and shame.

"What did you say, Amy?" Andrew's voice cut with a tone she had never heard. "You kissed someone? You're crying because there's a picture of Bree and you *kissed* someone?"

"I'm crying *because* I kissed someone," Amy choked out. "I'm sorry, Drew."

He marched in a small circle before her, yanking his fingers through his damp hair.

"I'm sorry. I promise, it was only a kiss."

Andrew abruptly turned and grabbed the stack of pictures and threw them at Amy. The images scattered like leaves around her: boobs, beaches, beer, and Bree. She picked at the nail polish she'd painted while waiting for Andrew.

"Only a kiss? I broke up with Bree because I caught her kissing someone else. That was 'only a kiss,' too!"

"Are you breaking up with me?"

He took a deep breath and sat beside her, crushing the glossy pictures beneath him. She looked into his eyes, seeing hurt more than anger. She felt an urgency for Andrew to forgive her but was overcome with dread.

"Please say you're not breaking up with me. I always want to be honest with you, and I'm sorry, Drew."

"Who knows that you kissed this guy?"

"Only Veronica."

Through puffed cheeks, he exhaled, letting his lips flutter. "I'm not breaking up with you," he said, seeming to decide in that moment. "I'm glad you told me, but this won't happen again. No extracurricular kissing."

She was grateful that the familiar Andrew was peeking out, grateful that he wasn't ending it. First he had saved her from Paul, and now he was saving her from herself.

Chapter 20

A FLURRY OF DEADLINES, papers, and exams marked the weeks after spring break. Freshman year was coming to a close. Weather on campus turned mild, and the moment temperatures hit 50 degrees, shorts replaced sweats. Amy invited Veronica to spend a weekend in Newtown, a retreat from school to study before the final crunch.

"How is it that Jenny has been to the York Manor before your best friend has?" Veronica teased on the trip to Connecticut.

Entering the white colonial on a hill, Veronica noted how different it was from her Newport friends' homes. With a stab of regret, she pushed away the ingrained snobbishness that crept into her thoughts. The home was modest but tidy and welcoming.

Veronica took in the country decor, ginghams and plaids, floral prints and baskets. The smell of a home-cooked meal greeted them, Mr. York's standard pot roast, and he proudly gave the girls a tour of the seedlings growing in the kitchen window, readying to be planted in his freshly turned vegetable garden.

Around the dinner table that night, Veronica felt at ease with the Yorks and their comfortable banter. She laughed with Mr. York as she told stories of Amy doing laundry and her kidnapped toothbrush. Within her enjoyment, she felt longing. It was so unlike the Warren family dinners, yet without her brother at home, she was struck by the similarity of being the only child at a family meal and she filled with missing him.

Over the weekend, between study sessions and cookie breaks, the girls worked on photo albums of freshman year and their spring break. They carefully lifted the clear plastic off the sticky pages, cut construction paper shapes, and lettered titles on colored scraps, laughing at the memories. Carefully snipping around tines and blades, Amy added thick borders of utensils and silhouettes of forks, knifes, and spoons, subtly labeling as she went. Veronica's book was void of silverware shapes as she lined up the edges of her "Party Pix" and neatly arranged the snapshots. She noticed Amy place the shape of a knife next to the only picture they had of the Bennett brothers.

Piecing together the images of her first year away from home, Veronica realized she had mapped a series of changes in herself. Glancing between the Yorks' small, love-filled home and the pages before her, she glimpsed the effects of her upbringing on her impressions. She was awash with gratitude for the perspective and determined to branch away from her parents' views of the world.

IN A RUSH OF TIME, freshman year was over. Packing up, Veronica pondered life since arriving on campus in August, the changes as dramatic as a baby's first years: from an infancy of the unknown, to crawling through changes in awareness and relation-ships, to toddling surely into new understandings of herself and into deeper friendships. Over the summer, she would miss Amy, her endless snacks and teeth brushing, her optimistic outlook on everything, and their twin-like ease of connecting. *The phone bills will be big*, she thought, and shrugged, secure in knowing they would live together sophomore year in the coveted and newly remodeled Watson dorm.

While Amy's absence would leave a hole, another would be filled. Doug Bennett was also returning to Newport for the summer. The two had not seen each other since spring break, but the older Bennett brother had called regularly to talk with Veronica, who wondered after each call why she hadn't looked into paying extra to the phone company to get a line in their room. Next year. She was done with shared pay phones and calling cards and pledged to use some of her money from her summer job at the Preservation Society of Newport County to ensure some privacy.

After spring break, Veronica noticed a nervous twinkle in Amy when they talked about Doug, as if speaking of him were entwined with his brother, as if the mention of Zach's name exposed something in Amy. Veronica was torn about Amy's kisses with Zach if only because of their dishonesty to Andrew, but she understood the desire. She was relieved to learn that Amy had told Andrew the truth and was impressed by his loyalty to her.

Zach had sent Amy a few letters, and Veronica had watched her read them slowly, digesting the meaning behind the words, enjoying his paper flirtations, only to tuck them into her yellow box. Close as they were, Veronica asked about her feelings only once after spring break and accepted Amy's response. She had said, "I'm not entirely sure how to feel, V, he's definitely a knife and I'd be interested if I didn't have Andrew. But I do have Andrew and I'm happy. He's been there for me and he forgave me, so I can't think about Zach Bennett."

Veronica knew that Andrew loved her best friend and knew that he and Amy were good together. Doug had begun to restore her trust in guys, allowing her to see Andrew without filtering him through an Eric-tainted lens. She had to admit, he was a catch. He was a superstar on campus and loved by anyone who knew him. He had smarts, athleticism, charm, and friendliness. He embraced life and did everything with enthusiasm. He befriended everyone in his path and Veronica realized that he'd won her over, too.

Part Two ♡

1992–1993

SENIOR YEAR AND MOVING ON

Chapter 21

"WHERE IS ANDREW TAKING you? You're so dressed up." Veronica sat on her bed in the Kappa house, chatting as Amy got ready for her Valentine's Day dinner.

"I have no idea, he just told me to wear something nice."

"Here, take this." Veronica hopped up and pulled a cashmere scarf from her closet. "Remember freshman year when he forgot about Valentine's Day? I couldn't believe you weren't more upset."

Amy looped the scarf around her neck and shrugged. "Yeah, that stunk, but every Valentine's Day it's like he's still trying to make up for that first year."

"Boyfriends are supposed to be on top of that day." Veronica had guidelines and she was holding Andrew to her standard. "They at least have to remember birthdays, anniversaries, and Valentine's Day."

The knock on the propped open door set them both to giggling. "Man on three." Andrew made the required sorority house announcement too late and they wondered if he'd overheard Veronica's "Rules for Boyfriends" from the hallway.

At the restaurant, Amy felt proud walking into the fancy dining room with Andrew. He looked gorgeous. His butt fit just right in his khakis and his freshly cut hair made him look older. By his side, as he gave his name to the hostess, she imagined someday being his wife as she had countless times before. Mrs. Andrew Gabel. Andrew and Amy Gabel. She pictured her byline one day in the *New York Times,* Amy Gabel. Or would she use Amy York Gabel?

"Why are you smiling?" Andrew asked, taking her hand and following the hostess to their table.

"I'm happy."

Everything was perfect. Amy watched the candle reflect in Andrew's eyes, and she savored the feeling of his hand on hers. She leaned across the narrow table and he met her in the center with a kiss that tingled her heart and between her legs. Yes, she was happy.

Andrew fished in the pocket of his navy blazer and presented a cube-shaped box to Amy, a card in a red envelope beneath it. Her chest fluttered and she gingerly opened the envelope, her eyes searching past the printed sentiments to his words.

Dear Amy—
I love you. I love us. I hope you accept my way of asking you to Be Mine. Happy Valentine's Day!
Love,
Andrew

Tears welled in her eyes and she whispered, "I love you."

Carefully peeling the tape off the thick wrapping paper, Amy unwrapped the box, lifted the lid, and peered beneath it. Stuck into a cushion was a pin with the Sigma Chi cross symbol. The Greek letters were centered in the cross and the pin was edged in tiny pearls. Amy gasped and a youthful squeal escaped her.

"Pinned for Valentine's Day! Drew, it's the best gift!"

As a show of commitment, a fraternity brother could give his girlfriend a lavaliere or, more rarely, a brother would take it to the next level and give her a pin—and then suffer the wrath of his brothers. Earlier in the year, after a Sig Ep brother lavaliered one of Amy's Kappa sisters, the poor guy was dunked naked into the icy autumn water of the Clinton Square fountain in downtown Syracuse. What was it with college boys and nudity? As Andrew leaned across the table and pinned his letters on her, she wondered what humiliation it would trigger for him.

For the girls, being pinned or lavaliered resulted in a different kind of event. Without sharing who it was for, one sister would arrange a candle-lighting ceremony, and with everyone singing softly in a circle, a candle was passed. The white candle circled once for friendship and sisterhood, the second time around was for a lavaliere, a third time around meant a pinning, and if the candle looped a fourth time, someone was engaged. When the flame reached the girl being honored, she would reveal herself by blowing out the candle, which filled the dim room with shrieks and a swarm of hugs.

Andrew had given Amy a lavaliere for her birthday junior year, and he endured the embarrassment of being delivered, stripped and bound with duct tape, to the front porch of their sorority house after the candle lighting. Veronica had organized the ceremony and sat beside Amy, breathless, as the candle circled the group. After the reveling and excitement had simmered, the doorbell rang persistently until the sisters still lingering opened the door and screeched for Amy to come. Andrew lay trembling, curled on his side on the slate steps, frosty in a Syracuse November, his eyes seeking the one he suffered for. Amy gathered a blanket to wrap him and scissors to unwrap him, yanking at delicate skin and hairs as she went. Andrew had been a sport, and "I love you" were his first words as Amy unstuck the silver tape from his mouth. That night, Veronica had said approvingly to Amy, "Andrew really showed his commitment tonight. He's got to love you to go through that!"

Amy would get to have another candle lighting. It was a dream Valentine's night, just like a movie scene. She stood, held Andrew's face in her hands, and kissed him. "I love you." She felt his hands on her hips and a tap on her shoulder.

Jenny stood grinning at them. "Oh my gosh! I can't believe I'm seeing you two here!" She gushed a little too loudly for the serene restaurant.

Before Amy could ask, Jenny continued. "Isn't this just the best place? This is my second time here with Frank."

She tipped her head and darted her eyes to her right in an action meant to be subtle but bubbled out of her in full Jenny grandness. Andrew and Amy looked to the corner, where an older man, perhaps in his late forties, sat alone leaning back and peering at the menu an arm's length away. He adjusted his glasses with his other hand and squinted.

"Is that your father?" Shocked at her date's age, Andrew blurted the question with a hush in his voice.

Amy pinched him and Jenny winced just a bit before gleefully jumping to share the tale: "I needed some help with a scene, so I was waiting outside in the hall for office hours—"

"He's your professor?" Amy whisper-shouted, surprised that she could still be surprised by Jenny's male selections.

Seeming pleased, Jenny continued: "So we were in his office and Professor Howard—I mean Frank—told me how impressed he was with my work. I wanted his advice on how to portray my character's feelings of shame in my monologue. He was so helpful, he closed the door and worked on it with me for a whole afternoon."

Amy stole another glimpse to where the professor sat. His hair was thinning on top, but combed straight back, it pooled into a clump of longer hair at the base of his neck. His nose was prominent—huge, actually. *What does Jenny see in this guy?* At that moment, as if he knew eyes and attention were on him, Frank Howard looked directly toward the threesome. His mouth tugged on one side, then pulled into a full but crooked smile, exposing large teeth that crowded against one another. When he stood and walked over, his height shocked Amy; he couldn't be more than an inch taller than she was at her petite stature. Jenny, who was a head taller than Amy, had to look down to the short and skinny professor.

"How do you do?" Frank darted his hand out to Amy first, then Andrew, the four of them standing awkwardly among the tables and drawing stares. Frank's voice was deep with a slight raspiness that didn't fit the rest of him, and his posture and stance emitted a confidence that bordered on arrogance. Jenny rushed to fill the gap of silence.

"Frank has been with the VPA program for almost twenty years."

VPA, or the School of Visual and Performing Arts, was the same school that Matt's friend Laura would be in as a theater major, Amy realized; she was still one of the few female names Matt had ever shared.

"Isn't that amazing?" Jenny brushed her fingers across his chest and the professor pulled himself taller under her touch. His shoulders were deliberately held back so that it pushed his breastbone forward. Amy envisioned a swaggering, cocky cowboy firing a toy cap gun and pressed her lips together to keep from smirking. The professor's stance seemed superior and dismissive, and Amy chuckled in her head at the complete juxtaposition between his actual appearance and what he was projecting. Maybe VPA was right where this spoon acting like a fork belonged. Frank Howard was a spork in the flesh.

"We laugh about how I was a new professor the year Jenny was born," Frank burst into a snorting, cackling laugh, and his off-center smile widened beneath his tremendous nose. Amy smiled politely, and she noticed a faint flinch from Andrew at the piercing sound of Frank's laugh. Before the talk could continue, Andrew graciously wished them a good meal and he pulled out Amy's seat.

On the drive home, Amy fingered the Sigma Chi pin on her chest and shifted deeper into Andrew's side. She was snuggled in, shivering as the borrowed car heated.

"I just don't get it, I mean, I know her dad left them and I can't imagine how terrible that must feel, but I still don't get how she can just flit between so many guys. How can that make her happy?"

"It's like she's searching for something," Andrew said.

"Or someone."

Chapter 22

IT WAS DANCE MARATHON weekend, when students would stay awake and moving for thirty hours to raise money for the Muscular Dystrophy Association. Students and local bands performed and entertained the crowd while monitors ensured that no one slept, chasing people from between bleachers or stacks of tumble mats.

Entering Manley Field House on Friday evening, Amy, Veronica, and the Kappa Kappa Gamma Dance Marathon team stomped off the late March snow and opened their bags for inspection. Having neither Jolt Cola nor alcohol, the girls were permitted to enter the darkened gym. They wove through the milling crowd to the Sigma Chi and Kappa meeting place as the thick bass of the Beastie Boys pulsed around them. Sigma Chi pledges scurried to help Amy and her friends with their bags and added them to the pile as Andrew twirled Amy in their first big dance move of the event.

All around, guys were scamming on girls, who acted ditzy and flirted back, until a squealing microphone corralled the students. "We are taking on the challenge of dancing for those who cannot," began the opening ceremonies, which droned on with emcees, Muscular Dystrophy Association representatives, and

student council officers giving speech after speech. The participants undulated with anticipation and the volume increased, until
a special guest hushed them. A toddler stricken with MD slowly
walked onto the stage crutched by his parents. His frailty contrasted the vibrant student body. With the reason they were there
clearly before them, the marathon began.

Hours of music of all kinds stretched before them. Steel drums
followed rap groups, Garth Brooks crooned after Salt-N-Pepa.
The Divinyls touched themselves, R.E.M. lost their religion, and
Madonna justified her love. New wave fans jostled against head-
bangers, dance teams rocked it to Janet Jackson and Paula Abdul,
and Sinéad O'Connor drifted into En Vogue. Finally, around
three in the morning, it was Matt's turn to perform. Amy grabbed
Veronica and some sisters and made her way to the front of the
stage. Matt's acoustic versions of classic rock ballads soothed the
sleepy room, and people slowly puddled to the floor. A few groups
waved their arms to keep moving. Amy beamed up at Matt, solo
and confident onstage, gifting the audience with his voice.

Dawn Nichols, a Kappa from the pledge class behind hers,
turned to Amy. "Oh my gosh! I totally pegged Matt as a spoon,
but up on that stage it's like he's transformed into the coolest steak
knife. His music is clutch!"

Amy was taken aback at her assessment. She found herself
slightly offended at Dawn calling him a spoon, even though she
had also given him that label. It felt negative and accusatory coming from someone else.

"What do you call that? Maybe he's a spife or a knife-oon? Or
a temporary knife? What about a masquerading spoon?" Dawn
cracked herself up, doubling over as Matt crooned on, mesmeriz-
ing the room.

Veronica shook her head, amazed at how Amy's UCS had
endured and been handed down like precious family traditions.

Amy didn't like any of Dawn's labels for Matt and a protectiveness swelled within her. As he finished his set, she went backstage to find him.

"That was awesome, Matt. I love hearing you sing."

"Thanks, Amy. Come on, I need some water."

The DJ tried to rally the crowd, and the organizers from the Greek Council worked to get people back on their feet. With the help of Vanilla Ice, the dancing resumed. Matt and Amy leaned in a vacant corner, talking easily.

"What time are the Vampires playing?" Amy asked, wanting to see him perform again.

"I think around lunchtime tomorrow, or I guess it's today already."

"I can't stay up all night like you guys do. This no-sleep thing is killing me."

"Midnight rehearsals work. Schoolwork, then jam time."

"It's a good thing you've got the whole house to yourselves."

"Amy! There you are," called Dawn. She was still dancing to "Goody Two Shoes," an old Adam Ant song, as she approached them. Her face was red and her hair matted to her forehead, defying its perm. "Come on, you've been gone forever. Andrew's looking for you. Hi, Matt! You did a sick job up there," she cooed.

Dawn yanked her arm. With a wave back to Matt, Amy dug for some energy and rejoined the dancing. In a mob within the mob, she danced with Andrew, Veronica, Dawn, a crew of Kappas and Sigma Chis, and a mingle of friends. David Bowie blended into Huey Lewis and the News, INXS gave way to Yaz, and Billy Idol mixed into Marky Mark. Taking breaks, she jotted down notes and interviewed people for the school newspaper and magazine stories before dancing again. People stumbled from drinking smuggled booze, and the crowd shouted lyrics from early '80s favorites. As the synthetic sounds of "Electric Avenue" squawked, a girl in Dr. Martens deliberately shoved Amy, sending her stumbling. She righted herself as the girl's group formed a force, draped in black clothes, and advanced toward Amy. Seeing the mob of pink-streaked hair, Andrew raced to her defense.

"Back off! What do you think you're doing?" he yelled, raising his voice above the leather-clad local band.

"She stole my boyfriend. Saw 'em kissing in the corner."

"What?" Amy said as Andrew spun toward her, asking the same question.

"I don't know what she's talking about, Drew."

His face was stern.

"I swear; I haven't kissed anyone but you!"

He turned and barked at the accuser. She jingled a chain at her side and took several steps closer to Amy. Her spiky black hair poked toward Amy's face and she smelled of alcohol and Poison perfume. Suddenly, the girl's black-rimmed eyes widened and she sobered for a moment.

"Oh. It's not you. Shit." She stormed off, her posse stomping behind her.

"What was that about?" Andrew demanded. "Did you kiss someone? Why did she think you kissed her boyfriend?"

"I don't know, you heard her, she made a mistake. She's drunk. Don't you trust me?"

His shoulders relaxed. "I do. I trust you, Aim, sorry. I was embarrassed and for a minute it felt like freshman year after spring break."

"There's been no one since that one time, I promise. I've always told you the truth. You can trust me."

"I know. I know." He rubbed the back of his neck. "Why are you laughing?"

"Listen." The Violent Femmes and the Syracuse dancers sang "Kiss Off."

"That waste-oid can go kiss off!" Andrew pulled Amy to him and they joined the chanted counting.

And three, three, three for my heartache.

They were still dancing as the smell of coffee veiled the middle-school-boy odor that pervaded the field house, and the scent of soap mixed with bananas and breakfast as the locker room showers filled with sweaty dancers getting clean. There were still seventeen hours to go.

Chapter 23

AS THEY HIKED UP the front steps to the house already vibrating with noise, they noted the symmetry. Their last fraternity party of senior year and first big party of freshman year were both at Sigma Chi, neatly bookending their college days.

"Our last Syracuse party. Let's hope that tonight is nothing like that first time," Veronica said.

"It still shakes my insides thinking about it, especially when I wonder what would've happened if Andrew wasn't there to save me."

"We've also had tons of good times here, so let's make tonight like those and avoid the P-word."

"Thank God he's gone and graduated."

Every brother knew Amy and greeted her with broad smiles, friendly hugs, and pecks on the cheek. She'd been selected the Sigma Chi Sweetheart for her senior year, an honor voted on by the entire fraternity and awarded only when there was someone special to choose. Amy was treated like royalty among the brothers, the house sweetheart and their fraternity president's girlfriend. She participated in their philanthropic events and was invited to formal dinners at the house to which the guys always wore jackets and ties.

Amy heard a familiar voice call out her name above the bass beat that palpated her heart.

Veronica saw Jenny first and let out a little mumble: "Oh, boy, I'll go get us some beer."

"Amy! Amy!" Jenny bobbed up to her. Her breasts greeted Amy first, perky and escaping from the tank top she wore under her overall shorts, one shoulder strap fastened, the other hanging loose. Her pink eyelids accented her green eyes, her lips glistened a sultry mauve, and her bare feet were tipped in bloodred. She was a mélange of trendy colors unfashionably mashed together.

"Hi, Jenny, I haven't seen you in a while." Amy thought of their February meeting at the restaurant with Professor Spork.

"Yeah, not since the night we ran into you and Andrew at Varsity Pizza," Jenny recalled without hesitation.

Amy raised her eyebrows and thought back. *Oh, yeah, we did see her there. When was that?* Jenny had been with a guy who looked like a fork without him even opening his mouth. She seemed to have collected all the forks around campus in her time at Syracuse. The guy at Varsity wore a flannel shirt with the sleeves torn off at the shoulders, combat boots, and a smirk on his face that screamed out, *I'm a cocky son of a bitch; you'd be lucky to be with me.* Amy had to refrain from rolling her eyes when Jenny introduced them.

"So are you still with . . ." There was no glimmer of a name in Amy's mind for Lumberjack Fork. "Are you two still together?" Amy asked, already knowing the answer.

"Oh, Corey, no. He met some bimbette on spring break. But he can bite me. He wasn't my type anyway."

Amy forced the corners of her lips to stay neutral.

Jenny leaned into her secretively. "He was a shrimp fork!" She burst into laughter and cracked her gum near Amy's ear. "A big asshole with a little, tiny dick! Get it? A shrimp fork!"

Amy joined her laughing; she loved the additions to the Utensil Classification System and how it had grown since her father created it that night at Bella's. She grieved only her best friend's continued rejection of the system. For all of her tidiness, how could Veronica not see the usefulness and accuracy of the UCS? All four years, guys neatly fit the definitions: Eric was a giant serving fork, Doug (and Zach) were knives, Andrew, of course, was a steak knife, and computer-pro Matt was her sweet nerdy spoon friend. It all matched up.

"No, now I'm seeing Dennis," Jenny said. "You must know him, being the Sigma Chi Sweetheart and all."

Amy's head moved up and down while her mind searched for words to respond. Of course she knew Dennis. He was the typical player, the classic mack daddy, the very definition of the highest order of forks. Dennis was a pitchfork squared.

"Yup, I know Dennis. You can do so much better than him, Jenny," was all Amy could say truthfully, picturing him during March Madness, when he'd sauntered into the Sigma Chi house leading a giggling girl up to his room. He led her not by the hand, not by walking beside her, but with his left hand sunken into the back of her pants and his right hand flinging a thumbs-up to anyone who looked their way. He paraded her past Amy and the group of brothers and girlfriends watching Syracuse play in the Elite Eight on the living room TV.

"Do you think it's a little weird that Dennis told me that he knows all about girls' 'period underpants'? He told me never to wear my period undies around him."

"Yeah, that's a little strange."

"He even keeps trying to show me the 'right way' to give a hand job, like I don't know how to do that. That's not what bothers me, though." Jenny glanced around then leaned closer to Amy. "It's that he told me how he taught other girls how to do it, using his dick, of course, and then he compares me to them."

Amy felt the old familiar frustration and sadness creep in as Jenny talked. Amy wanted to shake her and lead her away from

Dennis at full speed. Instead, she put a hand on Jenny's arm and repeated, "You can do so much better than him."

"Oh well, no biggie, he's fun to be with anyway, and he sure is hot to look at." She shrugged.

"Where are you heading after graduation?"

"Back home to California," Jenny said, bubbling with forced enthusiasm. "I'm going to live with my mom for a little while, waitress and save some money, then I'll probably try to get into the movies or something." She flipped her yellow hair over her shoulder as the bubbles fizzled from her voice.

Amy searched for a silver lining around the cloud she felt. "I bet your mom will be glad to have you home. You should do some painting, too, you're really good at it."

Jenny didn't ask Amy what her plans were and she made a sharp-angled turn from peppy to serious.

"You know, I will always remember the time you took me home for Thanksgiving," Jenny said, her gaze on Amy's shoes instead of her eyes. "It really meant a lot to me. And your dad . . . well, your dad was the bomb. Tell him I said thank you. You were a good friend to me, Amy." She took a deliberate breath and raised her eyes to Amy's face. "You're really lucky."

AMY TOSSED ANOTHER KERNEL of popcorn into her mouth. "Can you believe we're graduating this weekend?"

Andrew was studying for his last final exam, and she and Matt were having a movie night at his apartment before she met Andrew back at his place. Matt opened the blue-and-gold Block-buster video case and slid *When Harry Met Sally* . . . into the VCR. It was three years old, but it was Amy's favorite movie, edging out *Say Anything* as her top pick.

"Do you really think it's true that men and women can't just be friends? We're friends," Amy said. "Don't you think Harry is totally wrong?"

Matt shrugged and didn't answer. He moved his guitar to the chair and lifted the popcorn from the coffee table. He nestled in next to her and balanced the bowl half on her leg and half on his, the way they always did. Amy kept talking even as she popped more kernels in her mouth.

"What's it going to be like being so far apart? And what am I going to do if I need help with my computer stuff at work?"

"You've got your computer word processing down pat now; you'll kick butt at the *Observer*, knocking out those top stories, your byline everywhere. Besides, the city's not that far. I can visit when I'm at my parents'. And there are these things called phones. You can call me with any questions or even just to tell me you miss me."

His smile wrapped around her. His once straggly hair was trimmed away from his face and around his ears, clipped for job interviews, and contacts replaced his glasses. Amy saw something new in his familiar brown eyes and in that dimple that she loved: a handsomeness emerged in a way she hadn't recognized before.

Amy was moving to New York City after graduation for a reporting job at a five-year-old newspaper, the *New York Observer*, and Matt was remaining in Syracuse to work for the computer technology department of the Lockheed Corporation while he stayed on at the university to begin a graduate program.

"And I'll send you postcards from sunny Syracuse."

"Matt," Amy said softly, "do you think Andrew and I would stay together if he weren't moving to New York City, too?"

"You're the only one who knows the answer to that," Matt said.

She sat pensively for a moment.

"But, I mean, do you think we *should* stay together? We've

been going out since freshman year, and what if there's someone else I should be meeting and I miss him because I'm with Drew?" Amy took a breath and continued, talking to herself more than to Matt. "Of course, I love him, he's amazing. Sure, sometimes I get upset and feel a little like I have to compete for his attention with all he does and with him always wanting to have friends around, but what couple doesn't have those kinds of things to deal with? Right? He's great at school and sports and, well, everything, and he got that great finance job. Bear Stearns is a big deal. He's not jealous, he's fun to be with, and everyone loves him. I know we're meant to be together, forget I'm asking. Never mind."

Matt shifted his arms behind his head and leaned back against the couch. Amy noticed his T-shirt rise at his waist, revealing a taut abdomen. Her eyes traveled along the line of hair trailing from his navel to his—she stopped herself and tried to pull her eyes away. She pretended to look into the popcorn bowl but glanced beyond it back to his exposed midriff, hoping he couldn't see her eyes. Her stomach fluttered, either from the tingle of discovery or the bare wonder of the momentary sensation never before associated with Matt.

"You have to do what you feel is right, Amy."

She lifted her eyes to his.

"There's nothing I can say about your relationship with Andrew. I can help you with computers, but you have to figure out your heart on your own."

She nodded. "How come you never talk to me about any girls? We talk about everything, except we hardly ever discuss girls you date."

Matt shrugged. "I don't feel like I need to talk about that stuff. Besides—"

"What do you mean? You can talk to me about anything, even your romantic conquests. Come on."

"I do talk to you about everything. Everything else. I've got nothing to hide from you, but what would you want to know, anyway? There's no one serious, there's not much to say."

"Hmm. What's your type of girl? Who's the girl you've spent the most time with?"

"You." He laughed. "My time with you doesn't leave me much time for other girls."

She nudged him, feeling relief jumbled with curiosity. He hit the play button on the remote. As the first old couples started telling their love stories, her worries about Andrew eased and she rested her head comfortably against Matt's shoulder. She let her eyes sweep to the edge of his shirt. It covered him again. She sighed, threw a handful of popcorn in her mouth, and watched the on-screen tales of love.

A POUNDING AT THE door woke Amy. She blinked her eyes open just enough to see Matt lift his head and stretch his neck. The knocking returned and the two rubbed their eyes and searched the room, trying to make sense of what was happening.

"Oh no, Matt! What time is it? We fell asleep."

Matt stood and padded to the door as Amy gathered the bowl emptied of popcorn and refilled with two drained Rolling Rock bottles and some Popsicle wrappers. Matt unlocked the door while his fingers brushed his sleep-filled hair. Andrew burst in as the latch released.

"Hey, Matt, is Amy still here?" His voice was filled with worry.

Matt began to answer but Andrew stepped past him. He saw Amy moving toward the kitchen and followed her into the outdated linoleum room with its 1970s appliances and avocado-green countertops.

"Aim, what's going on?"

"We must've fallen asleep. What time is it?" Amy replied, squinting at the stove for a clock.

"It's three thirty in the morning! I got back to the house and you weren't there," he accused. "You said you'd be there after your movie."

"I'm sorry, I fell asleep during the movie. Come on, let's go. Did you just get home? You were studying late," she noted, floundering to connect the dots.

At the door, she gave Matt a hug, then slid into her flip-flops. From the corner of her eye, blinking through the sleepiness, she thought she saw Andrew bump his shoulder into Matt on his way to her side.

Chapter 24

THE PIERCING SOUND CUT into Amy's dream, filtering into the images. In her dream, there were Christmas lights everywhere and Andrew's mouth was open wide as if the buzzing sound was coming from him. The ringing shrieked through her heart and reverberated down her spine, and then she was shaking back and forth.

"Amy! Amy, get up!" Veronica's voice wedged in and found her through the slumbering fog.

Amy startled to attention and robotically reached for the pile of fire-alarm clothes stored beside her bed, a practice that lingered from freshman year. She mindlessly lifted the sweatshirt, forcing her head through the hole as she yanked leggings on under her nightshirt. Her arms, by habit, found their places.

Their room in the Kappa house was dim, and the red numbers on the clock radio announced 2:28 a.m. The gleam from the streetlights and the campus beyond seeped in around the edges of the curtains. Amy walked toward Veronica's silhouette and they stumbled out the door into the hallway lights. She squinted against the whiteness and leaned against Veronica, relying on her stability.

Amy felt as though she could taste the buzzing and touch

the light as they herded down the hallway and the three flights of stairs. A cool night breeze crept up to them, even in May there was a chill in Syracuse after sunset. Amy wrapped her arms around herself and pulled her sweatshirt up at her neck without effect. Her ears throbbed in the sleepy outdoor air, and voices drifted away, lost in the expanse of the night.

"FOUR YEARS AND I'M still waking you up for fire alarms," Veronica teased Amy as they waited across the Kappa driveway for the fire department.

All the sisters who lived in-house gathered on the grass and the terraced steps that led down the hill to Comstock Avenue. The alarm rang out through open windows, and as sirens rose in the distance, brothers from Sigma Chi, next door, started trickling onto their front porch. They draped over the railing and threw themselves on the filthy, torn couch, watching their neighbors.

"Hey! You girls all right?"

"Wanna wait over here?"

"What's with the hair, girls?"

"Now we'll see who's shacking up over there!"

The friendly taunts punched the night air. Veronica thought back to the parents' weekends the two houses had hosted together, the semiformals, the casual hangouts, and the bid night parties. She laughed, remembering the late August weeks when they had all arrived back on campus early to prepare for rush, when the girls spent hours in song practice on the front steps of the stately brick house. In the middle of the night last summer, Veronica had woken in a panic; she was hearing rush songs and thought they were missing a rehearsal. She stirred Amy from sleep and roused her from bed, becoming more alert as she hurried to join the singing. It was dark and Amy grumbled, but Veronica insisted they couldn't miss a rehearsal. Amy was the one who had noticed the time, almost four in morning, and stumbled sleepily toward the sound of the music.

"Veronica, come here," she had said, laughing and leaning out their window. "Very funny, guys! You got us! Let's all go back to sleep now!"

When Veronica joined her at the window, she saw a bunch of their friends sitting on the roof of Sigma Chi with a boom box, playing back the tape they had recorded of the girls singing.

Before the fire trucks arrived, Veronica looked between the houses and glanced up to the roof where the guys had perched that night. Movement from the side door of the Kappa house— the door no one ever used—grabbed her attention. In the darkness, she couldn't tell who it was, but she saw silhouetted heads come together in a whispered word, or in a kiss, and then the body, who was clearly male, slunk away behind Sigma Chi. He scurried out of the shade of the houses and into a patch of lightness. Veronica gasped. Even in the dimness, she was sure it was Andrew. She walked away from the others and toward the house to see which sister uncoiled from the shadows.

"Stay back, please," barked a firefighter as she approached. Following his orders, she stopped and pulled her unruly curls away from her face, squinting as Dawn Nichols stepped toward her. The fireman redirected his reproach toward Dawn: "Ladies, off the driveway, onto the grass, please!"

Veronica stalked over to her and spoke through gritted teeth: "Andrew Gabel? You're fooling around with Amy's boyfriend?"

Dawn's face registered shame and she stammered, "I didn't— we didn't do anything really. We just—we only kissed and hooked up a little. Only a little." She looked stunned and scared. "Please, don't tell Amy, she's always been so great to me. Please."

Veronica turned on her heel, giving Dawn her back. She knotted her hair into a twist at the back of her head, thinking, knowing she had to be honest. Amy would be heartbroken. She was completely idealistic when it came to Andrew, totally devoted and unable to use her reporter's eye on him. *She is so stuck on him being her "perfect steak knife,"* Veronica thought, *too stuck.* Thinking through their years together, Veronica couldn't count the times when Andrew was too preoccupied with other activities and left Amy in second place behind those pursuits, but besides seeing him with Donna after the Pan Am crash, he'd never given any indications of being a cheater. Sure, he always commanded a room and was happiest in social settings surrounded by friends and new people to meet, but as far as Veronica knew, he had been loyal to her best friend. She felt sickened with disappointment.

Compelled to tell Amy, she went to find her roommate just as the firemen exited their house, announcing, "All clear!"

Back in their room, Veronica broke the news as gently as she could. Amy sobbed until morning, her eyes puffy and bloodshot, her nose rimmed pink. Veronica sat up with her, feeling Amy's grief along with a misplaced guilt for having been the one to tell her the news. As the house began to stir, there came a timid knock at their door. Protectively, Veronica left Amy's side to answer, instead of granting the usual invitation to come in. Dawn stood there, her shoulders hunched, her eyes swollen like Amy's.

"Can I talk to her? Please?" she sniffled.

Veronica planted herself, blocking the doorway.

"Who's there?" Amy said in a hushed voice.

"Her."

"It's okay, V, let her in."

Dawn moved slowly, cowering toward Amy's bed as if trying to not take up too much space in the room. Her voice caught as she spoke. "I'm sorry, Amy. I'm so sorry. I want you to know that nothing really happened. It was just a kiss and a little fooling around, that's all. Really. And it was all my fault. I've always liked him and I saw him out at Faegan's last night. I was drunk and I know it's no excuse, but then I walked back here with him. He was looking for you. I pretended to check your room and told him you weren't home." Dawn hiccuped and took what seemed to be her first breath since beginning. "I brought him to the back study room. I wasn't thinking, I just did it, I just kissed him and—well, I'm sorry."

Amy was out of tears. She squeezed her scratchy eyes shut, seeing more clearly with Dawn's confession. Dawn padded out of their room, seeming even smaller than when she had entered.

The whole time Dawn had talked, Veronica noticed Amy had looked away, toward something on her bookshelf. Veronica followed her gaze to a snapshot of Amy and Andrew smiling cheek to cheek, a dried corsage resting beside the frame.

"I'm breaking up with him," Amy resolved, blowing her nose as punctuation.

WEARY AND COVERED IN sleeplessness, Amy marched next door to the Sigma Chi house early enough to avoid most of the still-sleeping brothers. She found Andrew just waking up, alone in the single suite reserved for the fraternity president. He greeted her with his wide smile and outstretched arms, then startled when she crossed her arms over her chest, unmoving, and burst into tears anew. She couldn't hold it in for another moment.

"I can't believe I'm saying this, but it's over. I never thought that you . . ." Her heart and mind flapped like a sail in the wind, and she didn't know how to pin down her thoughts into words. "You've sometimes been distracted or a little far away emotionally, but I never expected—I never thought you could cheat on me."

Andrew protested. "Cheat on you? What are you talking about?"

"You messed around with Dawn. Last night. I know all about it, she told me everything."

"There's nothing to tell. I was there for you, and she just kissed me, that's all, just a quick kiss, just like you and that guy from spring break freshman year. I forgave you then, you should forgive me now—it's the same thing."

His words stung, but still she pushed back. "You're holding that over my head? That's not forgiveness. Is that what this is? Payback for freshman year? We only kissed; we didn't hook up. That was three years ago and this isn't the way things are supposed to happen. We're about to graduate, to move to the same city. I thought you were 'the one.' How could you fool around with someone else? We're breaking up." Sobbing, Amy turned and left his room.

Wearing only his boxers, Andrew followed her into the hallway, calling behind her in a muted tone: "Don't do this. You have to forgive me. Give me another chance, Aim, I'll show you it was nothing. I'm sorry. Don't go. Please."

The fraternity was rising, and brothers were peering out doors and lining up in the hallways, staring at Andrew, their leader, who was unaccustomed to negative attention, unfamiliar with being rejected. As Amy stood on the landing at the turn of the staircase, she sensed the desperation in him, felt her own embarrassment mix with his. He begged her in a loud whisper. Leaning over the railing of the stairwell half-naked, he pleaded. Amy heard the crack in his voice, felt a squeeze in her heart. She looked away from him. Down the hall, she saw a brother leave the bathroom; she glimpsed the panels of the toilet stalls in the wedge of space before the door fell shut again.

Her stomach clenched from the memories of that bathroom. She grasped the huge finial on the railing beside her. She felt an overpowering bond to Andrew beyond loving him; he had saved her when she needed saving, had rescued her when she was vulnerable.

"Please, Aim. Please."

She returned her eyes to him. He looked sincere in his sorrow, in his remorse. He was more emotional than she had ever seen him and she was drawn like a yo-yo back to his palm. Everyone was watching; she felt like she had to save him from this shame. Slowly, she climbed back to Andrew, resolving to forgive him with each step.

Chapter 25

AMY DRAGGED OUT PACKING the last of her things, slowly putting them into the same plastic crates she'd brought in 1988. She sat on the floor and opened her childhood Treasure Box. She pored over the party pictures from four years of formals and pledge days, neat scraps of wrapping paper from special gifts, the pressed rose petals and secret admirer notes from four Valentine's Days, all with her initials. She fingered the bundles of letters and cards tied together with lengths of grosgrain ribbon, the letters from Zach Bennett after freshman year's spring break bound together in their own pile. It surprised her that she still fluttered at the thought of him, and she wondered if they'd see each other in New York City. Though Doug and Veronica had decided not to pursue long-distance love after their summer together, they stayed in touch and got together in Newport. Veronica had not so discreetly shared details on Zach and let Amy know that he was working in Manhattan.

How strange to be untethering herself from the home she had known for what felt like more than four years. How monumental it seemed to be stepping out, a woman with a real job, into real life, her college days through. Four years ago, at that first floor-meeting on Brewster 8, she had looked around the circle of faces, strangers from all over thrown together by a computer to live side by side for a year. Her floor mates were united by their nervous anticipation, each unknown to the others. They were suddenly living all the typical graduation card expressions: "reaching for dreams," "another chapter," "a fresh start," "a new beginning." Perhaps even, for some, a blank slate. They could feel the reality of it all vibrating around them, universally wondering where 1988 and their college days would take them. Amy thought of the parallels in life as she was again about to receive graduation cards with the same wishes for a bright future. She was, one more time, on the cusp of something wonderfully brand new.

A postcard slipped from a stack of papers. Amy grinned, holding up the *Footloose* picture of Ren McCormack. She hadn't thought of this trinket, which had been important enough to bring to school, in years. She ran her fingers over the image. Before the Kappa fire alarm, she thought she had found her Ren in Andrew, but now she wavered. Her father's thinly concealed urgency for her to find someone flickered to her mind. He worried about her, concerned in his old-fashioned way that she find a man to care for her as he aged. It had always been the two of them and it had always been easy to make him happy, to make him proud. She wondered now if she was holding on so tightly to Andrew for her sake or for her father's.

Maybe this was just a bump with Andrew, just a small slipup, she thought. Everything had been great between them after she confessed to kissing Zach; they could get through this indiscretion, too, she told herself. She set the postcard aside with her uncertainty then continued through the keepsakes.

She scanned through her Panhellenic rush schedules, the freshman-year fire-alarm tally sheet (eighty-three in all), her Kappa bid letter, the ransom note for her toothbrush missing a few of the pasted letters, and a picture she didn't remember having. It was of her and Matt, faces smooshed together, smiling out at her older self. Her hairstyle marked it as their sophomore year. It was like seeing the two of them with outside eyes. They looked happy and comfortable, like they were sharing a private knowledge. The boy she had stumbled upon in the computer lab had been a constant in her time at school. They'd been friends as long as she and Andrew had been a couple.

Gazing at the picture, she recalled slivers of phrases and snippets of times when her dad or Veronica had shared tactful concerns about Andrew and offered thinly disguised suggestions of how Matt liked her as more than a friend. How often she'd dismissed them, Amy realized. As a faint scent of Old Spice wafted up from the box, she considered the words she'd ignored. Thinking of Matt, Amy felt a surge of compassion and belonging. She felt safe with him, her favorite spoon; he was a friend who understood and accepted her, who was familiar and always present for her. *Does he think of me as more than a friend?* Amy skeptically puzzled the question her father and friend had posed more than once through the years.

Dubious, her focus shifted to a snapshot of Andrew. She smiled at his good looks and his success, at his public display of love for her in giving her his pin. She cherished his attention and understood how everyone loved being around him. Amy was comforted by his ease in every situation. *I'm only questioning Andrew now because of what happened with Dawn. It's normal to feel nervous at a time of big changes in life,* she justified, concluding that Matt was just a friend. He had never once indicated he was interested in her in any way other than friends. Andrew was her steak knife. And because of that label, Amy tucked her doubts with the pictures into her Treasure Box.

"IS THIS REALLY THE CHECKOUT LINE?" Amy asked the girl standing beside the Syracuse poster display. The girl nodded and rolled her eyes. "All the way back here? Wow! Well, this line always goes fast, I bet it won't be too bad," Amy said.

"It's crazy, isn't it? I think we all waited until the end of the year to pick out our Syracuse memorabilia," the girl commented. She was shorter than Amy and just a little "fluffy," as her friend Pam liked to describe the size between skinny and chubby. Her pale eyes smiled even when her rosy, cherubic mouth didn't.

"I know, I bought tons of SU stuff freshman year then not too much after that. Now I feel like I need to stock up before leaving." Amy hugged the orange-and-blue apparel to her chest and dangled mugs from her fingers.

"I did the same thing. Everyone in my family got Syracuse sweatshirts, T-shirts, and car stickers for Hanukkah and birthdays my freshman year."

"Yup, and Syracuse baseball hats and umbrellas and magnets . . ." Amy laughed as they took one step closer to the registers they still couldn't see.

"Amy! I'm so glad I ran into you before we leave!" Amy heard the voice and shifted the clothes lower so she could peer over the pile.

"Kate, hi!" Looking around, Amy found a clearance display of winter hats and dumped her pile onto them, freeing her arms to hug Kate.

"Where are you off to?"

"New York City. I got a job at a small weekly newspaper, the *New York Observer*. They're pretty new—they just started publishing five years ago—but they print on pink paper. Isn't that cool? How about you?"

"That sounds perfect for you. I'm going back to Ohio. I'll live at home and start grad school for education in the fall."

"A teacher like your parents. That's great." Amy realized that the cherub-faced girl was politely turning her body away from their conversation. "Oh, Kate, this is, uh . . ." She smiled at the girl. "Sorry, we never introduced ourselves. I'm Amy, this is Kate."

Her sweet mouth grew into a smile. "I'm Laura. But it's okay, go ahead, catch up. I'm not going anywhere."

The line shuffled forward. Amy scooped up her selections and Kate moved alongside with them. Her eyes scanned the line curling through three departments.

"Before I go to the end of the line," she said, loud enough for the people giving her watchful looks to hear, "I have something for you." While shuffling through the basket on her wrist, she explained, "I saw this and had to get it for you. I was going to swing by the Kappa house to drop it off, but it's perfect that I'm seeing you now."

She held her hand behind her back and had that bursting look of someone who can barely contain a surprise. Then she thrust her hand forward, presenting Amy with a package of Syracuse toothbrushes. Amy's laugh turned heads from both directions.

"I love it! Seriously, that is so funny! Thank you, Kate." Amy side-hugged her freshman friend.

"Okay, so give them back. I have to pay for them, then I guess I'll have to drop them off at the house after all."

"I'll wait for you in the atrium. We can grab one final Schine cookie together." Amy was ready for an afternoon snack and the chocolate chip cookies at the student-center dining hall were her favorite.

Once Kate had followed the queue to find the end, Laura turned to face Amy again.

"So, what did she get you that was so hilarious?"

Amy recounted the tale of the Great Toothbrush Kidnapping, then peppered Laura with questions about home, what school she'd studied in, and her postgraduation plans.

"I was in VPA, a theater major," Laura began.

Amy's mouth popped open, then clamped shut. Her eyes widened just a fraction, but enough for Laura to notice and interrupt herself.

"What?"

"Nothing. Well, it's just that, do you know Matt Saxon?"

"Oh my gosh, yes! How did you make that connection?" Laura asked.

"You dated him, right?" Amy couldn't stop herself. Since freshman year, she had wondered about Matt's secret Laura. Because Matt always tended to brush over the topic of dating, saying little even in response to Amy's inquiries, she remembered one of the few names he'd ever mentioned.

"Well, not really. I mean, yes, a couple of times. We went out on Valentine's Day freshman year. After that, he took me out to dinner and once to the movies. I thought we would go to his spring formal, but he didn't ask me."

Amy felt a blush climb her neck and hoped that her bundle of clothes hid it. She had been Matt's date to that formal freshman year. Andrew understood that Amy was a stand-in date for Matt; he teased Amy about it but had never protested their friendship. In all their time together, Matt had never come on to Amy, had never even reached to hold her hand except to help her off a bus. Amy heard Laura's voice continuing as she wondered why Matt had taken her to that fraternity formal if he had another sweet, available date option.

"Matt is such a great guy," Laura said with conviction and wistfulness. "He would make the best boyfriend."

Amy raised her eyebrow, pondering Laura's assessment and marveling at how a long line can open up strangers to one another. She glanced at the gift tucked in her pile for Matt, a navy necktie with a pattern of tiny orange S's for his new job. Giving it a moment's thought, she supposed Laura was right. She was another person who saw Matt in a way that Amy hadn't. It was true, she realized. Matt would make someone a great boyfriend.

Chapter 26

VERONICA REACHED OUT AND straightened Amy's graduation cap.

"I liked it off to the side—I think it adds a little style," Amy said, and kicked up her heel, catching a pouf of air under the rented blue gown. She twirled the honors cords around her neck.

Veronica laughed but left her matching gold cords where they belonged as they headed across campus to the graduation ceremony.

"We're grown-ups now," Veronica said, thinking about her new human resources job at the Saks Fifth Avenue corporate offices. "Full-time jobs in New York City and no more summers off." Her stomach tumbled at the realization.

"I'm really glad we're doing this together."

"I feel like I'm different in so many ways from four years ago. For one thing, I came into college hanging on to my high school boyfriend and we didn't even get through freshman year," Veronica said without regret.

"And you've had dates with an interesting assortment of silverware since then. Jeremy the silver-plated knife, Sean the ladle—he was such a big, goofy nerd—and remember Jeff? That pompous, gigantic butcher knife."

"Oh, brother." Veronica recalled nights giving Kate and Amy details of the one-time-only dates while the two of them dissected the guys with the UCS. "You and your silverware labels."

"Yeah, and I came in without anyone and I'm leaving with a steak knife."

Veronica rested her hand on Amy's back but said nothing. She wasn't as quick to forgive Andrew as Amy had been. The image of his silhouetted figure leaning in toward Dawn still made her angry and stirred up visions of Eric and Jenny at another fire alarm, snuggled up in her purple blanket. She thought of their psychoanalysis of Andrew through the years and all the confidences Amy had shared along the way. She had listened as her roommate described Andrew's emotional reaction to her breaking up with him, she had listened to her reasoning and justifying and rationalizing. It wasn't that Veronica didn't like Andrew, but she worried that Amy's romantic comedy standards would leave her heartbroken. She worried that Andrew was too magnetic, too much like a character in Amy's favorite movies, too appealing to everyone he met.

"I'm psyched that we'll still be living together. I can't imagine not having you for a roommate," Amy said, interrupting her thoughts.

"Me, too. It's crazy to think that we're best friends just because we were randomly matched up freshman year." Veronica retucked a bobby pin through her red curls and into her cap to secure it. "Come on, we're over there."

Lining up in their designated and rehearsed order, Amy was between Trevor Yoland and Dan Young. Veronica was in the row in front of her only two people down. Over her shoulder, she saw Amy craning and searching. Veronica wondered where her parents were among the blur of colors. The crowd of parents, families, and faculty filled every seat in the vast Carrier Dome, and she took in the moment, scanning the stadium like a slow-moving security camera recording the details. Armfuls of congratulatory bouquets, flashes of cameras, banners, and flags. If she focused, she could see a child on a lap, a grandma's face, but without sustained concentration, the individuals knitted into a mob of celebration.

"Amy!" Veronica heard someone call, and she noticed Amy's row of graduates standing and shifting their legs to the side, allowing Andrew to pass. He made his way through and clutched Amy in his arms, swathed in blue polyester. Veronica faced forward again, but her peripheral vision caught the couple, and their words were almost directly behind her.

"You look hot in a dress," Amy teased.

"I needed to see you one last time as a college student."

"Thank you."

"I was looking for you, too. Here." She dug into the small bag by her seat for a package wrapped in thick navy paper. "Happy graduation, I couldn't wait to give this to you."

The lightness left his face and his jaw fell slack. "Uh, thanks, I didn't know we were getting gifts for each other."

Veronica could tell that Amy forced a nonchalance into her voice. "It's okay. Open it." Amy had used the last bit of her summer waitressing money to purchase the watch; she had returned to the jewelers every day for a week, dragging Veronica along, trying to decide on the best one for Andrew. She finally selected one with a brown leather strap and a rectangular face and paid extra for the engraving on the back, *For All Time*. She'd bought it before the kiss, before the almost-breakup. Veronica was deliberately trying not to turn, but knowing how much this meant to her friend, her head drifted to the side, keeping Amy's face in view. She was watching Andrew put it on his wrist.

"I love it! You're so good to me, Aim. Thanks."

"There's an inscription," she said, but her words were swallowed in the drone of the dome.

Andrew nudged Veronica's shoulder and handed her a disposable camera. "Hey, Veronica, can you take a picture of us?"

He pulled Amy close and they posed, marking the moment.

"Thanks! Congratulations, Veronica!" Turning back to Amy, he said, "Here's one for you." He gave her a second cardboard camera and a kiss, then excused his way back out to the main aisle just as the band started playing to corral the crowd's attention. Veronica reached her hand back, hovering across Dan Young, and squeezed Amy's outstretched hand.

Amy leaned toward her. "I expected to feel happier when I gave that to him."

AS NAMES WERE CALLED, echoing rhythmically around her, they nudged at Veronica's memory: a familiar name from a group project, someone a friend had dated, one of her sorority sisters, an old Brewster floor-mate. Acquaintances, classmates, true friends, and strangers marched across the stage to accept their diplomas. A history of names stirred emotions all the way through the alphabet.

Veronica was fixing the strap of her sandal when the voice reverberated through the microphone: "Isadora Jennifer Callista."

She bolted upright and hit her head on the seat in front of her, connecting the name spoken with Jenny. *Isadora?* She turned to see Amy's questioning expression that matched her own. Jenny pranced toward the congratulatory receiving line, her blond hair swept behind her shoulders. Even from row Ty–Xh, Veronica could see that Jenny's robe wasn't zipped up all the way. Instead of fastening at her collarbone, it dipped, exposing cleavage. She stepped toward the dean, and his chin seemed to rise, as if working to keep his eyes on her face. Jenny reached out to shake his hand and retrieve her certificate but stumbled. Her high heel appeared to get stuck behind her and she fell toward the dean. Like one would to catch a tottering child, he put his hands out to steady her, but instead of grasping her armpits, he caught her squarely by the breasts. His action kept Jenny upright, but instantly, the dean pulled back, as if he had touched flame, and then he held his hands up in a show of innocence as Jenny's bare foot hit the stage, balancing herself inches from him.

A murmur replaced the hush of the stadium. The two paused for only a beat, standing face-to-face, and then Jenny bent to pick up her shoe, giving the student section a clear view of what the dean had just felt up. With a coy curtsy, she limped offstage, leaving the dean with his hands still hovering in the air.

Veronica turned back and caught Amy's eye. "Oh my God," she mouthed. Until the recent Sigma Chi fraternity party, they hadn't seen much of Jenny since leaving Brewster tower behind. Every now and then they ran into her around campus or out on M Street, but many of the early relationships of freshman year had fizzled. Veronica was relieved that, when no longer living side by side, Amy had been able to ease away from Jenny and her antics.

Behind her, Amy rested the camera in her lap, waiting through *D*, *E*, and *F*. She lifted the camera as the speakers moved on to the *G*'s. " . . . Manuel Luis Fuentes, Bridget Kelly Fyfe, Karen Claudia Gabardi . . ." She slid her finger over the grooved disk to advance the film and prepared for her shot as they got closer.

" . . . Danielle Ashley Gabbert, Andrew William Gabel . . ." Amy snapped at the faraway platform, trying to preserve Andrew's passage. Her photo albums and frames were filled with images of the two of them: Amy and Andrew with groups of big-haired girls and boys with their hair parted down the middle, a little too long in back; the two arm in arm at football games, on beaches, at formals, huddled by campfires. Soon she would add pictures of them in graduation caps and gowns to the collection.

Veronica looked back to Amy and pulled a curl away from

her face as Amy took her picture, too. She noticed Amy feel for Andrew's Sigma Chi pin, which Veronica knew was tacked to her dress under the robe. She had arranged Amy's second candle lighting, as she had the first for her lavaliere. So few pinnings happened that the whispers grew as the candle started around the circle for the third time. Veronica sat next to Amy, and before the candle had fully left her hand, Amy had blown out the flame, announcing her pinning, and was tackled by a bevy of sisters. It was Andrew, Veronica realized, who had given her those treasured memories, who had made her friend feel loved and special. The thought softened her to him as the names continued their rhythmic march.

THE MORNING AFTER GRADUATION, Veronica woke before Amy and headed downstairs. At the foot of the stairs, Veronica made her usual loop into the communications room to check the bulletin board one last time. She saw an envelope tacked on to the board addressed to Amy and pulled it down. The house was still quiet as Veronica made herself a cup of coffee, returned to their room on the third floor, and silently leaned the envelope against Amy's alarm clock, the first place she would look when she awoke.

"What's that?" Amy's groggy voice croaked.

"Sorry, hope I didn't wake you. I don't know, I found it on the board."

Rolling onto her back and examining it, Amy said, "It's Matt's handwriting." She tugged out the slip of paper, scanned it and read it out loud.

Meet me at our computer lab at 10:00 Sunday morning.
Love,
Matt

"Is he kidding me? There is no way I'm doing computer programming. I already have my diploma and barely scraped through those awful computer classes."

Veronica laughed as Amy slogged out of bed and padded down the hall to brush her teeth on their last morning in this house, on this campus. They were marking off everything with a bittersweet finality.

AMY PULLED THE DOOR OF THE computer lab at 10:02 a.m. Locked. She looked around, knowing there would be no one in sight with the key, or the authority, to open a whole facility for her. She tried the door again, shaking it back and forth as if maybe one more time would prove it wasn't locked, and then she scanned the area for Matt. Why had he told her to meet him there? Maybe the note was old and she had the wrong Sunday. While she considered what to do, Amy sat on the low stone wall beside the entrance and took out the granola bar she'd grabbed from the kitchen.

With a clank that made Amy jump, the computer lab door opened from the inside, hiding her behind it. She stood to peek around the door and nearly smashed her face into Matt's as he peered around the opposite way.

"*Ah!* You scared me!" they both said, laughing.

Matt held the door open and waved her in. "I'm so glad you got my note. I wasn't sure it would get to you in time."

"What are we doing here? Is this place even open?"

"I have connections. Important computer lab connections." His grin drew one out of her. It was impossible not to smile around Matt.

He led her into the familiar room stocked with machines. She stopped short in the doorway, overcome by a rush of feelings, from the fear she had those first weeks to the relief Matt gave her, like aloe on a sunburn. She recalled the small jokes and big conversations they'd had in their corner. Their corner. The corner where their friendship had begun, where it had grown.

She followed Matt to their nook. She'd done it so many times, she could navigate those tables blindfolded. The screens were all dark and the keyboards neatly tucked in for the season. Matt pulled out her chair for her and sat facing her. From his sweatshirt pocket, he removed a gift wrapped in creamy yellow with pink spots. Amy loved it already. She turned it over in her hands before delicately guiding the ribbon over the corners of the box and slipping a finger under the folds.

"I love how you can leave your stuff all over your floor but you unwrap gifts and open envelopes, which are kind of meant to be ripped, like they were rare historical documents."

"Letters and gifts are as precious as any old proclamation. Besides, I like to make it last as long as possible." She held the box with restrained anticipation. Like Russian stacking dolls, she opened the lid to find another box within.

Matt dragged his thumb across his chin; he was smiling and watching Amy's every move. She laid the outer shell beside the computer then glanced up at him before lifting the hinged top of the leather box.

"Oh." She stared at the silver charm bracelet, her eyes brimming with tears and her breath catching in her throat.

"I thought you could add to it for different milestones in your life," Matt began as she studied the charms he'd chosen. "There's a fleur-de-lis for Kappa, and the Syracuse *S*," Matt explained.

Amy fingered the last charm, her name in capitals. "And my name."

"Your initials. The first three letters of your login to remind you that you can do anything."

She threw her arms around his neck with such energy that it pushed Matt back in the chair and Amy fell onto his lap, their bodies touching unlike ever before. The room stood still for a splinter of time before Amy pulled herself upright and sat again, wondering why she felt nervous.

"You are the sweetest, most thoughtful friend in the whole world," she thanked him. "I can't imagine what my life would be like if I hadn't met you."

Looking from her charms up to Matt, she saw his eyes glisten.

Chapter 27

"HOW CAN YOU TWO have so much stuff to move in?" Andrew slid a box on top of another, adding to the towers of cardboard along each wall of the snug city apartment. A tuft of his sandy hair, newly trimmed, stuck to his sweaty forehead. "If it's this hot in June, summer in the city is going to be deadly."

"At least it's not raining," Amy said, plopping a box down and kissing him.

Veronica and Andrew conspiratorially rolled their eyes at her relentless optimism.

Amy and Veronica had decided on a smaller place in a doorman building, forgoing some space for security. It was on Thirty-Seventh Street and Third Avenue, near the entrance to the Midtown Tunnel, and had two tiny bedrooms, a galley kitchen, and a fair-sized living room. Amy scanned the parquet floors, the freshly painted walls, and the large window overlooking Third Avenue and the Empire State Building in the distance. It was all theirs.

Her T-shirt and jeans were dusty, and her brown hair was pulled up into a high, straight ponytail. She'd long ago given up coaxing it to curl and was thankful that hairstyles were straightening. Dressed in similarly grubby attire, Veronica had a wide cloth bandanna keeping her thick red curls from her face. Her parents were vacationing in Italy and had hired a small moving service to help Veronica transport some large things from Newport. The crew unloaded the few items of furniture the Warrens were handing down, along with cartons of new pots, small appliances, and too-fancy dishes they had packed up for their daughter's first apartment. Veronica had found a parking spot in front of the building's entrance on Thirty-Seventh Street, and she trekked in and out with armfuls of garment bags and crates of neatly organized CDs she'd driven down from Rhode Island.

The parade of assorted movers crossed one another on the elevator and in the corridors. Andrew pulled his shirt up and wiped his face, then sat in the middle of the room with an audible exhale. He had been especially attentive and available to Amy since she had climbed the stairs back to him, vowing to show her it was the right choice.

"Just a few more trips and everything should be in," Tom York announced, carrying in two giant suitcases. "That doorman of yours is a nice fella. Even still, I'm happy I'm leaving you in the city with Andrew to look after you for me."

"You're so old-fashioned, Dad, I can take care of myself, you know."

"Don't you need me?" Andrew adopted a wounded look and her dad laughed.

"Come on, let's leave her to unpack all those clothes while we bring up some more."

Andrew hopped up to follow him to the waiting car. Amy watched her dad clutch Andrew on the shoulder and was glad that having Andrew in her life gave her father peace. He had done everything to give Amy a youth to treasure, and she deeply wanted to make him happy and proud. She pulled the luggage to her new room and peered out her window. It filled the whole back wall and overlooked an overgrown courtyard, letting in brightness but no sunlight.

"Amy? Where are you?" Veronica's voice echoed through the unfurnished space.

"In here!"

Veronica appeared at her door, eyes wide and full of meaning that only a best friend could discern. Behind her stood an olive-skinned guy carrying a stack of boxes. Veronica's eyes crinkled with her smile as she directed him to the door next to Amy's. Amy followed them into Veronica's room, where the bed was already made with a new coverlet in ivory with small green leaves scattered across it. It was the only sign of hominess in all of their four rooms.

"This is Joey DiNatali," Veronica introduced, her eyes glittering. "He lives right down the hall, apartment 202."

Joey had black hair combed back with gel, holding it stiff. His black Led Zeppelin T-shirt stretched snuggly across his broad shoulders and chest. His muscular arms, firm even at rest, bulged against the edges of the short sleeves, and a gold chain glinted at his neck. When he and Veronica stood apart from each other, it was hard to tell who was taller.

"How about I cook you ladies dinner tonight?" Joey offered after the introductions, his eyes on Veronica. Joey had a faint accent, the New York–Northern New Jersey twang.

The roommates had planned to order in food and eat between unpacking and decorating. Amy was looking forward to being alone with Veronica setting up their first apartment together. She turned to Veronica, willing her to decline.

"That sounds great," Veronica answered. "Doesn't that sound great, Amy?"

Amy pushed out a smile. "Yes. Thanks, Joey."

The trio drifted out of Veronica's room to the short hallway. They still had hours to get some work done before dinner, Amy reasoned, plus Veronica was clearly interested and it *would* be good to know their neighbors.

"Where do you want these, Aim?" Andrew's voice called from behind three small boxes with a spider plant balanced on top.

"Here." She scooped up the plant and pointed into her room. "Joey, this is Andrew. Andrew, Joey. He lives down the hall," Amy said as Andrew passed. He grunted a hello beneath the load and squeezed through the narrow space.

"Okay, so I'll see you later, seven thirty?" Joey said.

Veronica walked him to the door and Amy chuckled as her friend watched him until he waved from the other end of the hall and let himself into his apartment.

Once the moving helpers had cleared out, Amy and Veronica tore into boxes and cleaning supplies and set up their new home with the Red Hot Chili Peppers CD as their sound track, and evening crept into the city. The handmade wind chimes that Kate made with silverware stolen from the dining hall were the first thing Amy hung in their new apartment. They dangled from the ceiling fan in the living room, tinkling as the blades moved the sticky air.

"I still can't believe Kate stole those," Veronica said, hammering a landlord-approved hook into the plaster.

With a few pictures on the walls, the shower curtain hung, and the kitchen fully unpacked, Amy sat on the floor of her room. She leaned against her bed while Veronica showered in their newly scrubbed bathtub. The light from a small lamp sitting on a box created yellowy shadows. Surveying her new home, Amy felt energized from the physical labor of the day; she swooned with anticipation of life in the city and the greater freedom within the tugs of responsibility. Sitting in her own apartment, with her own job and her own salary, mature and proud, she had arrived at being a grown-up.

"Your turn," Veronica called into the dimness as soap-scented steam poured from the bathroom behind her.

VERONICA KNOCKED ON THE door marked 202 clutching a bottle of Chianti that her parents had sent. Joey had invited Andrew, but he had prior plans to meet a group of work friends downtown at Aces & Eights. Andrew had spent no time at home after graduation, but instead moved into the city and started his job, and he was already immersed in post-college city life.

"How do I look?" Veronica asked again before the door opened.

"Why are you so concerned about how you look?" Amy teased.

Veronica answered with a smirk.

The smell of fresh garlic and olive oil greeted them as Joey opened the door and gave them each a friendly kiss on the cheek. He gently rested his hand on Veronica's back as he led them into his apartment, and she inhaled his aftershave. He was dressed in a neatly pressed black button-down shirt tucked into slim black pants; his only accessories were the gold chain at his neck and a dishtowel thrown over his shoulder. Carrying his glass of red wine to the living room, he poured two more glasses and handed them to Veronica and Amy.

Joey's apartment had some of the same features as theirs, but the floor plan was different. His two bedrooms were unequal sizes; the larger was his bedroom and the other was set up with bookshelves and a desk housing a computer on half of it. To the left was his kitchen, which was small but bigger than Amy and Veronica's hall-like one.

They sat in his living room with the same view of the Empire State Building, which was lit up in red, white, and blue for the upcoming Fourth of July holiday. The rooms were decorated in a bachelor style with a modern edge: black lacquered furniture, Lucite accent tables, huge canvases of abstract art, and dark contrasting tones. It was clear that Joey wasn't fresh out of college; he was established and settled in a more adult way, even if his taste didn't match her own. Veronica wondered how old he was and how she could discreetly slip that into the conversation.

Joey noticed Veronica observing. "Cousin Alessandra helped me pick out some things when I bought this place." He pointed to the leather couch, inviting them to sit while Frank Sinatra crooned in the background. "Tell me about yourselves."

Veronica sat on the edge of the cushion and summarized hometowns, college majors, and new employment statuses, smiling nervously as she spoke. Joey's ankle crossed his opposite knee, and the delicate wineglass rested in his thick hand as he listened attentively, asking for details and clarifications. His eyes left her face only when she paused in conclusion. Then he turned his attention to Amy.

"So, Andrew's your boyfriend? What does he do?"

"He's an investment banker at Bear Stearns. I'm not really sure what that means." She chuckled and sipped her wine.

"And you grew up in Connecticut, huh? I talked to your dad down in the lobby a little bit today—he's very proud of you."

"I'm really lucky to have him. Where are you from?" Amy asked, shifting into reporter gear.

"Jersey. Hoboken. I lived just outside the city my whole life, watched the World Trade Center being built. My whole family, we all felt a little resentful when the towers were going up, beating out the Empire State Building as the tallest in the city." He glanced out the window to the skyscraper. "My grandfather was a skilled mason. He came over from Italy and helped build it. We've always felt pride in that building; it's part of our family's history."

"Wow, that's so interesting! Have you seen the movie *An Affair to Remember*? It's incredibly romantic."

"Sure have. My mom and I are big old movie fans."

Veronica sat deeper into the couch as she followed their conversation, listening for clues into Joey's life. She crossed her legs casually and waited to learn more, happy that her best friend was a reporter.

"Your family's still in Hoboken?" Amy asked, taking another bite of the antipasti spread on the transparent Lucite coffee table.

"Yup. Or close by. All the DiNatalis, Mezzinas, and Boccacinis—aunts, uncles, and cousins—stayed in the area. I'm the only one who left Jersey, and look how far I got. I came in for school, NYU, and never left. I'm actually the first in my family to go to college." His smile fell as his shoulders rose in a shrug. "Never graduated, though. The whole family treats me like a prodigy anyway," he said, his smiling returning, "it's kind of embarrassing."

Veronica's toes started tapping in the air.

"What did you study?" Amy said.

Joey sipped his wine. Veronica's foot bobbing slowed and she leaned forward.

"Well, I went in for medicine—it was my dad's dream for me, not something I was interested in, but I did it for him. I stuck it out for three years, but finally, I told him I really didn't want to be a doctor. So I switched into electrical engineering. He was mad at me for a long time, in that good ol' stubborn Italian way, but then he saw my business grow and he saw that I was happy. It wasn't long before he was back to being my biggest fan."

"Your business?" Veronica nudged him for more information, no longer able to sit quietly.

"Yeah, I'm an electrician. Didn't really finish all the requirements for an engineering degree. I started training and did apprenticeships while I was still in school. I took the licensing exam and became an electrician—that's why I never graduated. Now, I run a small business and have four other guys working for me. We keep pretty busy." Joey stood and started toward the kitchen. "Excuse me."

The CD player paused, rotated to the next disc, and then Ray

Charles joined the gathering of neighbors. Glancing to where Joey had disappeared, Amy leaned toward Veronica, whose foot was back to bouncing.

"He's really nice," Amy said in her softest voice.

Veronica nodded, then put her glass to her lips, the foot that dangled over her knee wiggling rhythmically. Amy swayed in her seat and mouthed the words as Ray sang "I've Got a Woman" before stuffing a marinated artichoke wedge in her mouth.

"Dinner will be ready in just a few minutes," Joey announced, coming back and refilling their glasses.

His living room was large enough to fit a substantial dining table; it was black with sleek lines and was set with candles and three place settings. Unadorned, contemporary-styled forks, knives, and spoons framed each plate.

"What year did you finish school?" Amy asked.

"'Eighty-six." He smirked and ran a hand over the side of his head, smoothing his immovable hair.

Veronica was quicker in calculations, and she lifted her eyebrows toward Amy, who was still tabulating his approximate age, invisibly using her fingers, Veronica knew.

"When's your birthday?" Veronica asked, still circling around the edge of the real question.

"March seventh." He grinned, visibly amused. "Do you want the year?"

"That would make it easier," Amy joked.

"I just turned twenty-eight."

Veronica let her gaze rest on Joey, acknowledging her attraction and disregarding the six-year age gap. They were officially adults and age didn't matter anymore. She could ignore his age, she told herself, but what about him not having a college degree?

Chapter 28

A DAY AFTER THEIR moving-in-day dinner at Joey's, they found a note tucked under their door. The envelope was addressed to Veronica in a boyish scribble. The words were few but revealed his interest.

Veronica—
I would love to get to know you better. Dinner again sometime? I'll be out of town for a few days for the 4th weekend. I'd like to call you when I get back, but I need your phone number.
Joey

He jotted his number beneath his name, though it was hard to tell the 4's from the 9's after the 212 area code. In the days after they discovered the note, Veronica analyzed every word and debated a reply, but she left for the holiday weekend without responding.

"He seems really nice and he's cute," Veronica confessed, "but he's not like the other guys I've dated. What would my parents think? I'm not even sure what I think."

"Just go out with him and see," Amy encouraged.

Veronica chatted about him on their train ride to Newtown,

where they spent the Fourth of July. She talked about him in the dark as the girls lay in Amy's childhood bedroom, and at the cookout, at the fireworks, and on the train home.

"He's just not really the kind of guy I thought I'd be with—he didn't even finish college. He is so different from Eric and Scott and Doug and, well, everyone I've ever gone out with."

"How did those guys work out for you?" Amy joked. "Maybe Joey is your steak knife."

Veronica ignored her and continued undeterred in her list of protests, then boomeranged back to all the reasons she wanted to see Joey.

"He really is sweet and an amazing cook—that alone blows away a bunch of the things on my 'ideal guy' list. Seriously, a guy who can cook."

"He was a great host and obviously does his own laundry and ironing, too," Amy said, adding to the plus column.

"His clothes. Some of his clothes are so, I don't know, so tight and dark, but they do show he's got a fine body. And his business must be successful to own that apartment. He seems like a great family guy, which I love, but do you think that could be a problem, too? What if he's a real mama's boy?" Veronica debated herself out loud.

When they returned to their building, they heard music as they passed apartment 202. Veronica moved quickly past and into their apartment. She pulled the worn note from her pocket and reread it. Still conflicted, she drafted a response, then edited it twice. Finally, she slipped the piece of paper under Joey's door with only her phone numbers written on it, labeled work and home. Then she waited. They waited.

"He's back in town, right? We did hear music from his apartment—that means he's back, doesn't it? Why hasn't he called?" Veronica said an hour after she left the numbers.

"What do you think he is, V? He kind of looks like he could

be a little forky, but he doesn't seem like a fork at all, does he? Can he look like a fork but be a steak knife? What would that be?" Amy giggled, knowing she was asking these questions to a non-participatory Veronica. "Are there any Italian utensils? Maybe he's a garlic press! Or a wine corkscrew?"

"Smelly or crooked, terrific," Veronica objected.

"A wooden spoon? Nah, he's definitely not a spoon. What about those Italian knife thingies, you know, the curved knives with handles on the sides? I think they're called *mezzalinas* or *mezzalunas* or something. Maybe he's an Italian knife," Amy decided, adding a new entry to the UCS, and Veronica smiled despite herself.

The next day, the girls returned home after work having met up to walk across town together. The light on the answering machine was blinking when they let themselves into the dim apartment. Veronica dropped her bag, stepped hastily out of only one of her heels, and limped across the room to press the play button.

"Hi, honey, it's Dad. I'm calling to—" *Beep*—Veronica hit the skip button. "Sorry, Amy, you can listen to it after, okay?"

"Hi, Veronica and Amy, it's Joey. Veronica, I'm calling to see if you want to go out this week. Maybe dinner on Wednesday? Give me a call, or just come by."

Veronica pattered her feet in a fast *Flashdance* move, making her curls swirl crazily. She squeezed her fisted hands near her face and couldn't extinguish her smile. She smiled through changing into spandex workout clothes and the Denise Austin exercise video she and Amy did together in the living room, she smiled through heating up dinner, and she smiled through eating.

WHEN THE DATE NIGHT arrived, Amy was in their kitchen chopping zucchini and onions for her favorite summer soup when Veronica's key turned in the lock.

"A postcard from Syracuse."

"Oh, let me see it." Amy brushed the onions off her fingertips and wiped her hands on her shorts before taking the card from Veronica. Despite her frequent letters, Matt's postcards had dwindled over the past month, from one a week after graduation to only every few weeks.

"I swear that boy has a thing for you!"

"No, he doesn't, we're friends."

"You share more with him than with anyone, except me and Andrew, of course. Are you sure *he* thinks you're just friends?"

"You sound like my dad, but yes, he's a best friend, nothing else. Would you like to hear what our favorite spoon has to say?" Amy asked affectionately. With the way Matt knew computers—better than most of the U.S. population—he had to be labeled a spoon.

Veronica smiled and let out an exasperated sigh. "I thought this fork, knife, and spoon stuff would subside once we were out of school."

"Why would you think that? The UCS is very useful," Amy said, and reread the postcard aloud for Veronica:

Dear Amy,

Went to the Finger Lakes with some friends for the 4th. Fireworks always remind me of you and the summers I visited in Newtown. Loved the story you sent, it's exciting to see your name in the paper. Keep it up! Miss you.

Love, Matt

Amy warmed in the air-conditioned apartment, thinking of the short but fun-packed days when Matt came to see her the summers after sophomore and junior years. Reading the card through again, she walked to her room behind Veronica, who went to change for her date with Joey.

From the bottom bookshelf, Amy pulled out the box her dad had built for her. Undoing the latch, she tucked in Matt's postcard, adding it to the others, and took a moment to peek at the tokens of memories in her Treasure Box: ticket stubs, a cork from the bottle of wine she and Andrew shared on their third anniversary feeling very mature, and a crown he made her out of twist ties from the grocery store during junior year's Christmas break.

Leaning into Amy's doorway, Veronica asked, "How do I look?" She spun around, modeling a fluttery red top and a four-inch-wide belt over slim jeans and flat sandals. "I still can't believe I said yes to this date. He's really not my type."

"You look great."

Waiting for Joey, Veronica paced, grinned, and sighed. The knock at the door came as she finished her sixth loop in front of their Third Avenue windows. She opened the door and turned her face nervously as he greeted her with a cheek kiss, her hair veiling half of his face.

"Are you trying to hide me behind that terrific hair of yours?" he teased.

Veronica blushed lavishly and, over her shoulder, she threw Amy a giddy smile, then followed Joey for their first date.

"YOU WAITED UP FOR me?" Veronica flopped beside Amy where she was reading in bed.

"Of course." Amy marked her page in Danielle Steel's newest bestseller, *Jewels*, and tossed the book aside. "So, how was it?"

"Oh my gosh, he is completely amazing. I'm not sure I've ever felt like this about someone before. He's so smart, and we talked about music and books, not that romance trash that you read." She smiled at Amy's shrug. "He's funny, too—we laughed all night. It was easy talking with him, and he's really good-looking. I couldn't stop staring at him through the whole dinner."

"Where'd you go?"

"You'd never believe this place, it's called Puglia's in Little Italy, and there's this guy who plays the accordion and sings old Italian songs. Joey knows him—Jorge is his name—and it seemed like he knew everyone else there, too. We had awful-tasting Chianti out of carafes and sat at long tables with tons of other people. It was the best!"

"Sounds like an intimate first date."

"He even bought me a rose from the guy who came around selling flowers." Veronica paused to take a breath. "Seriously, I think I really like him. What am I going to do?"

AFTER MONTHS OF GOOD intentions and busy schedules, a double date was finally arranged. As the foursome entered the Mulholland Drive Cafe, Patrick Swayze's restaurant on Third Avenue at Sixty-Third Street, Andrew said, "You look pretty, Aim."

She wore a new one-piece romper in a deep blue and modeled it for Veronica loving the way the wide legs flowed as she walked. He let Amy enter, then held the door for Veronica and Joey.

"This looks like a good pick, Amy," Veronica said. "You know the theme song from *Dirty Dancing* was my prom theme."

"Mine, too," Andrew said, and laughed.

"Mine was Phil Collins, 'Against All Odds.' I wore the best white strapless dress."

"My senior prom theme was 'Wonderful Tonight,'" Joey chimed in, "classic Clapton slow dance. I went with Gina Broncatelli. Her hair was so high that she looks taller than me in all the pre-prom pictures, but by the time they played 'Stairway to Heaven,' her hair looked like she'd jumped in a swimming pool."

They all laughed.

"I danced with Scott Moore to that one," Veronica said.

"Chrissy Conover," said Andrew.

"Mike Testani," Amy said.

"Ah, finally, a good Italian name." Joey gave Amy's shoulder a friendly squeeze.

"Right this way," the hostess announced as she gathered menus and led them between the tables.

They shared laughter, college tales, and appetizers; work sagas, long-winded jokes, and bottles of wine. Veronica radiated beneath Joey's attention and his touch on her leg. The way he listened to her made her know she mattered. Feeling heard gave her a comfort she hadn't known before, and it gave her a perspective she hadn't expected. Basking in Joey's attentiveness underscored how Andrew seemed to be distracted sometimes when Amy told him stories or spoke about her job. At dinner, she noticed him glance over Amy's shoulder, watching people at another table while she was talking to him.

"Great article in the *Observer* last week," Joey said.

"Thanks. I'm not sure if I'm happy or sad that I didn't write that piece on Kiki Kosinski; it's sure getting a lot of buzz."

"Your piece on Williamsburg was a spot-on profile of the neighborhood."

Andrew joined the conversation. "You wrote about Jerzy Kosinski's widow, Aim?"

The three of them stared at him. When no one spoke, Joey said, "No, that was another reporter, man. Don't you follow what your girlfriend's working on?"

"Sure I do. Yeah, of course. I just forgot." He hailed the passing waitress, giving her a grand smile.

After ordering desserts, Amy and Veronica excused themselves to the ladies' room.

"Joey is so into you. I see how much he likes you when he's hanging out at our place, but the way he is with you in public is incredible. He's definitely a solid steak knife, or did we decide on him being a *mezzaluna*?" Amy said, pushing open the bathroom door.

"He is amazing, so why have I not told my parents about him? They still think I'm single and my mom tries to set me up constantly."

In the stall, Amy wrestled and twisted to unzip her romper. Wiggling, she pulled it to her mid-back, and then she stretched her arms trying to grasp the zipper again.

"What's going on in there? You're making funny noises."

Amy laughed then grunted. "I can't unzip this dang romper and I really have to pee. Oh, got it!"

Noise from the restaurant swept in with the open door, then muted with its closing.

"This guy is a total fake. I can't believe you and Jake thought I'd like him. Can't you see that he's such a phony?"

"It's just a date—you don't have to marry the guy."

"I can barely stand to eat with him. Every word out of his mouth is putting a price tag on something. 'My new stereo with the five-disc CD player cost me six hundred dollars,' 'You wouldn't believe how much I spent on this jacket,' 'I paid thirty grand for my car.' Which, by the way, is a ridiculous amount to spend on a car. That's like a whole year's salary. I can't stand it. Is he so insecure that he has to announce how much he spends on everything? I'm serious, Tiffany, I'm not going to make it through this dinner."

Amy and Veronica slipped to the sinks, passing the girls in matching skintight black miniskirts and feathered bangs. One had on the thick-heeled black shoes that everyone was wearing and the other had on classic black pumps. From the stalls they heard the girl in the metallic silver top go on: "How can you even be friends with this jerk? He's not even good-looking enough to act as cocky as he does. God, he's acting like some bigwig, some know-it-all. Who is he kidding?"

Metallic Girl was still complaining when Amy and Veronica left the bathroom. Far enough from the closed door, they burst into laughter.

"That was hilarious! What kind of utensil is that guy?" Amy challenged, not waiting for an answer. "I've got it! He's a plastic fork. Fake, superficial, plasticky, and he definitely sounds forky. Yes, that's perfect. Our very first plastic fork. Although, wait, do you remember that guy we met, spring break junior year in Cancun? What was his name? That guy who wouldn't leave us alone and kept talking about how much he spent on everything?"

"Oh my gosh, I remember him. Clinton or Clifford or something? He wouldn't stop throwing numbers around. He was so shallow and completely in love with himself."

"He must've been our first plastic fork."

Walking slower to their table of knives, Veronica asked, "Which one do you think they were talking about?"

They scanned the restaurant for another table with two guys sitting beside two empty seats.

"Over there," Amy said, pointing with her chin. "I bet the plastic fork is the one with the pink collar turned up," she added as they put their napkins back on their laps.

"And the 'very expensive jacket' on the back of his chair."

"What poor man are you two labeling now?" Andrew shook his head sympathetically.

"Just be glad it's not you this time, superstar," Veronica jabbed, not without a little honesty behind her words.

Chapter 29

HAPPY TO BE HOME AFTER a long workday, Amy heard the phone ringing in their apartment from down the hall. Searching for the right key, she moved quickly. By the time she stepped into the stuffy apartment, the answering machine had picked up: "Hi, Amy." The familiar voice filled her heart and she picked up the cordless phone from its cradle, stopping the recording.

"Matt, hi. I'm here." She hugged her friend with the cheer in her words.

"I'm so glad I caught you. I'm home and—"

"What's wrong? Your voice sounds hoarse. Wait, you're in Tuckahoe?"

The phone line was quiet except for the sound of him breathing.

"Matt? What?"

"My mom died last night," Matt whispered. The words crushed her; she fell onto the couch and cried with Matt. She felt the loss fiercely for him and his family, but also for herself. Mrs. Saxon had welcomed her like one of her own daughters and had filled a maternal longing for Amy. Now she was gone.

"ARE YOU SURE IT'S okay that I don't go? I've got this big meeting tomorrow that I really can't miss." Andrew tasted the spaghetti, leaning backward to avoid the steam.

"It's okay," Amy said absently. "I still can't believe Mrs. Saxon is gone. Matt said she just died in her sleep. They think it was a heart attack; his father tried to wake her up and she had already passed. It's so sad."

"You already told me that."

"She was the most generous person. You know, she started the food pantry in Tuckahoe and ran a community dinner." As Amy spoke, Andrew poked through the cabinets looking for the colander. "I went once when I was at Matt's and she hosted it like it was a dinner party in her home. She made everyone feel welcome and special. I just can't believe she's gone."

When he had drained the pasta in the sink, he turned to comfort Amy, his face moist from the task.

"I'm sorry, Aim. And please tell Matt I'm sorry, too."

She wiped her cheek where Andrew's face met hers. "Can you stay here tonight?" she asked.

"I can't, I've got to get into the office ridiculously early. You'll be fine, won't you? Veronica will be home soon, right?"

She set out two placemats on the small round table in the corner of the living room, then folded two paper napkins and laid out the silverware. As she went to place the knives, she realized this meal didn't need a knife and she put them back into the drawer.

THE LATE SEPTEMBER SKY was brilliant and clear as Amy boarded the Metro-North Harlem line to the Crestwood station, then got a cab to take her the half-mile to the Westchester Funeral Home. Through the scratched window, Amy spotted Matt, his tall build hunched and pacing the front lawn of the white clapboard colonial, hands tucked in his pockets. The slam of the cab door caught his attention. Realizing it was Amy, he jogged across the grass and pulled her into him with a force that surprised her. His dark hair tickled her cheek and she breathed in his scent, Old Spice and soap. He clung to her and Amy felt his back jerk in silent sobs.

The strain in Amy's shoulders told her they stood like that for a while, her petite frame supporting Matt's height and the weight of his sorrow. He straightened himself and pulled a tissue from his jacket pocket. Amy noticed he wore the Syracuse tie she'd given him for graduation. Without words, she pressed her palm into his chest. Beneath her touch, she felt a pen in his shirt pocket and thought fondly that he was still her spoon.

Matt finally spoke. "Why'd you take a cab? I would've come to get you."

"You've got enough to think about. I didn't want to bother you."

"You still don't get that you could never bother me." He took her hand and led her into the funeral home. She startled at his touch, his broad palm encircling hers. He had never held her hand like that before.

Matt led her to the front of the room, letting go of her hand as they approached the row of chairs behind his family. Amy quietly hugged his sisters, Kim and Rachel, and his father, Wayne Saxon. Seeing the tears and loss in their eyes, Amy started to cry. Matt handed her a tissue from his supply and sat her next to a young woman she'd never met before.

"Amy, this is Patty; Patty, this is Amy," Matt introduced in a whisper, then sat in front of them next to his sisters.

"I've heard so much about you," Patty said.

Amy dipped her face into the damp tissue, concealing a dim frown. *Who is this girl?* she thought. *And if she knows who I am, why haven't I heard about her?*

She balled the Kleenex into her palm and looked up at Patty. "How do you know Matt?"

"Oh, he hasn't mentioned me? Um, we've been going out for a few months."

Amy felt a blood pressure cuff squeeze her heart and the sourness of jealousy churn in her stomach. *Maybe she's why Matt's postcards have slowed down.* She was embarrassed by her response and grateful that she didn't need to talk as the family's pastor stood and led them in prayer. Amy couldn't focus on his words; she bowed her head and thought about Matt. Of course, she should be happy for him to have a girlfriend and she shouldn't be surprised. Why wouldn't he find someone? Yet why hadn't she considered it? Hearing the words of prayer, she blinked back tears for Matt and for his mother. And for herself.

AMY SCOOCHED INTO THE train seat by the window and waved to Matt until she could no longer see him standing on the platform waving to her. She immediately missed him. The sun had set hours ago while they sat on the back porch of Matt's childhood home. Guests' good-byes had been said at the restaurant after the service and cemetery, and she had joined the exhausted family— Matt, his dad, his sisters, a few close relatives, and Patty—as they told stories about Helen Saxon. Once, Amy found herself frowning when she saw Matt whisper something to Patty, realizing she was no longer the first girl to know his thoughts, no longer the main girl in his life. She watched Patty dote on Matt, noticed how she followed and clung to him, and Amy had to look away when Patty leaned her body into him or gave him a kiss.

When Matt drove her to the train station, Amy talked to him hungrily for the few minutes she had him to herself. She thought to lightly jab him for not telling her about Patty, but she said nothing, not wanting to tarnish their sliver of time alone.

Amy felt sleepy and worn as the train left the station and Matt behind. As the car rolled along the tracks, she rested her head against the burgundy plastic, slid her butt to the edge of the cushion, and wedged her knees against the seat in front of her. The stretch in her back made her sigh, a sigh of something releasing in her. She put her face in her hands and cried. All day, as tears hovered and dripped, she was reserved, but alone on the public train, she wept.

At the Fordham stop, she felt her seat lift when someone sat heavily in the aisle seat.

"Hey, honey, why are you crying?"

Oh, dear God, I am not in the mood. Amy stayed still, trying to ignore the deep voice, and kept her face hidden though she yearned to peek at the stranger.

"It's okay, don't cry. Do you want to tell me what you want?"

What? Her restraint dissolved and she lifted her head, just a little, to see a large man dressed in khaki slacks and a cheerful red blazer. He had on thick-heeled black combat boots that didn't match his age. There were no puffs of white fur and no pointy hat topped with a pom-pom, but his face looked just like Saint Nicholas's. His hair was the whitest of whites, and his thick white beard was clean and trimmed neatly at his chest. When Santa smiled at Amy, his eyes how they twinkled, his dimples how merry. She sat up, glanced around, and noticed that they were alone in the train car; she was trapped in the window seat. While Santa didn't seem threatening, Amy calculated her options and counted out four more stops before Grand Central. Her eyes were swollen and dry, her limbs felt jittery, unsure what to make of this familiar stranger.

He shifted his bulk side to side in the seat as he reached into his pants pocket. Amy clutched her bag and considered sliding under the seat in front of her when, in the softest voice, Santa spoke: "Here, honey, no need to cry." He held out his plump hand to her, something small and gray rested in his palm. Her arms were frozen against her, her eyes locked on his jolly cherubic face. With visions of Paul dancing in her head, she wished Father Christmas would dash away.

"You'll find your way. You're going to have a decision to make and you need to believe in yourself. A big choice is coming, but you'll know what to do if you believe."

When she made no move to accept his gift, Santa placed the object on the seat in between them. He rocked himself forward twice, gaining momentum, then stood.

"You'll know what to do if you trust your heart. Believe in yourself," he repeated, and walked forward, squeezing himself through the doorway and into the next car.

Amy felt her pulse electric in her chest. She looked at the seat beside her, the vinyl puckered into a gully. In the center lay a smooth, oval stone the size of a stretched quarter. She released her grip on her bag, and her hand trembled as she lifted the rock in her fingers. She rubbed the glossy surface, and her shoulders relaxed, her breath deepened. Feeling a ridge, she turned the stone over in her palm. Etched into the other side was the word BELIEVE.

EACH DAY FOR THE next week, Amy called Matt. For the first days, she called him in Tuckahoe. On the fourth day of calls, when he had returned to Syracuse, she shared her encounter with the mysterious Santa on the train. Matt gasped as she talked.

"I'm sorry, I knew I shouldn't tell you about this—it's too weird."

"No. No, it's not that. You know my mother loved Santa. Remember her collection?"

"Oh my gosh, yes!"

"It's kind of incredible to me that a Santa guy would sit with you on an empty train, give you that gift and message on the day we buried my mother. I'd like to think that it wasn't random. Thanks for telling me about him."

"A connection to your mom didn't cross my mind, but I haven't been able to stop thinking about Train Santa."

"I think my mom would've liked him."

Amy breathed with relief and comfort as she saw her Santa meeting in a new way, and she smiled, remembering Mrs. Saxon and her kind and giving nature.

Chapter 30

"I'M A LITTLE NERVOUS," Veronica said from the passenger seat of Joey's black 1986 Cadillac Eldorado. He'd spent the morning in the building's garage washing, waxing, and polishing his favorite toy.

"Aw, don't be nervous, they're gonna love you." Joey reached his hand out across the red leather seat to soothe her.

"Yeah, but your whole family is going to be there. That's a lot of pressure for a first meeting." Peering in the mirror of the red visor, Veronica reapplied her lipstick and ran a finger under her eyes to wipe away invisible smudges.

"I can't believe it's been three months since we started going out and you haven't been here yet. And sorry, but there's no way to meet just my parents, everyone has to be there for everything. We're here." Joey parallel parked the long Caddy easily into a tiny opening. "You'll be great! Just be you."

They mounted the steps of the Hoboken brownstone. The leaves of the few trees along the sidewalk had begun to turn shades of fall. Joey rang the bell, and a moment later the door buzzed and released for them to enter. He led her past a staircase that hugged the wall straight ahead to his parents' home and he opened the door. The roomful of bodies rushed toward them. Veronica was mobbed and brought into bear hugs and hearty kisses. Her cheeks were dotted with peaches, pinks, mauves, and reds, a sampling of Revlon's past-season shades.

"Joey, she's a skinny one," said Aunt Erma.

"You finally bring your girl around, s'about time," shouted Uncle Sal, grabbing Veronica into a squeeze.

From the mob of women, each of whose hair was coiffed and sprayed to stone, bellowed a loud voice: "Will you all step aside so I can get a look at my son's girl?" Filomena DiNatali stepped forward, wiped her hands on her apron, and welcomed Veronica with the most earnest hug of all. Then Mrs. DiNatali grasped Veronica's shoulders and held her in front of her. "Very pretty," she pronounced. Her lips were coated in hot pink, and her hair was dyed brown, curled under at her chin, and moved with her head.

"Nick, where are you?" Filomena yelled for her husband.

"Right here," he responded from a foot away. He held Veronica's face between his well-fed fingers and kissed her cheeks.

Despite the volume in the apartment and the jostling among strangers, Veronica felt more at home than in her own formal Newport house. She could not envision her parents within this family, and trying was like picturing a farmer on the Wall Street trading floor or a grown woman in a baby stroller. She couldn't make the images fit together.

The multifamily home housed Joey's parents on the main level, his cousins in the upstairs apartment, and his widowed grandmother, Concetta, in the basement apartment with her sister, Marie, who never married. The living room was bursting with people and vibrating with shouted conversations. On the walls hung pastel-hued prints of flowers, hand-colored portraits of Joey and his brothers, Little Nicky and Dominic, and vividly painted images of Jesus and the Virgin Mary.

Stretching to the edges of the coffee table was an antipasto platter layered with capocollo, prosciutto, soppressata, and mortadella heaped beside provolone, mozzarella, and chunks of Parmigiano-Reggiano. There were mountains of olives marinated with herbs and green stuffed olives. Dark purple kalamata olives rolled into roasted red peppers, and artichoke hearts piled against anchovies. The dining table on the far end of the room was lined with silver foil chaffing dishes, Sternos already burning. Whenever someone laid down an empty appetizer plate, a young girl or older woman swooped in to clean it up.

"Marie, what was that fella's name? The man at the deli? You know, the man at the deli?" Concetta hollered at her sister sitting beside her.

"Quiet, Ma, we can't hear the game," Uncle Cosmo yelled above the women.

For the first time, Veronica noticed the TV was on, the volume lowered. It was perched on an ornate wooden console next to a paint-by-numbers scene of *The Last Supper*. Joey was nearby being scooped up by his family.

"Ai, Uncle Nunzio, how'd you live wit dose two growing up?" Cousin Mario called out.

"Come on, honey, come with us." Cousin Ottavia and Aunt Tessie each took an elbow and led Veronica into the kitchen beyond the living room. The small, foyer-sized kitchen was bustling with women unwrapping cellophane from tinfoil pans, stirring sauces, tossing salad, and plunging cooking tools into soapy water. Ottavia wordlessly placed a bouquet of serving utensils into Veronica's hands, patting her knuckles before she turned to another task. Veronica scanned the platters of food, trying to decide which were best suited to spoons and which needed forks or knives. She took care with her assignment, mindfully matching each serving piece with a dish. Without directions, the women shuttled food from the kitchen to the table, like a choreographed performance. Veronica marveled at the chaotic efficiency and felt included within the commotion.

"Okay, boys! Dinner's on!" shouted Filomena, and the room quieted for only a second in response before the men heaved themselves from the couches and meandered to the buffet table, commenting on the food.

"Did Fil make her manicotti?"

"Gotta have some of that eggplant with extra gravy."

"Would you look at dose meatballs?"

Plates, heaped with food, balanced on laps and small folding tables. Some of the older ladies pulled chairs up to the edge of the serving table and ate as people filled their white plates.

"Ma! Real forks?" Dominic yelled.

Uncle Nunzio cut into his chicken marsala. "Real forks and real plates today, huh, Filomena?" he shouted with his mouth full.

"We've got a special guest to welcome to the family," Joey's mom called back.

"That's a lot of washing," Tessie muttered. "I still would've used the plastic."

Joey joined Veronica. "So, this is my family! You doing okay?" He kissed her. "They all love you, but not as much as I love you. Come on, let's get some food."

Veronica froze. Did he just tell her he loved her? The intimate moment felt somehow both natural and stunning in the midst of the family clamor.

"You coming?"

"Did you just—"

"Say 'I love you'? Yes, Veronica, I did. I love you." Joey grinned broadly and led her to the food, handing her a plate.

They sat in two folding chairs side by side. Veronica placed a bite of lasagna neatly into her mouth.

"Joey! You gonna keep her all to yourself over there?"

"Sorry, Uncle Sal," Joey said, "but for now, yes."

"How did you get to be so quiet?"

"Third child, twelfth cousin—I just flew under the radar." He laughed with a shrug.

"I like your family," Veronica said, unable to say those three magic words back to him.

Chapter 31

THE METRO-NORTH TRAIN CONDUCTOR approached, the sound of his hole punch clicking its way through the car. Andrew gave him their tickets, then returned his hand into Amy's. She leaned her head against his shoulder and thought about her train ride home from Tuckahoe. Santa and his words wiggled into her mind at random moments in the months since the funeral. Amy kept the BELIEVE stone on her nightstand, and when she rubbed its glossy surface, it washed her with a sense of serenity and sparked her confidence. The cars emptied, the Friday rush hour travelers trickling off as the train crept farther from the city.

"Bethel, next stop," the conductor called through the cars. "Only the three head cars will open at Bethel."

Amy gathered the two smaller bags at their feet, and Andrew hefted his duffel and Amy's hobo-style weekend bag from the shelf above. Out the window, Amy spotted her dad and Aunt Joanie waiting beside the tracks. With Andrew behind her, she moved to exit the train. Amy gave her dad the carefree, boundless hug of a little girl and squeezed her aunt. Tom York clapped Andrew on the shoulder as the two shook hands.

"Thanks for bringing my car, Dad."

"It's not so common these days to see people getting married right after college. Who's the couple?" Aunt Joanie asked.

"Owen and Holly—he's a friend of ours from Syracuse," said Amy. "We've only met her a few times, but they seem completely in love."

"Will Matt be there?" her dad asked.

Andrew turned to Amy at the question.

"Yeah, they're fraternity brothers."

"Tell him hello." Her dad closed the trunk. "I made sure you have a full tank of gas."

"Thanks, Dad. We'll meet you back here Sunday. I'm sorry we're missing your visit, Aunt Joanie, thanks for helping. Kiss Uncle Arthur for me."

The next day, Amy and Andrew wove through the New England roads past stone walls and drying fields. The First Congregational Church of Litchfield looked like a postcard with its white clapboard siding against the last of November's golden and red leaves. The bell in the clock-adorned steeple rang out eleven times, triggering a sentimental weepiness in Amy. On the stone path in front of the church, she snuggled herself into Andrew's side. Their fingers interlaced while they chatted with a group of Owen's friends and their dates; the only one Amy had met was Patty.

"So Owen's the first one to crash and burn," one joked, his girlfriend lightly poking his side with her elbow.

"Wonder if he'll ever be allowed to come out anymore."

"Not once the ring is on. Then it'll be 'honey, this' and 'honey, that.'"

Amy glanced around the cluster, a wrinkle between her eyebrows as Andrew said nothing and laughed along with the guys. The girls all smiled unobtrusively. Each one exempted herself, believing her guy wouldn't assume these things about their relationship. Amy wanted to speak up but suppressed the desire.

"No more late nights with the boys for the Owe-ster. He'll be all, like, 'No can do, fellas.'"

"All bets are off now. He's whipped and we've lost him."

Words and emotions were bubbling in Amy's stomach, something in their joking felt personal to her. Their jabs at marriage struck her heart and urged her to protect what she believed.

"Are you all kidding me?" she blurted. "Holly is a sweet girl; she's not a jailer. Owen is happy and wants to be married." She saw the stunned faces around her, and she felt Andrew subtly lean away from her, but still she couldn't stop herself. "Being married isn't some punishment, it's a partnership, a forever friendship. Clearly he is the most mature of all of you."

Amy punctuated her rant with her hands, gesturing higher and higher as she spoke. The women looked at Amy with admiration in their eyes while they stepped closer to their dates, distancing themselves from her as Andrew had. In the silence, Amy took a deep breath, shocked at her own boldness, and observed the blank faces until Kyle broke the stillness.

"The great marriage defender. Boy, you're in for it, Andrew," he muttered.

"Lay off, Kyle," Matt said, glancing at Amy.

She looked at him with gratitude and turned to Andrew, willing him to chime in, to support her and stand up to these guys. He stood beside her like a sculpture as she implored him with her eyes.

"Oh, right," he murmured, then spoke louder. "Amy's right, I mean, Owen's happy and we should just be happy for him."

Smiles crept into the guys' faces, but no one dared speak what he was thinking.

Amy let her lips part and then pulled them taut. She wanted to run away from the church, away from these people, away from

Andrew, but her feet stuck to the path beneath them as her eyes burned with threatened tears.

"We'd better get inside," Andrew said. "Come on, Amy." He took her hand in a demonstration of his masculinity and led her up the steps where ushers escorted them down the main aisle of the church.

Amy sat in the pew with an erect posture. Tension tightened her shoulders and jaw, and a sadness rested in her throat, even as Holly glided down the aisle on her father's arm. Amy pictured herself making that walk with her dad, but for the first time in years, with anger in her eyes, the end of the aisle was blurry.

Owen stood in his tuxedo, his clasped hands in front of him and his eyes fixed on Holly. Love painted his face. Amy's jaw softened in a smile, and Andrew lay his hand, palm open, on her lap. An offering. She paused then reluctantly placed her palm on his. He aligned each of his fingertips with hers, and Amy felt their pulses join as Holly repeated the words the minister recited.

"I, Holly, take you, Owen, to be my husband, to have and to hold, for better or for worse, for richer, for poorer, in sickness and in health, to love and to cherish, from this day forward until death do us part."

Amy dabbed at her eyes, adding another balled-up tissue to her fist. Emotions ricocheted through her and she couldn't help visualizing herself in Holly's white lacy shoes. She imagined standing at the altar of her family's church on Main Street, the one where her parents had gotten married, and where she had been baptized only weeks before her mother's death. She envisioned the pews filled with familiar faces of people who loved her, she saw her dad, and, as her indignation dissolved, she also saw Andrew's parents sitting across the aisle. Their fathers with coral roses in their buttonholes, Mrs. Gabel in cornflower blue.

She squeezed Andrew's hand when the minister spoke words she agreed with, and Andrew returned each with a reciprocal squeeze. As they stood for the benediction, Andrew nuzzled his nose into Amy's pin-straight hair and whispered, "I'm sorry for the guys. I love you, Aim."

Amy dabbed her eyes, hearing his words and what was missing from them.

THE SUNDAY MORNING SUN smiled into Amy's face before she was ready to greet it. She rolled over in the four-poster bed at the Litchfield Inn and pulled a pillow over her head. Andrew lifted the feather pillow and kissed her. "You need to get up, it's already nine thirty."

"Mmm," she said, pinching her eyes closed. She felt him kiss her head again, then sit on the edge of the bed. Peeking from beneath the white linens, she was happy that her first sight of the day was his muscled, naked back. "Mmm," she said again with new meaning.

"We're supposed to meet everyone for brunch downstairs," Andrew said, slipping on pants and brushing his damp hair with his fingers.

Amy hopped off the side of the high bed and headed to the steamy bathroom.

"Did you agree with what those guys were saying before at the church?" she asked with a toothbrush dangling from her mouth.

"Spit, I can't understand you."

Rolling her eyes, she spat and repeated herself, then continued. "Why do they have to be so negative about marriage? Do you feel like that, too?"

Andrew threw his things into his bag. "I don't know why you had to get all sensitive about that yesterday. The guys were just being guys. We're young and they were just horsing around. No one meant anything by it and you freaked out."

"Freaked out?" Amy clenched her toothbrush in her fist. "So, you think it's no big deal to act like once a woman gets married she becomes this, this different person who traps her man against his will? Do you ever even want to get married? Or do you think I'll ruin your life if we do?"

Andrew sighed heavily and sat on the ottoman, resting his elbows on his knees. "You're reading too much into this. Of course I don't think that. You know I love you and someday I'd like to get married. I'm not ready now, but someday I want to." He rubbed the bridge of his nose. "Is that what this is all about? Do you want to get married? I saw the way you looked at the ceremony."

Amy released a puff of air through her lips. "No, that's not what this is about. Of course I want to get married, but I'm in no rush. I was offended by the guys' comments. They were rude, and not just to Holly, who's really great, but to all women."

"Oh, so now you're a feminist?"

"What? Just forget it." Amy closed herself in the tiny white bathroom.

It seemed like too long before he tapped on the bathroom door. "Please come out, I don't like arguing with you."

When she answered only with a sniffle, he continued. "I've never seen you like this before—what's going on? We never fight."

Amy dabbed her face with water and let it gurgle in the sink. *Maybe we never fight because I don't speak up about what I'm feeling. Do I do that? Do I stand up for myself?* Amy asked herself the prying questions she would ask on the job before tentatively opening the door, leaving them unanswered. Andrew stood with his bag on his shoulder, waiting for her to emerge.

"I love you. You know I love you." He pulled her to him and stroked her hair.

Amy hiccuped. She stood in his embrace, her arms caught between their chests, leaving a gap.

"I don't feel like you get me," she said. "It feels lonely to be misunderstood.

Chapter 32

THE RENTED POCONOS LAKE house where they were spending New Year's Eve weekend was large and contemporary, with wide-open spaces and five bedrooms, each furnished with pairs of beds. Everyone claimed rooms with their bags; Veronica and Joey were sharing a room with Amy and Andrew. Friends of friends piled in and prepared to make memories with new acquaintances and longtime pals.

Cases of beer chilled on the deck and plates of cheese and crackers, celery and carrots, potato chips and onion dip, lined the counters and coffee tables. A group crowded around the dining room table in a lively game of Scattergories, and laughter was punctuated by the sound of billiard balls crashing together in the TV room.

Sitting on the stone hearth by the fire, Veronica took in the scene of friends new and old, glad that with all the drinking everyone was safe inside for the long weekend. She sipped and looked around: Andrew leaning across the pool table to make a shot, Owen handing Amy another beer, Andrew leaving his game to kiss Amy, Matt noticing Andrew kissing Amy.

"What are you doing alone over here?" Joey sat next to her.

"It's like I'm watching a movie. A romance. You see how Andrew is so attentive to Amy?"

"Been noticing since we left the city."

"Ever since that tiff they had at Owen's wedding, he's been the perfect boyfriend."

"Well, perfect is his thing." Joey smirked. "What are they doing up there?" From their seats at the fireplace, they could see the upstairs sitting area through the railing.

"Strip Scrabble. Looks like that guy Stanley's not doing too well. Tipsy and down to his underwear and slippers." They could see his fluffy slippers with the Syracuse mascot, Otto the Orange, popping from the toes like stuffed animal heads.

"Oh, crap, what's he doing now? Dude, Stanley, don't do that!" Joey called, getting to his feet.

Stanley had climbed over the railing and was trying to balance and walk across an exposed beam. "Dude, get down!" Joey called, running toward the stairs. Pool balls cracked together, U2 blasted through the open house, and no one seemed to notice what was happening above them. The other strip Scrabble players—Holly's friends Josie, Emily, and Marcus—were standing in various stages of undress, trying to prod Stanley off the ledge. Joey ran up the stairs, and as Stanley started to let go and teeter onto the beam, Marcus and Joey each clasped an armpit and lifted him like a drunken rag doll over the rail to safety.

"Thanks, man," Marcus said to Joey. "He's a good guy, but always been a bit of an idiot when he drinks."

"I'm sure Amy's got a utensil for that," Joey said to Veronica, who had followed him.

The Scrabblers put on their clothes and joined the party downstairs with Joey and Veronica. Amy rolled herself away from the card table and across the wood floor on a cushioned chair to put her empty can on the kitchen counter. Andrew grabbed her a new one and sent her wheeling back to the table, where Owen caught her before she crashed. She squealed, full of delight like a toddler on a swing. Back at the table, she tried to keep a straight face as she called Matt's bluff: "Bullshit!"

Matt threw down his cards, laughing at being snagged.

"She got you!" Patty kissed his cheek and left his side while the dealer started shuffling the cards.

From the edges, Joey said, "You'd never be able to play Bullshit; it requires lying."

Veronica smiled, nestling into his arms as they watched poker faces and people hiding cards.

Hours later, Owen yelled, "Come on, everyone! It's almost midnight," and they all congregated around the TV.

"Who played tonight?"

"The Village People and Barry Manilow."

"And I think Slaughter was supposed to be there, too."

"What's Tori Spelling wearing? She's got more twinkles than the ball."

Couples sought their other halves and sorted themselves around the room as the countdown clock ticked away the time until 1993. Andrew scooped Amy onto his lap and nuzzled into her. Veronica could tell Amy had drank too much and left to get her a bottle of water. "Thanks, V," she slurred as she gulped it down.

"Should we be worried about her?" Joey asked.

"She'll be okay. She usually throws up when she drinks too much, then she's better."

"We're sharing a bathroom with her." Joey raised his eyebrows.

"It's okay, I'll take care of her, or Matt will."

"You mean Andrew?"

She shook her head. "In school, whenever Amy got a little drunk, it seemed like it was either me or Matt holding back her hair, wiping her face, and making sure she was okay. Andrew was usually still off partying."

"Nice."

"When you're the life of the party, duty calls. But you know he's a good guy, even perfect boyfriends have their flaws."

"*Ten! Nine!*"

"Would you be including me in that assessment?"

"*Six! Five! Four!*"

Veronica smiled at him and joined in the countdown: "*Three! Two! One!*"

"Happy New Year, Joey." She fell into his kiss and the room around them melted away.

As the early hours of 1993 crept in, people found their way to beds, couches, and corners. The TV droned behind quiet conversations and one couple's tearful argument. The dramatics drifted upstairs, mixing with metered snoring and stifled whispers. Snuggled in bed beside Joey, Veronica heard Amy noisily tiptoe into their room followed by Andrew, then the familiar sounds of her nighttime routine in their shared bathroom.

"Is she brushing her teeth?" Joey whispered to Veronica.

She laughed, no longer surprised by her friend's compulsion despite her drunkenness.

"Her teeth will be sparkling but her clothes will be in a heap on the floor."

The water shut off and they could hear the slapping sound of Amy's feet stumbling against the tile floor. Then it started. Amy was getting sick, and Veronica leaped out of bed to help her friend. From the darkness, she saw a white hand stretch out in front of her and she screamed.

"Oh, sorry, Veronica, it's me. I've got her." Andrew had been feeling his way to Amy's side, too. Veronica stepped back and let him go to her.

From the bed, she heard Andrew's soothing voice comforting her: "It's okay, Aim, I got you. I've got your hair, it's okay."

After a few moments, Andrew flushed the toilet. "Let me wash your face. Don't drink any water. You're brushing again? Okay, here." He was patient and sweet with her, and Veronica smiled, pulling the sheets under her chin and cuddling into Joey.

In the dark, she watched Amy's figure shuffle back into the room with Andrew guiding her to bed. He tucked her in, then rounded the bed and climbed in beside her.

Veronica heard Amy's loud whisper before she went still. Andrew must have heard, too, because even with her mumble, her words were clear: "Thank you, Matt."

Part Three

1993–1994

FORKS IN THE ROAD

Chapter 33

"GO AHEAD, OPEN IT," Andrew encouraged. "I told you I'd never forget Valentine's Day again." He grinned proudly.

"But it's past Valentine's Day, it's practically Easter."

"Well, I didn't forget Valentine's Day, did I?"

"What does that have to do with—"

"Just open the present." Andrew was smiling like a child and tapping his toes impatiently.

The small box was wrapped clumsily in cream paper speckled with pink dots. Amy's stomach fluttered as she turned the box over to untie the ribbon and untape the seam. He had tried his best and his effort was more attractive to her than if some lady at the store had wrapped it flawlessly. Andrew wasn't a gift-giver; she had accepted that over the years, and when he did get her something it meant even more for its scarcity. She smiled into his green-gray eyes, those happy eyes that she felt could see into her. The paper tore as she peeled off the three pieces of tape sealing the backside. Maybe this was it, the small box she'd been waiting for, hoping for, dreaming of. *But it's just an ordinary day in his ordinary apartment. This is an odd way to propose,* she thought.

"Oh, just open it, Aim. Rip into the paper," Andrew teased,

and leaned forward from the edge of the leather couch in his Upper East Side apartment.

"I like taking my time with presents, and you know I like to save paper from the special ones. You're making me think this is a special one."

Andrew smiled widely, nodding. "Come on, open it," he pleaded.

Amy unfastened the sides and pulled out a heavy-duty cardboard box. The top was imprinted with the Lord & Taylor signature and red rose logo.

"Oh, it's not from Lord & Taylor, I just used the box from there," he preempted as she jiggled the lid off.

The flutters in Amy's heart flew into her stomach when she peered inside. It was shiny and golden, resting on the fluffy foam square, but it was not at all what she had expected. It hung from a chain made of tiny silver beads. A key.

Amy's mouth hung open. "I, uh . . ."

"You're surprised! That's just what I'd hoped!" Andrew pulled her into a hug. "You'll move in with me, won't you? It'll be great to live together, Aim, and so much easier for us. You can rearrange and redecorate stuff if you want to, so it feels like your place, too."

Amy nodded, her head bobbing like a metronome to a silent beat, unable to speak.

VERONICA SAT CROSS-LEGGED AT the end of Amy's bed. "Wait, so this is his idea of the next step after going out four and a half years?"

"I don't know, it was a month ago we had that big talk. Maybe he thought moving in together was what I meant."

Veronica watched Amy stroke the BELIEVE stone, thinking this must be the big decision Train Santa had prophesied.

"You're a reporter, you specifically talked to him about getting married," she prodded. "It was a month ago, but you've recounted that talk over and over, analyzing it up and down and backward. You discussed getting married, right?"

"Well, I told him I wanted to, and that my dad's getting older and I would love to give him his wish of seeing me married. I guess I figured that telling him those things was enough. He didn't say he *didn't* want to get married."

Veronica started to point out that Amy had fretted over this very detail, that after their talk, he hadn't said that he did want to get married, either. He had used the word "someday," and Amy had flipped it around and around trying to figure out: When was someday?

"You know, we're only twenty-three, you've still got a lot of time for getting married."

"Yeah, but my dad's sixty-eight, and I know he would like to see his grandkids. And if Andrew's my steak knife, what difference does age make? When you know, you know. Right?"

"Do you know?"

Veronica noticed a whiff of a pause before Amy answered, "Yes."

AMY LEFT THE BAGS of clothes for donation in the lobby and, buoyed by the April air, returned to the apartment humming off-key. As she passed 202, the door swung open.

"Joey, you scared me." She laughed and greeted him with a hug as her heart raced.

"Sorry. Veronica's not home, right? Do you need a hand packing?"

"Thanks, come on in, it's just me."

"You've been a great friend to me and you're Veronica's best friend," he began when the door closed behind them.

"Yeah?" Amy encouraged, tipping her head to the side and pulling out a chair for each of them.

"Well, we've been together for over eight months and she's never brought me home to meet her family. I sometimes wonder if she's even told them about me." Joey's voice was filled with sincerity and tinted with pain.

"Have you asked Veronica about it?"

"Yeah, I've brought it up. There are always reasons that she goes back to Newport alone, like work schedules, her parents' traveling, or something, but"—he shook his head and swept both hands over the sides of his gelled black hair—"I just get this sense that she's hiding something from me."

"I don't know, Joey, Veronica can be a bit private about family stuff, but we both know she really cares about you," Amy reassured him, but diverted her eyes. She didn't want to go any further into the topic for fear of sharing something that Veronica hadn't already told him herself.

She passed Joey an open box. "The bottom three shelves are my books. Fill 'er up."

He clutched groups of paperbacks, moving slowly, pensively. His eyes, brimming with questions, tugged at Amy to say more.

"Listen, Joey, talk to her. Okay?"

"THERE YOU ARE, JOEY. I just knocked on your door." Veronica dotted his cheek with kisses. "What are you doing here?"

Joey and Amy were draped on the furniture, Rolling Rock bottles dripping with condensation in their fingertips even in the cool early-spring temperatures.

"Grab a beer with us. We got a ton done. All of my books and CDs are packed, the front coat closet is finished, and Joey helped me take that rickety old cabinet I had in my room down to the street for the garbage."

Veronica opened a Coors Light with the familiar sound of the aluminum tab unsealing and sat next to Joey. She kissed him and he smiled at her.

"I'm glad you're home. I love you."

"Me, too," Veronica said, and then she exaggerated a frown at Amy. "I still can't believe you're moving out."

"It's been a long run as roomies. I'm going to miss you."

"What if this new Chelsea girl is like *Single White Female,* or takes forever in the bathroom?" Veronica moaned.

"Don't complain in front of me," Joey said. "I told you to move in with me."

"You did?" Amy sat erect. "He did?" She turned accusingly to Veronica.

Veronica shifted in her seat and glanced to the floor. "Only the other night. I just haven't had the chance to tell you yet."

"She said, 'No.'"

Joey caught Amy's eye, and she felt a pang knowing he was right. Her friend wasn't fully letting him in.

Chapter 34

ANDREW STOOD AT THE counter sorting mail as Amy unpacked her CDs, mixing them into his collection. "Are you putting those together with the same genres of music?" he called through the large rectangular opening between the kitchen and living room.

"Kind of."

"Here's a postcard already from your buddy. What's the computer geek up to, anyway? It's gotta be lame still being in Syracuse."

Andrew tossed the card across the counter. The postcard slid as if on ice, gliding off the counter and skimming across the wood floor, where it stopped under the corner of the area rug—the rug that scratched at Amy's sense of taste like a knife scraping across a ceramic plate.

"He's doing great, working on some big information system for the U.S. government," she started to explain, but Andrew had lost interest.

Amy got up from her spot on the floor and crawled the few feet to retrieve the card. The front was a picture of the Syracuse quad in full spring foliage, crisscrossed with its paths. She smiled, thinking of playing Frisbee there with Andrew and crossing those sidewalks with snow shoveled waist-high on either side. Seeing the picture of the quad brought back memories of the Phi Psi golf tournament freshman year, the stumping visit of presidential primary candidate Bill Clinton, and the ordinary lingering through the years. She flipped the postcard to read Matt's note.

Dear Amy,

   Thanks for your call on my mom's birthday. You're the best to remember—it was a hard day for me. I got the promotion! Thanks for the encouraging letter. I'm working on some really cool stuff. There's talk of a merger with Martin Marietta, busier than ever. Congrats on another great byline! Proud of you!

   Love, Matt

No mention of Patty, Amy noticed, but then, he never did mention her.

"Andrew, did you read my article yet? I'm dying to know what you think."

"Not yet, I've just been so swamped." Andrew tossed an envelope into a pile and a catalog into the garbage. "Want to go away somewhere this summer?" he asked her, holding up a travel agency brochure filled with fancy, happy beach photos.

In all their years together, they had never taken a full week's get-on-a-plane-and-go-away vacation, just the two of them. She was holding a Smiths disc, deciding where to file it. Amy dropped the orange case and sat on the stool across from him at the counter.

"A real vacation together? Yeah!" she said, beaming. "Where to?"

"I don't know, you pick someplace, but I'd rather go to a beach or island than some kind of touristy adventure trip."

Amy kneeled on the stool, leaned across the Corian counter, and kissed his lips with a playful smack.

"This will be so much fun. I'll stop in at that travel agency near my office tomorrow at lunch and get some ideas," Amy said, opening the trifold pamphlet and staring at the images of romantic destinations.

"I'M A HUMAN RESOURCES manager, Joey, I can't just take a day off and not follow the protocol. I need to set an example," Veronica spoke quietly into the phone. "You know I'd love to head out a day early, but the rules are the rules. Let's leave tomorrow after work like we planned."

"All right, I was hoping to beat the traffic down to the shore, but I'll fit in another job."

"We'll still have all weekend, and I'm approved for Monday off like we decided. It's better having the day after Easter off anyway—then we won't need to rush home on Sunday." Veronica tidied a binder and hole-punched papers as she spoke to him.

"Your parents are okay with you not going home for Easter?" Joey asked softly, wondering more than his words exposed.

Veronica punched a group of pages then said, "They'll be fine. I'm calling now. See you tonight."

"Bye, I love you."

"Me, too."

Veronica replaced the receiver with precision and snapped together the rings of the binder with a clank. *I love you, Joey,* she thought with a knot in her stomach. *I do love him and he treats me better than any other guy ever has. So why can't I say the words?* When she was alone, Veronica practiced in front of her mirror, saying, "I love you, Joey," over and over, believing the repetition would help the words come out when she was with him. But they never did.

"HONEY, I'M SO GLAD you called, I have the Curtises coming for Easter dinner. Do you remember their son, Ian?" Susan Warren rattled on the moment she heard her daughter's voice.

"Yes, Mom." Veronica tried to keep the impatience from her

voice. "Don't you remember all the times we've hung out since you introduced us freshman year? But that's why I'm calling."

"You'll be up on Friday night, right? I hope you're not planning to come on Saturday morning because I've already set up a day for the two of us. We're getting manicures—I got appointments with my favorite two girls—then we're going to—"

"Mom," Veronica interrupted.

"What is it? You don't want a manicure?" Her mother's voice dropped.

"No, Mom, it's not that. I'm calling to tell you that I'm not coming home for Easter this year." Veronica spoke the words quickly, then held the phone away from her ear and closed her eyes, waiting.

There was silence, and Veronica worried that she was missing her mother's words so she pushed the phone to her ear in time for one more beat of silence and then the guilt.

"Well, if that's what you want, your father will be so disappointed to hear it. And that nice Curtis boy, he'll be alone with us old folks," she started.

Veronica just sighed and listened.

"Wait, what are you going to do for Easter? You'll go to a service, won't you? Who will you be with? I feel like we never see you anymore. Is there something you're keeping from us?"

Veronica couldn't lie and couldn't answer, either. She inhaled, deciding what to say, but her mother continued: "We won't be around next weekend, you know, if you wanted to come up then instead, I mean. That's the week your father and I head to Washington for that fundraiser. I do wish you could meet us there. I hear the senator's son is available and I'm sure your father could make an introduction."

"Mom, I'm sorry, I've got to go now, I'm at work," Veronica said. "I just wanted to let you know."

"Well, okay then. Good-bye, honey, we'll miss you," her mother said. "Happy Easter."

Veronica heard the dial tone and whispered, "Happy Easter, Mom."

"CAN WE DYE EASTER eggs tomorrow?" Amy asked. "I love coloring eggs."

"I'm sure my sisters, or at least Heather, would do that with you," Andrew answered, pulling out of the rental car parking lot and onto the West Side Highway toward the George Washington Bridge.

As they headed into New Jersey, Amy pulled out a few tapes and fed the *Footloose* sound track into the cassette player. "Okay, flashback time." She danced in her seat to "Footloose," "Let's Hear It for the Boy," and "Dancing in the Sheets," until she was out of breath and her face muscles were sore from her constant smile.

"You're hilarious. I think you may rock the car right off the road," Andrew teased as they eased onto Interstate 80 westbound toward Sparta.

"I love this next song." Amy clapped.

"More than the last ones? I'm in trouble."

She was already moving to the beat under her seat belt when Bonnie Tyler started wailing and Amy joined in on the first words.

Where have all the good men gone, and where are all the gods? Amy belted out the lyrics, singing freely off-key and letting go of New York City and her workweek. She pumped her fists and flipped her head forward, letting her brown hair shake around her. *I need a hero! I'm holding out for a hero till the morning light!*

"You've got your hero right here," Andrew said, smirking as the song ended. "I'm a hero just for letting you sing the whole drive."

"Very funny."

"I haven't heard that song in ages. Okay, my turn to choose?"

He turned on the radio, adjusted the dial and tweaked it to Stone Temple Pilots.

Andrew pounded the steering wheel to the beat through Pearl Jam and Nirvana as Amy's head lilted to the side and she dozed off despite the high-volume rock. He pushed in the Soul Asylum cassette and lowered it to let her sleep a little longer as he exited onto Route 15 north. Pulling onto Farmbrook Road, Andrew stopped the car and gently stroked Amy's cheek.

"Aim, we're here. Wake up, we're here."

Her eyes eased open and she rubbed a kink from her neck as Andrew entered the garage door code. Hearing the rumble of the door, Heather and Stephanie ran out to meet them.

"Andrew! Amy!" Heather, a high school junior, took Amy's arm and led her into the kitchen. "I'm so happy you guys are out for the weekend. You're staying in my room like usual, Amy, I have it all set up for you, come on."

Wendy Gabel laughed as her daughter tugged Amy through the kitchen.

"Hi, Mrs. Gabel," Amy called over her shoulder.

"I'll say hello when Heather sets you free."

Stephanie, a freshman in college, liked Amy, but she missed her brother and was stingy about sharing him. She stuck to him as she would all weekend. Andrew always wanted to be around family and friends, and people always wanted to be around him. Amy understood Stephanie's desire to have him all to herself, even just for a little while.

ON SATURDAY MORNING, Amy woke and shot out of bed when she saw the time, 9:38. *Crap!* she thought. *I don't want to look like a complete slug. I hope I'm not the last one up.* She tugged on a sweatshirt over her pajamas, brushed her teeth, pinched her cheeks for some color, and headed downstairs. From the foyer, she heard whispered voices in the kitchen. *Good,* she thought, *maybe they're being quiet because others are still sleeping.* Just in case, she tiptoed toward them.

"Well, sweetie, I don't know what you two are waiting for. Your dad and I were already married at your age. She's a wonderful girl and if you love her, I don't know why you don't propose," Mrs. Gabel said.

Amy froze. She looked back toward the steps and debated going quietly back up and then thumping down a little to make herself known. She was hidden by the dining room wall, and she hunched behind it, wondering what Andrew's response would be.

"Amy," Heather yelled behind her. "What are you doing there?"

The question forced her to emerge from the entry into the breakfast room, fully lit with eastern sun. Mrs. Gabel's eyes darted up and Andrew turned in his chair.

"Morning, Aim." He put down his coffee and stood to hug her. "Sleep good?" he asked, rubbing the back of her head. She nodded, gently leaning her head into his hand, and then she bent to give Mrs. Gabel a hug as Heather disappeared into the family room and flipped on the TV, filling the room with the voices from a *Fresh Prince of Bel-Air* rerun.

"Good morning. Yes, I slept great. Heather's bed is comfy. But I'm sorry, I had no idea it was so late."

Waving a hand that it didn't matter, Mrs. Gabel made her own apology with a lowered voice. "I'm sorry you two can't share a room here. We know you live together, but we're trying to set an example for Steph and Heather," Mrs. Gabel explained again, as she did every time they spent the night in Sparta.

"Really, it's okay, Mrs. Gabel, I don't mind at all. We still sleep in separate rooms at my dad's house, too." She noticed Mrs. Gabel's shoulders slacken with the reassurance.

Amy poured herself some coffee, adding sugar and light cream.

"Go easy, that has caffeine," Andrew teased, knowing Amy's accelerated, jittery response to coffee. She cradled the mug in her palms and inhaled the aromatic steam, enjoying the experience of the coffee more than the substance of it.

"I hear you're going to Saint John this summer," Mrs. Gabel said.

"Mom, just let it go," Andrew snapped.

"What a fun trip that'll be. Do you want some eggs?" She ignored Andrew's admonition and started preparing to cook without Amy's answer, which was always affirmative when it came to food.

"I'll do the toast," Amy offered, hoping to intercept another remark from Andrew; his tone had surprised her.

"Do you two have anything special planned for your trip?"

"Mom! Knock it off!" Andrew barked, shocking Amy frozen.

Mrs. Gabel gave her son a mother's look that held meaning at any age, but Amy saw hurt in her face.

"Wendy, can you come in here a second, please?" Roger Gabel called to his wife, popping his head into the kitchen. "Oh, good morning, Amy."

Alone, Andrew stood behind Amy, holding her hips as she put slices of bread into the toaster. "I missed you last night." He kissed behind her ear. "So, how much exactly did you hear this morning?"

"Oh, not much." She felt his sigh on her neck. "But I *am* wondering why you don't propose."

Andrew exhaled with deliberation. He let go of her hips, patted her bottom playfully, and said, "Someday."

Amy bit her lip as she slammed down the toaster lever. She was tired of that word.

SHOWERED AND DRESSED, AMY sat in the kitchen with her notebook, working on a story, when Mrs. Gabel sat beside her.

"Amy, can I talk with you for a moment while Andrew's upstairs?"

Amy put down her pen, grateful for the mother-daughter-like moments with Mrs. Gabel.

"I love my son. He's like the sun, bright and big, a huge shining star. He's a wonderful son and brother and has always made us proud. But everything has always come easily to him. I sometimes wonder if I've failed him because he's too accustomed to things orbiting around him and going his way. He hasn't often really had to commit himself to anything"—she took a breath and leaned toward Amy—"or anyone."

Amy crumpled her brow, confused by what she was saying. "Do you think he doesn't love me?"

"Oh no, honey, he loves you. That I know, he truly loves you, but think about what *you* want and need in a relationship—"

Before she could go on, Andrew thumped down the stairs. Mrs. Gabel touched Amy's hand and whispered, "Roger and I love you, too. Give it some thought."

"Ready to go, Amy?"

"Go where?"

"We're going over to my buddy Brian's house, he's got some new Sega games. Some guys you know from last time will be there and you know Bree. Ready?"

Amy gathered her things as Mrs. Gabel hugged her son and then Amy, giving her a light squeeze on the shoulder.

At Brian's, Amy sat on the basement couch and watched the guys battle one another, grunting and cheering like middle school boys. She was the only girl and rolled her eyes to herself, thinking of their day jobs. Besides Andrew's intense finance job, one was in med school, another worked for an accounting firm, and Brian was in sales for a pharmaceutical company. With the joysticks in their palms, they all looked, and acted, fourteen.

"Hey, guys," Bree's sweet voice sang out as she came downstairs. Andrew looked up and away from the screen, and sounds cried from the game and the fourteen-year-olds chorused, "You're out of the tournament, Gabel!" Bree made the rounds, kissing the guys, then plopped on the cushion next to Amy. "Looks like the usual fun."

"Yup. We haven't seen you in ages. How's D.C.?"

"Pretty good, I'm learning a lot, but I'm not sure politics and the world of lobbying is for me. I'm considering a move. How's life as a big-time New York journalist?"

"Oh, very glamorous, you know, waiting for court decisions, sitting through city council meetings, begging for interviews and anything quotable. But I love it and my boss is incredible. She's always encouraging me and has taught me so much about writing and the business."

"You're lucky, my boss is an arrogant pig. Total fork. You know, I still use that. Taught it to all of my roommates."

"I still do, too, and Veronica still won't admit that it works. Have you found any good knives?"

"Our capital is filled with forks, poking and jabbing anyone that gets in the way of their ambitions. I haven't had many good dates." She lowered her voice and fixed her eyes to Andrew's back. "You're lucky you've got Andrew. I blew it with him in high school. Sorry. That was so long ago it's not even worth talking about, but it's hard to find a great guy like him. Hang on to him, Amy."

Conflicting ideas fought like video game ninjas in her mind. Mrs. Gabel's words challenged Bree's, whose thoughts contested Mrs. Gabel's, and to Amy there were no clear winners. *Orbiting around him, not had to commit, truly loves you, hard to find, hang on to him, my steak knife, someday.* She was fighting on both sides of the ring, her own dreams and wishes struggling to be contenders.

Chapter 35

"THIS PLACE IS SO cute," Veronica said as they pulled into the gravel drive of the loaned cottage.

"My buddy said the beach is just a few blocks' walk, it must be over there." Joey had a sharp sense of direction and turned his head like a compass, discerning the way. "I'll get the bags, you go ahead and have a look inside." He tossed her the single key dangling from a pewter anchor key chain. An anchor, the symbol of hope that graced the Rhode Island state flag, she noted.

Veronica skipped up the few wooden steps and crossed the front porch. She fiddled with the lock and creaked the door open. A closed-up, damp smell greeted her as she stepped into the main room with its sand-worn wood floors and a stone fireplace. The walls and ceiling were made of narrow interlocking wood slats painted a crisp white. The living room was open to a small kitchen and two bedrooms were to the sides. Veronica pulled the tab on the white wooden louvered shades, letting in the early April light and puffs of dust.

"How do you like it?" Joey asked, plunking down their weekend duffels and three brown paper bags of groceries.

"It's perfect."

She peeped out each window, circling the perimeter of the

house. For their room, she chose the pale yellow bedroom with its iron bed, cream-colored bedspread, and mountain of yellow and blue throw pillows.

"Hungry?" Joey asked while opening cabinets and pulling out cutting boards, knives, and pots. Soon he was chopping garlic and escarole. "I'll start the sauce for dinner, and how about some *pasta e fagioli* for lunch?" He handed her a glass of wine and they toasted. "Happy Easter, *dolcezza*."

She smiled at the term of endearment he'd taken to calling her and sipped her wine, feeling everything in her body relax into the weekend holiday. She stood beside him and picked up a knife. "Give me something to chop."

"No, you sit. Seriously, these knives are terrible." He slid two blades against each other in his never-ending quest for the sharpest knives. "You're more likely to cut yourself—"

"With a dull knife," Veronica finished his sentence.

"Oh, just you sit and tell me about your family while I cook." He stopped midsharpening and looked straight into her eyes with a yearning in his own. "Tell me."

"What do you want to know? I've told you about them. My parents travel a lot since I've been out of the house, my dad's retired and golfs a lot, and my mom is eternally entertaining or hosting some fundraiser or another."

"Yeah, you've told me those things, but I want more, Veronica, I want to know you. Really know you. You never talk about what your life was like growing up or anything about your brother. I don't even know his name."

Veronica drew her knees up to her chest, hooking her heels on the edge of the seat. For a moment, she rested her head on her knees, then looked up and took a slow breath.

"My brother's name was Henry," she spoke slowly, "he was four years older than me."

Joey stared at her wordlessly.

"I was in sixth grade, he was a sophomore in high school when he got sick. At first it seemed like a bad cold or something, a virus; he couldn't do anything but sleep, but he wasn't getting better." Without a sound, Joey stood beside her, his hand on her back.

"The doctor said it was the flu, he was just supposed to rest and drink lots of fluids, you know, the typical recommendations for a bug. I remember strings of doctors, sitting in waiting rooms, and seeing him get sicker and sicker. In the shortest time, it seemed he changed from my athletic, fun big brother to a pale, withered sick person." Joey didn't move, his eyes locked on her, as if not wanting to interrupt the moment, and she went on. "He was throwing up a lot and he started acting strange, too, like he was really confused, but he was a smart kid and a good student. It wasn't like Henry at all. He was in and out of the hospital a couple of times in the first week. They did a million tests but kept sending him back home with no answers. They guessed meningitis and one time they even suspected a drug overdose. My parents went crazy—Henry was a good kid.

"The night he couldn't stop throwing up, my dad called the ambulance." Tears dripped down Veronica's face as she relived it. She felt Joey's arms wrap around her shoulders and knees, holding her together more than he knew. "My mom went with Henry in the ambulance and my dad and I followed the flashing red lights. The whole way to the hospital, I watched the lights looping around and around. It was February and I remember the way the red lights reflected against the snow on the ground." Her voice was quiet and halting, caught on the memories and every vivid detail.

"At the hospital, they told us that his liver was failing. They put him into a coma and on life support, but he kept getting worse. My parents didn't let me see him. I think they thought it was better for me. No one let me see him. I wanted to hug Henry, to tell him I loved him, but they wouldn't let me see him." She let out a sob and let herself heave in Joey's embrace.

"It's okay, go ahead," Joey whispered, drying his own tears on his shoulder.

They cried together, wrapped up in each other, freeing a loss that whipped around and drew them closer. Time stretched backward and stopped completely as they clung together in the little cottage. Calming slowly, Veronica stood. She led Joey by the hand to the blue-and-white sofa. She leaned against his chest and nestled herself into his arms before speaking again.

"We were at the hospital all day for the next two days. My parents took turns going into the ICU, but on the third day, he was brain-dead. He stopped breathing as soon as he was taken off life support. I was in the waiting room all alone when my dad came out to tell me." Veronica pressed her face into Joey's body, letting him absorb her tears. He stroked her hair rhythmically, tenderly. "I never got to see him. I never got to say good-bye."

When she eventually lifted her face, she dabbed at the wet mess she'd made across Joey's shirt. He hugged her back to him.

"What was it—why was he so sick? It wasn't just from the flu . . ."

"No, when they figured it out, it was too late. He had Reye's syndrome."

Joey shook his head, questioning. "They think he must've taken a medication or used some acne cream that had an aspirin ingredient in it. They never really knew how he got it, but it was just too late when they finally figured it out."

"I'm so sorry, *dolcezza*. Thank you for telling me about Henry."

Veronica looked into his dark eyes, noticing every eyelash and the faint lines at their edges. She held his gaze and released the words.

"I love you, Joey."

Chapter 36

THE SUN HAD ALREADY TUCKED below the tall buildings on the June evening. A passing bus puffed out gray exhaust and a pigeon bobbed beside their feet, pecking at sidewalk crumbs. "Do you think he's going to propose on vacation?" Veronica asked as she and Amy sat outside the Manhattan café.

"It would be romantic, wouldn't it?" Amy smiled. She leaned back and ran her fingers over the familiar charms dangling from her bracelet. "Though, sweet as he is, Andrew's not always so clued in to grand gestures or to small details for that matter."

"I want to be the first to know if he does."

Amy played along with the what-ifs, allowing herself to believe it could happen. "I'll call from the airport when we land. Wait, did he talk to you? Do you know something? Did he ask you about what kind of ring I want or something?" Amy fired questions to Veronica's shaking head. "Hold on, do you know what kind of ring I want in case he does ask?"

Veronica chuckled. "A round cut diamond, channel-set baguettes on the sides, platinum setting, got it."

"I haven't talked about it that much."

"What about that magazine clipping you've had tucked in your jewelry box forever?"

"Well, fine, you are my best friend and you're supposed to know these things. Oh no, but I don't know what you want. How do I not know what you want?" Amy gasped, sending Veronica into full laughter.

"That's because, my friend, I have no idea, and there's not a chance of you needing to know any time soon anyway."

"You must know, or have some idea about what you'd like."

"I'd love something simple, something completely unshowy. I think a solitaire would be just right."

"There we go," Amy said as the waitress set down their drinks. "Thank you. How are things going with Joey?"

"Ever since I told him about Henry at Easter, I feel like we've gotten closer and closer."

"That's great!"

"Yeah, but . . ."

"What?"

"I still haven't told my parents about him and I don't know what to do." Veronica twisted a red curl around her finger. "He's been amazingly patient even though I really haven't explained much."

"What's to explain? You love him, he loves you."

"Always the romantic, but things aren't that simple. You know my parents, they like things just so. They have certain expectations for me and my life, and I don't want to let them down, but I also feel like I'm being unfair to Joey. How do I introduce him to them?"

"You say, 'Mom and Dad, this is my boyfriend, Joey.' It's been a long time and you love him. Your parents will understand because they love you."

"I'm scared to rock the boat and I also worry that, well, that—"

"That you're embarrassed of him?" Amy finished.

Veronica bit her lip and nodded. "Everything's okay here in our world, but stepping into my life in Newport just feels like a whole different thing. When I picture that scene, I avoid doing it. Even at our age, I still want their approval."

"I get that, I do, but you're a grown-up now, making your own money and living on your own. They'll be okay. You don't have to follow their rules anymore, you know."

"Oh, my *dolcezza,* always the rule-follower." Joey stepped between the neighboring tables and kissed both girls. "What rules are you worried about now?" He grinned at Veronica.

"What rules isn't she worried about?" Amy answered for her, secretly shaking her head at Veronica to convey that he hadn't heard what they were talking about. Amy diverted him with another question. "What's going on with you, Joey?"

"Lighting up the world, kid."

"Bad one." Amy laughed and Veronica playfully hit his chest with the back of her hand.

"Where's Andrew?" Joey asked, looking at his watch.

"He should be here soon. He's been working a lot. Our vacation next month will be good for him. He really needs to get away from this constant work and late nights."

The trio chatted and waited for Andrew before ordering appetizers. After an hour, Amy left to call his office from the restaurant pay phone. No answer. She tried their apartment and his friend Buzz, but no answer at either. Amy returned to their table as Andrew arrived, out of breath.

"You will not believe what just happened," Andrew said as he slid out the iron chair next to Amy, pecked her on the cheek, and, with quick greetings across the table, launched into his story. "So I'm waiting in the subway for the damn six train and this guy walks over to me, slaps me on the back, acts like he knows me."

The server hovered, waiting for them to notice her. Andrew gave his order and dove back into his tale.

"I'm sure I don't know him, he's not even a little familiar, but he acted so much like he knew me that I hesitated, thinking maybe it was a client or someone I should've remembered." Andrew removed his suit jacket and hung it over the back of the chair. "He kept his arm on my shoulder as he was talking to me. It felt like he was holding me a little too long, so I pulled out of his grip and stepped backward into this other guy who was right behind me with his hand in my back pocket. By the time I understood what happened, the guys were already busting ass up the stairs and out to the street."

"Drew, are you okay?" Amy clutched his arm.

"Yeah, yeah, I'm fine now. I bolted up after them but they were gone."

"What did you do? Did you go to the police?" Veronica asked.

"There's a precinct station right by the Fifty-First Street subway, so I went over there."

"What were you doing on the subway? You could walk here from your office," Amy wondered.

"Meeting. The police took a report and all, but I'm sure they'll never get anything from it. They sat me at a desk with a phone book where I called my bank to report the stolen cards and I was able to get my credit card company's number from information. Man, what a hassle, now I've got to go get a new driver's license, new hotel rewards cards, and all that crap." Andrew took a long draw of beer from the bottle as it was set down before him.

"Well, that's one way to get out of paying the bill," Joey joked.

Even as she laughed along, an uneasiness settled into Amy's chest that she couldn't explain.

Chapter 37

ANDREW WAS EDGY AS THEY packed for vacation. He sighed intermittently, tossed clothes together instead of folding them in his usual neat manner, and even snapped at Amy when she suggested he bring a light sweater for the evenings.

"I know how to pack, Amy. I'm a big boy now."

Quietly, she left him alone, reasoning that he must be stressed preparing to be away from work for a week. She struggled to ignore the nudge in her gut and the little stab at her heart. *Is this what being together for nearly five years looks like? Does it just become ordinary and testy?* Her optimist's heart lifted her spirit. *Everyone has tough days and grumpy moods,* she thought, *or maybe Andrew is nervous because he's planning something big while we're away. Maybe he's trying to figure out how to pack the ring without me seeing it.*

Their flight left at 7:05 p.m., and they had two hours before leaving for the airport. She still had a few things to pack, but she plopped on the couch and sat with a magazine to give him some distance.

"I'll be right back," Andrew said, slipping into flip-flops and heading out the door.

"Wait, what? Where are you going? We're leaving soon."

Amy dropped the July *Vanity Fair* on the cushion beside her, hearing herself spew the checking-on-you words that guys resist. A memory of the banter at Owen's wedding made her inhale sharply.

"I'll be right back," he repeated, softening his tone. "I'm just running to the store."

When he'd gone, Amy returned to their bedroom to throw in final accessories, her makeup, and toiletries. On Andrew's dresser, she noticed he'd left things askew: drawers were left with clothes spilling out and the handsome mahogany box, where he left his coins at the end of the day, stood open. Amy wondered whether to tidy it for him or leave it, and she smiled at the backwardness of the situation. She tucked the clothes into the drawers, then went to shut his box. Inside, she saw the watch she'd given him for graduation. *He never wears that anymore,* Amy thought, remembering how excited she was to give it to him. Without touching it, she slowly closed the lid, thinking of their years and the hidden words inside, *For All Time.*

"THERE'S OUR CHECK-IN LINE," Amy said, rolling her suitcase toward the counter.

When Andrew had returned from the store, his mood had brightened. He'd tossed her a pack of Freshen Up gum and a kiss, and they'd caught a cab to La Guardia.

"Next!"

They approached the attendant together.

"Itinerary and driver's licenses, please," she said.

Andrew reached into his back pocket, pulled out his wallet, and fished for his license. Amy froze with her hand in her unzipped carry-on. His license was the same. The same crackled edges, the same picture with his head tipped to the side just a tiny bit, the same peeling ORGAN DONOR sticker in red. His license was the same as before the mugging. Then she noticed the gently worn stitches of the leather wallet, a slightly faded black; it was thick with cards and receipts and had shiny spots where it bulged.

"You have your wallet," she blurted out.

"What? Oh. Yeah, the police found it. The guys dumped it, just took the cash," Andrew explained, lifting his luggage onto the stand beside the clerk. "I can't believe I forgot to tell you."

Amy's forehead wrinkled and she looked down to resume digging for her own license. She handed it to the clerk, who glanced between her photo and her face, returned the ID, then turned her back to put stickers on their luggage handles.

It's not very likely that he would get his wallet back, she thought, in reporter mode. *Did he make up the whole thing? But why would he invent a story?* Amy felt the questions whirl; small doubts she'd pushed deep crept their way out.

"Gate E," the airline agent said, and pointed with the boarding passes in her hand. "Have fun, Saint John is a beautiful place for a honeymoon."

Andrew thanked her with exaggerated friendliness, and Amy forced a smile as they headed toward the security line.

"Honeymoon? What made her think that?" Amy blew a dismissive breath through her lips. Andrew took her hand, free from extra luggage. She left her hand passively in his, questioning her suspiciousness, rattled by the swirl of feelings.

"Maybe we'll end up having our honeymoon there someday," he said with a wink. "I'm sorry I've been a little testy. I didn't get that new position I was hoping for, they gave it to some guy from Goldman."

"Oh, Drew, I'm sorry." *Ah, that explains a lot.*

"I've never been passed over for something like this, for something that I wanted so badly."

She squeezed his hand supportively, unsure of how to help him and thinking of his mother's words: *He's too accustomed to things orbiting around him and going his way.*

They passed a newsstand and the thick issue of *Brides* magazine caught her eye. She sighed, anticipating the day when she could buy those magazines and plan her dream wedding.

"THIS PLACE IS AMAZING," Amy said, throwing open the balcony doors and breathing in the salty island air. "Let's get into bathing suits," she added, already stripping.

The sheer curtains ruffled as the breeze welcomed them. Andrew slid his arm around her bare waist, a finger under her chin, and gave her a sensuous kiss full of expectation. He led her to the bed, leaned back into the white feathery covering, and pulled her down on top of him. Amy responded to his touch, savored the passionate kissing. Their kisses at home had become rote, ordinary daily pecks, and Amy missed the drawn-out, soap-opera-style kissing sessions that used to go on forever. She helped him take off his clothes, then threaded her fingers behind his head and clenched his golden hair into her fists.

Everything felt new again, experimental with the excitement of discovery. Each touch was startling and electric. She quivered with the flutter of his fingers and spread her thighs wide, inviting more. Andrew was her movie star, her hero who knew all the right things to do.

They were eager yet patient, taking each other to the edge then retreating, leaving them with sumptuous yearning until the ecstasy of friction, skin against skin, hips against hips, made Amy cry out as Andrew trembled and stiffened and collapsed to her side.

"I love you, Aim," he murmured as they began their vacation.

"WEAR THAT WHITE DRESS I like," Andrew requested as Amy browsed her choices, clinking the hangers in the closet. "I made reservations at Anna's for tonight." He stood behind her and hugged her to him, sprinkling her neck with kisses.

"That expensive place overlooking Cruz Bay? What's the occasion?"

Andrew answered with more kisses along the tan lines on her shoulders from four days in a bikini.

Amy giggled. "You're all salty." She let the drips from her clean hair wash away the beach again. The fluffy towel slipped lower. She retucked its edge at her armpit and held up the simple white cotton dress, slim with skinny straps.

"This one?"

"Mmm," he answered, wiggling out of his bathing suit and revealing his approval. He flicked the bathing suit with his foot to his hand and hung it on a bathroom hook before stepping into the shower.

Amy chuckled, heady with the sensation of falling in love.

THE SKY GLEAMED ORANGE and pink, casting glitter over the turquoise Caribbean waters. Amy shifted in the chair and turned to look over her shoulder, watching the sunset like a child watching a butterfly land on her wrist. Her body felt heavy with relaxation, her heart light with content. The week together in paradise had stirred old feelings and reignited something between them.

"To us!" Andrew's voice pulled Amy back to him. "To us and our future."

Amy lifted her glass to meet his, smiling. He looked beyond her to the horizon and she gazed at his face; every curve and speckle was familiar. She had touched every spot of his smooth skin, knew his taste and his smell. She was his and he was hers.

"I want you to be my wife, Aim, we're good together," he said and swallowed hard. "We're good together, aren't we?"

"Yes. We are." She glanced around. He wasn't reaching for anything: one hand was on his glass, the other in her hand. There was no small box in sight. Amy glimpsed the bottom of her wine-glass—maybe he'd slipped the ring in there while she was staring at the sunset. She sipped carefully and checked the glass with every taste, even as it was clear there was only white wine in the crystal.

Appetizers were served, the most elegant presentation Amy had ever seen. When the entrées were presented, she noticed every detail, took in the scents of the food and admired the way they looked like art on the canvas of the plates. She observed Andrew's actions with fervor and kept her eye on their waiter for clues. Before dessert, she excused herself to the ladies' room.

Amy examined her reflection in the mirror and patted some pink into her tanned cheeks. *He wants me to be his wife*, she thought, *he's never said that before*. In all the times they'd talked about getting married, he had never used the word "wife." It felt different to her and the word swam like a goldfish in her heart. She slid the wand of gloss over her lips and pressed them together before she went back to Andrew.

The table was cleared, the signs of a meal swept away. She scanned the table, bare but for teacups and fresh utensils. Her napkin had been refolded and placed at her seat. Andrew was looking at the dessert menu as she pulled out her chair across from him.

"Want something?" he asked, peering above the menu. "Should we share the mango cheesecake?"

"Um, sure, that sounds good." She would have preferred the chocolate mousse, always her favorite, but thinking that maybe the cheesecake was part of his plan, she agreed.

The waiter placed the rich slice, drizzled with a mango coulis, between them. Andrew pushed the plate closer to Amy and picked up his fork.

"Go ahead, Aim, it's your favorite," he said with his hand hovering over the cake, waiting for her to take the first taste.

This is it, Amy thought. She grasped her fork, touched the tips of the tines to the creamy triangle, and pressed through the wedge slowly, carefully, like an archaeologist excavating a fossil. Her fork slid through the smooth cake and hit the plate. She let the fork's handle drop into the crook of her hand, then placed the bite into her mouth. Just in case, she pushed her tongue through the sweetness, then swallowed down the cake. She stuck her fork in again, poking in two places before scooping some up. Her heart fluttered as Andrew took bites from the other end of the cake. *He's avoiding the ring.* When the last piece, streaked with fork marks, sat on the plate, she noticed the giddy tremble in her chest had vanished, leaving her heart still.

WHILE ANDREW WAITED AT the carousel for their baggage, Amy said, "I'm going to call Veronica."

"What? Now? We just landed, can't it wait?"

"It'll only be a minute—I told her I'd call when we got back." Amy weaved her way between travelers to the pay phones.

On the third ring, Veronica answered.

"It's me."

"Where are you? What happened? Did he propose? Are you engaged?"

"I don't know. I mean, no. No." Amy's voice was soft.

"What do you mean?"

"Well, he arranged this amazing dinner at a fancy place with a table overlooking the water and the sunset. He even picked out what he wanted me to wear and he told me that he wanted me to be his wife."

"Oh my God, Amy, that's great. But then, what do you mean you don't know?"

"He never actually asked me to be his wife. And no ring. He didn't give me a ring."

The line was silent. Amy waited for Veronica to say something, to explain this to her, to make her feel better.

"Veronica?"

"I'm here," she whispered. "Did you ask him about it?"

"I couldn't even talk at first, but he kept asking me what was wrong, like he didn't even get it. Finally I told him I thought he was proposing, but he just said what he always says, 'Someday.' He hugged me and explained how he's putting in all these hours at work to move up, that now isn't a good time, that we're still too young. He just missed out on a promotion so he's really stressed. He gave me all these reasons, and I know they make sense, but I'm tired of waiting for 'someday.'" Amy's words came out with her tears. "I was more disappointed than I thought I could be. I'd gotten engagement into my head and all week everything was incredible. We had an awesome time; it was like we were the perfect couple on the perfect vacation. Everything was perfect except"—Amy lifted the edge of her shirt and dabbed at her eyes—"except no ring."

Chapter 38

"YOU'D HATE IT," VERONICA SAID, smoothing another dress into her weekend bag. "It'll just be all of my parents' friends and their boring small talk. They host this garden party every August and it's tedious. I don't even want to go." She sat beside Joey on her bed and laid her hand on his thigh; his faded Levi's button-fly jeans felt smooth on her palm. He leaned against the headboard, eyes fixed on the ceiling, his hands folded over his chest.

"You don't really want to come, do you? I'll only be gone two nights, it'll give you some time to help your mom with her tomato plants," Veronica continued, filling the silence. "She'll be so happy to have your help staking them, and you've been meaning to get out there to help your dad with—"

"Just stop, Veronica. Stop making me the reason you're going without me." Joey stood up and kissed her cheek. "I don't know what's going on, but this isn't about what's best for me. Be safe, I love you."

Veronica watched him leave her room, heard him say good-bye to her roommate, Chelsea, and startled at the sound of the door clicking behind him.

THE TRAIN RATTLED ON, whooshing past Connecticut towns and finally into Rhode Island. Every seat was filled with people heading out of New York for the late-summer weekend. Veronica stared out the window. Her book lay closed on her lap, the bookmark unmoved. Absently, she fanned the corners of the pages and pictured Joey's old Eldorado pulling into her parents' driveway. It didn't matter that it was clean and polished. She shook her head to herself and bit her lip at the image.

She grabbed a taxi at the station to get to Newport without interrupting her parents, who were preparing for the party: managing caterers, directing tent builders, and overseeing florists. The cab rolled toward her childhood home. The trees along both sides of the driveway were filled with men on ladders stringing white lights, and the grand house stood before them.

"Whoa, you live here? This is some place," the driver commented with a whistle.

"It's my parents' house," she said, seeing her old home as an outsider. It was an impressive property with everything manicured and flowered to perfection.

The driver jumped out to open the trunk. He laid Veronica's bag on the walkway and lingered, waiting for payment, as the front door burst open and Gerald Warren's big personality and tall stature bounded down the stairs to greet his daughter.

"You made it." He pulled Veronica into an embrace for a moment before reaching into his pocket to hand the driver the fare and a generous tip then returning his attention to his daughter.

"Wait until you see what your mother's been up to this time." He grinned, pulling her into their conspiratorial tradition of teasing Susan Warren about her grand entertaining style.

Veronica sighed and took what felt like her first breath since leaving the city.

VERONICA SETTLED INTO HER childhood bedroom, redecorated from the jarring turquoise color she chose in high school to a more mature sage accented with creams and a calming gray blue. For the first time, she realized what a sacrifice it had been for her mother to allow her to pick that terrible aqua that Veronica had loved. She felt a softness toward her mother, a woman who, after Henry's death, redoubled her philanthropic efforts and was constantly volunteering and raising money for Reye's awareness and other worthy causes, if often leaving Veronica to grow up and figure things out on her own.

Susan Warren was good at communicating what she expected of a Warren offspring, but she struggled at being fully present and available. Veronica was organized and mature and rose to the occasion as best as a teenager could. Being a levelheaded realist, she knew her mother loved her, and though it stung, Veronica knew her mother was staying afloat by keeping herself busy in the wake of losing Henry. All those years had passed and she was still busily fundraising.

"Sweetie, Daddy said you'd arrived." Veronica's mother swept into her room. She held her daughter's shoulder and kissed her cheek. A coral Chanel lip print marked the spot. "We'll have a little dinner on the veranda, then you'll help me set up the gift bags."

"Of course, Mom."

Her mother turned to leave the room.

"Mom," Veronica said softly. Her mother stopped and turned back to face her. "Mom, what would you think if . . ."

"What is it, honey?" She stepped closer.

Veronica took a deep breath. Her gaze followed the delicate handwoven pattern in the silk rug beneath her feet. Hiding the truth about Joey was pulling her away from him and away from her parents. The leaves on the rug tangled into vines where ivory-colored birds perched. In the pattern, only one bird was flying; the others stood still, never venturing from solid footing.

"What would you and Dad think if I brought a boyfriend home?" She lifted one foot from the branch.

"Well, that would be lovely, Veronica." Her mother's eyes sparkled and she held her hands together at her chin. "You have a boyfriend? Does he work on Wall Street? Oh, I bet he's so handsome in his suit and tie. Where is he from? What do his parents do?"

"I'm not saying I have a boyfriend, Mom, I'm just asking what you'd think of me bringing someone home." Veronica closed her wings and put her foot back on the woody vine.

"Well, it would be wonderful. You know, we've already been to three weddings of our friends' children just this year. The good ones are getting scooped up, Veronica. Maybe you'll meet some of the single boys at the party tomorrow. I can make some calls . . ."

"No, Mom, please don't, I'm fine," Veronica whispered, "I'm fine."

VERONICA HOPPED OUT OF the shower and reexamined the tea-length floral dress she'd draped on the bed. It had tailored short sleeves and a scooped neck, though not scooped enough to expose her collarbones. Her low-heeled shoes sat on the floor beneath, and the matching jewelry rested beside it on the matelassé coverlet. It looked like something her mother would wear: too mature, too staid, too proper, even for a Newport garden party. She pulled her weekend bag back out of the closet. She'd unpacked everything except the new dress Amy insisted she buy. Veronica was hesitant about it, but Amy assured her that it was flattering and in style, saying, "Get out of your comfort zone and don't be afraid to show a little shoulder, V." *Easy for her to say with those skinny shoulders*, she thought lightheartedly.

Veronica shook out the long satin slip dress, the emerald-green fabric floating on the air. She pulled the dress over her head. With only a wiggle, it slid down her curvy body and fell into place. The bias cut accented her full chest and slimmed her hips. Veronica let a smile escape and spun in front of the mirror. She opened the hidden drawer in her dresser and retrieved the diamond tennis bracelet, a graduation gift from her parents that she chose not to bring to New York. She clasped it on to her wrist, ran her fingers through her curls, and slipped into heeled silver sandals.

"Okay, here goes. I'm stepping out of my box, Amy," she said aloud to her friend states away, and she ventured to the backyard to join the first guests.

Susan Warren waved to her from across the stone patio. She raised her eyebrows at her daughter for a flash of a second, then recovered with a pleasant look as Veronica approached.

"Honey, this is Hugh Curtis, your father's accountant, his wife, Jane, and their son, Ian," she introduced.

Ian and Veronica smiled at each other. "We've met," they said together.

"You introduced us Thanksgiving break years ago," Veronica said, nudging her mother's memory. "And we've hung out a bunch of times since then."

"Oh, lovely, you two can catch up," her mother said obliviously, turning to the Curtises, chatting away as she held a hand on Jane's back and headed toward the white-clothed garden bar.

"It's been a couple years. How are you?" Ian asked, his eyes full of genuine interest and his tone reminding Veronica of his mature nature.

"Good. I'm good, thanks. I'm in New York City, working in human resources. How about you?"

He grinned at her, his madras bow tie lifting with the upturn of his mouth. "I'm glad to hear about *what* you're doing, but *how* are you doing? Is that bossy guy who interrupted our dinner still after you? Are you happy in the city?"

Disarmed, Veronica stepped back and away from his questions. The heel of her sandal sank into the grass and she lifted her other foot for balance, but she toppled with the edge of her dress fluttering in the fall. All at once, her heart skipped, her arms grasped at air, and in a flurry of seconds, she braced herself, praying the satin dress wouldn't show off more than her shoulders.

Suddenly, her face was pressed against buttons. She blinked against crisp white linen and breathed in Calvin Klein Eternity. Veronica felt Ian's hands gently standing her upright, and she tucked a curl behind her ear, blushing.

"Oops, sorry," she said, searching the grass with her bare foot for her sandal.

"Here you go." Ian bent and held it for her like the prince slipping the glass slipper on Cinderella.

"Prince Butter Knife," Veronica thought, shocked that her years-ago label for him was the first thing that came to mind.

"What?" Ian asked, standing again.

"What?" Veronica reddened. *Crap, did I say that out loud?* "Oh, God. Nothing. Thanks for catching me—I mean, for not letting me fall."

"Quite a graceful way to avoid answering my questions." Ian smiled with kindness spilling from his eyes. "Let's get a drink and you can tell me about your life."

They sat on a white-cushioned wicker couch on the low-cut lawn. Vases of late summer black-eyed Susans and white wild-flowers decorated the accent tables. Ian drank his beer from a glass and Veronica sipped a fruity pink cocktail.

"I've forgotten what you asked me," she said, linking one ankle behind the other and angling herself to face him. "Well, I've kind of forgotten."

"Is there something you're trying to forget?"

"No, that's not it. Oh, what the hell, we haven't seen each other in a couple of years—why is that, by the way?"

"You're stalling."

"Fine. I may as well just lay it out there. I've been seeing this guy but I'm not sure how to introduce him to my parents. He's not exactly the kind of guy they expect me to be with."

"What kind of guy is he?" Ian's long, thin finger traced a drip of condensation on his glass.

"He's amazing, he's so good to me. I feel happy when I'm with him and lost when I'm not." Veronica's shoulders relaxed under the silky straps.

"So your parents wouldn't expect you to be with someone who makes you happy and who cares for you? You're losing me."

Veronica exhaled, then leaned forward and lowered her voice. "He's an electrician." She looked up, waiting for Ian's response, but his face remained open and thoughtful. Veronica glanced around the party, taking note of her parents' positions, then continued. "He runs his own company. He went to college but never finished—he was the first in his family to go, but he's still in a blue-collar profession. He drives a huge old car, a Cadillac or something with ugly red leather inside." She remembered when he'd polished the seats to gleaming before taking her out one time. The leather was so slick that at the first right turn, Veronica slid across the seat, the loose seat belt stretched, and she landed almost at Joey's side before the car straightened and sent her careening back to the passenger door. Their cheeks were streaked with tears from laughter and Joey had to pull the car over to catch his breath.

"You're smiling at that ugly car," Ian pointed out.

"Yeah. And his family is so different from mine. They're so much more, I don't know, down-to-earth. He's one hundred percent Italian and his parents and most of his aunts and uncles were born in Italy." The skin around Veronica's eyes crinkled and the words poured out of her with enthusiasm. "They're great and so much fun, really loud, but fun. And they welcome me and make me feel comfortable. He's an incredible cook, too."

"Sounds like this guy's a real problem: company owner, responsible, good cook, friendly with a fun family, and he makes you laugh." Ian smirked.

"Forget it."

Ian reached for her arm, his hand soft and nonthreatening against her bare skin, and she relaxed against the cushion, sighing.

"I'm sorry for my sarcasm. Our families have some set ideas about things, it's true, but we both know that even with all these fancy parties and high-end finery"—Ian swept his hand out like a ringmaster introducing the sword swallowers—"appearances aren't everything. Even though we want our parents' approval, it's more important to find what makes us happy. That's what really matters."

He looked to his lap and twirled the glass in his hands.

"What?" Veronica asked. "Your turn."

Ian looked around the party as Veronica had, taking in the locations of his parents and noting who was nearby, and then he moved closer.

"I get it. I understand what you're feeling more than you know."

Veronica waited. Ian shifted, glanced behind her, and inhaled audibly.

"Only a few people know. I haven't told my parents, either, because, same as you, it doesn't fit into the way they think things should be." He looked down, then right into Veronica's eyes. "I'm gay."

"I guess that would be hard to tell them. Have you found someone? Someone who makes you happy?"

He nodded.

Veronica thought about the AIDS epidemic and all the questions and uncertainties. She had seen the trailer and news coverage surrounding the new Tom Hanks movie, *Philadelphia,* coming out in December, and it worried her for Ian.

He nodded again. "This is part of why we haven't seen each other. Though, I wish we had, you've always been easy to talk to. I've had a lot to think about, to figure out."

Ian handed his empty beer glass to a passing server. He stood to return a wave from someone across the rosebushes, and then he leaned down to give Veronica a good-bye peck on the cheek. Through her curls, he said, "I get it, but stop hiding your electrician."

Veronica watched Ian's skinny body walk away, his pressed khaki pants loose at his hips. His appearance didn't match his confidence, she thought, feeling the familiar fondness for him. She took in the sloping lawn and the tent draped with flowers, filled with bejeweled and coiffed guests. They sparkled, sipped, and small-talked. She tried to picture Ian there with another man. Impossible. Then she envisioned Joey mingling among them with a maroon button-down, his stiff, gelled hair, and his gold chain. Using every bit of her power of visualization, she could not make him fit into the scene.

Chapter 39

THE BUZZER STARTLED AMY as it always did. Andrew got up from beside her and pressed the talk button. "Yeah?"

"Food's here," the doorman squawked through the intercom.

"Okay. I'll be right down."

As the apartment door closed behind Andrew, the buzzer zapped again. Amy jumped slightly, then walked to the button, laughing at herself for being jarred every time.

"Um, food's here from another guy?"

"Thanks, Sam. Andrew's on his way down, he'll get them both."

They had decided on sushi and Indian food because they couldn't choose. It was a cozy Sunday evening. They had spent the rare free day together meandering in Central Park and around the city. They'd stopped to rent videos, Andrew letting Amy choose, and after much deliberation, she finally selected *The Firm* and *Sleepless in Seattle*—a little suspense and a little romance.

"Sam cracked up at the delivery guys lining up for us tonight." Andrew tossed his wallet on the side table and set the armfuls of stapled brown bags on the coffee table. "This has been a really fun day, Aim. I've missed the two of us just hanging out together." He kissed her temple, started the movie, and sat on the edge of the couch while Amy laid out the food containers.

"Oh, almost forgot, I got yesterday's mail. Here." He laid a postcard with a photograph of a sunset behind the Carrier Dome on the table. "That's all there was. I've never known a guy who writes so often, and he doesn't even really say anything."

"You read them?" Amy held the postcard up like she was guarding a winning poker hand.

"It's not like they're in an envelope or anything. I mean, the mailman and the guy who sorts our mail could read Matt's notes, but they're so dull who would care?" Andrew tucked a piece of tuna sashimi into his mouth.

"They're not dull! He tells me about things in his life and asks me about mine," Amy said defensively. She read the words written in Matt's familiar, angular handwriting.

The TriStar Pictures Pegasus ran toward them on the small TV screen as *Sleepless in Seattle* started. Amy read Matt's note one more time; he asked her about going up for homecoming in October. She hadn't thought about it but nodded at the idea.

"Let's go to homecoming this year." Amy dabbed a paper napkin at a drip of soy sauce on her lip. "Then again, you already know the idea from reading Matt's postcard."

"Sure, sounds fun. Your movie's on." Andrew portioned some basmati rice onto his plate and began scooping the lumpy green mush and the red sauce with chickpeas over it.

When Annie Reed was hiding in the broom closet with her radio and the red telephone cord hanging out, Amy said for the third time since the movie began, "I love Meg Ryan." Andrew laughed, hugging her closer to him. The boxes and dishes, napkins and containers, lay on the coffee table, rice drying on the plates. Andrew had tried to tidy it up, but he let Amy overrule him, snuggling up and dimming the lights.

Just before Meg Ryan and Tom Hanks finally meet on top of the Empire State Building on Valentine's Day, the phone rang.

They paused the movie, listening and waiting for the answering machine to pick up.

"Amy? Are you there?" Veronica's voice asked through the room.

"Go ahead," Andrew said as he stacked the plates and gathered the empty boxes to take to the garbage chute.

"You're back," Amy answered, and strolled to the window, missing the view of the Empire State Building that Veronica could be seeing as they spoke. "How was your weekend?"

"Well, I thought about everything with Joey the whole weekend, and I think I'm going to invite him to my friend Bitsy Everett's wedding next month."

"That's great! I'm sure he'll be very excited to hear that," Amy said, returning to the couch. "Want to go to homecoming this fall? Andrew and I are planning to go. Maybe you can bring Joey to that, too."

"Let's take one big journey into my past at a time, but that does sound like fun. I already booked a room in case we wanted to go, remember?"

Andrew returned to the apartment. He put his mouth next to Amy's and called into the receiver, "Hi, Veronica. My turn again, I'm hogging Amy tonight, bye."

"She says hi and good-bye."

Clicking the off button, Amy tossed the phone onto the cleared table.

"She's bringing Joey to a wedding next month with all of her old high school friends."

"It's about time," Andrew said, reaching for the VCR remote. "I don't get why he hangs around waiting, not knowing where he stands."

Amy looked directly at him. "Like me?"

"What are you talking about? Like you, what?"

"Like me not knowing where I stand."

"You know where you stand—we live together for God's sake. I love you, you know that."

"Yes, but are we ever going to get married? We've been together for five years. Owen and Holly have already been married for almost a year and they only met two years ago, and now Karen and Mark and Molly and Michael are married, too."

Andrew blew air out, letting it vibrate his lips.

"Forget it, just hit play."

"Amy, let's not ruin a great day. We'll get married. We will. I love you. Trying to get this promotion is killing me, but one day, we will."

He hugged her to him, optimistically kissing her all over her face and neck.

"Maybe I'll even meet you on the top of the Empire State Building on Valentine's Day." His words pulled Amy's face to his like a magnet; her eyebrows lifted and a smile played at the corners of her lips. As the screen filled with Tom Hanks's face looking completely in love, she laid her head against Andrew's chest, appeased one more time.

Chapter 40

VERONICA TAPPED THE LUXURIOUS wedding invitation between her fingers. She gazed out the window as the highway streaked past the black Eldorado. Then she added her foot to the rhythmic tapping sound, hitting it against the dash.

"You're a real one-woman band over there." Joey grinned, drumming out a complementary beat on the steering wheel.

"What? Oh, sorry." Veronica stilled herself, sitting on her hands. "It's just four more exits, I think."

"Mystic exit, right? Okay. So the bride is Bitsy, but she goes by Elizabeth now so I shouldn't call her Bitsy," Joey quizzed himself.

"I should never have told you that. Don't let that slip out or she'll kill me. We haven't been allowed to call her Bitsy since senior year, when she tried to reinvent herself for college. It never really stuck, but she practically had a nervous breakdown when the yearbook editor left a 'Bitsy' caption in there."

"Okay, got it, and Elizabeth is marrying Jackson, who is some publishing bigwig. His family has mountains of money and he grew up with more pimples than they have dollars."

"Oh, God, I'm in trouble. You wouldn't mention that, would you? I think I gave you way too many background details." Veronica was tapping the invitation against her fingers again.

Joey laughed out loud. "Man, you're a nervous Nellie about this wedding, as Aunt Tessie would say."

"I'm not nervous," Veronica said flatly, and laid the invitation on the seat beside her. "I just haven't seen this group in years."

"You'll be the talk of the wedding, you're so beautiful, and I'm afraid you may outshine Bitsy the Bride."

Veronica fought it, but then she chuckled, relaxing. "How do you always know how to make me laugh? One mile, exit ninety."

They wound through the old whaling town, following the directions Veronica had handwritten on the back of the wedding envelope. "Park over there. It's such a nice day, we can walk a little bit," she said, pointing to an empty area in the back of the parking lot. "This is where the reception is. If we park here, we can walk to the church and then already be here after the reception."

"Very efficient planning," Joey teased, parking and following her toward the church.

Veronica smiled and greeted friends briefly as she directed Joey to a pew in the back of the sanctuary. From her seat, she politely nodded and returned small waves as long-ago classmates sought eye contact. When the ceremony was over and Elizabeth and Jackson had exited the church, Veronica excused herself to find a restroom. Joey waited at the doorway, observing the receiving line, the birdseed pelting the couple, the crowd dispersing, and then the couple riding away in their Bentley, until Veronica returned.

"Sorry I took so long. My stomach's a little queasy."

"Are you okay?"

"Thanks, I'll be fine."

Looping his arm around her, they walked back to the Eldorado to retrieve the professionally wrapped wedding present. Veronica straightened the new tie and smoothed the white shirt she had bought Joey for the wedding. Finally, she patted the lapel of his gray suit and, clutching the gift with both arms, led the way toward the reception.

The room, elaborately decorated in an upscale coastal theme, overflowed with flowers in whites and pale yellows, which perfectly coordinated with the bridesmaids' dresses, which were perfectly coordinated with the napkins, which were perfectly coordinated with the groomsmen's bow ties and cummerbunds. Carefully placed seashells ornamented the centerpieces, and place cards were neatly hand-calligraphed. The band played favorite oldies intermingled with versions of Top 40 ballad hits, from Eric Clapton to Boyz II Men to Mariah Carey. Veronica placed the gift on the designated table and, after scanning the place cards for who they were seated with, located table number seven.

"Are we sitting with anyone good or are we relegated to the cousin table?"

Veronica's face remained serious. "We're with some old friends from our group"—she paused—"and an ex-boyfriend."

"Don't worry, I can take him, whoever he is. I'll knock him out if he makes even one move for you." Joey grinned, putting up mock fists.

"Stop it," Veronica whispered. She lightly grabbed his hands and pushed them down. Glancing around, she surveyed the roomful of faces from her past.

"Which one is he? Wait, let me guess. I bet he's a real preppy boy, but that's about everyone in here," Joey said with a hushed voice as he examined the guests milling around the room in pastels and post–Labor Day madras. He noticed someone looking straight his way. Joey recognized how he was using his buddy as a shield in a typical move, pretending to talk and laugh while he stalked his ex-girlfriend's boyfriend. This was the guy. He had beach-blond hair neatly combed across his forehead, meticulously styled to look casual.

"That's him. In the pink shirt by the bar." Joey smiled. "Want a glass of wine?" he offered quietly.

"Um, yeah, but how did you know that was Eric? You're not going to say anything to him, are you?"

Joey grinned and Veronica straightened her shoulders, creating a small space between her and Joey.

"Have a little faith," he teased, but Veronica remained stiff and serious.

"Cabernet, please," Veronica said with a sigh.

JOEY STOOD IN LINE at the bar while dates, juggling handfuls of drinks, balanced their way through the waiting mass of men.

"Never seems to be enough bartenders at these things," Joey commented to the guy beside him who wore a pale blue shirt under his suit jacket; a Rolex peeked out at his wrist. The guy grunted with a nod, then turned away and clapped a neighboring guy on the back. Joey rolled his eyes and stepped up to place his order, catching the pink-shirted ex in the corner of his eye. He maneuvered away from the bar line and sipped his vodka, straight up with a twist.

He wandered his way back toward table seven, where he saw Veronica's handbag on the table, her wrap hung over the back of the corresponding chair. Browsing the room, he found her standing just outside the ballroom doors on the terrace among a group of women. He admired the dip in the back of her dress. She worried it was too revealing, but Joey had reassured her and repeatedly complimented her until she conceded and wore the dress.

The September sun glinted off the water of Long Island Sound and the smell of salty air poured in through the doorway. Couples and girlfriends were squeezing their way back into the ballroom while others jockeyed to claim space outdoors. Joey stood aside, allowing a group to pass. From there he could see Veronica and he heard a burst of her laughter, a sound he craved when they were apart. Her voice carried in on the breeze, making him smile, proud to be here with her. The entry was clearing and Joey moved forward to join her.

"No, no, we're just friends. I could never go out with him—he's just my electrician," Veronica told the semicircle of friends. "You know, I got the plus-one invitation and needed someone to bring."

He stood frozen. He held her glass of wine extended toward her, unable to retract his arm. He watched the widening eyes of her friends; one tried to discreetly catch Veronica's eye and, with a guarded hand, she made a slicing motion across her throat.

"He's really not my type, you know," Veronica continued, unaware as another friend stared at Joey without disguise, her mouth gaping. "Why do you all look so shocked? I told you we're not together."

Veronica turned and gasped with her whole body, knocking her friend's drink down her dress. She opened her mouth to speak but was numb. Joey placed her glass of wine on the cocktail table beside her, then turned and walked away.

Joey felt dizzy and focused on making his feet move one after the other. He walked with his back erect and his eyes fixed on the main lobby door they had entered. He crossed the ballroom in deliberate strides.

"Hey, buddy, watch it," Pink Shirt called after him, dabbing at his hand with a cocktail napkin.

Joey burst out into the parking lot. The afternoon sun was high and he felt spotlighted in its brightness. His throat clenched and his chest heaved like he was onstage alone and had forgotten his lines, exposed and vulnerable. He heard his name in the distance and kept his back to the building. He squeezed his eyes, then wiped at them with the back of his hand. When he reached the car, he leaned against the hood for support and gulped for air. The black metal burned under his palms and he pressed harder, wishing that pain would eclipse the pain in his heart.

VERONICA SAW JOEY'S BACK confidently retreating from her, watched Eric say something to him as he passed. She couldn't think clearly, yet thoughts overwhelmed her mind and fear over-flowed her heart. Her head throbbed like a warning light in thick fog. Her vision was singular and she followed Joey's back as fast as her heeled shoes allowed.

"Joey!" She forced her mouth to form the word, to call out to him. "Joey!"

Breathless, Veronica yanked off her shoes and, crossing her hands over her chest, ran to him. "Joey."

She stopped short, leaving a distance between them. Now that she had raced to catch him, she couldn't speak. No words, or too many words, scrambled around inside her and she was afraid of what she'd done. Joey stood neutral and hard to read. He stretched to his full height and pursed his lips, holding in anger, rebukes, or tears.

"Joey, I'm so sorry. I don't know why I said that. You know that I love you. You know that, right?" Veronica begged him, willing her hurtful words erased.

The sun beat down on the exposed skin of Veronica's back. The squawk of a seagull overhead and the faint sound of music from the building gave her the feeling of being outside of something, of life continuing around them, though to her, it had stopped.

"Joey?" she pleaded.

His chest rose as he inhaled, then with a tender voice, in almost a whisper, he said, "I can see you are trying to sabotage a really good thing. You know that I love you. I love you very much, but you need to figure this out on your own." He handed her his car keys. "I'm leaving. Think about what you want because this isn't about me. I know who I am and I know what I want. I'll get a cab to the train. Leave the keys with the garage attendant when you get back."

"Joey," she sobbed.

He shoved his hands into his pockets and walked away.

Chapter 41

"DON'T GO KISSING ANYONE, Aim." Andrew nudged Amy as he carried her bag down to the sidewalk to meet Veronica. "I know how much you love making out."

Amy punched his arm and reached up to kiss him. "I save all my kissing for you. I wish you could come. All the Sigma Chis will wonder where I'm hiding you and you'll miss the big homecoming game."

"Wish I could, too, but work beckons. I called a few of the guys this week to let them know I've got a deadline and asked them to keep an eye on you."

"It sounds like you don't trust me. You know I've always told you the truth."

"Of course I trust you, I just want you to be safe." He patted her rear. "Have a great time. I'll be waiting for you to come home Sunday night."

Veronica pulled up in her parents' shiny new car, on loan for the weekend. "Hi, you two. Ready to go, Amy?"

"Whoa! Nice wheels. I can't believe you're driving a Lexus. You're one of the first people I know with one." Andrew examined it with admiration. "Awesome."

With a final kiss good-bye, Amy slid into the front seat while

Andrew waved, his eyes caressing the car. Veronica drove cautiously, obeying the traffic rules and keeping within the posted speed limits, even as Amy teased and urged her to go faster. They alternated between long, analytical discussions about Joey and the Incident and loud, carefree sing-alongs. At the first sign for Syracuse, fifty miles outside of the city, the sky darkened and a few raindrops speckled the windshield. The duo laughed at the familiar bad weather and broke into new snacks for the final leg of the trip.

"I just don't know what to do," Veronica said for the umpteenth time as she stuck a potato chip into her mouth. "Should I just knock on his door? No, I couldn't do that. What would I say? I've tried writing him a couple letters but they never sound right. What if I call him? Should I call him?"

Amy inserted a few yeses and words into Veronica's monologues as she tried to work things out, speaking her options and feelings aloud, reviewing her actions over and over.

"I feel horrible, I was such a jerk. He probably has a new girlfriend. I've totally lost him, I'm sure of it. And all because he didn't fit into some dumb outward idea of what I expected in a boyfriend. But he *was* what I want in a boyfriend in a million ways. I was so stupid. He is—well, was—the best boyfriend. I don't know what made me lie—I never lie. How could I have lied and been so awful?

"I felt so judged and so looked down on by all those old friends, and it just came out. I was sick to my stomach the whole time, but I still kept denying we were together. It was really hard to say those things, but these girls wouldn't stop asking me about the 'slick guy' I was with. They said it with such disdain, but that's no reason to be dishonest. I can't believe I lied. I can't believe I let appearances and people I don't care about make me hurt Joey so badly. I deserved to get caught, I deserve to feel miserable." Amy let her talk, recognizing her crisis of integrity.

"Do you know I haven't seen him once in the building? Actually, I did see his back one time in the lobby, but I couldn't even say hello to him. I was so ashamed and also scared of what he might say to me. I just watched him. I was standing by the elevator and he walked out. Walked away like he did in Mystic." Veronica went on until they came to the Syracuse exit and she pointed the car through the familiar streets.

"It's strange to be back here, isn't it? Hard to believe we graduated a year and a half ago," Veronica commented, gathering herself as they passed M Street and turned up Crouse to the only on-campus hotel. Thanks to her efficient planning, Veronica had secured a room a year prior on the chance they decided to return for homecoming weekend. "Let's check in, clean up, and head out," she said with an unconvincing brightness.

Amy squeezed her friend's arm. "I'm sorry, V, I wish I could make it better for you."

"MATT!" AMY SPOTTED HIM from across the quad and ran. It was early Saturday afternoon. Amy and Veronica had caught up with their Kappa sisters on Friday night, and then, after sleeping in, they had wandered the campus, went to part of the homecoming game, and shopped on M Street until Amy's designated meeting time with Matt.

The space and time since their last visit vanished with the ease of true friendship. They settled beneath a tree on the speckled blanket of orange and yellow leaves as Amy took in Matt's thick eyebrows, his Traveling Wilburys T-shirt under a plaid flannel button-down, his worn-through Levi's, and the familiar stubble emerging from his fresh shave.

"You're still wearing those Converse high-tops and ratty old jeans. Going right from rocker to grunge, are you?" Amy joked, sticking a fingertip into the hole in his knee.

"Nah, always rock 'n' roll for me. You know fashion's not my thing. I'm just a computer geek wearing what's comfortable, at least outside of the office."

When he smiled at her, Amy felt like she was the most important person in the world. Matt's focus was intent, affable, and comfortable.

"I miss you," she said. "Writing and calling isn't the same as sharing our everyday details. We used to know each other's schedules and the small things in our lives, but now I feel like we can only get to the bigger stuff. So, let's have it, fill me in on the details."

Amy hesitated, then came out with what she most wanted to know: "Where's Leslie?" He and Patty had broken up a few weeks after the New Year's Eve party and Matt never willingly shared anything about his dating life with her. He finally mentioned Leslie after Amy's prying over the summer.

Matt shrugged. "We just dated a few times, it was nothing serious."

Amy worked to keep the relief from her face and voice, and said only, "Oh."

"I have something for you," Matt said, diverting the discussion. He dug into his pocket and pulled out a tiny organza pouch.

"What? Why?" Amy carefully untied the ribbon that cinched it closed.

"For your birthday. It's only a few weeks away and I won't see you until Christmas."

"You're so thoughtful, Matt." She jiggled the pouch, letting a small silver Santa Claus charm fall into her palm.

"It's for Train Santa, to represent you coming to my mom's funeral and for always remembering her with me. You know, I'm still amazed by the strange appearance that day. It's hard to believe it was over a year ago."

"As weird as it was, that jolly ol' elf comes to my mind way too often. Thank you. Look, I always wear the bracelet." She tugged up her sleeve to show him. Unclasping it, Matt helped her add the charm to the others he'd chosen since graduation: an apple for New York City, a newspaper for her first big story. She wiggled her wrist, letting the meaningful tokens jingle.

Music blared from somewhere beyond the quad and bounced off the buildings. Amy picked up a newly fallen leaf and spun it by its stem. As she watched it twirl between her fingers, she asked, "So . . . Leslie didn't work out, are you dating anyone now?"

Matt playfully rolled his eyes and leaned back against the tree. As Amy looked up from her spinning leaf, a flash of brown streaked in her peripheral vision. Too fast for understanding, the whirling object cracked into her temple, hurling her backward onto the ground. She couldn't focus her eyes—there were only blurred colors. For a moment, she wondered where she was, then she heard someone calling her name, a cacophony of voices, pressure on her head. Her head ached and she lifted her hand toward it, but even as she felt skin, her head had no sensation.

"I can't feel my head." Amy formed the words, but they sounded outside of her.

"It's okay, Amy, I have my hand there, you're touching my hand," Matt explained softly.

She held on to his hand and his voice among the chatter, letting her eyes fall closed again.

"Is she okay, man?"

"Shit! She's really bleeding a lot!"

"God, I'm so sorry, I can't believe that got her square in the head."

"Why'd you miss the toss, asshole?"

"I'll get her to the health center." She heard Matt's voice among the ebbing tones. "Here, take your weapon."

"Matt? My head hurts. What happened?"

"You got pegged by a rather fierce football. Go slow, I've got you." As she tried to sit up, Matt held one hand to her bleeding head and the other guided her. "Take it easy, rest there, don't sit up all the way yet."

"Your shirt." Amy saw splotches of blood down the front of him and realized that he had pulled the long shirtsleeve past his hand and was using the balled-up cuff to press against her bleeding head.

"Aw, this old thing, you told me yourself I need to update my clothes."

Amy leaned against his chest, getting her balance. Matt shifted and followed her head with his palm. She felt his free arm wrap around her and sensed his breathing slow until it seemed he was almost holding it. She relaxed into him and they were both still. Beneath her ear, his heart beat in sync with the pulsing at her temple. She breathed deeply, filling her lungs from their very bottom and smelling Matt, before she leaned back, sitting upright.

"I think I can stand up now."

Matt startled and carefully peered under his sleeve at Amy's head. Blood soaked the plaid fabric and trickled into her hair when he released the pressure.

"It's still bleeding. Here, let me hold your head this way—yup, like that—then wrap your arm around my waist, okay, lean on me, go easy," Matt coached, positioning her. Walking together as if connected in a three-legged race, they started for the health center. Amy realized that the only other time she'd been to the campus clinic was when she had a stomach virus junior year. Matt had taken her that time, too, borrowing a friend's car while Andrew gave a class presentation.

After a short distance, Matt asked, "Do you need to rest? Sit here a minute."

He guided her to a smooth stone plank covered in fall leaves.

It was a moment before Amy realized they were sitting on the Kissing Bench. The bench was a gift from the graduating class of 1912; the tradition evolved through the years, but the legend was that a couple who kissed on the bench would eventually get married. Amy thought of the time she had tugged Andrew and, only half teasingly, had him kiss her while they sat on the bench, which was then covered in an early December snow. She wanted to believe in the tradition but wondered when Andrew's "someday" would arrive.

"HI, MATT. OH MY God, what's all that blood? What happened to you, Amy?" Seeing Matt's stained shirts and the white bandage on Amy's face, Veronica covered the few yards across their hotel room, repeating, "What happened?"

The stat care visit had taken hours, but Matt and Amy condensed the saga for Veronica. They decided to forgo their night out on M Street and instead ordered Chinese food and sat on the two double beds to eat.

"Are we seriously getting old?" Veronica asked, catching the dangling noodles with chopsticks and tucking them little by little into her mouth. "Who stays in at our age?"

"Either we're old or it's stitches and a concussion keeping us from hitting the town."

Veronica coughed on her noodles, laughing. "Right, forgot for a minute why we're sitting in a hotel room on a Saturday night of homecoming weekend."

"You should go out, Veronica," Amy insisted again. "This shouldn't have to ruin your weekend. You, too, Matt, you both should go out."

Ignoring her continued urging, Matt said, "That concussion sure hasn't affected your appetite," and he scooped more broccoli and chicken onto her paper plate.

"Oh, I almost forgot," Veronica said, then finished chewing and swallowing before she continued. "I ran into Kate this afternoon, Kate Anula from Brewster? Guess what she told me."

"How is she?"

"Great, she just got married."

"That's quick. I got a letter from her last spring and she said she'd met her steak knife. It only took her months, and I'm still waiting on my steak knife years later."

"Just another example of how the whole fork, knife, and spoon thing doesn't work. Anyway, they're both teachers in the town where she grew up. But that's not the part I wanted to tell you."

"Steak knife? Spoons? What's that?" Matt asked.

Veronica hit her forehead with her palm. "Oh, brother."

There weren't many guys who knew about the Utensil Classification System, but year after year it trickled out. One night sophomore year, Amy and some Kappa sisters started ticking off the types of guys they'd spotted that night. Andrew said it was like he was listening to another language; he could understand each individual word but couldn't decipher them to make any sense. In hysterics, the girls dramatically filled him in on the forks, knives, spoons, and everything in between, all while Veronica twisted a curl, waiting for the descriptions she'd heard a million times to end.

"What am I?" was Andrew's first question.

Veronica had answered him: "It doesn't matter, the whole thing's gotten out of control. Your girlfriend thinks she can label any guy with this system of hers. It's ludicrous."

"Sounds a little crazy, but what am I anyway?" Andrew turned to Amy.

Veronica sighed as Amy assured him that he was her steak knife.

Once Andrew found out, though, he would ask Amy to peg someone on the spot, never with any discretion. Whenever a guy

LEAH DeCesare

heard someone else being called a butcher knife or a serving spoon, he would put down his pool cue or his pizza slice and instantly be curious. "What am I?" he'd ask as soon as he got a whiff of the categories.

Amy was shocked, sprinkling a few grains of rice on the hotel bedspread as she scooped out more. "You've really never heard me talk about the UCS?" Then, to Veronica, she asked coyly, "Should we tell him?"

Veronica shrugged. "Don't involve me, you know how I feel about it. Go ahead, you're going to tell him anyway, but I'm warning you, Matt, you're about to peek into another one of Amy's romantic notions. I can't convince her that the whole thing falsely categorizes people and follows all sorts of arbitrary rules."

Amy jumped in before Veronica could continue her arguments against the UCS. "There are three types of guys: forks, knives, and spoons . . ."

Throughout the summary, Matt was shaking his head but smiling, appearing both intrigued and puzzled. Amy summed up: "Basically, cocky jerks are forks, nerdy geeks are spoons, and knives are the biggest category, where we'll find Mr. Right. And that's our shorthand way to label guys."

"Speak for yourself," Veronica muttered.

Matt was quiet for a moment, his thumb stroking his jaw. "So, it sounds like I'm a spoon." He looked back and forth between the silverware labeler and the disbeliever. "But just because I'm a computer geek doesn't mean I can't be someone's knife, you know. I'm not sure your system would hold up under much scrutiny. I might have to agree with Veronica on this one."

Veronica burst out laughing and reached over the white cartons to give Matt a high-five. "And that is why we don't tell guys about this," Amy said, deflated, "you just don't get it. Guys are always analyzing themselves and no one ever likes it unless they're a golden steak knife."

Matt chuckled. "Fine. I'm a spoon and proud of it. Pass the lo mein, please."

Veronica handed over the container from the array balanced on the bed in front of her. "I still haven't told you what Kate said."

Amy nodded, her mouth full.

"She ran into Jenny last night."

"She's here? How's she doing?" Amy mumbled through noodles.

"Jenny only told Kate that she works in a restaurant."

Matt followed the conversation with his eyes, eating an egg roll.

"She asked Kate if she had your New York phone number."

"My number? Why?" Amy's forehead wrinkled and she winced as her stitches pulled beneath the gauze.

"I asked Kate that, too. She didn't know, but she said that Jenny also asked about you and Andrew."

"Hmm." Amy chewed the end of a chopstick.

"Kate told her that you're living together and that you're waiting for a ring."

"She said that? He keeps me guessing, that's for sure. Did I tell you he mentioned going to the top of the Empire State Building on Valentine's Day?"

"That would be right up your romantic alley. Maybe that's when he'll propose." Veronica's enthusiasm fizzled as that triggered another thought. "I really blew it with Joey. He made last Valentine's Day like one of your fairy tales. I don't know what I'm going to do. I should never have lied."

The phone rang from the nightstand like an intruder. The red message light fluttered with the ringing. Amy's mouth was full;

she looked to Veronica to answer, but she was locked in with cartons of food on the bed in a crescent around her. Matt was sitting on Amy's bed, leaning against the headboard. He rested his plate on his lap, reached over, and picked up the phone.

"Hello?" Matt shrugged and repeated, "Hello?"

He covered the mouthpiece. "No one there," he said, clarifying the obvious, then tried again. "Hello? Hello?"

"Oh, just hang up, Matt," Amy said, and giggled. "It's probably some drunk kid making prank calls. Pass the dumplings, please."

Chapter 42

PULLING UP TO THE FRONT OF Amy's building, Veronica said, "It was fun going back to school together. Tell Andrew I'm sorry for getting you back late, but I couldn't pass up Sunday morning Bloody Marys at Faegan's. Besides I really needed to have you to myself this weekend. Thanks for listening to me go on and on about Joey. You're a good friend, Amy."

Amy hugged her, then hopped out and bounded into the lobby toward the elevators.

"Hi, Sam," she said to the doorman, and the ding of the opening elevator doors welcomed her.

She knocked on their apartment door. "Hey, Drew, it's me," she called.

She dropped her bag and fumbled to find her keys, wondering where Andrew would be. Before she could unlock it, the door swung open, and she greeted Andrew by throwing her whole body into his. He stiffened and held his arms at his sides, waiting for her to let go, and then he closed the door and turned abruptly toward her.

"What are you so cheerful about? You come back late and happy after spending a weekend all snuggled up with your nerdy boyfriend." Andrew's tone cut and the accusation stunned Amy into wordlessness. Memories flickered of how he'd snapped at her before their vacation and the way he spoke to his mother at Easter.

"I can't believe I've been so naive. All this time I trusted you when you said he was just a friend and right under my nose he's sending you postcards and calling you, I should've guessed it, but I couldn't imagine my girlfriend being interested in someone like him."

A vein on Andrew's forehead pushed itself through his skin, pulsing blue. Amy had never witnessed this intensity in him. She stared from the popping vein to his eyes and shook her head, making it throb slightly.

Amy found her voice and it rose in defense. "What are you talking about? Matt has never been anything but a friend. He's a kind and decent person and has never so much as tried to hold my hand."

"That's not what I heard."

"I have no idea what you mean." Amy's head hurt, and she pressed her bandage and moved from the entry to sit on the couch. Her motion shifted Andrew's attention to her injury.

"What's that? What happened?" Andrew sat beside her, his voice softened. "Did he do something to you? Did he hit you?"

"Are you nuts? What is wrong with you?" Amy spat the words at him, ignoring the pain it caused. "I was talking—nothing but talking—with Matt on the quad when some guys whipped a football that whacked me in the head. It wouldn't stop gushing blood so we went to the health center and I got a few stitches. Matt is a friend, a really great friend, but that's all. Why are you so suspicious all of a sudden? What's going on, Drew?"

He folded forward, leaning his head into his open palms. As if there could be only one voice between them, when Amy found hers, Andrew went mute. Her insides vibrated like a nervous foot tapping. Seeing his hunched body motionless beside her, she suddenly felt sad for him. Slowly, like reaching to touch an unknown dog, she rested her hand upon his back and felt the rise of his breath, the exhale.

"What is it? What's wrong?" she whispered. "I haven't seen you like this before."

In the slowest of movements, Andrew straightened himself, leaving his hands over his face. He rose until his back was against the sofa and his head fell back.

"Shit, Aim, I'm sorry."

She sat still, waiting for more. Andrew dropped his hands to his lap and released his breath in a loud sigh.

"I'm sorry I yelled at you, sorry I didn't trust you. I love you and don't want to lose you. When Buzz called and said he saw you and Matt together, I've been going crazy here waiting—"

"Buzz? I didn't see him all weekend. Why would he say that?"

"He said he saw you and Matt hugging and all over each other in the quad, and that Matt wouldn't let go of you. Then when I called your hotel room Saturday night and Matt answered, I just thought . . ." Andrew drifted off, visibly trying to disassemble the picture he'd conjured and reorder the pieces into a new image of truth.

Amy let a small laugh escape; it wasn't a laugh of humor or joy, but of relief.

"Chinese food with Veronica," Amy said, and Andrew wrinkled his brow. "Saturday night. Veronica, Matt, and I stayed in because of my head, and we had Chinese food in our room. And as for Buzz, he should mind his own business. He doesn't know what he saw, because all Matt was doing was keeping me from bleeding everywhere. He should've just come over to say hello. Your buddy can be the worst gossip, and he really got it wrong."

"I'm so sorry." Andrew threw his arms around her, trying to get a do-over of her original greeting. He gingerly avoided her bruised forehead but pulled her to him so tightly that she had to strain to take a breath. "I'm sorry," he repeated into her hair.

They made their way to get ready for bed and the workweek ahead. Amy left her bag packed and picked through it for what she needed, then went to brush her teeth. The toothpaste was squeezed in the middle. Andrew always made sure it was neat and flattened from the bottom. With her finger, she wiped a blob of toothpaste off the tube. *Andrew really isn't himself,* she thought.

Amy chatted about the weekend as she slipped into her pajamas and dabbed lotion on her face keeping it away from her bandages. "We went to an amazing school. I'd forgotten just how great it is. The music blaring all over campus, the Crouse chimes ringing, the craziness of M Street, the Greek houses on the hill and on Walnut—it felt like we'd just left and at the same time like we've been gone forever. It's such a strange trick of time.

"Oh, you changed the sheets. Wow! I go away for the weekend and you become Mr. Domestic? I like it." She slid in beside him and thanked him with a kiss. "Do you remember kissing me on the Kissing Bench? You know what that means, right?"

Andrew nodded with a half-smile and shut off the bedside lamp. He rolled toward Amy, hugging her to him and molding his body to fit hers.

"I'm sorry," he murmured again.

As Andrew's body flinched into sleep, Amy lay awake thinking about her weekend, and her welcome home.

Chapter 43

A NEW HABIT, VERONICA slowed her pace when she walked past Joey's apartment door. She was both afraid and hungry to see him. She held her breath, listening for any sign of him on the other side of the door. His absence had created an echo in her life, a hole she had dug all on her own. She unlocked her apartment and glanced down the hall again before letting the door click behind her.

"Chelsea?" She sighed into the quiet, relieved that she was home alone.

Dropping her workbag and kicking off her heels, she hung up her suit jacket and sat at her desk. She pulled out the last thick, creamy sheet of Crane stationery. Underneath were ten unused envelopes and nine half-completed, semi-started letters to Joey. This time she wanted to get it right. She pictured him finding her note, forgiving her and loving her again. She had lain awake countless nights composing the most beautiful letters, and each night, she fell asleep envisioning herself slipping that eloquent note under his door, the letter that would fix everything. But when she woke, the words were gone. She wanted to write how she missed how he made her feel, how she felt more truly herself with him than anywhere or with anyone else. She wanted him to know that she loved him, that she really loved him for who he was, just the way he was.

In the months since he left her standing in Mystic, she realized that he was exactly the right person for her. Why had she struggled to fully accept him? That was the kernel that she had worried and examined since September. In that time, she had figured out what she wanted and she knew that she wanted him. She picked up the pen and wiggled it within the crook of her thumb, waiting for the right words.

Dear Joey—

I am so sorry I hurt you. I wish I could take it back and never have caused you pain. I understand if you have moved on by now, and I wouldn't blame you, I was so horrible to you.

I want you to know that you were the best thing that ever happened to me and I'm sorry I messed it up.

Veronica stopped writing and dropped her head to her desk, letting tears stream onto her arms and splatter the letter. The ink blurred under the drops. As quickly as the emotions had overcome her, they shifted into determination and courage. She sat up and wiped her eyes across her blouse sleeve, leaving a streak of black mascara. Grasping the pen, she wrote from her heart then finished with, *Please forgive me,* and signed, *Love, Veronica.* She folded the letter in half, sealed it into an envelope, and wrote *Joey* across the front. Before she could analyze it another minute, she walked down the hall and tucked it under his apartment door, deep enough that she couldn't retrieve it.

Veronica turned to leave, then instead, she paused and knocked on the door: three solid knocks. She stepped away, second-guessing, and when silence answered, she sat against his door still listening for him inside. She hugged her knees up to her chest and pressed the curve of her back against the door, unconcerned that her skirt hiked up, exposing her control top panty hose at the hem. The knob clicked and she fell backward like a child tumbling on a play mat. She looked up with mascara-smudged eyes to see Joey peering down at her. Veronica rolled to her side, used the doorframe to stand up, and tugged her skirt into place before facing Joey. The creamy envelope was nowhere in sight.

"Hi," she said. "Um, thanks for letting me in."

He glanced over his shoulder into the apartment, then back to Veronica.

"Oh, God, oh, you have someone here. Oh my God, I'm sorry, I'm leaving." Veronica stepped into the hallway.

"Come in," Joey said softly, and led her to the living room with his hand lightly on her back, like the first night they met.

He directed her to the couch, then sat a cushion's width from her. Being beside him after so long apart, Veronica acted on impulses. She reached across the space between them and tentatively took his hand in hers, relieved that he let her. Her fingertips trembled as they drifted across his callouses. She fixed her eyes on his. He looked different, older somehow, but yet the same, or maybe even better. Could it be true that she was sitting beside him again? That he had invited her inside? The words she'd been wanting to share with him for months streamed out. They flowed without edits, poured without restraint, and revealed the truth in her heart.

"I love you, Joey, I am so, so, so sorry. I hope you can forgive me. I've thought of nothing but you since Mystic and I know now, I know without question, that I want you. You've made me a better person and I need you, Joey. Please tell me you haven't found someone new, I couldn't—"

Joey let go of her hand, stopping her words. Veronica held her breath, afraid of what it meant, afraid that he was going to ask her to leave, afraid that he couldn't forgive her. Her heart was choking and the familiar sobs surfaced. Tears masked her vision until a blink sent them rolling down her face and she could see clearly again.

Joey was crying, too. Silently, tears fell through his dark stubble as he clasped her face with both hands and pulled her into a kiss. She felt the prickle of his unshaven cheeks, felt the fire at her lips as he moved over her with raw desperation. The world fell away around them, and Veronica was spinning and flying and sailing above herself. Their salty tears mixed together like a potion healing the hurt.

"I love you," Veronica said breathlessly into his mouth.

He touched his forehead to hers and grasped a handful of her curls, holding her head cradled in his palms.

"I forgive you, Veronica. Thank you for finding your way back to me."

Chapter 44

"HAPPY BIRTHDAY!" AMY HANDED Veronica two boxes wrapped in flowered paper, tied together with yellow ribbon.

"I couldn't tell this was from you, you and your cheerful colors." Veronica handed her November birthday sister her present before opening the gifts.

Tucked into tissue paper, Veronica pulled out Amy's BELIEVE stone.

"You're giving me your Santa rock?"

"I figured you need it. You had a big decision to make, and like Saint Nick said, you knew what to do."

"Thank you, that's really special."

"Open your other gift, it'll come in handy this weekend."

Veronica unwrapped the second box and burst out laughing, "Thanks, I love it, open yours." She swirled the soft, brick-colored scarf around her neck.

Amy understood her laughter as she unfolded a cozy pink scarf from Veronica.

"I'm nervous, but excited to introduce Joey to my parents and show him around Newport. Are you sure about giving me your Santa rock? I think we should share it for whenever either of us has a big decision to make. Andrew has seemed so attentive and doting since homecoming that a big decision may be coming for you, too." Veronica ran her fingers over the smooth surface of the stone.

"When he asks me to marry him, it won't be a big decision, I'm ready," Amy said. "Have been for years."

A loud knock at the door hammered out a rhythm.

"That's Joey!" Veronica jumped up and hugged him in.

"You two look ready for some cold weather," Joey laughed grabbing Veronica's bags, and the trio made their way to Joey's car.

"Have an amazing time," Amy said as they parted ways.

"Any advice for me?" Joey asked.

"Yeah. Just be yourself."

"Be myself. Is that what you want me to do, Veronica?"

"Yes, be yourself. I love you just the way you are, no matter what my parents do or say, I love you. Who knows how they'll act. We'll just have to hang on for that one, but don't say you weren't forewarned," Veronica teased him while pushing away her own worries.

When Veronica told her mother she was bringing her boyfriend home for her birthday, Susan Warren had gushed. Veronica knew her mother would want to entertain, but she made a birthday request to have a low-key weekend with the freedom to come and go as they wanted with no social obligations, and in return, she promised her mother that she and Joey would have her birthday dinner with them on Saturday night.

"Ready?" Joey asked, closing their luggage into the trunk of his Eldorado and climbing into the driver's seat.

"Let's go."

Veronica would have normally insisted that Joey drive with two hands on the wheel, but when he held her hand across the red leather bench seat, she clung to it and didn't let go. They barely noticed the thick Friday afternoon traffic out of the city as they laughed and talked. Veronica told Joey about her homecoming trip to Syracuse and Amy's football accident as the sun set at their backs.

"Wow, sounds like Andrew overreacted," Joey said. "He's fine to hang out with now and then, but sometimes I don't really trust the guy. He's a little too perfect."

"It's like Amy's transfixed on the whole steak knife thing and I worry sometimes."

"When we're all together, I often get the sense that he's got somewhere he'd rather be, like there's something he's missing out on."

"He's always been Mr. Life-of-the-Party, and I know what you mean, he can definitely seem distracted."

Veronica felt the need to fill Joey in on every detail of her life when they were apart, and he, too, knit together the gap between September and November. They both realized they had each put their lives in slow motion with little of consequence happening without the other.

"Did you date anyone?" Veronica whispered, not really wanting to know.

Joey answered slowly. "I went out on a couple of dates"—he glanced from the road to look at Veronica—"but no one was you, *dolcezza.*"

She smiled at the affectionate term; she had missed his sweet name for her. Out the window she watched as they passed the Mystic exit. The green sign screamed at her: EXIT 90—MYSTIC—1 MILE. Silently, she sent up a simple prayer: *Thank you for not letting me lose him.*

Veronica dozed as they traveled out of Connecticut into Rhode Island, on the winding back roads past the University of Rhode Island and over the Jamestown Bridge.

"Wake up," Joey said, touching Veronica's arm. "We're at the second bridge, where to now?"

Veronica directed him through the old cobbled streets of Newport and along the water to her parents' house.

"You maybe could've warned me a little about this," Joey said, sweeping his hand across the expanse of the windshield as they rode down the driveway. Even in the dark the house looked enormous and the grounds glowed with landscape lighting.

Veronica bit her lip and shrugged her shoulders. "Home sweet home."

He parked the car and carried their bags up to the front door, where they stood together, Veronica's hand on the grand door handle. She kissed him. Then she took a breath and blew it out like she was already blowing out birthday candles. "Here we go," she said more for herself than for him.

The door pushed open into the deep foyer, and Susan and Gerald Warren were already walking from the living room to greet them, as the alarm system would have chirped an alert of a car entering the driveway gate.

"Mom, Dad, this is Joey DiNatali. Joey, this is my mom and dad, Susan and Gerald Warren."

Joey bypassed Susan's outstretched hand and gave her a genial hug. Veronica stiffened, then saw her mother's face fill with a genuine smile—she even appeared grateful. Then, knowing how the men in Joey's family collided in embraces, Veronica wondered if he would hug her father, too, certain that wouldn't be as comfortable, but she watched as Joey read the situation with ease and gave her father a strong gentleman's handshake. Veronica exhaled: step one, done.

"Joey, welcome, we're so happy you're here. Come in, leave the bags. Would you like something to drink?" her mother said, taking Joey by the elbow and leading him into the living room. Her father rested his hand on her shoulder and they followed, smiling at the forever hostess.

Settled into the formal living room, Veronica wished they would have chosen the more casual family room for their first visit. Joey had selected his clothing to make a good first impression: he wore pressed gray pants and a black button-down shirt that had a broad white band running vertically down the left side. Veronica caught herself both enjoying the spot of his exposed chest and wishing he had buttoned one more button. He crossed one ankle over the other knee and conversed easily with her parents. She felt a blush come to her face, sorry that she had doubted him, sorry that she had almost lost him because of her fear of this very meeting.

"So, Joe, what do you do for a living?" her dad asked. Veronica tapped the air with her foot, watching her father's face as Joey spoke.

Proudly, he said, "I'm an electrician. I run a good business; I have six guys working for me now. Just two years ago I had three, so we're growing well."

Gerald Warren nodded through Joey's answer. Finally, he took a sip of his Scotch and said only, "Hmm."

After more interview questions, and catching up on Veronica's life, Susan Warren jumped up. "Let's have some dinner, shall we?"

Her parents led the way to the dining room, and Veronica laced her fingers through Joey's and squeezed. Her mother had the table set with an autumn theme; the browns, coppers, and rust tones were elegant in the orange candlelight. Susan sat Joey across from Veronica as she and Gerald took opposite heads of the table.

"Please, help yourself," Susan invited, sliding the shrimp and scallop curry dish toward Joey.

If we have to be in the dining room, at least it's family-style serving, Veronica thought.

"So maybe tomorrow, Joe, you could take a look at my lighting setup by the pool. I think something's hooked up wrong because all summer I've had to jiggle the switch to make those lights work," Gerald said, heaping seafood onto his china with the silver serving spoon.

"Gerald!" Susan scolded. Veronica felt unsettled by her father's request and grateful for her mother's rescue. Then Susan continued. "You have people to call for that—you don't need to bother Veronica's, um, Veronica's boyfriend on his day off."

Veronica looked at Joey, who graciously held a smile on his face.

"No problem, I'd be happy to take a look. This is delicious, Mrs. Warren," Joey said, looking her in the eye.

"Joey's an amazing cook," Veronica told her parents. "He makes the best eggplant Parmesan ever."

"An electrician who cooks—now that's a combination you don't hear every day," her father said, taking a bite.

"Well, I guess if you get home earlier than people in office jobs, you have time to learn to cook," her mother said. "I don't know many men working on Wall Street who are home in time to prepare dinner."

Veronica fought to swallow her food through her closing throat. She looked at her parents, who seemed unaware of their rudeness, their judgments. The very fight she'd struggled with, the fight she had finally overcome, was being projected through them.

"So, Joey, do electricians have to go to college?"

"Stop it!" Veronica shouted, hitting her palm on the table. "This is exactly the reason I didn't want to introduce you to Joey."

"Well, honey, you've only just started dating, it can't be that serious, now," Susan Warren said with a tinge of hopefulness.

"We are serious and we've been together for almost a year and a half."

Her parents gasped, forks frozen in the air above their plates.

"And you've never mentioned him before?" her mother accused. "And to think, we've raised you to always be able to talk to us about anything."

"Anything that fits into your mold of what is proper, of what looks good to other people. Outside of that there's no room for openness. Do you have any idea how that's affected me? I knew from the start how perfect and right Joey is for me, but because I was hung up on the wrong things I almost completely ruined everything. It's taken me this long to bring him home because I was worried about what you would think." Veronica shook her head, sad that she'd been right.

"Even though I'm a grown woman living on my own, I still feel like a little girl filling in the hole of a brother who died and needing Mommy and Daddy's approval. Well, I'm done. I don't need your approval anymore and I know Henry would have been happy for me. I love Joey. He is kinder and better to me than all of those 'boys from nice families' you've fixed me up with, Mom. Isn't that what you want for me? Don't you want me to be happy?" Veronica pulled air into her lungs then exhaled into the silence.

Her hands were balled into fists and her heart raced, knowing she had just broken a long list of unspoken rules. She felt both freed and burdened. Her father laid down his fork and stared at his daughter; her mother's face crumpled, her shoulders shaking. Joey sat with his hands in his lap, unmoving. She saw a glimmer in his dark brown eyes that communicated, *Did you really just say all that?*, *Are you okay?*, and *Thank you* all in one look.

Veronica's mother dabbed at her eyes with her linen napkin and pushed back her chair. Veronica worried that she'd hurt her mother's feelings, that she'd gone too far, but she remained confident in the conviction of her words. She feared her mother would walk out, but instead, she took a step toward Veronica, leaned and wrapped her arms around her, and continued to cry.

"I'm sorry, I am sorry you've ever felt like that. I'm sorry that I've made you feel like that." She stroked Veronica's curls and tucked one behind her ear like she did when Veronica was in elementary school. Turning to Joey, she said, "Joey, forgive us. We can be foolish old parents. Thank you for loving our daughter. Gerald?"

Gerald was sitting back in his chair as if watching a debate on television or listening to one of his committees present a report, and he startled slightly when his wife addressed him.

"Yes, yes, that's right." He went to Veronica, too, and she stood up to accept their hugs.

"Joe." Her father walked to the other side of the table and clasped Joey's shoulder with his left hand while giving him his right hand in their second handshake of the night. The gesture was his apology.

Blowing out a sigh, Veronica wondered how many imaginary candles she'd be extinguishing on her birthday weekend.

SATURDAY MORNING, VERONICA HOPPED out of bed onto the birds on her rug. *I'm that flying bird now. I'm soaring free,* Veronica thought with a fullness in her heart. She tapped on the guest room door, which swung ajar; Joey's bed was made and the morning light poured in the windows. She skipped down the back staircase to the kitchen.

"There you are." She kissed Joey, who sat beside her mother with coffee, a folded newspaper, and an old photo album on the table in front of them.

"Morning, sweetheart. Joey and I are just getting to know each other a little bit. Coffee's made."

"Your mother and I just finished off today's crossword puzzle," Joey said, lifting the mug to his smile.

"Right, of course, something you two have in common."

"Joey tells me you told him about your brother."

Veronica became a statue pouring cream into her coffee; she knew mentioning Henry last night may have gone too far. No one talked with Susan Warren about her son. His name was scarcely mentioned and only in hushed tones. It was silently decided years ago that it was better to hold it deep down. Veronica had always wondered, *Better for whom?* She had yearned to talk with her parents about Henry, to laugh through old memories and pictures, and to cry, too. Crying was okay. Who were they trying to protect in tamping down the subject? Veronica or Susan?

"It's okay, sweetheart, it was quite a lovely way to start the morning, showing Joey pictures of your brother. Of Henry."

Veronica's eyes grew wide. Her mother had mentioned his name at normal volume, and she seemed happy.

"Do you want to see?"

Veronica almost ran across the kitchen to go through the photos with her mother. She couldn't understand this shift, this sudden willingness to talk about Henry, but she didn't want it to disappear. Joey gave Veronica his seat beside her mother and looked on with love. They meandered through the pages, pointing and saying, "Do you remember when . . . ?" and "Oh, look at this," speaking snippets of memories. They traveled through Easter egg hunts with sister and brother in sweet matching outfits, they rambled along beaches and Cape Cod dunes and through vast flower gardens. They saw Henry lift his little sister onto his shoulders, pull her in a sled behind him, and tuck her onto the back of his bicycle. They trimmed Christmas trees, posed before the Rhode Island State House, and watched Henry make the winning goal again and again.

"Thank you, Mom." Veronica hugged her mother, wiping a tear from her eye.

"Really, I should thank you and Joey. I was up most of the night thinking. About everything. And as stunned as I was by your speech, I realized that we needed to hear it. We needed your honesty. So thank you, my love." Patting Veronica's hand, she kissed her and left the room, her long bathrobe floated above the floor behind her. She hadn't dressed or put on makeup before coming down. She was being herself; a self she had, for too long, stored away.

"SHE'S A BEAUTY! THOUGH that was the year they made the mistake by making the Eldorado smaller—the '86 was only 188 inches long, you know," Gerald Warren said, running his hand along the hood and giving Joey's car an affectionate pat. "I had the Commemorative Edition Eldorado in '85. That one was just short of 205 inches. It was the last year they made that version."

"I know that car. A buddy of mine fixed one up—it was in real mint condition," Joey said.

"Boy, that was a good car, all top-of-the-line features for that time. She even had gold wheel center caps and emblems on the taillights. Where's Veronica taking you today? Out and about in Newport?"

"I left the plans to her, but I think there's a mansion tour on the itinerary."

"Better you than me. I'll be waiting for you with a stiff drink when you return, and Susan's got a birthday dinner planned for tonight. Promise, it'll be nothing like last night." Gerald nodded his head toward the house. "Let's go in, they'll be wondering what's happened to us."

HAPPY BIRTHDAY TO YOU, happy birthday to you, Joey and the Warrens sang to Veronica from their seats in the darkened dining room. The candlelight twinkled on the ceiling and walls, and Veronica remembered how she loved to watch birthday candles as a child. She waited until they finished singing; she filled her lungs and closed her eyes and made a wish for her twenty-fourth birthday, even though she sensed that her wishes were already coming true.

"What did you wish for?" her father asked, sliding the knife toward her for the first cut.

"Dad, you know I can't tell you."

"Joe, I'm sure you've noticed that Veronica isn't one to break the rules. Nope, we never had to worry about her missing curfew or throwing a party while we were out." Gerald laughed from his belly.

"What do you mean, Dad? I can break the rules sometimes. One time I took your car without permission and you never knew."

"You mean the time you drove it to the end of the driveway, then put it in reverse and came right back?" He laughed even harder, and Joey, Susan, and Veronica joined him. "Is that all you've got?"

"Open your present, sweetheart," her mother said, handing her a blue Tiffany box.

Veronica received the gift with a flush in her cheeks.

"Oh, let us spoil you." Her father waved his hand for her to open the box.

"Daddy picked these out for you."

She untied the white ribbon and lifted the lid. Diamond stud earrings glittered out at her.

"Oh my gosh, Dad, Mom, thank you so much, they're incredible." She unfastened her simple, classic gold hoops and screwed the Tiffany diamonds in their place. Turning her head side to side, she noticed Joey looking down and nibbling small pieces of his cake.

Veronica's mom kissed her head and cleared the cake and their dishes. "Turn off the kitchen lights when you're done, kids. Happy birthday, my love. Just leave the rest, I'll do it in the morning—no working on your birthday."

"Happy birthday, honey, we're glad to have you home," said her father with a kiss. "Night, Joe."

And the Warrens climbed the stairs to bed.

Alone and snuggled together in the family room, Joey stared into the waning fire, thoughtful and silent.

"Is something wrong, Joey?"

He remained quiet for a long moment before answering. "I just keep thinking that I'll never be able to provide for you the way your parents do."

"But you don't—"

"Wait, let me finish. I can give you a nice life, I can give us a good life, but not a life like this." He threw his arms out in a large Italian gesture. "Now that I'm here and I can see the differences between our upbringings, I understand better why you didn't bring me here sooner. We really do come from different places," he said, his voice drifting away.

"Joey, what are you saying?"

"Here's my birthday gift to you," he answered, holding out an envelope and a small wrapped package.

Inside the envelope was a handmade card. Joey had sketched a caricature of the two of them smiling with huge teeth. Veronica chuckled and looked at him with amazement; she hadn't known he could draw. He was showing her more of himself, she realized. Inside, she read in his boyish script:

To My Dolcezza—

You are my light, my breath, and my happiness. My heart is yours. The pearl is said to bring clarity and grace. You have brought me both. Your open eyes and open mind have brought you back to me. I love you. Happy birthday.

Yours forever,

Joey

Tears clouded her sight as she read the last words, *Yours forever*. Never could she have imagined receiving such a beautiful letter—that kind of writing wasn't even on her "perfect guy" list. This was beyond anything she could wish for, and now she wondered if their weekend trip had changed his mind. Did he feel differently since he'd written this in New York? Her stomach constricted with worry.

"This is the best letter I have ever gotten. Ever. I love you." She kissed him.

She turned to the package in her lap, peeled the paper off, and lifted the fuzzy, hinged box cover. Pearl earrings pierced the cardboard backing.

"Oh, Joey, they're beautiful. This is the best birthday, I have you and I am the luckiest girl alive." Veronica reached to her ears to replace the diamonds with Joey's pearls, but he darted his arm out, stopping her.

"No, it's okay, leave those in. Let's go to bed."

Veronica flipped off the kitchen light and followed Joey upstairs. She kissed him in the hall outside his bedroom, spotlighted by a puddle of November moonlight.

"Thank you, Joey. I love you."

"Me, too." He kissed her cheek and closed the guest room door behind him, leaving Veronica to agonize if she had wished hard enough on her birthday candles.

Chapter 45

VERONICA CALLED HOME TO wish her parents a happy Thanksgiving. "Thank you for checking on us, but don't worry, sweetheart, your father and I will be just fine. Of course we'll miss you, but we understand. Everyone will be sorry not to see you and meet Joey at the annual Thanksgiving eve party tonight." Susan Warren both reassured Veronica and made her flush with guilt. "You have fun with Joey and his family. Please tell them happy Thanksgiving for us."

"Thanks, Mom. Happy Thanksgiving, and tell Dad, too." Veronica hung up the phone and slumped on the couch.

The late November sun had long ago disappeared behind the buildings, and twilight gave way to the artificial glow of the city at night. The Empire State Building was lit in Veronica's favorite all-white lights, not yet covered in blue for Hanukkah or in green and red for Christmas. She lifted herself from the sofa, and pressed her face against the picture window, watching people pass on the sidewalk below. She saw a woman hail a cab, an old man pull his hood up, and a mom with a stroller struggle to get onto a bus. She looked uptown to see the line of taillights and traffic lights stretching out of view. Newport felt far away when she was here with Joey right down the hall.

Since returning from Rhode Island, Veronica sensed things were different between them, shifted somehow. It felt like a widening; it was indecipherable yet lingered like a splinter in your palm that reminds you with every touch something's there that shouldn't be. Whenever the splinter zinged Veronica, she tried harder, gave more of herself, but she hadn't talked to Joey about it. She closed the curtains, switched on a lamp, and left the city outside for the night. Tomorrow, she pledged to herself, tomorrow she would talk with him.

ANDREW AND AMY ARRIVED in Connecticut on Thanksgiving morning, their arms filled with New York bakery-fresh breads and pies, and flowers from the corner market for Aunt Joanie. Amy smiled at the familiar and happy smell, the smell of home, family, and Thanksgiving warmth. Amy called out, announcing their arrival, as they dropped their bounty onto the kitchen counters.

Her father came to greet them from the family room with the faint scent of fire on his sweater, trailed by Uncle Arthur. Aunt Joanie bounded down the stairs, grabbing Andrew and Amy into hugs. "I'm so happy you're here. Everyone else should be arriving by two. Do you want a snack before you help me peel potatoes?" She grinned, removing plastic wrap from a platter of cheese.

As the three men went to refill the woodpile, Amy and her aunt chattered and chopped.

"How are things with you two?"

"Good. Really good, actually. Veronica swears that he's going to propose this Christmas. Or else at Valentine's Day."

"What do you think?" Aunt Joanie asked, leaning into the oven to baste the turkey.

"Sometimes I feel like he's ready and that he's going to ask me, like on Saint John last summer, but then other times, I don't know.

Other times, I feel like he's just going to keep putting it off and I can't picture it ever happening."

"Mm-hmm."

"I don't know. We're happy, so I guess I should just be grateful for that, right? I want him to be really ready before we get married, and I know that if I want a strong marriage, then I need to make some compromises, so I'll wait until he's ready."

"Are you ready?"

"It's the next step."

"Being a wife doesn't mean waiting for him or compromising who you are. It means being able to be completely you before joining yourself with another. You should make each other better. There was a time I needed to learn that. I was young when Uncle Arthur and I got married. It took some time to figure out that I needed to truly be myself, and even longer to learn *how* to do that. Arthur has always been my best friend. I wish that for you, sweetheart."

Amy let her aunt's words drizzle into her idealism as she busied her hands wondering if she and Andrew made each other better.

JOEY KNOCKED AT VERONICA'S door promptly at ten a.m. He wore a patterned sweater that fit closely, showing off his strong build, and the gray pants he'd worn to her parents' house. Veronica grabbed her coat, handbag, and hostess gift for Joey's mother. She had on a classic navy shift with a cashmere cardigan and Joey's pearls were in her ears.

Joey turned across Forty-Second Street toward the Lincoln Tunnel as beside him, Veronica tapped her foot, her navy pump flipping on and off her heel.

"You don't call me *dolcezza* anymore," she blurted out, her well-scripted opening forgotten.

Joey fixed his gaze forward, but his arms stiffened against the steering wheel, pushing his back deeper into the seat. Veronica watched his Adam's apple glide up and back before he spoke.

"I don't?"

She shook her head, looking at her lap.

"I don't, you're right."

She waited for him to go on, but silence assailed her ears.

"Why, Joey? I'm so confused. I finally got the courage to bring you to meet them, to see where I grew up. I finally thought I'd figured things out and it seems like instead of making things better, it made you love me less."

"*No!*" He was emphatic. "No, Veronica, I love you. I told you I will love you forever and I meant it."

"Then what? What is it? Did I do something wrong? Did I hurt you again? Please tell me."

Veronica noticed that he'd pulled over; they were parked in the small lot of the Market Diner on Eleventh Avenue. Joey turned his whole body to face hers, unlatched the seat belts, and slid her across the red leather to him. He ran his hands down her arms to find her hands.

"Listen to me, you did nothing wrong. I love you, *dolcezza*, I love you." He looked down, shaking his head. "Sometimes I—" he started, but pressed his lips together and shook his head again. "I try hard to not act like my pigheaded Italian father with his Mediterranean machismo, but I grew up with the belief that the man is supposed to take care of his family, to care for them in many ways, but first of all, to care for them financially."

Veronica stroked the tops of his hands with her thumbs; she saw his strength in them. She wanted to speak, to protest, to relieve or console him, but she could tell that he was only pausing to neaten his thoughts.

"When I met your parents and saw how you were raised, I saw that even with my business and its success, I will never be able to give you the life you grew up with. I will never be able to match that for you and it breaks my heart." He slowed to take a breath and Veronica could no longer wait.

"But I don't care about that! Don't you see? I love you and I want to be with you and the money doesn't matter, I don't need all of that."

"You say that now, and I believe you mean it, but what about in five years? Ten years? What about when we have children and you want them to sail and ski, to play tennis and dance, go to private school and have perfect outfits—" He waved a hand through the air. "What about then?"

Joey restarted the car, and they headed for the tunnel.

"Never doubt my love, *dolcezza*."

The planner in her had already envisioned life with Joey down the road, married life with babies, toddlers, and kids with backpacks and crayons, but in that moment, sitting in the Eldorado on Eleventh Avenue, she knew that she had pictured her childhood, with her privileges, with her plenty. Even adding in her salary, they wouldn't get close.

THE DOOR AT THE end of the hall was wide open, voices spilling into the corridor, and as Veronica and Joey entered, the volume crescendoed to greet them.

"Ai, they're here." Mario slapped Joey on the back, knocking his cousin forward.

"Wat? D'you have traffic? We been waiting for you," Uncle Cosmo said, shoving a forkful of slippery red peppers and a slice of fresh mozzarella into his mouth.

"Let me through! Let me hug my son and his girl!" Filomena strong-armed her way to the door. Her sweater, veined with golden threads, sparkled out behind her bibbed apron patterned with kitchen utensils. Veronica chuckled every time she saw the forks, knives, spoons, ladles, whisks, and spatulas scattered on the apricot-colored apron. Joey's mother carried a wooden spoon in her hand, which pressed into Veronica's back. The apron's edge tickled her nose as Filomena squeezed both of them into her short torso, one with each arm.

"Ah, my boy is home! I'm a lucky mama with all three of her boys here. Thank you for bringing him home," she said to Veronica, clasping Joey's face between her palms, the spoon stuck out to the side of his head. "Come, eat! You need some meat on those bones." Filomena took Veronica's full body and pointed it toward the coffee table, where the standard spread filled the broad surface. Plastic cups filled the spaces between the food platters.

A band of men lounged on the U-shaped sectional sofa that took up most of the apartment, their attention divided between the television and the antipasti before them. When Veronica spilled into their domain, they shuffled and lifted themselves from their spots to say hello.

"There she is. Come here." Uncle Sal smooshed her into his scruffy face.

"Where's my brother been hiding you? We don't see youse two so much no more," Dominic said, giving Veronica a hug and looking around for Joey.

Nicky, Joey's oldest brother, embraced Veronica and yelled in her ear for his wife: "Yo, Tina! Bring da baby."

Veronica had been included in the baby shower for Tina, which was held at the local Knights of Columbus hall with more than seventy-five girls from toddlers to ninety-something-year-olds. Joey drove her out, then spent the afternoon with his brothers, cousins, and uncles drinking beer and watching football with no female interference or service.

Tina approached with baby Francesca cradled in her arms. Tiny earrings glinted below a lacy pink headband with straight black hair sticking out.

Veronica peered at Francesca. "She's beautiful, congratulations."

"Wanna hold her?" Tina asked, snapping her pink bubble gum. She handed Francesca to Veronica, who was still wearing her coat, and slipped through the men into the kitchen.

"Here, let me help you." Cousin Ottavia swooped to her side and took the baby. "Give me your coat, you'll die of the heat in here." She juggled Francesca in one elbow and Veronica's coat in the other and easily passed the baby back to Veronica's uncertain arms. "Here, sit," she commanded, then swatted her brothers, Orazio and Pasquale, on the knees, creating a spot for her on the couch.

At first Veronica just gazed at the slumbering child, amazed that she could sleep amid the shouting and hollering, but soon she, too, was deaf to the noise and was alone with Francesca. Something fluttered in her heart as she envisioned being a mother, holding her baby with Joey beside her. Tears bubbled picturing Joey as a father, swinging their daughter, reading to their son, running beside them holding on to bicycle seats. When she looked up, the voices drummed around her again at full volume. She scanned the room and saw the parade of familiar commotion. Uncle Nunzio was snoring, his feet propped up on the coffee table beside the tray of prosciutto; Orazio reached behind him and pinched his wife Angela's full rear; Angela lurched and slapped his hand, grinning. Veronica looked away as Uncle Cosmo scratched at his crotch.

Over the back of the couch she could see into the kitchen, set apart by a half-wall, where Filomena, Aunt Erma, Cousin Alessandra, Cousin Ottavia, and Aunt Tessie stirred, chopped, floured, scooped, sautéed, and basted. The women laughed while they worked, shouted while they garnished, and flailed their arms while they arranged. In the corner on the far side of the apartment, Joey's grandmother Concetta and great-aunt Marie sat in peach upholstered armchairs pulled side by side.

"That young fella at the bakery, the one with the big nose," Marie yelled to her sister, "I'm telling you, Connie, he shorted us two rolls."

"Count them again, Marie, that boy did no such thing. Maybe you ate them on your way home."

Veronica smiled at the muddle surrounding her and then at Francesca as she stirred in her sleep. Veronica saw the love that her babies would grow up with, within the family where she felt belonging.

"I'm gonna feed her now before we eat, then Nonna wants her," Tina said, scooping up her baby and nodding toward Concetta. "Thanks for holding Frannie."

"Here, take my seat." Veronica stood and let Tina sit between the two old men.

"Good sitting with you, dear," Pasquale said to Veronica as she tried not to block the view of the TV.

"Did you miss me?" Joey asked, reentering the apartment with his brothers and cousins, bringing in crisp air and their empty beer bottles. "Do they have you helping yet?"

Veronica leaned up and kissed him. His cheeks were pink and cold, and his lips tasted of Budweiser. "I'm on my way to the kitchen now. I've been holding Francesca." Veronica winked and walked by him.

Aunt Tessie marched past her collecting dirty paper plates and plastic forks. "Come on, give me the forks," she said to the slouch of men. "I'm gonna wash them up to use again."

No fewer than fifteen tinfoil pans rested in stands above Sterno flames. The lineup reminded Veronica of sleepaway summer camp meals. The buffet was set with towers of Styrofoam dinner plates and a basketful of plastic utensils rolled in paper napkins and tied with curly ribbon.

"Pretty earrings," Angela said.

Veronica touched the pearls reflexively. "They were a birthday gift from Joey."

"What'd Joey give you?" Nicky asked. Veronica couldn't understand how he'd heard the comment through the noise.

"Ai, Joe! Nice earrings! They pearls? Look at Mr. Big Bucks buying his lady pearls!" Nicky bellowed across the room.

"Lemme see." Marie waddled toward her with Concetta at her side.

Aunt Tessie grabbed Veronica's earlobe. "Woo-ee! Real pearls, how'd you like that?"

"He never bought his mama pearls!" Filomena joined them, leaning over the ladies to see. The scent of L'Air du Temps and Jean Naté that had been saved for too many years wafted around them.

"How glamorous!" Ottavia said, her deep-set eyes growing wider.

Veronica caught Joey's eye. He leaned against the wall, gave her a half-smile, and shrugged as his family's pride honored and embarrassed him.

Filomena's call boomed, ricocheting to another subject: *"Dinner!"*

Dominic stood beside Veronica. "You're really part of the family now. No more fancy plates and forks for you," he yelled, then threw his head back in heaves of laughter.

"Pipe down over there," Filomena shouted. "There are too many of us for real dishes, Donny, now go fill your plate."

"You're always causing a ruckus in this calm family." Joey smiled and looped his arm around her waist. She caught her breath with his touch.

"Joey, I love your family and I love you. I want to be a part of your life in every way, to raise a family with you. We'll be happy with these wonderful people around to love our kids along with us."

His face brightened and his lips tentatively turned up at the corners. "But what about—"

"So what if our families are as different as, as, I don't know—salami grinders and canapés. And who cares that our backgrounds are totally mismatched? Aren't all the great romances about love across barriers?"

At the buffet table, Veronica handed him a dinner plate and a napkin roll, then took them for herself. "And ours isn't even a real problem, we just have different families. You're my best friend, nothing else matters," Veronica effused, resolved.

Chapter 46

THE SMILE WAS AUTOMATIC when Amy saw the postcard in the mailbox.

> *Amy—*
>
> *See you in the city for Christmas—how's Thursday the 23rd? I'll leave my car in Tuckahoe, take the train in to see you, then head back home for Christmas Eve, good? Hope you had a great Thanksgiving, sorry we didn't swing getting together. Love hearing about your boss—she sounds very supportive. Can't wait to see you—less than a month.*
>
> *Love, Matt*

Perfect, Amy thought. She was going home for Christmas Eve on Friday, and she would get to see Matt first. She pushed open the apartment door with her foot. "Hello?" she called out as she did every time she entered. No answer. She flipped the light switch and the buzzer rang. "Ahh!" Amy yelled, and pulled her hand back as if she'd touched flames. The buzzer zinged again, impatiently calling her, and Amy flinched. *Every time,* she thought, pressing the button to respond. "Yes?"

"Your pal Veronica is here. I'm sending her up," Sam announced as he had dozens of times since spring.

Amy stuck a shoe in the door and went to change out of her work clothes. In her underwear, she let the hot water run over her hands and wrists, chilled from the bite of December, and splashed hot water onto her face and neck. She heard the door clunk closed. *That was quick,* she thought.

"I'll be right there."

Amy reluctantly turned off the faucet and buried her face in a towel. Heavy footsteps approached the bathroom. She quickly dried her eyes—the solid, even steps couldn't be Veronica's. Amy yanked the towel from her face and peeked around the doorframe. She screamed at the darkened silhouette.

"Crap, Drew! You scared me to death!"

Andrew laughed. "You shouldn't leave the door propped open." He whistled looking her up and down. "I like coming home to you like this. Let me join you."

She gave him a kiss, then re-buckled his belt for him. "Veronica's on her way up, keep your pants on," she teased. "I'm going to put some on myself."

"I'll get it," Andrew said, answering Veronica's knock.

As the two women settled into talking position, Andrew poured them glasses of wine and then went into the bedroom to change.

"So tell me all about it," Amy prompted, and she sat back, sipping her wine, ready to hear the story of Veronica's Hoboken Thanksgiving.

"See you later, Aim." Andrew was out of his suit and tie, but still dressed nicely in khakis and a button-down straight from the dry cleaners. "Going out for a bit."

"Oh. Okay. I thought we were making pasta for dinner. What are you doing?"

"Just meeting up with a few people from school: Cooper, Buzz, Dan, Bree, and a few other guys." He started for the door.

"Bree? She's in town?"

"Yeah, she lives here now," Andrew said, rubbing the back of his neck.

"In the city? Bree O'Connell lives in the city? Since when?" Amy asked, sitting more upright with each question that popped in her head and directly out of her mouth. An old twang of jealousy stabbed at her gut.

"I don't know, since around Memorial Day, I guess." Andrew shrugged.

"She's been here since May and you never mentioned it? We've never had her over or gone out with her?" Amy's voice was rising with her posture.

"You sound like you're mad. Are you mad? It's not like you two are really friends. Besides, we've been busy with stuff: there was Fourth of July, then Saint John, and leaving the city to go to the beach in August, and the fall has been so swamped with work and homecoming and stuff." He shrugged again. "Do you want to come out with me?"

Amy stared at him and took a deep breath, thinking, *You didn't even come for homecoming.* "No, I'm hanging here with V. Tell everyone hello for me."

Andrew gave Amy a kiss. "I won't be late, promise," he said, then turned with what was almost a hop. He tucked his wallet in his pants and left.

"So, what are you thinking?" Veronica said after the door clicked shut.

"I don't know. I guess he's right, it's been busy, but he should've told me that Bree moved here, don't you think? I can't understand why he didn't because it's not that big of a deal and things are good with us."

Veronica squinted at her friend. "We've been best friends for a really long time. I know you're optimistic and all, but you're okay with him just going out with his ex-girlfriend? The one he never told you lives here."

"They went out in high school. It was over seven years ago." Amy heard herself using Andrew's defense, then got truthful. "I do get a little jealous, but I trust Drew. You've known me long enough, and Andrew, too. Nothing's going to happen. He just didn't tell me that Bree's living in the city now, that's all."

"For seven months, Amy. You can't only see the bright side of things. You need to be more honest with yourself."

Amy was quiet. An almost-thought flurried across her mind then crystallized into words.

"You don't think he could be shacking up with her, do you? He's been working a lot of late nights."

The door handle jiggled, silencing them. They stared as the door swished open and Andrew walked in behind it.

"I decided to stay home with you girls," he said, untucking and unbuttoning his shirt, revealing his white crew neck undershirt. "I'll call Cooper at work to let him know I'm not coming—hopefully I can catch him—then I'll start the pasta. You staying for dinner, Veronica? It won't be as good as Joey's sauce; I'm just opening a jar of Prego."

Andrew grabbed the cordless phone and walked to their bedroom, yanking on the antenna and dialing. Veronica's face mirrored Amy's with widened eyes and brows raised, both wondering if he'd heard them and why he changed his plans.

AMY WATCHED ANDREW KNOT his tie in the mirror's reflection. She loved the intimacy of observing him get ready in the morning, grateful she was the only one who got to do that.

"You were smart to take the day off. I wish I could've," Andrew said.

Amy adjusted the pillows against the headboard. "I'm going to finish my Christmas wrapping before Matt arrives around lunchtime. Will you be home to get the tree and decorate with us? I want to string popcorn and cranberries."

"I still don't understand why you're putting a tree up now—it's two days before Christmas and we're leaving the city." Andrew faced her and ran his fingers through his still-damp hair.

"I've tried to get you to go with me for weeks. I've always had a tree, every year. I can't miss this year. You know I love Christmas and decorating and wrapping presents. I'll get a small one and we'll have time to enjoy it when we get back before New Year's."

"I should be home by dinnertime. Are we ordering in or going out?"

"I thought we could order from the Thai place, and I baked those Christmas cookies you've been swiping for dessert."

"Sounds good, but go ahead and pick out the tree with Matt, and don't wait for me to start decorating."

"Aw, really? All right, we'll save you some cranberries to string but I can't promise we won't eat the leftover popcorn." She tucked her legs under her and kneeled forward to kiss him. He pulled her to him, kissing her deeply and caressing her breasts beneath her nightshirt.

"That's the way to head into the office, bonus that you like to brush your teeth the second you wake up. Can we have some time alone together tonight? I want to give you your Christmas present before we leave tomorrow."

"You got me a gift?"

"Very funny. I've gotten better at remembering occasions, haven't I? I even wrapped it on your fancy wrapping station out there." He left their bedroom and from the living room called back to her, "Are you going to clean up all this stuff out here?"

"First thing, Mr. Tidy."

After he'd gone, Amy got to work preparing for Matt's arrival. She ate breakfast, wrapped boxes, and packed up the gifts for home. Something was nudging at her even as she hummed along to Christmas carols. It was as if there was something she knew but couldn't retrieve, something within her that wouldn't surface.

She cleaned up the paper scraps, price tags, and ribbon cuttings. A receipt caught her eye. It was from the jewelry store Michael C. Fina. *My gift from Andrew is from Michael C. Fina?* She put the receipt aside without looking at it, guarding the surprise. She disciplined herself and went to shower with a skip in her step.

The receipt called to her as she dried her hair and touched some mascara to her lashes. She let herself touch the slip but walked away to brush her teeth again. The force of it pulled her back, and finally, she had to peek. She lifted the paper. She unfolded it and gasped as the buzzer startled her.

With the door wide open, she waited for Matt to turn the corner. When she saw him, she ran toward him and leaped into his arms, wrapping hers tightly around his neck. The bang and click reminded her that she hadn't propped the door.

"Uh oh," Amy said.

Matt laughed and looked at her bare feet. "Where's the super's office? I'll run down and get the key."

"Well, if you take the elevator to level B, when you get out, there's a hallway to the left. You need to go to the end of that but don't go in the door marked 'manager'; instead there's a blue door right after that, and you need to go in there and up a few stairs. Go right or, no, maybe that's a left, but in that area, there's a door with a sign, that's where he should be."

Matt frowned as he visualized each step of the directions. Amy chuckled at him.

"Forget it, I'm coming with you. Give me a piggyback."

Matt bent down and Amy climbed on his back.

"Am I choking you?"

"Not at all," he said, hoisting her higher and hitting the B button in the elevator.

Amy guided him through the basement hallways.

"I hope you don't come down here alone." His voice echoed and his sneakers squeaked above the drone of a fan motor.

"That door." Amy knocked on the door over Matt's shoulder and thought of the time that she and Andrew had gotten locked out. Andrew sent her to find the building superintendent while he carried up the last of their luggage from the lobby. She had shuddered and ran through the halls as quickly as she could to get out of the basement, where the pipes clanked and noises came from the vents. This time, she was grateful to be with Matt.

The super coughed as he corralled them into the service elevator, an express route from the dungeon of the building. "Maybe you should give a neighbor an extra key."

"Thank you," Amy chirped, dodging his cough as he unlocked the door. Matt handed him a tip and followed Amy inside.

"First, lunch, then we pick out a tree," Amy announced, tying her L.L.Bean duck boots.

The local café was busy but Matt and Amy found a small table in the back. They talked easily, tasted each other's choices, and laughed at tales of work and the same-olds of Syracuse. After sharing a chocolate mousse, they walked across an avenue and down a few streets. The trees were lined up by size, and the smell of pine replaced the scents of subway steam and pretzel carts. Amy chose a spruce that barely reached her waist. As the tree guy tied it up for her, she pulled out her wallet to pay.

"That fella's already taken care of it, ma'am."

Amy turned to look for the lady old enough to be called "ma'am" but only saw Matt behind her.

"Thanks, Matt, it's the perfect city Christmas tree." He lifted the pine onto his shoulder and she walked beside him on the way back to the apartment. They dodged other pedestrians, part of the holiday hustle, and shared comfortable quiet.

With him half hidden by evergreen branches, Amy gave voice to the knot in her stomach. "Matt? I'm pretty sure that Andrew is cheating on me."

Matt stopped and set the tree trunk on the sidewalk, concern in his face as he listened to her.

"I think he's been sleeping with Bree. I've had a feeling something was off for a little while, I just didn't want to believe it, so I've been ignoring the signs. Then I found out Bree has been in New York for seven months. Veronica had some suspicions, too, but I didn't listen." Amy bit her lip and studied a snag in her mitten. "Then today I found the receipt for my Christmas present. It was for two necklaces. I know that doesn't seem like proof of much, but I know Andrew and there's no way he got me two necklaces."

Matt gathered Amy into his right arm and put the tree on his left shoulder, and they walked the few blocks back to the apartment in silence.

"A LITTLE TOWARD ME, yup, that's straight." Amy held the top of the tree while Matt tightened the trunk into the stand. He crawled from under it covered in needles.

"Well, that's one fresh pine."

They laughed and together picked sharp needles from his hair and shirt, every so often Matt jumping with an "ouch" followed by Amy giggling a "sorry." They twined white lights around the tree as Christmas carols played on the stereo.

"I love the sparkle of Christmas lights." Amy flipped off the apartment lights and stood back admiring their work. The

December evening was already a deep indigo, and the tree lights cast a lusty glow through the room.

"You get the beers, I'll get the popcorn," Amy said, gathering the bowl she'd popped before getting locked out, the dish of fresh cranberries, spools of thread, and sturdy sewing needles. Working by the light of the tree, they sat on the couch with the bowls balanced on the cushions between them like they used to do for their movie nights. They sipped beer and shared stories of their childhood Christmases.

"My mom always made Christmas so special, it's not the same without her. For a religious woman, she loved Santa Claus, she really saw him as a saint and an image of kindness and love instead of a commercial character. Every year, she made sure we went to see him, even when I was too old for it, I still had to have my picture with Santa." Matt's eyes twinkled with the memory of his mother and the glint of the Christmas lights. "She loved her Santa collection and said she covered our mantel with the antique figurines to welcome him when he came down the chimney."

Amy's string of alternating popcorn and cranberry touched the floor. She pricked her finger and stuck it in her mouth, sucking away the sting. Matt had strung a few kernels, but his hands were idle as he spoke.

"I remember when I learned the truth about Santa. I was nine or ten when Kim and Rachel blindfolded me and dragged me to the basement. They pulled off the scarf and I was staring at the gift-hiding place. I was crushed and ran to my mother crying. She hugged me and talked to me—her voice was so soft as she helped me to believe in the magic and spirit of Christmas in a new way. She made it okay." Matt was smiling, back in his mother's arms. "She made Christmas good. You're like her in that way. Thanks for a fun day, Amy, I'm really happy to be here with you."

She rested her popcorn string in her lap and leaned toward Matt. She crossed into his space and drifted forward. The ceramic bowls clanked between them, but neither looked away from the other. Moving slowly, her lips hovered without touching his, deciding. She paused, holding her breath but feeling his, lingering with lips parted, their mouths only a thread apart. Expectation and hopefulness coursed through her; she wondered if she was shaking outside like she was shaking inside.

They were two magnets facing the wrong way, an invisible field holding them apart. *Kiss him.* It was more a feeling than a thought. Then, as if one magnet suddenly turned over, she pressed her lips to his. It felt new and old both. Exciting and comfortable. Her heart pulsed, fluttering her chest and thrumming her ears. Everything in her prickled with faint surprise and unbounded pleasure. She surrendered herself and there was nothing in the world except the two of them until bright light filled the room.

"What the hell is this?"

Chapter 47

ANDREW STARED AT THEM, fists at his sides. The knot in his tie that had been flawless that morning was loosened and lopsided at his throat.

"I'm out working my ass off all day and this is what I come home to? I trusted you, I believed you when you told me you were 'just friends.'" Andrew paced behind the couch, dragging his fingers through his fine hair.

Amy stood to respond and saw that she had placed herself exactly between Andrew and Matt. Andrew moved closer to her, positioning himself above Matt, still seated on the couch.

"I've been so nice all these years, letting you be friends with him, bringing you his boring postcards from my mailbox. I never worried about him, never thought you'd go for a total nerd. Cut him off now, this is over, whatever this is." He waved his hand between her and Matt. His forehead was damp, and blue veins bulged through his reddened skin. "How could you embarrass me like this? Tell him now that you'll never talk to him again, that this is through."

His voice commanded her to look at him, but she turned away, her gaze falling on Matt, who said nothing but held her with his eyes. She knew the downward slope at the corners of his eyes by heart, knew the way they creased with his smile or drooped when he was thinking.

"Say it! Tell him, Amy!"

She faced Andrew. His glare made him unfamiliar to her.

"No," she said calmly. "No, I won't do that."

Andrew took a step backward, wavering in his stance. He turned away from them and held his head down for only a second before he spun around. Matt stood and moved to Amy's side. He was taller than Andrew, and slimmer, and his movement seemed to anger Andrew more.

"You're choosing this geek over me? We've been together for all these years and you're going to throw that away for this loser? Don't talk!" Andrew ordered, holding his palm up to them. "I can't believe you'd pick him. I'm your perfect knife, remember? He's just a spoon, a dorky, dweeby spoon. I'm the one who saved you when you needed help, I was the one who was there to rescue you in that bathroom, and I'm the one who can protect you. I forgave you once for kissing someone else, but this is—this is too much."

Gulping air through his flared nostrils, Andrew pointed as he escalated: "You've been waiting and waiting for me all this time, even acting like my wife. Well, I guess it's a good thing I never proposed to you. Oh, wait. Wait, I know what you're doing. You're trying to make me jealous so I'll give you a ring. Is that it? I knew you'd wait around for me. Bree was sure you knew we're sleeping together, but I told her you were clueless and you'd wait for me no matter what. You even bought that stupid story about me being mugged when I left my wallet at her place."

Amy's mouth fell open as he confirmed suspicions and revealed details. His blundered confession escalated his fury. He stomped over, grabbed the top of the tree and threw it across the floor. Lights clinked on the wood but stayed lit. Pine needles tinkled down and water spilled from the stand, puddling on the rug that

Amy detested. Christmas lights were everywhere and Andrew's mouth was open wide in a shout of rage. Amy had a fleeting sense of déjà vu.

He pounded his fist to his forehead and dug a heel hard into the floor. With imperceptible motion, Matt shifted himself in front of Amy. Andrew started to talk but instead exhaled forcefully, shooting spit droplets into the air, then grasped his shaking head with both hands.

As Andrew seemed swallowed in his storm, Amy spoke, with precision and firmness in her voice. "I don't know you anymore. Leave. Leave now. I'll pack my stuff and be out tomorrow, but get out now."

Andrew rocked from one foot to the other. He was too far away, but he swung a fist in Matt's direction, a last posture of intimidation. Matt's arm shot out in front of Amy like he was protecting her from stepping into traffic.

Andrew walked past them toward the door. Papers were strewn where he had dropped his briefcase; it lay half zipped on its side spilling its contents. He stooped to gather the files into messy heaps. As he jammed dangling papers into his case, a streak of her Christmas wrapping paper toppled out. Andrew snatched up the small box, threw it in, and pressed the briefcase closed without trying to zip it shut. Balancing the jumble on his knee, he opened the door, kicked it with his foot, and slid out, letting the door bang closed behind him.

Inside Amy, everything was rushing and darting about, but outside, her only movement was a tremor in her hand. They stood until the distant chime of the elevator stirred Amy. She ran to the door, turned the deadbolt with a definitive clank, and threaded the chain lock into place. Matt was beside her as she slid down the door and collapsed to the ground, crying and shivering. He stroked her hair, peeling it off her face and smoothing it down her neck and back. Her ribs opened with her breath and slowly she quieted, comforted by Matt's arms around her, wishing him not to stop. His chest vibrated with his words so that she felt them in her face before hearing them.

"I'm sorry," he said.

She held her hand to his heart. "But, why?"

"Because that was completely awful for you and I'm sorry."

"I'm sorry I made you a part of that but I'm glad I kissed you."

"Me, too. I've wanted to kiss you since you first bumped into me freshman year." He smiled, tucking a ribbon of hair behind her ear.

"I didn't know it, but I wanted that, too."

ON CHRISTMAS EVE MORNING, Amy haphazardly filled the brown boxes and luggage Thomas York had brought into the city. Sam secured a spot in front of the building entrance and, in hurried trips, Matt, Veronica, and her father carted Amy's things into his waiting car and shuttled them to Veronica's apartment.

She and Matt had talked and dozed on the couch throughout the night, connecting in a new way. Years of unspoken feelings surfaced and Amy viewed the past with a refocused lens. The predawn hours filled with realizations, reversed perspectives, and shared stories retold with the filter removed. Amy was awed by the simple touch of Matt's hand on hers and overwhelmed by his kiss. His devotion flooded her with wonder and she felt at home in his presence. By the time they were awakened by Sam buzzing her father up, Amy's face was crisscrossed with indents from Matt's shirt.

Armfuls of clothes still on hangers, suitcases of books, and boxes filled with toiletries and shoes returned to Third Avenue. They laid her few framed posters across the top and tucked in garbage bags of throw pillows and a year's worth of acquisitions.

Amy made quick decisions, leaving their shared items and most of the household things she'd brought, working to finish before Andrew came back.

She had righted the Christmas tree and given it some water, leaving the lights plugged in overnight. Her home of the past year felt foreign. The dreams and expectations the apartment had held were tarnished like her perception of Andrew. This wasn't the romantic comedy ending she'd scripted.

On the bookshelf, she studied what had been one of her favorite pictures of the two of them, taken when neither was aware of the camera. Andrew draped his arm over Amy's shoulders, his face full with a smile, bonfire flames casting it golden. *I thought he looked like a movie star.* In the photo, she was staring at his face, contentment brimming from her eyes and her smile. Amy tilted the frame in her hand as if seeing the image for the first time. In it she was completely riveted by him, love stamped all over her, and Andrew was looking away, holding her to him, claiming her, but smiling elsewhere.

"Any more stuff, Amy?" Veronica asked, dragging the handcart Sam had lent them behind her.

Amy put the picture back in its place. "Nope, I think I've got everything I want to take. I'm glad you're here, V."

"I'm always here for you. I guess your Santa guy was right after all. Deciding to leave Andrew after all these years—that's a big one."

"No kidding. I'm pretty rattled by the whole thing"—Amy shook her head—"but it's the right thing."

"I'm giving you back your BELIEVE stone. It's your turn to use it."

She smiled, "And we get to be roommates again. Chelsea won't mind?"

"She'll be fine, she's out a lot. We can share my room."

"Are you even there anymore?"

Veronica grinned and shrugged. "Now and then. It'll mostly be your room and I'll just use it as my closet. Joey and I are heading to his family's tonight for Christmas Eve, then driving to Newport tomorrow. Call me at my parents' house."

"All set, kiddo?" Amy's dad and Matt entered the propped door.

Hearing her dad call her "kiddo," having her loyal friends beside her, and leaving behind a history, tears sprang from Amy's eyes. All three stepped forward with arms spread to comfort her, then paused to allow the others space. Amy laughed with tears still dripping. She pulled them all into an embrace.

Taking Veronica into a solo hug, Amy said, "Enjoy spending your first Christmas together."

"My turn," said her father, pulling Amy into him. "I'm proud of you, honey, this can't be easy. Come on, Aunt Joanie and Uncle Arthur are already in Newtown waiting for us with a Christmas Eve dinner."

He turned to Matt, clapping him on the back. "Let's go."

Amy twisted the apartment key off her key chain and placed it on the small table by the door. She scanned the dim apartment by the light of the tree and stepped out. She swallowed hard as the door closed behind her. She was locked out for the last time.

"Bye, Amy, sorry to see you go," the doorman said.

"Merry Christmas, thanks for everything, Sam," she said handing him an envelope.

Matt opened the passenger door for Amy and gave her a sweet, clandestine kiss as her father walked to the driver's side. She felt desperate to keep him close; she didn't want to say good-bye or wait until Tuesday when she would see him again. He closed the door, framing her pleading eyes in the window, then opened the backseat door and slid into a small cubicle of space among the things Amy chose to bring back to Connecticut.

"What are you doing?" Amy asked, spinning around and peeking between the seats at Matt.

Her father answered, turning on the ignition. "We're taking Matt home on our way."

At least I still have him to Tuckahoe, Amy thought, knowing she would have to feel that longing at his departure again in a short time.

Chapter 48

ON THE DAY AFTER Christmas, Amy found her dad reading the paper. "Come on, Dad, let's go for a drive."

His eyes twinkled as he rose from his seat. "Hmm, what's going on here? Are you old enough now that you're turning things around on your father?"

She grinned, leading the way to the garage. Behind the wheel, she lowered the radio, leaving the Top 40 of 1993 counting down in the background. She navigated the familiar Newtown roads, deciding how to begin.

"Dad, I want you to know that I've really taken your advice seriously all these years."

"What advice would that be? I'm quite sure I've given you a lot." Her dad chuckled.

"Since you told me about the forks, knives, and spoons, I'd been looking for my perfect knife and I thought I'd found him. I know you worry and want me to find someone. I've thought about that a lot." She glanced at her dad, who was turned toward her with an affectionate look of concern on his face. "This whole thing with Andrew has made me realize that I'd been clinging to an idealistic view of him, of us as a couple. I'd always labeled him as my perfect steak knife and I couldn't let that go. I had this image of what our relationship should be, of how Andrew should be, and I kept trying to make it work even when so much around me said it wasn't right. I still compromised and gave up my needs to stay together and make it work."

"Compromising doesn't mean giving up part of yourself. You both need to be fulfilled and work together toward common goals."

She nodded. "I suddenly see that. I see a lot of things in a new way now. While I was waiting for Andrew, Matt was waiting for me. I can't believe that I never saw it before. Andrew wasn't going to commit to me and I took Matt's friendship for granted. I kept insisting that we were just friends. Yeah, I know, stop laughing, Dad, I get it now. But what I didn't understand before was that the relationship I've been searching for happens between best friends. I think I've gotten the whole fork, knife, and spoon thing wrong. Maybe Veronica is right."

Amy's dad reached across the seat and rested his hand on her shoulder. "Amy, that talk at Bella's was never meant to stifle you or to narrow your views, it was your old dad's way of helping you navigate college boys without me."

"Wait, what? You mean you don't believe in the UCS, either? After all this time, I've been so sure it worked."

"Well, I still think you can put most fellas into one of those categories, but, honey, it was a guideline, a metaphor. I wanted to help you but I'm afraid that maybe you've held on to it a bit too tightly. If I gave you the impression that you needed to find someone for my sake, I am so sorry. What I want most is your happiness, whoever that is with. Sure, I'm getting up there and would love to walk my girl down the aisle before I kick the bucket—"

"Cut it out, Dad, I need you around."

"But this is your life and you don't need a man to make you happy. You have to be happy and whole without a man first. Having a boyfriend or husband isn't your end point, and when the time works out, you'll know the right man for you, even without using a labeling system I made up."

"Now I can see all the times you and Veronica tried to point things out to me over the years. Some reporter I've been, I dismissed it all, always justifying things and standing up for Andrew. It's time to stand up for myself."

"It sure sounds like you've done a lot of growing up, sweetheart, I see a lot of your mother in the woman you've become."

"That means so much, Dad." Amy took a deep breath, bracing to ask him one of the biggest questions on her heart. She pulled the car into the Blue Colony Diner, parking so she could completely focus.

"Do you think it's crazy that I want to be with Matt now, so soon after breaking up with Andrew?"

He paused, framing his thoughts. "You've known and cared for each other for many years and it's clear to see that Matt adores you. If you feel that way about him, I don't see why the timing should matter too much, though a little time for yourself would be a good thing, I think. But, honey—"

"Yes?"

"Be sure you know yourself and what's in your heart. Remember, you have to value and love yourself first."

"That's just it, Dad, I see that I wasn't being true to myself during a lot of my time with Andrew, and I'm comfortable with Matt like with no one else. I'm really me with him. I've never felt like I had to pretend or sacrifice anything. It's like the lights went on after a movie, and now that my eyes are adjusted, I can see it all so clearly."

Her father smiled. "I'm behind you whatever you decide."

As they started to drive home, number thirty-two on the charts came on the radio. Rod Stewart sang as if just for Amy: *Fill my heart with gladness, take away all my sadness, ease my troubles that's what you do.*

CHELSEA WAS AT HOME in Maryland for the week and Veronica and Joey weren't returning to the city until sometime on New Year's Day. The Warrens had invited Joey and Veronica to a private New Year's Eve party at Marble House, the historical summer cottage of Cornelius Vanderbilt's grandson and his wife. Their plans left Amy the apartment to herself for the week.

Amy's train from Connecticut arrived in Grand Central at lunchtime on Monday. To accommodate the extra bags from Christmas, she hailed a cab instead of walking the few blocks to her old apartment. She felt the comfort of being home alone and the strangeness of being alone in someone else's home. From the countless hours she'd spent there with Veronica, she was accustomed to Chelsea's additions, her furnishings and framed prints on the walls, but it felt different in their absence. It was like going back in time to a new beginning.

Amy went right to work moving and organizing the heap of boxes and clothes they had stacked hastily in the entry on Christmas Eve day. Veronica offered Amy her bedroom until she figured out where she would live. Secretly, Amy wished that Chelsea would move out, leaving Veronica and her to be roommates again, but she also wondered how long it would be before Veronica and Joey would make the decision to live together. Life was changing for both of them.

Once she was settled, Amy heated herself a can of soup and sat at the table in front of Chelsea's stack of entertainment magazines. Thumbing through a July issue of *Entertainment Weekly* featuring "Tom Hanks Grows Up" on the cover, she glanced at stories about the movie *The Firm*, U2, and Clint Eastwood. The phone rang and she lifted from her chair to answer, then realized it wasn't for her to answer anymore. She lowered herself, and as the phone kept ringing, she rejected an October issue of *People* with a shirtless Fabio on the cover and skimmed November headlines: "Michael Jackson Cracks Up: Sex, Drugs and the Fall of the World's Biggest Star" and "Oprah Opens Her Heart in a Tough TV Movie."

The answering machine picked up. Amy took a spoonful of soup as she listened to the familiar greeting and looked for the page with the cover story on "The Richest Women in Show Biz." After the beep there was silence, but she could tell someone was on the line. Then she heard a throat clearing: "Um, Veronica, hi, um . . ." Amy dropped her spoon, splashing chicken noodle soup onto Madonna's face. She stood over the machine not breathing as the message continued. "It's Andrew again, and um, I was checking to see if you were back yet. I tried to call Amy at her dad's house but I got the answering machine and I don't want to leave a message there. Um, I'm just wondering if you know where she is. I need to talk to her. Please tell her I need to talk to her." Sadness leaked from his voice and she could picture him weaving his fingers into his hairline. There was another pause. She heard him inhale and sigh before he hung up the phone.

Amy watched the red light blink. She hadn't noticed, but it must have already been blinking when she arrived; the digital number on the machine showed 3. She hadn't pictured talking with Andrew; she hadn't thought about having to see him. There was nothing he could say to erase all he had said, repair all he had revealed. There was nothing that would change the truth that she now saw clearly.

She got a napkin to wipe up Chelsea's magazine and the phone rang again. She froze, feeling like Andrew could see her, like he knew she was there. Laughing at herself, she realized it was the doorman ringing, the bell much more pleasant than the crass buzzer at Andrew's apartment. She had already shifted back to labeling the place as his alone. Walking to respond, she hesitated. What if it was Andrew? What if he was there? The tingling call rang out again. She pressed the button. "Yes?" she asked carefully.

"You have a visitor."

"Who is it, please?" Amy had the presence of mind to ask instead of giving her usual, careless response of "Send 'em up."

She waited, holding the button down. There was a shuffling as the doorman covered the receiver, then he returned. "He says his name is Matt."

Again, she stood in the doorway like she had at Andrew's only four days before. She held the door open with her body, impatient for him, but this time she waited. Waited like he had for years. He jogged to her and swept her into the apartment with an unwavering hug. The door clanked closed and they were locked in.

"You're here a whole day early." Amy jumped into his arms and linked her legs around his waist.

"I couldn't wait another day to see you. I'm only off until the second and I want to spend every moment I can with you."

They had talked on Christmas Eve after midnight church services into the wee hours of Christmas morning, and again later on Christmas Day, and twice the following day. It was as though Matt had stepped into her view, and now that she could see him, she couldn't bear to be apart.

"Six nights and days all to ourselves," Amy tabulated between kisses.

He carried her to the living room, her legs still clasped around him. Kissing with the passion of the reunited, no one and nothing else existed. Heat and energy vibrated between them, crescendoing. Without timidness, Amy shimmied out of her jeans, pulled her shirt over her head and threw it to the floor. She stood before him as an invitation, a gift. Wordlessly, Matt unlatched her bra and ran his fingertips along her collarbones, the outside contours of her breasts, down her ribcage. He barely touched her but created a storm of emotions in Amy. It was the most sensuous thing she had ever felt and a tickle fluttered through her from her solar plexus to the swell between her legs.

She wanted more of him and slid her hands under his shirt, gliding them across his chest as she lifted it over his head. He unbuttoned his Levi's, stepped out of them closer to Amy, and pressed his body into hers. Her breath caught at the sensation of his skin against hers and she leaned into him, inhaling his scent as it mixed with her own.

She touched his taut abdomen and trailed her finger from his navel along the hairline to beneath the band of his boxers, remembering the glimpse years before. Now it was hers to touch, she thought, allowing her hands to explore all of the man whom she knew so well but hardly knew at all. Matt shuddered and cradled her face between his palms, kissing her deeply.

He carried her down the hall and rested her on the bed like a precious stone on a velvet pillow. Amy felt dizzy as Matt's finger traced her belly button, her hips, and her pubic bone before slipping beneath it. She arched into his fingers, which touched her in just the right place, in just the right way.

"Oh, God," she sighed.

It was exquisite torture. Anticipation and eagerness coursed through her; he was all she wanted as he eased himself into her, steadily, slowly. Amy couldn't stand the agony of waiting. She flipped on top and rubbed herself against him, hungry for release but hoping it would never end.

"Oh, Matt!"

He matched her pace and grasped her hips, moving her faster. His head turned upward and he breathed slowly, lingering and giving until Amy let out a cry. She clenched her fingertips into his back and held her breath to prolong the ecstasy as she felt Matt tremble beneath her.

Their bodies entwined, sweaty in the cool December afternoon, as their breathing slowed in sync.

"Amy Melissa York, I love you."

His voice was filled with love. No one had ever spoken her name with greater tenderness.

Chapter 49

AFTER CHRISTMAS, FROM TUCKAHOE, Matt had called all over New York City for New Year's Eve dinner reservations, several hostesses laughed at him trying to book so late. One manager even asked, "Sir, do you mean for December 31, 1994?"

"It's a special occasion," he said, trying a new tactic at one restaurant, only to have the host respond, "For you and everyone in the world tonight. No tables."

He persisted with his sisters cheering him on, making suggestions, and looking up numbers in the Manhattan phone book for him. It was a couple years old but they always made sure to keep one in the house.

"This would be so much easier with my computer access from work. The World Wide Web is making everything more accessible," Matt told Kim and Rachel as they dictated numbers and called out, "Wait, I found one," "Try this."

At last they got a reservation that wasn't in the early-bird-special time frame; the host was quick to explain that a cancellation caused the opening. It was at a place called Magoo's and Matt worried that it would be as awful as the bald cartoon character he pictured, but the menu printed in the phone book offered a good selection. He asked if they used butcher paper on the tables, and when they said no, he took the reservation.

ON THEIR FIRST MORNING together, Amy and Matt ventured out for supplies and returned with a bag of bagels, bottles of wine, and some champagne for New Year's Eve. Along with basic groceries, they got a stash of Blockbuster videos. From the time of his arrival, they never left each other's sight. Food was ordered up—Mexican, burgers, sushi, Italian—and they prepared a few simple lunches in the galley kitchen. They tangled together, hungry for each other, between, during, and after meals.

Thursday afternoon, the phone rang, but Amy ignored it and kept kissing Matt. She stiffened as the long beep receded and Andrew's voice filled the room.

"It's me. Again. Um, I guess you're not home yet, or you're not giving Amy my messages. Or maybe you are and she's just not calling me. But please, Veronica, please tell Amy I need to talk to her. Tell her I still love her and I'm sorry. I messed up. Tell her that. Please."

Matt watched Amy as the words wedged into their time. She released him and walked to the phone. She reached toward it, but instead of answering, she popped open the lid of the answering machine and removed the tiny cassette, tossing it into the drawer of the small table.

"Remind me to tell Veronica where I put that," Amy said, returning to Matt's lap.

"He's called before."

"Only once while I was here, just before you arrived."

"Are you okay, Amy?" He paused. "Things have changed fast."

"In some ways it's been quick, but I can't believe all these years I was looking in the wrong direction. I love you, Matt, and I finally see what's real."

IT HAD BEEN DAYS since they'd left the apartment and Amy protested when he suggested they go out for New Year's Eve. "Besides, there's no way we'd get a table tonight."

"I made a reservation," Matt said proudly.

"You did? When? How?" Amy was properly impressed by the gesture as much as the achievement, and so she was persuaded. She showered, and for the only time that week, she did her hair and put on makeup. She slipped into a little black dress and wore high heels, then clicked down the parquet hallway to where Matt waited; it had been almost an hour since they'd seen each other. He stood to meet her and breathed, "My God, you're beautiful."

He lifted her and spun her around. "Have I told you that I am in love with you?"

"Keep saying it." She laughed, giddy with his affection all the way to the restaurant.

"Here it is, Magoo's." Matt paid the taxi driver and surveyed the outside. He opened the restaurant door for her. "I'm a little worried that you're seeing the place before I can check it out."

"This is cute, Matt," she said, stepping inside.

The small rooms were dark but glistened with strings of white lights draped all along the ceilings. White linens covered the tables and contrasted with the old chestnut paneling, and different-colored glass jars glowed with candles at each table.

"Do you still think Harry was wrong?" Matt asked after they ordered drinks.

"Who's Harry? Wrong about what?" she asked, sliding the amber glass candleholder to the side.

"In *When Harry Met Sally* . . . You always thought Harry was wrong."

Understanding dawned. "I guess I was wrong. Maybe men and women can't be just friends." She linked her ankle around his under the table. "How long have you known?"

"Since the first day in the computer lab."

"No way." She shook her head, taking his hand in hers.

"I've known, Amy. All along."

"Why didn't you ever—why didn't I know?"

He smiled and removed his hand from hers. Amy looked at him, her eyebrows questioning. Matt held up his knife; it twinkled with the reflection of the little lights above them.

"You were focused on your steak knife."

His comment reminded her that he knew about the utensils.

"*You're* my perfect steak knife," she said, hardly realizing her ingrained insistence on using the UCS.

"I don't know all the ins and outs of your elaborate system," Matt said with a grin, "but I think I'd like to stay a spoon and be your perfect spoon."

"Well, it turns out that I had the labels all wrong and you are definitely my knife, Matt Saxon. You are smart, witty, kind, and completely incredible. You're perfect for me. And that makes you my steak knife."

AFTER THEY RETURNED FROM their New Year's Eve celebration at Marble House, Veronica and Joey said good night to the Warrens. It made her happy to see her father pat Joey's back and smile with genuine fondness. Her mother kissed Joey's cheek and squeezed his hand before following her husband upstairs. They were acting quite affectionate and a little excitable, and Veronica wondered if they'd had too much to drink at the party.

Joey made a small fire and they cuddled on the family room couch. Veronica rested her hand on his chest, slipping her fingers into his unbuttoned tuxedo collar.

"How should we ring in 1994?" she teased.

Joey reached into his pants pocket. Before she understood

what was happening, he knelt, held her hand, and, like a magic trick, a shimmering solitaire diamond was on her ring finger.

"Will you marry me, *dolcezza?*"

Veronica threw her hands to her face, knocking Joey in the jaw.

"Oh, I'm sorry!"

"You're sorry?"

"No, no."

"No?"

"I mean no, I'm not sorry, I mean I'm sorry for hitting you, but yes. Yes, I'll marry you!"

Veronica leaped forward to hug him, and in her enthusiasm, she jabbed Joey in the chest with her knee. He rolled backward onto the floor, laughing as he grasped his heart. She snuggled next to him on the floor. They kissed, her red curls cascading around their faces, until a spark crackled from the fire, startling Veronica. She flinched away from the ember and batted at her dress and Joey's arm, her elbow poking into his ribs and her knee pressing into his crotch.

"Ow! Do I need armor to be your husband?"

She swatted his shoulder. "You're already wearing some. You're my knight in shining armor, my shiny silver steak knife. I sound like Amy, don't I?"

"I like her happily ever afters."

"Maybe she was right after all, this steak knife thing does work. I'm so happy we're engaged, Joey. I can't wait to tell my parents and Amy tomorrow."

"Your parents know." He grinned.

"You asked them? Oh, thank goodness!"

"Of course. We Italians can be a bit traditional, too."

Carefully, she laid her body on top of his. Her glittering gown covered them both like a blessing.

Chapter 50

MATT AND AMY WELCOMED 1994 making love as the ball dropped in Times Square just a few long blocks away. As he unbuttoned his shirt, her heart quavered, amazed at the love she felt for him, and grateful to be able to fall asleep in his arms.

Early on New Year's Day, the ringing of the phone woke them.

"Let the machine get it," Amy said, rolling over.

"You took the tape out, remember?" Matt adjusted his body to mold against hers and was back asleep instantly.

The phone persisted. Amy begrudgingly wiggled out of Matt's hold and ran to the living room to yell at, then hang up on, whoever was calling so early on the first day of the year.

"Hello?" she said with sleep oozing from her throat.

"Amy! You'll never guess what happened! I wanted to call you last night but it was too late to call," Veronica chirped.

"It's too early to call now," she teased, but her friend's cheer brought Amy to full wakefulness. "What happened?"

As Veronica gushed about her engagement, Amy squealed like a twelve-year old girl. "No way! Oh my gosh!" Amy spoke away from the receiver to Matt, who had roused from her shouts. "They're engaged! Joey proposed last night. They're engaged," she shrieked again.

Amy lay back on Veronica's sofa and listened to her share every detail. She punctuated the story with "He got on his knee, oh, that's so romantic," "I can't believe you punched him," and "You said that? Poor Joey!"

"I'm so happy for you, Veronica. Tell Joey congratulations for us."

Amy felt a tightness in her face and a lightness in her chest as she disconnected the line. She had smiled throughout the proposal story aware that she was still waiting for her own, but for the first time in a long time, she felt serene and fulfilled without anticipating a ring.

"I CAN'T SAY GOOD-BYE." Amy held tightly to Matt, his car idling on the street beside them. He had reluctantly packed his things, letting the sun set before he could no longer delay the long drive north to Syracuse.

"Soon, we won't have to." He kissed Amy. "I'll come back in two weeks, we can talk every day until then. Tomorrow, I start my New York job search."

"I can't wait to be in the same city again. And this time I know what I have in you."

His hand on the back of her neck anchored her. She felt secure with him while still feeling whole within herself, more herself than she'd ever felt before. Amy hadn't realized the accommodations she'd made to be with Andrew, the thousand little betrayals of herself to justify his aloofness or his lack of attention. The recognition stung, igniting a fresh gratitude for how unrestricted and open she could be with Matt.

VERONICA AND AMY BRAINSTORMED wedding themes and flower ideas, color options and invitation styles. They created a list of possible wedding venues, and during lunchtime their first day back at work, Veronica had three appointments scheduled, one for the next evening.

She and Joey decided to plan the wedding themselves, in their own way, in their home of Manhattan, geographically between both families. They wanted something wonderful but casual and approachable. Susan Warren was already trying to persuade her daughter to look at the Plaza and Tavern on the Green, but Veronica appeased her temporarily by assigning her mother to look into photographers. Filomena DiNatali was vying for a wedding palace in New Jersey with a huge statue-filled fountain in front and pavilions dappling the lawns. Joey distracted her by having her shop for groom's cakes.

After work, the cab dropped Veronica, Amy, and Joey at Twenty-Ninth Street at the East River. They entered the Water Club and asked for Dora at the reception desk. Veronica reached into her workbag for her newly purchased wedding notebook, a binder that she had organized with color-coded labels and tabs and filled with lists and timetables torn from magazines. Approaching from down the hall, Veronica heard a familiar voice that she couldn't place.

"Hi, Amy. Hi, Veronica."

Amy spun, her face divulging her confusion and utter surprise. "Jenny?"

Veronica hesitated, then gaped in shocked recognition.

"What are you doing here? I thought you were in California."

Jenny's blond hair was cut into a professional bob, and her slim skirt and suit jacket were stylish yet demure, her blouse unbuttoned only enough to reveal a small gold pendant. No part of her breasts was visible, Veronica noticed. More than just her appearance seemed different. She had a maturity. Of course, they'd all grown since leaving Syracuse, but there was something else new about Jenny that Veronica couldn't define.

"I work here now. I moved to the city in November. I've been trying to reach you since the summer, Amy. Can you guys go out for a drink after our appointment tonight? Maybe just us girls?" she said, flicking her eyes at Joey.

"Yeah, sure," Amy replied, turning to Veronica for confirmation.

"Yes, let's do that, but we're supposed to be meeting with Dora."

Jenny smiled and glanced down at the folders in her arms. "That's me, I go by Dora again now."

Amy crinkled her forehead. "Again? I don't understand."

"I know." Dora smiled. "There's a lot to explain," she said, glancing sideways to gauge the proximity of her coworkers.

"Jenny—I mean, Dora—this is my fiancé, Joey DiNatali. Joey, this is Dora Callista. We lived on the same floor freshman year."

Dora presented her hand to shake Joey's. He released Veronica's hand to accept the gesture. Veronica's gaze drifted over Dora, who was smiling and asking questions. Joey politely engaged her, posed questions of his own, and animatedly told her the story of how they met, beaming and holding Veronica proudly to his side.

"I knew she was the one for me the second I met her, those crazy curls flying everywhere." He kissed the side of her head. "I cooked her my best sauce the first night we met." Veronica smiled; she loved hearing the story from Joey's point of view.

"Let me show you around," Dora offered.

Veronica opened to the first page in her notebook and clicked her pen, getting to business. "Okay, then, Jenny, uh, I mean, Dora, how many can the Water Club accommodate?"

Dora handed Veronica a sleek folder. "This has all of our menus, floor plans, and other information."

She gave her freshman-year floor-mates the tour, talking about seasons and checking date availability. "We'd love you to have your wedding here, Veronica and Joey. And, Amy, I can't wait to hear all about you and Andrew. Is it true you may be getting engaged soon, too? Let me grab my coat and tell my boss I'm leaving. Wait here," Dora said, and slipped into the offices before Amy could explain that she had changed guys like Jenny had changed names, both returning to something comfortable, familiar, and more truly themselves.

AS THEY WALKED THROUGH the small restaurant, Dora held her shoulders back in a confident posture, parting discussions and turning heads as she went. *That hasn't changed*, Amy thought.

"It's ladies' night here tonight. Open bar until eight as long as we buy an appetizer," Dora explained as they settled into a corner table and ordered.

"Tell us how you became Dora," Amy started.

Jenny looked at her hands folded on the table in front of her. "I was always Dora growing up, short for Isadora. My mom named me for her grandmother and my dad gave me my middle name, Jennifer, just because he liked it. He would whisper 'Good night, Jenny-Doe' when he put me to sleep. He always called me Jenny-Doe, putting my middle name first. He was the only one who ever called me Jenny."

Dora paused at the interruption of the waitress delivering their glasses of wine and fried zucchini. She left her glass untouched and went on. "When he left, I tried to make everyone call me Jenny, but my mom and aunt, my first grade teacher, they all kept calling me Dora. I even started writing Jenny on my drawings and papers, but it only lasted a little while, and eventually, I stopped trying to change my name. I was Dora, no one called me Jenny once he left, not until college. My mom argued with me about going to Syracuse. I had my mind set on it for years, but she didn't want me to go on a wild-goose chase.

"My dad sent me one card. It was the only contact he made after disappearing. The card was for the first birthday he missed, my seventh. It had purple balloons on the front and he wrote it to Jenny-Doe and signed, *Love, Daddy.* Of course, I saved it, the envelope, too. There was no return address but the postmark was Syracuse, New York.

"It was dumb, but I thought if I lived closer, if I called myself Jenny, that maybe I could . . ." Dora rolled her eyes and shook her head. "It sounds so stupid now, but I thought I could find him. Or that he would find me. But of course he could've found me all those years and never did. It was a stupid fantasy."

Amy reached across the table and touched her hand. Dora's nails were neatly manicured and painted a tasteful geranium, the only touch of color in her dark city outfit.

"After coming home from school, I tried to live as Jenny, but my mom could never call me anything but Dora. To her, I was always Dora." She rubbed her temple, then leaned closer to Amy and Veronica before continuing. "Back at home, I bounced around a lot between guys, like I did in college. I was waitressing and working doubles and meeting all kinds of men.

"One night, about a year ago, this guy was eating alone at one of my tables. He was probably in his forties, and he was coming on strong all night. He was gorgeous and I was flirting back. When he finished eating, he waited for me, drinking at the bar until my shift ended. I left with him and he took me to the bar in his hotel, down the street from where I worked, which was real fancy. He bought me drinks, said the nicest things to me. He was so grown up and incredibly good-looking, and he clearly had money—he kept taking out this Motorola DynaTAC cell phone. Have you seen one of those?

"Anyway, I had a lot to drink, but I remember the night clearly. His name was Vince and it all hit me that night. We were at the bar and he answers his phone, and clearly he's talking to his wife, telling her he loves her, to have a good night and to kiss the kids for him, that he'd see them the next day. It was disgusting, and in my head I was shouting, *Fork! Fork!* I thought of how many guys I'd been with who were jerks and how I never felt happy with any of them. I thought about how none of them ever really cared about me. I felt sick. I walked out and away from Vince and, for once, I felt like I was doing something for myself."

"Good for you, Jen—uh—Dora," Veronica said.

"I heard what your dad told me all those years ago on Thanksgiving, Amy."

"My dad? What did he tell you?"

"You don't remember? Thanksgiving night when we went for the drive?"

"I remember the drive, but I'm not sure I remember exactly what he said." Amy could recall only her shock as Jenny revealed that her father had left.

"I always remembered it, but I hadn't really gotten it until that night with Vince and his fancy phone. It was like I saw myself helping this guy cheat on his wife, I saw myself being used and taken advantage of, not being loved. I hated it. Something clicked and I understood what your dad told me. He said, 'Believe you are worth being loved and don't ever settle.'"

Hearing her dad's advice loop back to her years later, Amy thought about Andrew and how she'd tried to fit him into her picture of perfect. She realized how she had justified away her gut feelings and suspicions. *My God,* it dawned on Amy, *I would have been settling for so much less if I'd stayed with Andrew.* Somehow, like Jenny, she had also missed the real meaning of the lessons she'd heard from her dad.

Dora set her glass down, the clink startling Amy back to the table as she continued. "All through college and after even, I was confusing attention with love. I was selling myself short over and over and over again. I was searching for something that I could never find, never catch hold of . . ." Her voice drifted off and her face looked pained. "That night it was like a secret unlocked in my head and I realized that I didn't feel that I was worth loving. I would never have consciously admitted that before. I didn't know it, but it suddenly struck me that I had always assumed men would leave me, that no one would bother to stick around. But now I work every day on feeling that I'm worth being loved."

She smiled at Amy and Veronica, who stared at her, attentive and impressed. "I'm not willing to settle anymore. I haven't been with anyone in a year. I'm single. Totally single and happy about it, for now. I even started painting again; I'm taking a watercolor class at NYU." She lifted her glass, toasting herself. Amy and Veronica joined her, genuinely glad for her.

"I owe you an apology," Dora said abruptly to Veronica, who managed to swallow her wine before she coughed. "I'm sorry about everything. It took me a while, but now I know that sex never made any guy love me. I had it all wrong and I hurt a lot of people, including you." She spoke calmly, with peace in her eyes. "I've been wanting to tell you that I'm sorry for a while."

They could feel her sincerity, and without a word, Veronica leaned to embrace Dora, whose shoulders eased beneath the hug.

"I'm learning to wait for the real thing. You've found that with Joey, I can see it."

"I have. He's the real thing for sure. It took me too long to realize it, but thank God, he was still there when I figured it out. I found true love in an unexpected place."

"Clearly, he completely adores you, Veronica. That's what I'm looking for, someone who is crazy about me—"

"Hi, I'm Todd."

Veronica, Amy, and Dora turned toward the low voice. Todd was gawking at Dora as he tilted his back toward the other girls. He was athletic, his shoulders tugging at his shirt seams, and he was handsome despite his nose, which was angled as if it had been broken and never set straight. The crookedness somehow added to his physical appeal.

"Can I buy you a drink?"

Veronica and Amy exchanged a look. *Here's where Jenny flips her hair and heads off with the cute fork.*

"Todd, is it? Thanks for the generous offer, with the open bar and all, but my friends and I were just catching up." Dora delivered the line with finesse and a new assuredness with men that Amy and Veronica had never seen in her before.

Veronica held her glass to her lips to hide the smirk. Todd clapped his hand over his heart, feigning a wound as he retreated to his pack of cackling buddies.

Dora winked at Veronica. "Now I can spot a fork a mile away and steer clear. I've finally gotten it down after being a fork magnet for years. I definitely dated a whole drawerful of every kind you can imagine. I'll have to show you the fork earrings I made in a jewelry workshop. I wear them to remind me what to avoid."

"Remember?" Amy interjected. "Veronica doesn't believe in the UCS and I'm starting to think she's right."

"Actually, it makes a lot of sense," Veronica announced after Dora excused herself to go to the restroom. "See how well that just worked to screen out forky Todd? You were right, I've found the elusive steak knife and I can see that it totally works."

"V, it's just something my dad made up. I took it too far."

"But think about all those forks you pegged and—"

"I missed the fork in my own bed. How effective was that?"

"Maybe he was good at hiding it, maybe you were too intent on him being your steak knife and missed it. Maybe there are some labeling mistakes, but the structure is solid."

"How is it that you're trying to convince me that the UCS works?"

They were laughing when Dora returned, and the three filled in the years, talking as they hadn't in school, the distance of time and maturity allowing a new friendship.

"I still think of my dad and wonder," Dora said. "It always comes to wondering why he left. But for all of my searching, I see that going out with everyone who flirted with me, and seeking validation through guys' attention, was all about me needing to figure out that I deserve love. My dad left me behind with doubts, without any experience of how boys think or act. I didn't know I was on a self-discovery mission all that time. I made tons of dumb choices." Dora shook her head to herself. "Growing up, I didn't have my dad to guide me, and as unsatisfying as it felt, I thought I was doing it the right way, whatever that means. I thought going out with lots of different guys was how you found someone to love you. But I was looking outside all those years instead of looking inside myself. I know it sounds all therapy-shrinky, but I've finally realized that his leaving was about him, maybe even about my mom, too, but it wasn't about me. I've also been able to see my mom in a new way. She really had it hard and did a lot to make the two of us a family."

Veronica stared at her, smiling, and she touched her fingers to Dora's. "I don't know what to say. You're amazing. I never thought about my dad's presence as helping to define me and my interactions with men, but I guess there's truth to that."

"Sorry to be so serious. Thanks for listening. I don't have many girlfriends." Dora paused, exhaled. "And thanks for forgiving me."

Veronica answered with a clink of her glass to Dora's.

"Amy, I also wanted to tell you that I'm sorry. I'm sorry that I hit on Andrew. It was a shitty thing to do, especially since you were always so good to me. I felt jealous. You had everything I wanted: a great dad and a hot boyfriend."

They looked at one another, seeing more, feeling deeper.

"Speaking of Andrew, how's he doing?"

Amy chuckled. "My turn to catch you up on things."

Veronica chimed in: "Andrew turned out to be a fork in knife's clothing."

Chapter 51

ON A LATE JANUARY weekend visit home, Amy woke up in her childhood bedroom. The smell of coffee drifted up to her as she lay in bed, peaceful and content. Boxes and crates from her move out of Andrew's apartment were still stacked in the corner of her room. Most of them were unmarked, filled hastily with her belongings in no order, but one box, under two others, was tilted, and she could see the stars she'd scrawled on the side with a fat black marker.

She slid out of the sheets and her bare legs goose-pimpled at the touch of the the cool winter air. Wrapping herself in a throw blanket, she shifted the cartons, sat beside the starred box, and released the crisscrossed flaps. She lifted out her Treasure Box and rested it in her lap, unclasping the lid. The hospital bracelet from her homecoming accident rested on top of the blurry graduation picture of her and Andrew taken with his disposable camera before the ceremony. She moved aside the fire-alarm tally sheet and the letters from Zach Bennett. She carefully picked up sections of papers and memories and laid them out beside her until she found what she was looking for.

Her list was handwritten, originally in black ink, but additions and edits were visible in different shades of blue, in varying widths of black. The pale green copy paper was folded into eighths. The edges of the folds were worn and softened, and the creases were so embedded that the sheet tried to fold on its own as she held it. The title of the chart was neatly printed: *Traits of My Perfect Husband.* Amy chuckled at herself. On her girlhood list, she'd set out to define her ideal man, believing she could script him, or perhaps conjure him. She put everything she thought she wanted on the list, every characteristic that had mattered most to her. There were three columns across the top labeled *Extremely Important—Nonnegotiable, Moderately Important—Willing to Compromise,* and *Unimportant—But Nice.* Trust was at the top of her list, and she realized how often she had doubted Andrew. There were so many little lies and the taunting lie of "someday." She thought she knew the list by heart, but as she read, her smile melted into a dropped jaw, her mouth fell agape.

How had she not seen it? In all these years, how could she have missed it? Her list described Matt. Not just the top priorities, but he fit the trivial wishes, too. Amy looked at her list thinking that for all of her idealism, she'd set the bar too low. Matt gave her things that she hadn't even dreamed of adding to her list. He was so much more than she could have imagined. Pulsing with emotions, she let the paper fold upon itself and tucked it back into the box. There was no perfect guy, she knew in her maturity, just a perfect fit.

She worked backward, replacing the piles she'd removed, thumbing through them as she went. There were squares of wrapping paper from gifts she'd received, tickets to a play Matt had taken her to, the first Valentine's Day card he'd given her and others for each year since. Professional, labeled party pictures from formals, semiformals, rush parties, and pledge nights documented her college years.

A mix tape, a gift from Matt, was under a pizza receipt with a dots game on the back, a game she'd saved because she'd finally crushed Matt. She glanced at her freshman-year transcript with A's lining the columns, even in computer programming thanks to her personal tutor. A dried-up, deep red rose petal fell out from between the notes, and there was the golf tournament score-card and years of postcards from Syracuse. She rubbed the petal between her fingertips. Matt had been there all along.

There was a tap on her door, then it slowly cracked open and her father's head peered into the room.

"Over here, Dad," Amy said, leaning forward to be visible among the boxes. Tom York, in his moccasins and flannel bath-robe, wove his way to his daughter and sat beside her on the floor.

"You're happy," he said, smiling broadly, and Amy reflected it back with a definitive nod. "Matt's a good person. I'm happy that you finally noticed him," he teased with a wink.

"You really knew?"

"Honey, it was clear he's loved you for years. All those summer and vacation visits, his notes and calls to you. You honestly didn't see it?"

Amy slumped back against a pile of boxes, looking down at the memories encircling her. "I was so sure it was Andrew I was supposed to be with. Marriage was supposed to be our next step. I guess I never saw beyond that."

"It worried me, seeing you giving up little bits of yourself for Andrew."

Amy nodded and handed her dad a picture: it was Amy dressed up for Halloween with Matt beside her holding a guitar. She was the tooth fairy, dressed in a twinkly, sequined ice-blue dress, with wings, a tooth-shaped wand, and a pouch around her neck filled with quarters.

"What is Matt dressed up as?" her dad asked.

"Some rock star I can't remember. That was sophomore year.

Andrew decided to stay out after the Halloween party fizzled. Matt walked me to my dorm, then hiked across campus back to his."

Tom York listened, then handed the photo back to Amy and took the new one she was giving him.

"That's us at the James Taylor concert. Andrew wasn't into him but I really wanted to go, so Matt took me. And this one is Matt and me volunteering with my Kappa sisters, senior year. We donated books and read to kids at the city library. Matt borrowed a friend's car, drove a group of us downtown, and stayed to read to the kids." Amy looked at her father. "He's always been there for me."

EARLY ON FEBRUARY 14, 1994, Amy caught a cab to the Empire State Building to do a story on the first year that Valentine's Day weddings were being allowed at the midtown landmark. She had a contact who got her in early and she felt triumphant interviewing some of the winning couples before their staggered ceremonies on the eighty-sixth-floor observation deck. Her photographer got crisp shots and, after witnessing most of the historic weddings, she was eager to write the piece formulating in her mind. As she descended the elevator, she smiled, envisioning romantic movie scenes and happy couples.

"Amy!" Jarred from her reverie, she scanned the busy lobby. Businessmen and -women in dark suits ebbed and flowed through the marble space. "Amy!" She heard it again but could still see no one she knew.

A touch on her back made her turn, and she was face-to-face with Andrew. She startled at seeing him, his face as handsome as when she first fell in love with him and his eyes greener than she remembered, but his hairline seemed higher and his sandy hair thinner. Someone bustled by, knocking her closer to him.

"How have you been? What are you doing here? Can you grab

a bite?" He threw the questions out, not giving her time to answer, and guided her out of the traffic flow.

She looked down at the pattern in the marble floor, gathering herself. Matt had consumed her thoughts and heart for the nearly two months since the last time she'd seen Andrew. An unsettled feeling clenched her chest, and nostalgia mixed with her new truths. Her mind drifted back to freshman year and meeting Andrew, to how things had once been. The memory of those early days with Andrew and all the years since spiraled around in her mind.

"Let's get something to eat. Come on, there's a café right here. Please." His voice was light and friendly, his eyes sparkled at her, and his smile lassoed her into the nearby restaurant. She still hadn't spoken a word as they sat at a small table in the bustling café. Her mind whirled, trying to peg down why and how he'd become a fork. It wasn't just the cheating, it wasn't the Donnas and Dawns and Brees alone that defined him as a fork. It was the accumulation of falsehoods, the way he yo-yoed with her feelings, the detachment and dismissiveness. How had she been so wrong?

"I—I can't stay," Amy began.

"A quick snack. Or just a cup of coffee? Decaf? Please, Aim."

"Don't call me that. What do you want? Why are we here?"

"I want to talk with you, just sit for a minute. I'm so sorry. I can't stand the thought of you not loving me anymore. It's over with Bree. Done. She felt terrible about things and dumped me, and then she met some guy. She moved to Pennsylvania with him."

"I'm not upset about her anymore. She wasn't our problem. Your cheating just helped me see that. You were right when you said I was always waiting for you. I sold myself short and stuck around when I shouldn't have. I didn't believe in myself enough to leave you, and I wasted a lot of time trying to make something work that wasn't going to."

"No, you're wrong. What about that silly stone you always played with? It said to believe in us."

"No, it meant—"

"We were good together. I know I took you for granted sometimes, but we worked together."

"Maybe for a little while at school, but we hung on too long."

"It kills me to think of you being mad at me. Are you saying I've really lost you?"

"I'm not mad at you." Amy stood. "I hope you find a way to be happy without having to be perfect."

As she crossed Thirty-Fourth Street, she looked up at the building towering above. She thought about all it represented to the city, to America, as the tallest building for more than four decades. She thought of what it meant to those who had built it, like Joey's grandfather, and to those who had gotten married there that very day, and she thought about what it meant to her. It was so much grander from its base than from her living room window, but it was a constant in her grown-up New York City life. Its language in lights, its confident spire, its historical pride. The only time she couldn't look upon it from her home in the city was when she lived with Andrew.

Chapter 52

THE MAY WEDDING DATE created a cascade of activity and a flurry of preparation all spring. A cancellation opened the weekend, and when Dora called, Joey and Veronica scooped up the date. They agreed that a shorter planning time worked in their favor since both mothers had too many ideas to offer in the arrangements. The date was settled, the guest list was growing, and it was past time for the parents to meet.

Nerves jangled in Veronica as she reined in her hair for the meeting in the city. Joey's calm centered her; his touch soothed her. She needed his composure on the cab ride and at the restaurant as her foot bobbed rhythmically. His parents were already seated when they arrived.

"Joey! Veronica!" they shouted through the room. "Over here!" Filomena waved to them in case they hadn't heard her.

When her parents arrived, Susan Warren delicately reached out her hand to greet Joey's mom, who flew past her outstretched hand and pulled Susan into her bosom in an energetic hug. Veronica's mother was slender and appeared to be swallowed in the shorter, pudgy woman's embrace.

Throughout dinner, Veronica worried as Gerald Warren asked Nick DiNatali to repeat himself every time he said "earl" for "oil" or "yuge" for "huge." Nick's hearty laugh and boisterous story-telling resounded, and her mother seemed to be whispering to balance the volume.

"Joe, did you tell your dad about my old Eldorado?" The men chattered about cars and "earl."

Susan's eye widened only enough for Veronica to notice as Filomena shouted to Nick seated beside her, "Nick, pass me the bread, would you?" She served her husband generous pieces of bread and oil, though both sat in front of him, before taking a small heel for herself.

The mothers bonded over a shared love of dirty martinis and stuffed mushrooms. Veronica was grateful for the common threads, however small. They shared stories about their children sitting with them and avoided any controversial topics like politics, religion, or the wedding. Filomena wanted "yuge" Italian cookie platters for favors, and Susan wanted to give Simon Pearce handblown glass. Filomena favored a DJ who was the godson of a family friend, and Susan wanted a well-known sixteen-piece band. Joey and Veronica danced between their parents' visions and their own wishes for their nuptials. The Warrens insisted on paying for their daughter's wedding but worked to respect the couple's choices and tried not to intervene. Not too much. They were all finding their way in their new roles.

Filomena launched into another story. "When Joey was a little one—"

"Ma, please."

Ignoring him, she bragged on: "From the time he was small, he was always the smartest boy in his class, smartest kid in the whole school! He helped all the other kids, always had the A's. Everybody loved him! And he always does good at everything: he can fix a drain with his uncle and cook with his mama. Did you know he can draw, too? And he can solve any crossword puzzle in no time!"

Politely, Susan latched on to that tidbit. "Oh yes, he's wonderful at crosswords. It's something Joey and I have enjoyed doing together on his visits to Newport."

As the evening wore on and the cocktails emptied, the couples laughed together and forged a connection, one that might never extend beyond the realm of their offspring, but one that was amicable and respectful nonetheless. When desserts and espressos were served, Filomena slapped the table, jostling it and sloshing her own coffee.

"Veronica, you call us 'Mom' and 'Dad' now! No more of this Mr. and Mrs. nonsense," her future mother-in-law announced, loud enough for every restaurant guest to hear. Susan glanced around self-consciously as other diners gawked their way.

"Thank you, Mrs.—um, Mom," Veronica ventured. She waited, but her parents didn't make the same offer to Joey.

THE SPRING WAS FILLED WITH dress fittings, flower choices, and music selections. They traipsed around the city reviewing bands, tasting cakes, and selecting wedding rings. There were bridal showers and thank-you notes. Veronica received expensive vases and platters and china and silver place settings in Newport. In Hoboken, she got a chevron-patterned, hand-crocheted afghan from Aunt Tessie, satiny lingerie from Joey's grandma, and a fifteen-piece cookware set from Mom DiNatali.

They wrote their vows and met with the pastor, and Joey helped his parents make rehearsal dinner plans and come to terms with him getting married outside of their Catholic faith. Veronica overheard him talking with them on different occasions: "No, Ma, there's no priest, he's a pastor," "We're not having a Mass, there's no Mass in the Methodist church, Mom," "Yes, they still believe in God and Jesus," "It's a real church." When they were together, Filomena would cross herself and shake her head as she protested.

Veronica counted down the days, checking them off on the wall calendar tacked up in her office, twelve months of New York City firefighters, a Christmas gift from Amy. Even the hot men holding hoses couldn't distract her from her long to-do list. Every night, Veronica went home to her maid of honor, and they laughed and planned and reminisced before Veronica headed down the hall to Joey's and Amy got on the phone to Syracuse.

As a bare-chested Mr. May looked down from a ladder, wearing only a smudge of soot and his turnout gear, Veronica crossed off the second-to-last workday before her wedding.

"Tomorrow night Chelsea's away on a business trip. I'll stay here and we can have a movie night in pj's like old times," Veronica suggested to Amy that evening, holding up her next day's work outfit by the hangers. "I'll go to the video store on the way home—I'll get *Footloose*—and we can order in and spend both the second-to-last and last night here before I become Mrs. DiNatali."

Amy agreed, and Veronica padded in her slippers to apartment 202, dangling her suit high above the floor.

AS AMY HELPED VERONICA plan her wedding, Matt transferred his credits to NYU to complete his degree and accepted a job at a start-up, WP Studio. He would be working in a new technology area, building a city guide called Total New York on the growing Internet. Before relocating, he remained in Syracuse to finish a class and a project for Lockheed. He and Amy called and wrote letters, not letting a detail pass unshared. While juggling work and wedding planning, Amy helped him move into his temporary downtown apartment. Once settled into the city, they would take time to plan their next steps.

On the Thursday before the wedding, Amy was called into her editor's office. Her boss, Carolyn James, was a role model to her, someone who had become a mentor and friend. She helped guide Amy's writing and encouraged her career development. She challenged Amy to raise her hand for tough stories and pitch ideas that were bold and brave.

As Carolyn shared the reason for summoning her, Amy leaned forward in her chair, her heart beating rapidly and her breathing shallow.

"Think about it, Amy, this is a spectacular opportunity. I believe in your talent and know this would be an excellent assignment for you. I know it doesn't give you much time. The life of a journalist, right?"

Stunned, Amy thanked Carolyn and went back to her desk to call Matt; he was the first person she wanted to talk to. She was told he was out of the office and left a message. Amy wanted to talk with him in person right away, but their schedules were plotted. She had movie plans that night with Veronica, and he had a welcome dinner with his new team and the owner of WP Studio. It was important, she knew, but frustration mounted. He was so close, but she couldn't get to him. They wouldn't be able to see each other until the next evening, Friday, for the wedding rehearsal.

Amy walked the seven long blocks from her office on West Forty-Fourth Street to Third Avenue and arrived sweaty at the apartment that had been her first New York City home. The walk gave her time to think, and she wondered if maybe this was the big decision Train Santa had predicted, there had been several in a short time. Veronica wasn't home yet, so she showered and thought. Waited and thought. Stared out at the Empire State Building and thought. When Veronica finally rushed in with an armful of Blockbuster tapes, she was bursting to reminisce with Amy. They ordered food and pulled out old photo albums and laughed through the years and hairstyles, all while Carolyn's offer lingered in Amy's thoughts and heart. The night ticked on in rolls of giggles and remember-whens. It was a time of looking back before Veronica's new chapter. It was her friend's time and, not only did she need to talk to Matt, but Amy simply couldn't bring herself to tell Veronica the news.

Chapter 53

MATT MET AMY LATE in the afternoon before the rehearsal dinner. She hadn't slept much overnight. They sat on a bench in Bryant Park and Amy stroked a swatch of her stick-straight hair.

"I'm glad you could meet me before the rehearsal tonight, Amy."

"Me, too, I really needed to see you."

He leaned forward. His shirtsleeves were rolled, exposing his forearms. She stared at his masculine hands, his sturdy wrists, the knobby bone that pressed out at the sides, the strips of tendons. She had watched those hands for years, confidently making keystrokes, writing in her notebooks, rubbing his jaw.

"I've missed you with us being two hundred fifty miles apart, and now that we're finally in the same place, I have to ask you something," Matt began. "I've been thinking a lot about this, and yesterday I went out to see your dad." He kept talking to her puzzled brow. "I don't want to overshadow Veronica, but"—he took her hands in his—"'when you realize you want to spend the rest of your life with somebody, you want the rest of your life to start as soon as possible.'"

Amy instantly recognized her favorite *When Harry Met Sally . . .* movie quote. She widened her tired eyes as he slid from the bench and kneeled before her. "Amy Melissa York, I have always loved you and will love you forever. I want to be your steak knife. Will you marry me?" He beamed up at her and held out the platinum setting with a round cut diamond and two baguettes. It was her dream ring, the one in the picture in her jewelry box. A few tentative claps turned into a chorus of applause around them before the busy New Yorkers were off again.

She held the ring between her fingers, and tears welled and her face crumpled.

"What is it? What's wrong?"

"I don't even know how to tell you this. I couldn't sleep thinking about it last night."

"What? What is it?" He sat beside her again, worry in his eyes.

Amy looked into his face, taking in his deep brown eyes and the dimple through the scruff. Matt urged her with his gaze.

"I love you. I love you more than I've ever loved anyone, but there's something I have to do." She filled her lungs, then she let the words pour without stopping. "I've wanted to talk to you since I found out yesterday ... Carolyn offered me a yearlong assignment in London. I can't turn it down; I have to do this. I know you just moved here and that you've waited a long time while I figured things out. I want to be together, more than I can say, and I understand if you can't wait for me again. But, Matt, I have to do it. I haven't told Carolyn yet, but I've decided to take the job. I leave in a week."

A nearby young mother and her child threw pieces of New York City pretzel, and a mess of pigeons swooped around for the scraps. Their scurries mimicked Amy's heart. She fingered the ring, holding what she'd always wanted, the symbol of a love so deep.

He pressed his eyes closed and pulled her into his arms.

"Okay," he whispered, after a long moment.

They were wrapped in each other, clutched together, as the

sounds of the city park circled them. All around the bench, it was an ordinary day: dogs being walked, men in suits rushing by, old ladies strolling with market bags. On the bench, two lives took a new direction, finally together but branching apart again.

"I've thought about us for years, you've only had a few months. I'm proud of you. This is important for you. I'm going to miss you incredibly, but it's good you decided to go."

"I love you, Matt. I love you so much. You'll come to visit, won't you?"

"Are you kidding me? I'll be accumulating some serious airline miles." He kissed her. "What about your dad and Veronica? How did they react?"

"My dad was like you, supportive beyond reason. I have to call him; he must be going crazy knowing both of our secrets. I haven't been able to tell V yet. We're spending tonight together after the dinner, I'm going to tell her then. I can't believe I'll be gone when they get back."

Matt exhaled, "A lot of changes for all of us. Come on, let's get ready for the rehearsal. I'm spending every possible minute with you before you leave."

She held out the ring. "It's perfect. What should we do about this?"

"Please wear it. We can figure out the details for when you get back, but I want you to be my wife, Amy, no matter where in the world you are."

THE GROOMSMEN WERE LINED up beside Joey, looking sharp in their tuxedos. He beamed at them and out at the crowd filling the church. When the music began, he could not look away from the door at the rear of the sanctuary. He watched as the bridesmaids took deliberate steps. Amy grinned at him as she approached. She was the last to file down between the pews and the double doors swept closed behind her, but not before Joey glimpsed a wisp of white. He waited, holding his breath, his smile immovable, staring at the heavy, paneled doors. Anticipation shone from him like a prism in sunlight.

Without turning his head from the back of the church, he heard his brother Nicky, his best man, give a low whistle of air through parted lips, and his brother Dominic whispered from two people away: "Here she comes, man."

Both doors opened at once, revealing Veronica and her father framed, magically, in the entry. Daylight lit them from behind, but instead of silhouetting them, it created an aura, a golden glow around them. Joey inhaled and he felt a friendly pat on his shoulder. His gaze was fixed on Veronica slowly drawing nearer to him. Her smile was for him alone, her eyes locked on to his. He wiped his palms discreetly against his thighs then pressed a hand to his heart, feeling the paper in his breast pocket.

They stopped at the pew where her mother waited. Veronica's father lifted her veil and whispered in her ear, and she clasped him in a hug. Her mother rose and cradled Veronica's face in her hands, joy and love spilling through them. She kissed her daughter, and the trio turned to Joey as he stepped closer to receive his bride. With wetness in their eyes and hands joined, Gerald and Susan settled themselves in the front row together.

Across the aisle, behind his parents, Joey heard Aunt Tessie, who thought she was whispering: "Would you look at the lace on that dress, Marie? It must've cost a fortune."

Marie loud-whispered back, "All that red hair. How'd they make it stay up like that?"

"Where's the priest? Why isn't that fella wearing a collar?"

"You two keep it down," Concetta scolded.

"But no priest, Connie, and they're not crossing themselves," Tessie tutted.

A shaft of sunshine spotlighted Veronica as she stood facing Joey. It was only the two of them among two hundred well-wishers. Hand in hand, they climbed the three steps and joined their wedding party. The pastor greeted the gatherers and led the bride and groom in a declaration of marriage. The couple lit the unity candle, and then he invited the wedding party to sit for his sermon.

"Joseph, Veronica, throughout your life, you will be faced with fire alarms," the pastor began.

A hum of gasps and whispers vibrated from the Syracuse guests in the pews. Veronica turned to Amy; they gaped at each other with wide mouths hinting at puzzled smiles.

"What?" Joey mouthed to Veronica, who whispered, "I'll tell you later."

The pastor continued: "Life will have surprises, good and bad. It will have fires that are real and false alarms, but each will give you something to learn about yourself and about each other. Each of these alarms will reveal a truth to you. How will you respond and react? Will you put others before yourself? What sacrifices, what choices, will you make in the face of a fire alarm?

"Notice and appreciate when life seems calm and content. Be grateful for the lack of alarms in those times of tranquility and build your reserves of patience and love. Use the fire drills of life to practice kindness and respect for each other, as opportunities for self-improvement and growth as a couple. Joseph and Veronica, you are surrounded today by those who care for you. Learn to seek out extra support and turn to family and friends when a fire gets too hot. Your true friends will be there when the alarms are not false.

"Bolster and shield each other during the fires, big and small, in your marriage, be each other's safety net. Take time to explore what those fire-alarm moments mean. Work to prevent fires. Communicate truthfully to extinguish sparks of despair or frustration early, before they ignite. Use compassion and empathy, discussion and touch.

"While you put out the fires of loneliness and fear, continue to fan the flames of your love, and when that love changes from impassioned to contented, from new love to mature love, always nurture the embers in your hearts to keep your marriage strong and vibrant. Joseph, Veronica, we ask God's blessing upon you, today and forever. Amen."

Silence hovered as the pastor prayed and then directed the wedding party to stand. He blessed the rings and Joey pulled a note card from his pocket. Printed in his youthful scribble were the traditional vows they'd combined with those they'd written. Smiling, Joey focused on Veronica and spoke their vows straight from his heart, holding the card as insurance but not needing to refer to his notes. Then Veronica faced him, reciting the vows from memory.

"I, Veronica, take you, Joey, to be my husband. I promise to be true to you in good times and in bad, in sickness and in health. I will love you and honor you all the days of my life. I promise to give you the best of myself and to accept you the way you are. I promise to share my time, my feelings, and my dreams. I promise . . ." She paused, searching the ceiling for the next words. Joey offered his card to her, the congregation chuckled, and Veronica tilted her head with a smirk.

Her memory triggered, she continued: "I promise to grow alongside you, to encourage and support you as we both change, and to bring creativity and an open mind to our relationship. I promise to keep you my priority and to treat you with the respect and consideration of a lifetime friend. I promise to value and to love you in all ways."

Joey slid the ring on her finger and felt a wave of security as she placed the wedding band over his knuckle. The sensation of it lightly holding his fingers apart, the newness of the gold untarnished on his hand, the significance of its outward display of his connection to Veronica, all made his breath catch. He wiped a tear from the corner of his eye.

"Now that Veronica and Joseph have given themselves to each other by solemn vows, with the joining of hands, and with the giving and receiving of rings, I announce to you that they are husband and wife."

They were invited to share their first married kiss and, after a blessing of the marriage, were presented to the exuberant audience. Joey and Veronica walked up the aisle to the back of the church encircled in cheers and whistles. They slipped up the stairs to an empty alcove, allowing their guests to filter outside. Sitting side by side on a wooden bench, Joey reached into his breast pocket and handed Veronica an envelope.

"For you, Mrs. DiNatali."

Her face spread into a smile as she slid her finger under the flap and gingerly released the letter. The paper trembled in her hands as she read the beautiful words with a new understanding of Amy's romanticism. The love letter was the stuff of movies, of romance novels, of fairy tales; it moved her to tears that these words were for her.

"I love you so much, Joey, I am so lucky to have you as my husband." She tried the word on, enjoying the sound of it.

Chapter 54

AFTER A NEWPORT/NEW JERSEY segregated cocktail hour overlooking the East River and a lot of wine with dinner, the party loosened up. "I know we told the band not to play this song," Veronica shouted into Joey's ear, laughing. The dance floor bounced with the force of hundreds of feet stomping to *Celebrate good times, come on!*

"Guess they know better than us—it's clearly a crowd-pleaser."

Amy joined Joey's cousins and tugged anyone on the sidelines into the fray of dancing. Society women dressed in pale-colored St. John suits and strings of pearls swayed beside their custom-suited husbands, while Joey's cousins and friends twirled young ladies and Italian wives. A conga line bounded through the crowd. Orazio's belly hung over his black dress pants as he grasped the shoulders of a young colleague of Veronica's, who linked in turn to Aunt Erma, Cousin Alessandra, and Cousin Ottavia, all in ensembles of glittery golds and sparkling silvers.

Towers of cellophane-covered cookie trays filled a table against the far wall, and pouches of Jordan almonds in tulle bags sat at each place setting in elegant, handblown Simon Pearce glass dishes. The candy-coated nuts were an Italian tradition, five almonds signifying five wishes for the bride and groom: health, wealth, happiness, fertility, and longevity. How could Veronica veto that? They'd compromised and each family gave the favors they wanted, but the bold, energetic Italian traditions and personalities dominated the Manhattan ballroom.

The tarantella invited everyone to their feet. Joey's aunts danced with one another as the men sipped their sambuca in a circle around the dance floor. The old women sang and shook tambourines against their buxom hips. Susan Warren clapped her hands, trying to keep up as Filomena DiNatali pivoted her around, vigorously demonstrating the steps.

Ian grabbed Veronica and kicked his heels with her to the Italian folk music, making up moves as he went. They laughed together, and he spoke into her ear: "So you married your electrician after all."

"Yes, I got wise advice from a good friend," she replied with a wink. "And I'm glad you brought Robert."

With hands in the air, the crowd lurched from the tarantella to "Living on a Prayer."

"I'm getting a lot of stares, this is our first big outing together. Get it, outing?"

"Hilarious, Ian. Your parents seem good with it."

"They're coming around. It's been a bit of an adjustment for them, but I'm lucky, actually. They've been much better than lots of stories I've heard."

Joey took her hand from Ian as the band slowed it down with Journey. The crowd sorted into couples, faithfully. Veronica breathed in Joey's clean scent and squeezed herself deeper into his arms. Over his shoulder she watched couples dancing—Matt and Amy, her smiling parents, Joey's uncle Cosmo with her aunt Barbara—and she saw Dora holding her clipboard, talking with Zach Bennett. *He would finally be a steak knife for Dora,* Veronica thought, knowing that Amy had liked him more than she let on all those years ago.

She slowed the time in her mind. Consciously living in the moment, she told herself, *I am at my wedding. I'm here in the exact moments we've been planning for months.*

Joey swirled her around and her dress spun like an umbrella. Their friends whooped and cheered and circled around them, clapping to the beat of the next song. From the center, Veronica saw the melding of cultures. She saw her new sister-in-law, Tina, in a skimpy red sequined dress that barely contained her new-baby breasts dancing next to Mrs. Curtis in her camel Chanel shift. Angela, done up in more lace than an Italian bride, flounced beside Mr. Bennett, and Ian, dapper in his seersucker, dipped Aunt Tessie, who was laughing like a schoolgirl. Looking at the people around them, it was an odd but jubilant scene of merged mismatches. She and Joey had made this happen, this was their new life. It made Veronica burst.

As she gazed at the crowd from Joey's arms, her mother approached, motioning them to the edge of the dance floor. Susan Warren started to speak, then paused and began again: "Joey, it's not easy to have another boy call me 'Mom,' but I can't think of a better man to have as a son. We would be honored for you to call us 'Mom' and 'Dad.'" She touched her palm to his cheek for a moment, and Veronica cried through a beaming smile.

"Sweetie"—she turned toward her daughter—"we're thrilled for you. Henry would be, too. I know he's with us and would've loved to have Joey for a brother."

Her brother would be happy, and she was grateful they could talk about him again.

DORA SAW TO IT that the reception was going smoothly; they'd done the first dances, dinner, and the cake ceremony, all without a glitch. A friend of Veronica's family, Zach Bennett, kept finding her and flirting in the nicest possible way. Dora's heart fluttered, and finally, she trusted herself to recognize that he wasn't a fork. She wasn't sure what he was exactly, yet, but she placed him hopefully into the knives. Across the room, she saw him, his shirt-sleeves rolled at the wrists, talking with a plump old lady in a loose floral print dress—*Joey's grandma*, she thought, even more interested. Lost in her daydream, she hadn't noticed the band gather the single ladies, she didn't hear the telltale chords and taunts. She didn't know they were throwing the bouquet until it hit her in the face. Instinctively, she put out her arms, catching the stunning flowers between her chest and her clipboard. The room roared and cheered, and Dora blushed, grateful when the band started up again.

As the guests danced heartily, she knew she had something to do. She placed the bouquet in a vase of water and found the man she sought.

"Mr. York, I don't know if you remember me. I came home with Amy freshman year for Thanksgiving?"

He smiled in recognition. "Of course. Jenny, right?"

Dora didn't correct him. "I want to thank you for your advice to me. It took a while, but I can finally say that I believe I'm worth being loved."

He nodded and, like he would with his own daughter, he wrapped his arms around her. Dora held still, wishing his hug would last and last. She waited until he released her with a final pat and a kind smile.

"Thank you," she whispered before retreating to her office for a moment alone.

MATT HANDED AMY A glass of water with lemon the way she liked it and tugged her to the side of the room. She gulped it, breathless from dancing. She was giddy with the romance of the day and the break from dwelling on London. Her separation from Matt was never far from her thoughts, but she had confidently called Carolyn that morning to accept the dream assignment. It was done.

"Come sit with me." Matt pulled out a banquet chair in a corner behind a table of women with thinning hair sprayed high. She sat on his lap, wishing she could be even closer. Switching from admiring the new twinkle on her finger to examining and the charms that were always around her wrist, she came to the newest, Big Ben. Matt had given it to her before the ceremony. Fingering each charm overwhelmed her and she started to cry. Her tears wouldn't stop. They spilled happy and sad, excited and frightened, confident and nervous, all at once.

"I'm going to miss you, Amy. I love you."

"I love you so much." Catching her breath, she tried to stop crying. Matt held her as she heaved in sobs. Suddenly, she was laughing. Her body shook and her smile was covered in tears as competing thoughts and emotions collided. Matt handed her a cocktail napkin and she dabbed her eyes and blew her nose, gathering herself.

"I know you've been doubting the utensil system lately," Matt said, hugging her to him, "but maybe this will help you decide. Yesterday, a pregnant coworker was flipping through a baby name book and she looked up the name 'Saxon' for kicks. You'll never guess what it means."

Amy studied his face, hiccuping as she listened.

"It means sword or knife. Apparently, I've been your steak knife all along."

WHEN VERONICA'S FANCY WHITE shoes paused for a moment, Amy led her away. They left the reception room for the lobby outside the ballroom. The contrasting silence vibrated in their ears; they were alone except for a few balding men talking in a corner around a towering plate of cannoli. Veronica fanned her forehead, her face flushed pink and her curls unraveled down her neck. She flapped the skirt of her dress to get a breeze on her legs. Amy pointed to the couches.

"I can't believe I won't get to see you all the time," Veronica said, repeating a phrase she had spoken countless times since the prior evening when Amy shared the news. All of the news.

As soon as the bustle of the rehearsal dinner evening receded, and the girls were back in the apartment, Veronica noticed the glint on Amy's finger. Now that she had her own proposal story, Amy recounted it with infinite detail while Veronica held Amy's hand in one of hers, and a tissue in the other. The proposal intertwined with her move to England, and the two wove a blanket of surprise for Veronica. Together, they had cried and laughed, looked back and planned ahead.

Now, sitting outside the ballroom, Amy fished in her tiny purse and pulled out a skinny package.

"Since you've converted to a believer, it's for your first Christmas tree."

Veronica laughed, unwrapping the decorative silver handle then the edge of the knife.

"Oh, Amy, I love it!" Veronica held the knife up by the red velvet ribbon looped through the hole the jeweler made in the handle. It spun gently, finding its balance.

"Look, I had the guy at the store engrave it."

Veronica flipped it over and saw *1994—First Christmas* etched onto the blade.

The door swung into the sitting area, letting a burst of noise and drums escape.

"There you are," Amy's father said, sitting beside his daughter. "What's that?"

Veronica laid the knife in his hand. "Joey's my perfect steak knife."

Laughter chorused from the three of them.

"The knives were the nicest category of guys, weren't they? It's hard to believe you girls still use that fool thing. I'm afraid Amy took it too seriously." He squeezed his daughter's hand.

Amy shrugged. "Maybe, but I think I just made some labeling mistakes."

Veronica said, "To tell you the truth, Mr. York, I never bought into the whole Utensil Classification System. But I was wrong. That fool thing honestly works."

Discussion Questions

1. What traits do you see in Amy that represent young women today? What about Veronica? Jenny? Can you see yourself in any of the characters, either now or when you were their age?

2. What do you see as the main message of *Forks, Knives, and Spoons*?

3. Do you think men and women can be "just friends"? Why or why not? There are several instances in the book in which that line is crossed. Is there always an attraction on one end or the other? Name times in the story when Amy had a chance to see or notice Matt but she didn't. Why does it take Amy so long to recognize Matt as more than a friend when others around her see it?

4. What does Santa Claus symbolize throughout the story? Why is his message important?

5. People often say that college and grad school are *the* times to meet your future spouse and that later, as time goes on, it gets harder. Do you agree?

6. In the 1980s there were no cell phones, Internet, or even personal computers. Texting didn't exist, and meeting up face-to-face, talking on the phone, or sending snail mail

letters were the ways to socialize and stay connected. How do these differences affect college social life in this digital age as compared to in *Forks, Knives, and Spoons*?

7. Why do you think the author chose to set the story in the late 1980s? Does it impact the characters' choices and actions? If so, in what ways would the outcomes and characters' actions be different if it was set in modern day?

8. If trust was important enough to Amy to be on her "Ideal Traits of a Husband" list, why do you think she ignored or justified the many little fibs and lies Andrew told her? Does Andrew trust Amy? Should he?

9. What is the significance of Jenny changing her name? How does she change and grow through the story? Do you know someone like her?

10. How does the loss of Veronica's brother impact her relationship with Joey and the relationship with her parents?

11. Does Veronica's relationship to Amy influence her relationship with Joey? Do you think Amy acts as a stepping-stone to Joey? If so, in what ways?

12. Why do you think Joey was able to forgive Veronica? What allows Veronica and Joey to overcome the differences in their backgrounds and family cultures?

13. Why do you think Veronica's parents were able to come around rather quickly and be genuinely accepting of Joey? How do her parents, particularly Susan Warren, change through the book?

14. What do the fire alarms signify? In what ways did the pastor's sermon relate to the revelations during the alarms in their college years?

15. What kind of utensil would you label Andrew? Matt? Joey? Do you think Amy was on target with her labels? Can you fit people in your own life into the different Utensil Classifications? Amy believed in the UCS and Veronica didn't—where do you fall? Later, their belief in the system shifted. Did yours change at all?

16. Discuss the meaning of the Empire State Building throughout the story.

17. Amy finally got everything she wanted. Why do you think she made the decision she does at the end? Are you happy with her choices?

Acknowledgments

SINCE I WAS FIVE, I've wanted to be an author. I have many to thank for helping me realize this dream.

My early readers took the task seriously and provided thoughtful feedback. Thank you to Beth Bogdan, Dana Marnane, Stefanie Abate, Cindy Antonelli, Kelly Fichter, Jen Gaffney, Erinn Pisano, Amanda Mathieu and Amanda Hillegas. I'm grateful for Angela Lauria and Jeanette Perez who worked with me at the start of this journey with invaluable encouragement and big picture guidance.

Thank you to Brooke Warner, Crystal Patriarche, Lauren Wise, and the amazing team at SparkPress. Thank you to my fabulous, eagle-eyed copy editor, Nancy Tan, to Kas DeCarvalho for dotting, crossing, and redlining, and to my publicist, Sharon Bially and her team at BookSavvy Public Relations.

I'm grateful for all of my friends who have heard about the "fork book" for years and at least pretended to stay interested, and to everyone who has been inspired to add utensils to the UCS (many of which made it into the book).

A big shout out to Robin Kall, my constant cheerleader, brainstorming buddy, and connector extraordinaire. Thank you to the long list of authors who have generously shared their encouragement and wisdom with this new author, including Ann Hood,

Camille Pagan, Dawn Tripp, Allison Winn Scotch, Nicola Kraus, Jenna Blum, and Sarah McCoy. And a big high-five to all of the '17 Scribes authors. In memory of my friend Erica Shea, the kindest soul, who took my author headshot.

Many thanks to the DeCesare and Mezzina families for lending me some names and for the bountiful and boisterous celebrations together. And thank you to the Bogdans: Beth, Michael and Molly. Maybe my brother will finally read a novel in his adult life. I love you all.

To my mom, who made our home a story tale place to grow up, and to my dad, whose real life going-away-to-college talk inspired this book. I am beyond blessed to have you for parents.

Endless kisses to my three treasures who I hope I have taught to believe in themselves: Ali, Michael, and Anna. To Nick, my perfect steak knife, your limitless love and support are the best of all gifts.

About the Author

Photo Credit: Erica Shea

Leah DeCesare is the author of the non-fiction parenting series *Naked Parenting*, based on her work as a doula, early parenting educator, and mom of three. Her articles on parenting have been featured in *The Huffington Post*, *International Doula* and *The Key*. She writes, teaches and volunteers in Rhode Island where she lives with her family and their talking cockatiel.

A Letter From the Author

Dear Reader:

Thank you for being a part of my lifelong dream. Since I was a little girl, I have wanted to write books and you have just read my dream-come-true.

You may not be aware that reviews truly make a difference to authors. I would be so grateful if you could please take a moment to post a short review of *Forks, Knives, and Spoons* on Amazon and/or Goodreads. Those little stars matter.

THANK YOU!

Reach out to me at leah@leahdecesare.com; I love to hear from readers and book clubs.

Find me on:

GoodReads

Twitter: @leahdecesare

Pinterest: leahdecesare (I have a *Forks, Knives, and Spoons* board with 80s inspirations)

Facebook: leahdecesareauthor

Instagram: leah.decesare

See you online and in my inbox!

Leah

SELECTED TITLES FROM SPARKPRESS

SparkPress is an independent boutique publisher
delivering high-quality, entertaining, and engaging
content that enhances readers' lives, with a special focus on
female-driven work. Visit us at www.gosparkpress.com

The Year of Necessary Lies, by Kris Radish. $17, 978-1-94071-651-0. A great-granddaughter discovers her ancestor's secrets—inspirational forays into forbidden love and the Florida Everglades at the turn of the last century.

Satisfaction, by Andee Reilly. $17, 978-1-94071-663-3. After discovering her husband's affair, Ginny Martin impulsively hits the road and follows the Rolling Stones from L.A. to Oklahoma, striking up a friendship with Bree Cooper, a free-spirited drifter.

Elly in Bloom, by Colleen Oakes. $15, 978-1-94071-609-1. Elly Jordan has carved out a sweet life for herself as a boutique florist in St. Louis. Not bad for a woman who left her life two years earlier when she found her husband entwined with a redheaded artist. Just when she feels she is finally moving on from her past, she discovers a wedding contract, one that could change her financial future, is more than she bargained for.

The Legacy of Us, by Kristin Contino. $17, 978-1-94071-617-6. Three generations of women are affected by love, loss, and a mysterious necklace that links them.

First Rodeo, by Judith Hennessey. $16.95, 978-1943006038. Fast-paced and wildly entertaining, *First Rodeo* is filled with humorous scenes of city girl gone country, encounters with handsome cowboys, the struggles of the creative process, and a powerful message: the greatest love of all is the love you have for yourself.

25 Sense, by Lisa Henthorn. $17, 978-1-940716-30-5. Claire Malone just wanted to move to New York and live out her dream career of television writing, but by her 25th birthday, she's in love with her married, flirtatious boss. She struggles to hold it together—but can she break away without ruining her barely started career? *25 Sense* is about the time in a young woman's life when the world starts to view her as a responsible adult—but all she feels is lost.

ABOUT SPARKPRESS

SparkPress is an independent, hybrid imprint focused on merging the best of the traditional publishing model with new and innovative strategies. We deliver high-quality, entertaining, and engaging content that enhances readers' lives. We are proud to bring to market a list of *New York Times* best-selling, award-winning, and debut authors who represent a wide array of genres, as well as our established, industry-wide reputation for creative, results-driven success in working with authors. SparkPress, a BookSparks imprint, is a division of SparkPoint Studio LLC.

Learn more at GoSparkPress.com